Salvation Lake

Driftwood Beach

Back River

Tybee Island

North

Atlantic Ocean

©'02 jackie aher

NO
ENEMY
BUT
TIME

ALSO BY WILLIAM C. HARRIS, JR.

Delirium of the Brave

NO
ENEMY
BUT
TIME

WILLIAM C. HARRIS, JR.

St. Martin's Press
New York

www.stmartins.com

Library of Congress Cataloging-in-Publication Data

Harris, William, Charles, 1947–
        No enemy but time : a novel of the South / William C. Harris, Jr.
        p. cm.
    ISBN 0-312-26980-3
    1. Savannah (Ga.)—Fiction. I. Title.

PS3558.A662 N6 2002
813'.54—dc21

                                                    2002069833

First Edition: September 2002

10   9   8   7   6   5   4   3   2   1

In memory of

the Right Reverend Monsignor

Daniel Joseph Bourke,

the Last Lion,

and

Edwin "Eddie" Beranc,

a disciple of Christ,

a monk without monastery

Contents

II. WILL'S STORY

III. IN THE FULLNESS OF TIME

The innocent and the beautiful
Have no enemy but time.

               —W. B. YEATS, "In Memory of
                   Eva Gore-Booth and
                   Con Markiewicz"

I

Soldiers, Sailors, and Spies

I. God and Country

*Be as beneficent as the sun or the sea, but if your
rights as a rational being are trenched on, die
on the first inch of your territory.*

—RALPH WALDO EMERSON

As the East Coast Champion rattled and banged to a stop at
Union Station on West Broad Street, the heat and humidity
rose up from the station platform and enveloped the traveler.
He instinctively pulled at his collar, straining for room to breathe. As he
was about to step off the train, a strong black hand reached for his only
suitcase and said, "Let me help you with that."

Out on the street the porter asked in a thick accent, "You need a cab,
Father?"

Reaching in his pocket and pulling out a new dime, the priest
replied, "No, thank you. I think I'd like to walk. I'm going to the Cathedral of Saint John the Baptist. Do you know where that is?"

The porter accepted his tip and replied, "Yes suh, Father. It's on
Abercorn and Liberty."

As the young priest walked, the feel of Savannah began to surround
him with its smells and sounds. Just ahead he heard the cry of a street
vendor.

"Butterbeans, stringbeans, and fresh tomatoes!" shouted out a black woman with a basket of vegetables balanced on her head; then a street-car rumbled by, followed by a horse-drawn wagon driven by an old man wearing a large straw hat to ward off the sun.

It was a hot September in 1934, and there wasn't much of a breeze as the priest started up Liberty Street, looking for Abercorn. "Saint Joseph," he said to himself in exasperation, as he noticed his shirt was soaked with perspiration. Then he felt terribly homesick and wondered what his mother was doing back in Ireland. It had never been this hot in the town of Birr, never in his whole recollection. He had been told on the way down from New York that July and August were the really hot months in Savannah. "Lord have mercy," he said to himself, as he recalled that bit of information. Then the reason why he was in Savannah came to him again, and he mentally shrugged as he shifted the suitcase to his left hand.

Well, at least I'm safe. I'm hot as the hinges of Hell, but I'm safe . . . for now, he thought.

Michael Patrick Mulvaney, the only son of an elderly couple from the county of Offlay, looked up through the wide oaks shading his walk. He could see the twin spires of the cathedral reaching hundreds of feet into the blue sky, lording over all that surrounded them. He let his luggage drop to the sidewalk and stood there taking it all in.

Savannah reminded him of England, with its stately town homes, lampposts, elegant wrought-iron bannisters and railings. The people seemed to move slower than in New York, and they all had accents he strained to understand.

Father Mulvaney had volunteered to be a missionary in Africa but had been turned down because his bishop thought him too frail to endure the heat. "Holy Mother," he exclaimed, "I wonder if the bishop knows how hot it is here!"

When he arrived at the cathedral rectory on Harris Street, Father Mulvaney was warmly greeted by the bishop of Savannah, also a native of Ireland. With a smile and a pat on the back, the bishop escorted his new priest into the parlor.

"Sit down, Father, please. I've been waiting all morning for you," said the bishop.

Father Mulvaney took a seat in a high-winged chair. Overhead, a ceiling fan beat the air for all it was worth, causing the lace curtains on the windows to move gently back and forth. A droplet of perspiration ran down his nose and hung there for an instant before dropping on his coat sleeve. Bishop Keyes watched as the young priest mopped his brow.

"It's hot, I know, but we all get used to it with time," said the bishop; then he rang a small crystal bell. In a moment a massive black woman appeared in the doorway. She wore a well-starched gray uniform with an equally starched white apron. She was feeling the heat, too, and her face glistened with the sweat. "Yes suh, Bishop Keyes."

"Etta Mae, this is Fr. Michael Patrick Mulvaney. He's just arrived from Ireland. He'll be going to Saint Patrick's, but tonight he'll stay with us. I believe he could use a nice cool glass of iced tea with a sprig of mint."

Etta Mae did a small curtsey in the direction of Father Mulvaney, then said, "Yes, suh," and disappeared.

"Iced tea?" queried Father Mulvaney.

"Oh, yes," replied the bishop. "They drink their tea over ice here. No cream, just sugar and lemon. I prefer mint, when I can get it. It's really quite refreshing. You have so much to learn. We'll start your education over supper tonight, but first tell me about home."

Michael Mulvaney was uneasy talking about Ireland. It hurt him to think about it. Still he spoke of Dublin and Birr, of the weather and the southern coast. But most of all he spoke of All Hallows, the seminary he had attended. It was the same seminary that had produced Bishop Keyes. They laughed together about the places they had gone as seminarians to drink Guinness or Irish whiskey, but Bishop Keyes knew nothing about the real Michael Patrick Mulvaney.

After a dinner of more roast beef than he could possibly have eaten, corn on the cob, heaps of rice smothered in gravy, the new taste of corn bread and the peculiar taste of collard greens, the bishop motioned Michael back into the parlor.

"Will you have a taste with me, Father?" asked the bishop, as he went to the liquor cabinet and produced two cut-crystal glasses and a quart of Bushmills. Not waiting for a reply, the bishop filled the glasses; and as he did, he said, "These are from Waterford. My mother gave them to me years ago. We make the most exquisite crystal in Waterford. The Irish have a knack with that type of thing, you know." Then he held his glass up to Father Mulvaney in a toast.

"To you, Father, and to your success in Savannah and all the rest of Georgia."

He took a long sip, as did Father Mulvaney, and then, with a twinkle in his eye, said, "God was good to you in that he didn't send you here during Prohibition."

With glass in hand the bishop sat in a dark maroon leather chair and motioned for Father Mulvaney to take a seat in the one opposite him. With great wit Bishop Keyes talked about Saint Patrick's parish. Then he moved on to describe Savannah's politics and social structure. Michael found himself delightfully amused by his bishop; and for the first time since arriving in Savannah, he began to relax.

That night Michael Mulvaney didn't sleep much. It was hot, but the heat wasn't the problem. Everything swirled around in his head. He played that whole terrible scene over again and again in his mind. In the dark, on sheets soaked with his sweat, to the hum of a fan that only pushed the hot air around his room, Michael Mulvaney remembered it all. In his mind's eye he followed his arm as it brought the pistol to the back of the young British soldier's head. One quick shot, so much louder than he'd expected, then he watched his arm move instantly to the head of the other soldier and saw his face as it turned toward him in surprise. No time for an expression of terror on the lad's face. Then he felt the pistol recoil and watched as brain matter splattered out the back of the lad's head. As he lay in bed, so far away from it all, his heart beat as hard as it had that June day in Belfast.

"But he was a soldier, and so was I," he whispered to himself, perhaps for the ten thousandth time. "He was the enemy in my country," he told himself. "It was war," he repeated, "and it was him or me."

However, the British didn't see it that way. They weren't exactly sure who had shot their two young soldiers sent to rule the Catholics in their own country, but they had ideas.

Only four other members of the IRA knew who had killed the soldiers. A week later, two were captured and died in prison, refusing to reveal the name of the shooter. In Michael's mind, tortured to death, no doubt. It was then that Danny Bourke hit upon the idea of sending Michael to the seminary to take him out of harm's way.

"The British suspect everything, Michael, so I'm not sayin' you're safe in there, but it does lend a certain patina to your appearance of innocence," said Danny. "If you stay on the outside, you'll be in trouble again."

The arrangements were made; and much to the surprise and pleasure of his mother, Michael entered the seminary at All Hallows to become a priest. Only he had no desire, no intention of becoming a priest; it was just a place to hide. But it was an education for him, something he was not likely to receive on the outside. He wouldn't be doomed to run a pub as his father had done. He wouldn't have to smell stale beer every day and sweep the floors. He wouldn't be forced to watch boys he grew up with spend their money on whiskey, money that was supposed to go for their children's food and clothes. No, he would be an educated man. It wasn't all missals and catechisms, masses and rosaries. He would read the classics and learn about the world. There were no ignorant men coming out of All Hallows. It was the best in Ireland, perhaps the best in all of Europe. Just before he was to be ordained, he planned to say he was having second thoughts, give his deep regrets, and leave.

The Irish were different from many others of their faith in that Catholicism was at the core of their national identity. The Catholic Church was their constant touchstone in everyday life. Perhaps it was their way of existing in a cruel world where an alien power occupied their country, stole their crops, starved them to death, and sold off their land to others from across the Irish Sea. Whatever it was, Michael Mulvaney had been raised in this atmosphere and was, for want of a better description, fertile ground.

In his last year at All Hallows, Michael had a revelation of sorts. Not a vision, nothing at all like that. What he did have was a feeling, something that had been growing inside him over time; and before he was fully aware, he found himself wanting to be a priest. It was wonderful this feeling, this happiness inside him. So when June of 1934 came, Michael prostrated himself on the altar before the bishop of Dublin, was anointed with oil, received the gifts of the Holy Spirit, and became a priest forever.

2. The Patriot

Sighted sub, sank same.

—LT. DONALD F. MASON, USN
Message report while on anti-
submarine patrol, 8 January 1942

He could smell the men above and below him. After all this time, he could still smell them. He'd told himself he would eventually get used to the smells, but he hadn't. He hadn't gotten used to the cold or the dampness, either. Although he was daily pressed against the flesh of forty other men, he was alone. They were efficient, almost machinelike. He was different from them but had watched and listened as they explained their ways, and he had learned them well. He would use what they had taught him and then discard their ways . . . when it was all over. He would think as they thought to accomplish his end and then cleanse his mind of their right-angle, straight-edged, well-plumbed ideas . . . when he had done his duty. He gave not a whit for their country or their cause. He used them as they used him.

He had learned to kill from his brothers in arms; and when he had done so, he had not felt as though he had sinned against his God. He knew the sound of a rifle crack, the feel of its recoil, the image of a man struck down at a hundred yards. The memory of a man drowning in his own blood came all too easily to him. He was a patriot, a soldier in the service of his country. But why did he catch himself whispering short prayers for forgiveness? Was it because of what he had done with them?

"Seelöwe," whispered a breath foul with old sausage and strong, stale coffee, the kapitän wants to see you."

"Right, tell 'em I'm there in a minute."

Seelöwe's rack was in the senior ratings' quarters, just a few short steps from the officers' mess, and he could hear the ship's radio playing American music. He pushed the curtain aside and moved halfway into the cramped wardroom. He looked down at Kapitänleutnant Reinhardt Hardegen and said, in passable German heavily tinged with an Irish accent, "You wanted to see me, Kapitän?"

Kapitän Hardegen looked up and said, "I'll speak with you in a moment," then continued to fill out his log. "Surfaced 0951 hours, 7 April 1942, quadrant 6475 DB, off Ossabaw Island."

Francis Xavier Collins had been a passenger on the U-123 since she had set sail from Lorient, France, on March 2, 1942. He had been a member of the Irish Republican Army since his seventeenth birthday and, on the day after his twenty-second, had given himself to the Nazis in a devil's bargain.

In exchange for guns and ammunition, Francis would travel to Germany, where he would be trained in espionage and sabotage and then inserted onto the American coast. He knew the Germans were thorough and resourceful in their training, but he'd never dreamed just how thorough they could be.

On a clear, cold night in early November of 1941, on the west coast of Ireland, Francis had headed for the town of Ventry on Dingle Bay. There he'd boarded a small fishing trawler, which set out immediately for a rendezvous point in the Atlantic, ten miles west of the Blasket Islands. At exactly the time agreed upon, U-136, a type VIIC Atlantic-boot, surfaced fifty yards from the trawler. In less than twenty minutes, Francis had been exchanged for fifty Mauser K-98 rifles and five thousand rounds of ammunition. Five days later, via the Baltic Sea, he was in Germany at a place called Bergen-Belsen.

Francis was a likely candidate for the swap with the Germans because he was familiar with the United States, having visited relatives in America several times. He was acquainted with the different accents spoken along the Atlantic seaboard and could render a very passable imitation of northern and southern dialects. Another attraction was that he was an accomplished amateur actor, a talent that would surely come in handy as a spy. He knew how to handle a firearm and had tasted battle. There was only one thing about Francis Collins that gave the Germans pause.

At No. 72–76 Tirpitz-Ufer, in the imposing sandstone building in Berlin's central Tiergarten district, the legendary Adm. Wilhelm Franz Canaris, head of the Abwehr, the War Ministry's intelligence and counterintelligence service, expressed concern when he viewed a picture of Francis.

"This Irishman, he's too good-looking. He's got a face people can remember, especially the women. His eyes, they are like a woman's. He's almost beautiful. He doesn't look like a man who can kill in cold blood if he has to."

Sitting deep in the basement of the War Ministry in what the admiral liked to call the Fuchsbau or Foxden, he looked across the table at Allgemein Erwin Lahousen, the head of Abwehr's sabotage, and Oberst Hans Piekenbrock, the Abwehr's chief of espionage. They were the architects of Operation Pastorius, Canaris's plan for spying and destruction along the American Atlantic coast.

"Well, what do you two have to say about how this fellow looks? Couldn't you have come up with someone less conspicuous?"

Oberst Piekenbrock looked at Allgemein Lahousen, and then the allgemein leaned forward and said, "Not one who knows as much as this Irishman, or who is as good as he is. When he finishes his training, we'll know if he can kill or not. It's just a chance we will have to take."

With a shrug, Admiral Canaris closed the folder on Francis Xavier Collins, code name Seelöwe (Sealion), and accepted his only flaw.

Upon his arrival at Bergen-Belsen, Francis was assigned to a special SS facility. For three months, he underwent a grueling training period. Then, on a cold and bright day in late February, he was summoned to the office of Walther Kappe, who had been assigned by Canaris to oversee the training of all spies sent to America. Kappe was a beefy, bull-necked native of Germany, who had spent many years in the States before the war and was intimately familiar with all things American.

Francis took an instant dislike to the man. He was offended by his abrupt manner and the small, cunning eyes stuck into Kappe's piggish face, crowned by a sparse head of hair with sideburns that imitated Hitler's.

SS oberstgruppenführer Kappe was sitting on the edge of his desk when Francis was ushered into his office by an SS leutnant in an immaculate black uniform. The leutnant took his place by Kappe's side and gave Francis a slightly knowing and disturbingly evil little smile.

Kappe rose from his perch and strode about the room in silence for a moment, as if in deep thought. Then he turned and faced Francis.

"All of your instructors have rated you highly, Seelöwe. You should be very proud."

Kappe waited for Francis to reply, but he remained silent. Then Kappe took several steps away and wheeled suddenly to face Francis. In an accusatory voice, Kappe asked him, "Do you think you can kill a man in cold blood?"

"I've killed before, Kappe. I can do it again if I have to."

"With your bare hands, Seelöwe?"

"I've been trained by your boys to do it."

"But have you done it?" asked Kappe, with a wry smile.

"No."

"Well then, how do you know you can, my wild goose friend?"

"First of all, I'm not your fuckin' friend, Kappe. Second, I've been trained by those black suit boys of yours quite well. If I've got to, I can do it."

Kappe looked over at his leutnant and said, "Well, we shall see. Killing a man in cold blood with your bare hands isn't as easy as you would suppose," adding, with bitter sarcasm, "my friend."

Then Kappe moved behind his desk, as if to make an official proclamation, and said, "Operation Pastorius is of the utmost importance to the Reich war effort and receives the personal attention of the führer. The War Ministry has invested too much time and effort in you and your training not to be absolutely sure that you are completely capable of carrying out your mission. Admiral Canaris has expressed doubts that you are possessed of the necessary qualities to fulfill it with the precision and exactitude that is demanded from all agents of the Reich."

Without another word, SS oberstgruppenführer Kappe turned to his left and marched to the door on the opposite side of the room. With his hand on the doorknob, Kappe turned to Francis and said in a command voice, "Come with me."

He was uneasy, but Francis knew he had no choice and walked past the arrogant leutnant into a sparse, windowless room. Inside the room stood three burly SS men. On the other side of the room was a door. In the center of the room, seated on a wooden bench, was an emaciated man in prison garb. The floor had numerous dark stains scattered about. A rather delicate light fixture hung from the high ceiling. It appeared out of place in such a stark environment.

Without further ado, Kappe strode up to the prisoner and stood behind him. Then he turned to Francis and said, "This is what we want to know you are capable of."

In a quick and seamless motion, Kappe took the inmate's head in his arms, just as Francis had been taught, and snapped the man's neck with such force that Francis distinctly heard the vertebrae crack. Kappe nonchalantly stepped away and let the inmate's body fall to the floor, his skull hitting with a thud. Then he turned to Francis and announced, "That is what the War Ministry expects of you."

Francis was too stunned to fully appreciate the meaning of Kappe's statement. He watched in silence as one of the guards opened the far door and two teenaged girls with yellow Stars of David sewn to their gray prison dresses moved cautiously into the room. The guard motioned for them to remove the body, and they quickly began pulling it across the floor as the stench of released feces rose from its lifeless form and a trail of urine marked its path to the door.

She hadn't meant to, but one of the girls had caught the eye of Francis as she struggled with the corpse. For a moment they held each other's gaze. She had heard through the camp rumor chain that the SS was training a handsome Irishman, a man who had eyes that sparkled. But Gretchen Meyer had not believed these stories. Now she was startled by the beauty of this man's eyes.

As soon as the body had been removed, another inmate was led to the bench and roughly seated. Kappe turned to Francis, motioned to the inmate, and said, "Your turn, Seelöwe."

Francis stared coldly into Kappe's eyes, then said, "Fuck you, Kappe," and started toward the door. The leutnant stepped in front with his hand on his holster. Francis stopped, stood still for a moment, then turned to face Kappe.

Kappe had a hard smile on his lips; and before Francis could speak, he replied mockingly, "No, Seelöwe, fuck you." Then he shifted his stance and cocked his head back slightly.

"Let's get to the bottom line, as our American friends like to say."

With his left thumb tucked into his Sam Brown belt, just as the führer was fond of doing, Kappe continued. "You are going to show us you are capable of what is necessary, or the deal is off. That means no more guns for your comrades. They can just kick the British out of that stinking Emerald Isle country of yours with their bare hands," adding ironic emphasis on bare hands.

"You're fuckin' out of your mind, the whole lot of you. I'm not goin' to kill an innocent person just to prove something!" shouted Francis.

"Oh, but you will, Seelöwe, you will. As a matter of fact, you will kill this man if you want that little piece of shit island you dare call a country free of the British."

The inmate sat on the bench, understanding nothing in his stupor. Francis stared at the floor struggling with himself, knowing he was trapped in a monstrous situation. Then Francis clenched his jaw, looked directly at Kappe, and in an explosive movement, rushed the prisoner from behind. Francis grabbed the man's head and neck exactly as he had been instructed, and in one powerful motion broke his neck and let his body fall to the floor. A yellow star was attached to the man's uniform; and when he fell, he came to rest on his back, his face upturned to Francis.

The man's spinal cord had been crushed and partially severed. Death was not instantaneous but would come from asphyxiation due to paralysis of the muscles that controlled breathing. The only voluntary movement left was in his eyes and lids. He was paralyzed but conscious for the two minutes or so his brain had oxygen.

Francis looked at Nathan Eisenman, former teacher, father of three, and could see there was still life in his eyes. He could see tears well in them and then roll down his cheeks. Nathan blinked as the tears burned his eyes; then he looked directly at Francis.

Francis fell to one knee and put his hand on Nathan's brow and said in his best German, "Forgive me. You were doomed here to die for no cause. Now you have given your life for my country. I will not forget you."

One of the SS guards opened the door and roughly ordered Gretchen and her partner to remove Nathan's body. The girls approached Francis from his back and stopped, not knowing what to do.

Francis's head was bowed, and he rested his brow in his hand. Gretchen noticed a peculiar dark red birthmark on the back of Francis's neck, partially in his hairline. It was known as a port-wine stain, common enough, but the one on Francis's neck was distinctive because it was shaped like the boot of Italy.

Gretchen remained still until Kappe sarcastically said, "Herr Seelöwe, you are impeding the work of these two Jewish bitches. They have some garbage to haul out. Would you kindly step aside so they may go about their business."

Gretchen was able to look at Francis's face one more time as she tugged and pulled at the schoolteacher's body. As she pulled the corpse by the arms, air escaped from his stomach, causing a belching sound. Kappe roared with laughter, remarking to Francis that "the Jew isn't dead, only passed out from too much Oktoberfest beer."

Francis had heard that sound many times in the fitful dreams that followed since that day. He had seen Nathan Eisenman's eyes and heard his corpse speak the night U-123 surfaced off the coast of Georgia. He had not fully shaken the ghost from his head when Kapitänleutnant Hardegen called him to the control room and invited him to look through the periscope.

"What you are looking at are the lights of Tybee Island at the mouth of the Savannah River. The Americans have been kind enough to keep their coastline well lit at night. The fat, juicy merchantmen that sail the coast are beautifully backlighted for us. They make such easy and inviting targets. Very kind of the Americans, wouldn't you say?"

On December 12th, the day after Germany declared war on the

United States, Adolf Hitler and Grand Adm. Erich Raeder met and decided to send U-boats against the western Atlantic. It was then that Adm. Karl Dönitz initiated Atlantic Order No. Forty-six: Operation Paukenschlag—"Operation Drumbeat." U-123 was on its second patrol of Operation Drumbeat, and Kapitänleutnant Hardegen had not been pleased when he had received his orders to insert an agent onto the American coast. He felt it exposed his command to unnecessary risks.

When Francis had seen all of the Georgia coast he could digest, Hardegen ordered down scope and told Francis to come to his cabin with him. There, Hardegen opened the ship's safe and withdrew the rubberized pouch containing his orders.

"I believe this is for you, Seelöwe. You are to read and memorize the essentials. These," said Hardegen, holding up some other papers, "are my orders concerning you."

A slight smile creased Hardegen's lips as he reached up and removed a chart from the overhead rack. "Let's take a look at where we are to meet your ride to the coast." Then Hardegen spread out the chart of Georgia's coast on his bunk and pointed to a place on the map.

"My orders," said Hardegen, "are to take you to this location right here, about ten miles out from Saint Catherine's Sound, which is at the southern end of Ossabaw Island. We are to rendezvous with a shrimping vessel named *Dixie Warrior* at 0100 hours and turn you over to its crew. It's 2100 hours now. We'll travel on the surface recharging our batteries until we reach our rendezvous point. I suggest you have all of your equipment ready and get as much rest as you can."

Without another word, Hardegen placed Francis's orders, along with his own, back into the pouch and returned it to the safe.

The Germans had been very thorough in establishing Francis's false identity in America, and his family in Ireland had been equally thorough in establishing the circumstances of his death there.

According to all available documents, Francis had been raised in an orphanage run by the Sisters of the Most Blessed Sacrament in one of the rougher sections of New York City. He was the illegitimate child of a poor Irish girl who'd died during childbirth. The identity of his father was never established. Francis lived at the orphanage until the age of thirteen, when he ran away. What happened after that was murky and poorly documented. As with so many young men during the Depression years, Francis drifted from town to town, and records of employment were poor to nonexistent.

What actually happened was that the Germans had established contacts with a number of orphanages years before the war began. The actual Francis Quinn had died of pneumonia at thirteen and was buried in an unmarked grave near the orphanage. His death certificate was later removed from the Office of Vital Statistics in New York by a German agent. The birth certificate for Francis Quinn was all that existed. In addition, German agents in America had secured a Social Security number for the nonexistent Francis Quinn as well as other documents that gave weight to his identity.

In Ireland, the IRA had staged a boating accident in which he was lost at sea and his body never recovered. There were newspaper accounts of the drowning and a memorial service at the church where he grew up. Only select members of the IRA knew what had really happened. It was their plan for Francis to return after the British had been expelled from Northern Ireland and the country united.

In his bunk, Francis thought about these things and couldn't help admiring the thoroughness of his German handlers as he changed into the clothes provided by the Abwehr. They were those of a workingman, totally unremarkable, as they were intended to be. In his pocket was what appeared to be a fountain pen. It was actually a gun that fired a small bullet when its plunger was pressed against a man. The target's clothing would muffle the gun's report. But most important of all was the small briefcase sitting on his bunk. In it was the Auf radio used by German spies. The radio was a technological wonder and was fully capable of sending messages to German U-boats far out in the Atlantic. In his breast pocket were the best-forged documents in the world, and around his waist was a money belt containing ten thousand dollars.

The home port of the *Dixie Warrior* was the little fishing town of Darien, located on the Altamaha River about fifteen miles north of Brunswick on Highway 17. The boat had been purchased from its original owners six months before the war began by a man named Homer Peeples who said he was from Galveston. In actuality, he was Theodor Rowehl, a German national who'd been living in the United States since 1922. His buddy Ricky Suggs, who claimed to be from Mobile, was really Paul Fackenheim, another German national, who'd come to the States after his parents emigrated from Saxony just after the Great War.

Francis had very little to say to Homer and Ricky as they made their way up the coast past Ossabaw and Wassaw Islands to the Ambos Seafood docks at Thunderbolt just outside Savannah. When *Dixie Warrior* bumped against the dock, Francis was in the wheelhouse with Homer while Ricky jumped to the dock and tied off the lines.

Even though it had not been part of his orders, it had been Francis's intention all along not to leave anyone alive who could betray him. So while Homer had his back to Francis, watching Ricky secure the bowline, Francis jammed the barrel of his pen gun to the back of Homer's neck, killing him instantly. Ricky never heard the report and didn't notice that Homer wasn't standing at the wheel when Francis stepped onto the dock. He wasn't suspicious when Francis approached and extended his hand to say good-bye. Ricky didn't have time to react when Francis, with his other hand, jammed the pen gun against Ricky's right temple and dropped him with a muffled pop.

U-123 sailed on the surface, charging her batteries, until the first signs of dawn on April 7th forced her to dive and wait for the cover of darkness, when she would again be able to search for prey. For most of the day, she rested on the sandy ocean bottom in about fifty feet of water, fifteen miles off the beaches of Saint Simons Island. At eight that evening, Hardegen gave the order to blow ballast.

At 0200 hours on the morning of April 8th, lookouts spotted the large, wide shadow of the SS *Oklahoma,* a northbound tanker, and U-123 sent her to the bottom with a surface shot of one G7e torpedo or *Aal* (eel). Her next victim was the *Esso Baton Rouge,* another tanker headed north, which she hit with one torpedo; then she surfaced and shelled the burning ship with her deck gun. The sounds of the explosions rattled windows on Saint Simons Island and in Brunswick.

U-123 didn't tarry at the site of her victories but set a northeast course along the shallow coastline, looking for more targets. It was just after dawn on the 8th when Hardegen and his crew ran into trouble. They were sailing on the surface in fifty feet of water twenty miles off Tybee Island when the lookout spotted the USS *Spry* bearing down on them at flank speed.

Although she was small, *Spry* was fast and agile, much more so than U-123, and she started shelling the sub with her three-inch deck gun at two thousand yards, striking the conning tower of the U-boat.

Aboard the sub, sailors rushed to their battle stations, watertight doors were closed, and the U-123 slipped beneath the waves before *Spry* could score another hit. Deep water was what the sub needed to successfully defend herself. Hardegen and his crew were able to slip away from *Spry*, but the little corvette had taken a toll and sent out the alarm.

Hunter Field at Savannah dispatched two Lockheed PV-1 Ventura patrol bombers. One of the Venturas was able to spot the shadow of the sub as she moved, submerged, forty-five miles due east of Tybee Island. U-123 had no warning when the first depth charge was dropped. That explosion and the four that followed caused cracks and leaks in her hull, but still the sub pressed on.

The second Ventura from Hunter Field arrived on the scene as the first plane circled the sub, marking her location. The first four depth charges missed their mark, but the last struck U-123 amidships, and grave damage was inflicted.

Beneath the Atlantic, the situation was very serious. The sub was able to maintain trim, course, and speed; but it would be absolutely necessary to surface quickly and effect repairs. It was five in the afternoon of April 8th when Kapitänleutnant Hardegen gave the order to surface. The damage-control crews worked with undiluted fervor as they plugged leaks, sealed off ruptured pipes, and spliced severed electrical connections, while U-123 limped along.

Just as the sun was starting to disappear, another pair of Venturas attacked. The sub's only chance of survival was beneath the waves, and she dived in desperation as depth charges exploded all around. She was fifty miles from Tybee, in eighty-five feet of water, and her outline was obscured by the depth and the fading light; but all was for naught. All of her old wounds had been opened again, and she had received some fresh cuts that not even Hardegen could heal. The sub struggled for several more miles, but finally plowed into the ocean bottom, burying her bow in the sand and silt. There, shrouded by the dark and stillness of deep water, the crew of U-123 began to realize they could surface no more. Soon U-123 would be a ghost ship.

3. Tybee Island

*"There is no law of God or man east of
Lazaretto Creek."*

—Attributed to JOHN J. BOUHAN, ESQ.

Fr. Mike Mulvaney was tired and a little sleepy at eight o'clock
mass. He had been up most of the night with the widow and
family of George Price. George had been in the engine room of
the SS *Oklahoma* when she'd been torpedoed. He'd been horribly
burned in the explosions that followed and had died in agony on one of
Oklahoma's lifeboats. He left a small son, a young widow, and his pitiful
elderly parents.

The priest's sleep had been short and fitful, and having to fast before
his first mass of the morning nauseated him as he stood at the altar and
whispered the words "Hoc est enim Corpus meum" over the unleav-
ened bread he held in his hands. He hadn't paid much attention to the
congregation and didn't notice Francis Collins in the third pew.

After mass, while Father Mulvaney was in the sacristy removing his
vestments, Francis quietly appeared at the door. The priest noticed him
from the corner of his eye but maintained silence as he placed his chalice
into the overhead cabinet. Then he turned to Francis, crossed his arms
over his chest, and leaned back on the table behind him.

"I know this can't be anything good, Francis," said the priest.

Francis raised his hands in a silent plea.

"I'm not Francis Collins, at least not anymore. I'm Francis Quinn, Michael. Never call me anything else but that, unless you want me dead."

"Sweet Mother of God," said Mike, "I knew it was nothing but bad news you've brought me. What are you doing here?"

"Is there somewhere we can go that's very private?"

As Father Mulvaney maneuvered his car around the curves of Bonaventure Road, Francis marveled at the broad-shouldered oaks standing close to the narrow road. His eyes followed their stout arms, heavy with moss, reaching across the street. On either side of the road, azaleas, thick with blooms of lavender and white, fashioned a colorful skirt that lined the sides of the blacktop. The scent of wisteria filled the woods, and the vines wrapped themselves around telephone poles, their blossoms hanging like clusters of grapes.

More azaleas surrounded the car after they passed through the gates of Bonaventure Cemetery. Overhead, the oaks formed an unbroken canopy, with moss hanging in long, gray tresses.

"Charming place," said Francis.

Father Mulvaney made no reply and kept driving until they reached the bluffs overlooking the Wilmington River. He pulled his car close to the edge of the bluff and stopped.

"All right, Francis, suppose you tell me why you're here."

For an hour Francis recounted the deal the IRA had made with the Nazis.

"I'm here to spy on their shipbuilding, to find its weak spots, and to sabotage it if I can. I've got a contact here. It's been arranged for me to get a job at the McQueen Shipyard and then later to be sent down to the Jones yard in Brunswick."

"Good Lord, man, do you not know how dangerous this whole thing is?" asked Mike.

"Of course I do, but look what we've gained. Guns, lots of 'em, and I'm not the only one they're doing this with. It's a chance for a truly free and united Ireland. It's what you shot those two Tommies for, Mike. It's for our country. If the Germans win this war, they're telling me that all of Ireland will be free. I'd do anything for that. But if they don't win, then at least we've got weapons as good as the Brits; and at least we'll have a fighting chance."

"I'm back in the thick of it again." The priest sighed. Then he looked out over the river and continued. "I'd been wondering when what I'd done back in Ireland would catch up with me."

"You sound like you've lost some of your fervor, Mike," replied Francis in astonishment.

"For the cause, no. For some of the methods, yes," responded the priest.

"Well, are you an Irishman or an American?" asked Francis.

"Do I have to make a choice?"

"When it's our country you're talkin' about, you damn sure do," said Francis angrily.

Father Mulvaney looked at Francis and softly said, "I'm an Irishman, Francis, nothing can ever change that. But I'm not the same kind of Irishman I used to be. I'm a priest now, Francis, totally and completely a priest. It can't be washed out of me. I'm a changed man; and although I pray every day for a free Ireland, I'm a priest first."

"Well, that's a hell of note," barked Francis. "Our brothers in the Sinn Fein told me I could trust you with my life. Now you're sittin' here tellin' me you've got second thoughts on what we've both killed for."

"I'm just sayin'," protested the priest, "that what I did bothers me sometimes. I know it was an act of war, but it still bothers me. Seein' you today was such a shock; but don't worry, your secret is safe with me."

Francis shook his head and replied with a hint of sarcasm, "Well, that's nice to know." Then he turned, faced Father Mulvaney, and continued. "You don't have to do anything. Just help me if I ever need it and act like I'm a total stranger. One more thing, Mike. This is the last time you'll be hearing me with an Irish accent."

Francis then said in a harsh New York voice, "OK, Father Mulvaney, why don't ya crank up this heap and get me outta' here. I don't like this place; graveyards give me the creeps."

"Is there some place in particular you'd like me to take you?" asked Father Mulvaney, as he depressed the clutch and put the car in gear.

"A place called the Tybrisa Pavilion. I believe it's on Tybee Island.

There's a girl there I'm supposed to speak with. Can you take me that far, Mike?"

Although the summer season hadn't officially started, the warm spring weather and the large number of servicemen in the Savannah area erased the usually sleepy off-season at Tybee. While the old train to the beach was no more, and gas rationing cut down on car traffic, buses and army trucks filled with GIs were a common sight along Tybee Road.

A haggard old Trailways bus, burning more oil than diesel fuel, strained down the last stretch of Tybee Road just ahead of Father Mulvaney's '37 Chevy. Through the blue exhaust fumes, Francis caught his first glimpse of Tybee's Butler Avenue. It was a lovely boulevard, divided down the center by palmettos and oleanders, and running the three-mile length of the island. On either side of the street were white clapboard homes with green trim and wide-screened porches. Mike pointed out the newly opened DeSoto Beach Hotel, done in art-deco style, and then farther down the Spanish flavor of the Tybee Hotel. With the pressure of a war economy and all the workers it brought to the Savannah, both hotels were filled to capacity. At Sixteenth Street, Mike made a left turn and headed for the ocean and the Tybrisa Pavilion.

The Tybrisa was a grand structure that reached three hundred feet into the Atlantic. It housed a skating rink, dance floor, and fishing pier on the ocean side. On the beach side was a two-story building, with a bowling alley on the top floor and a bar on the bottom. The pavilion was the center of activity on Tybee, and all around servicemen wandered in and out of the various small shops and concessions that lined Sixteenth Street.

Mike pulled his car over to the curb in front of the bar that occupied the space below the bowling alley. A sign over the double doors at the corner of the building read THE RIPTIDE.

Francis looked over at Father Mulvaney and said, "This is where I get out, Father. I'm supposed to meet someone in this bar."

"Well, Mr. Francis Quinn, it's been nice meeting you," said Father Mulvaney. "Take care of yourself. With a war on, there're a lot of very rough characters about."

Francis shook the priest's hand and said in a low voice, "If I need you, I'll call."

Inside the Riptide, it was cool and dark. The smell of stale beer was mixed with the odor of cheap perfume and cigarettes. A jukebox played "String of Pearls" loud enough to drown out the laughter of four young GIs nursing tall glasses of beer in one of the booths. A picture of FDR decorated with American flags was on one wall, and on another was a poster with a drawing of a sinking ship. In bold red letters were the words LOOSE LIPS SINK SHIPS! An eighteen-year-old in a marine uniform was playing a pinball machine that allowed the user to shoot down Japanese planes for points. Every now and then bells rang and lights flashed as the eager player jostled and thumped the machine. The long bar had the obligatory mirror behind it, with bottles of whiskey stacked in front. Down at the far end, a skinny bartender sipped a cup of coffee and read the newspaper. He had well-greased black hair that had been combed back and emphasized a pronounced widow's peak. A Lucky Strike cigarette was tucked behind his left ear, and he absentmindedly picked at something under his shirt. When Francis took a seat in front of the beer taps, the bartender came over and, in a thick Bronx accent, asked, "Whadaya have, buddy?"

"How 'bout a Blue Ribbon?" replied Francis.

"You from Brooklyn, buddy?" asked the bartender, as he placed a frosted mug and a bottle of beer on the bar.

"Yeah," replied Francis.

"I thought so. I'm from da Bronx, and I can spot a Brooklyn accent a mile away. Whatcha doin' down here in hicksville?"

"Shipyard work. Say, have ya got a gal workin' here by the name of Grace?"

The bartender wiped his hands on the dirty apron tied around his waist and said, "Yeah, we got a Grace workin' here. Who wants to know?"

"Is she here now?" asked Francis, after he took a sip of beer.

"Might be. Like I said, pal, who wants to know?"

"Tell Grace that Francis from Brooklyn is here. Tell her that her old man's sick again with the dropsy."

"Sick with the dropsy, eh. That's bad. I'll go tell her right now."

A few minutes later a young blonde appeared with the bartender. Her eyes were light blue and cold. Her hair was shoulder length and pulled back on either side with a pair of silver barrettes. She wore a navy blue cotton skirt with a white, short-sleeved blouse, and her nail polish matched her red lipstick. Overall, she looked too well-groomed for the Riptide.

"You Francis from Brooklyn?" she asked.

"Yeah. You Grace?"

"Uh huh."

"Well, your mother said to tell you your old man's sick with the dropsy."

"Oh my," said Grace, with a pitiful look on her face, "that's bad news. I haven't seen the old man in a while. Why don't you come back to the office, where we can sit down and talk without all this noise?"

Grace turned to the bartender and said, "He's from my neighborhood, Sal. We're gonna go in the back and visit for a while. The old man's sick again. I don't want to be bothered, OK?"

After she'd closed and locked the door to the small office, Grace turned to Francis and said, "What's the price of eggs in Brooklyn?"

"Too damned high."

"How do you like your eggs, fried or scrambled?"

"I like 'em poached."

Grace looked satisfied then said, "OK, let's see the back of your neck."

Francis turned and lifted the hair on his neck, revealing his birthmark. Completely satisfied, Grace whispered, "We can't talk here, but I've got a place at Tybee—a little cottage on the back river. You come back at seven tonight, and you can walk me home. By the way, you're supposed to have a radio. Where is it?"

"Hidden in a safe place," replied Francis. "See you at seven."

The body of water that separates Tybee from Jesus Island and the miles of marsh to the west is known as the Back River. Grace's cottage was on the river, right at the point where it flowed into the Atlantic. It sat on a sandy lot, nestled among some crepe myrtles and scrub oaks. A wooden walkway led from the screened porch on the back of the cottage across a yard filled with crabgrass and cockspurs to a small dock house perched over the river on tilting pilings. When Francis and his contact arrived at the cottage, the sun was sinking behind the trees on Jesus Island.

The spring on the front porch screen door groaned when Grace opened it. She stepped in and headed for the kitchen.

"I guess you'd like a drink," said Grace.

While Francis watched, Grace reached into the cabinet above the stove and removed a bottle of Early Times, saying nothing as she took two water-stained glasses from the sink and placed them next to the bottle. Francis leaned against the doorjamb and watched her pull an ice tray from the tiny freezer compartment in the old refrigerator next to the stove. She held the tray under the water faucet then started to pound it against the side of the sink, trying to break some cubes free. After a brief struggle, Grace had two glasses filled with ice, and the cubes cracked as she poured the clear brown sour mash over them.

Without looking at Francis, Grace said, "Let's go out on the dock; there's a nice breeze blowing."

The sun had slipped below the horizon, and the sky had melted from hot orange to light pink. As the wind off the river moved through the screens, it made a low, whistling sound, and the smell of the marsh mixed with the ocean produced a relaxing balm. Thousands of crickets called out from their nesting places in the shrubs, and Francis studied Grace with a discerning eye. While she took a sip of her drink, Grace sized up Francis with equal intensity.

"I am your contact here," she said, "your only contact. Any orders for you will come through me. You know what you are to do. A job for you at McQueen's Shipyard has been arranged, as well as a place for you to stay near the yards. Other operatives will be arriving in the near future. You will be linking up with them for actions against the shipyards. You will get a copy of the Savannah newspaper each day and study the want ads. If I desire a meeting with you, there will be an advertisement that will say, 'Mixed breed puppies for sale, two females, one male, all black. Call 41920 after 6:00 P.M.' You will then meet me at the Riptide at 7:00 P.M. that evening. Can you remember all that?"

"Say it again, Grace, and I will."

Grace repeated the advertisement once more, slowly, and then Francis nodded and said, "I've got it. Now tell me about yourself, Grace. How did you come to work for führer and fatherland?"

"How silly do you think I am, Mr. Quinn? The less you know the better. But it should suffice for you to know that I believe in what I'm doing. Other than that, there is nothing further you need to know."

Francis smiled, wiped some of the condensation off the side of his glass, then took a long drink. As he did, Grace could not help admiring him. She thought he was more than handsome. Indeed, she thought he was beautiful and found it difficult to suppress the natural emotions and attraction that any normal young woman would have for such a man.

After a few minutes of small talk, Grace turned her glass up then said, "How about another? It's been a long day. Besides, it's getting cool out here. Let's go back up to the cottage."

Francis followed behind Grace as she walked toward the little house. He watched as the wind blew her skirt tight around her legs and admired the shape of her hips as they moved from side to side. While Grace mixed two more drinks, Francis studied the fullness of her lips and how petite and well-refined her nose appeared. He noticed the length of her eyelashes and the smoothness of her skin. When she turned to give Francis his drink, she caught him staring and could not suppress a smile.

Grace went into the tiny sitting room and turned on an old RCA radio. She fumbled with the dial and found some soft evening music on WTOC. It was dark, with the only light coming from a small bulb in the kitchen. It was enough for Grace as she settled onto the sofa, kicked off her shoes, put her head back, and closed her eyes.

"Mr. Quinn, you can come in and have a seat. There're a few more things we have to talk about."

Francis sat on the sofa and looked around the room. They were on a small sunporch with double windows on three sides, giving a panoramic view of the Back River and distant Jesus Island. The lingering effects of the sunset tinted the room in mauve.

"Now I know what Hardegen meant," said Francis.

"What are you talking about?"

"There aren't any blackout curtains on the windows," said Francis.

"All over England, everything is blacked out. America hasn't come to its senses yet, but they will."

"Listen," said Grace, "more operatives are due in the next few months. They are the ones who will have the explosives to carry out attacks against the targets you will identify. You will have until July at the McQueen Shipyard here in Savannah. Then you'll be sent to the Jones yard in Brunswick for the same purpose. In the meantime, you are to bring your radio transmitter here. You will supply me with weekly reports concerning all shipping and troop movements. I'll transmit them myself. Each weekend you'll pay a visit to me at the Riptide and pass on the information then."

"I understand," said Francis, in a halfhearted tone. "One question, Grace."

"Only one?"

"Yeah, how am I supposed to get back to Savannah tonight, and where am I supposed to stay when I get there? I slept out in the woods last night and don't look forward to doing it again."

"You stay here tonight, Mr. Quinn. In the morning you catch the bus back to town. I'll give you the address of where you're staying and the name of the man to speak with at the shipyard. Have no fear, everything has been arranged."

"I'm staying here tonight?"

"Yes, I've even got a suitcase for you with some extra clothes and shaving things. As I said, everything has been taken care of."

4. Bloodlines

But mark the rustic, Haggis-fed,
The trembling earth resounds his tread.
Put in his ample fist a blade, he'll make it whistle;
And legs and arms and heads he'll crop, like tops
of thistles.

—ROBERT BURNS, "Address to a Haggis"

No family could have deeper or stronger ties to Savannah than the McQueens. William Wallace McQueen, the patriarch in Georgia, had first set foot on the steep banks of the Savannah River at Yamacraw Bluff with General Oglethorpe in February of 1733. He'd aided Sir James as he laid out the city amid the oaks and tall pines that lined the riverbank. He'd fought by the general's side in 1742 at Bloody Marsh as his Scots Highlanders repulsed the Spanish and made everything north of the Altamaha River safe for British settlement.

When Ct. Casimir Pulaski was hit in the thigh by English grapeshot at Springhill Redoubt during the Battle of Savannah in 1779, William Wallace McQueen II caught the young Polish general in his arms and held him as surgeons stuffed bloody rags into his gaping wounds. Later he acted as a second to his cousin, Gen. Lachland McIntosh, when the hot-blooded McIntosh administered a fatal dueling wound to Button Gwinnett, one of the three signers of the Declaration of Independence from the colony of Georgia.

In 1752, King George II awarded William Wallace McQueen vast tracts of land in the new colony as payment for his services to the Crown. All of the barrier island, known then as Guale Island and later as Jesus Island, was given to McQueen.

When William Wallace McQueen decided to leave his birthplace of Kildrummy near the foothills of the Grampian Highlands in central Scotland, he never dreamed he would hold such wealth. His descendants raised long, flax cotton on Jesus Island and made it famous the world over for the length and texture of its fibers. Many of the sturdy ribs of the USS *Constitution,* better known as "Old Ironsides," had been harvested from the gigantic oaks that grew on Jesus Island.

At the beginning of the Civil War, William Wallace McQueen IV had been at The Citadel in Charleston. It was his gun on Morris Island that fired at the *Star of the West* as she tried to resupply Fort Sumter on January 9, 1861, and he participated in the bombardment of Fort Sumter the following April 12th.

His father, Robert Bruce McQueen, had supervised construction of the ironclads *Savannah* and *Atlanta* at the McQueen Shipyard and had been present when the feared Confederate warships were launched. After the war, he worked tirelessly to get the McQueen Shipyard productive again, and through his efforts helped put postwar Savannah on her feet.

Poor and disabled Confederate veterans were never turned away empty-handed from McQueen Shipyard or the front door of the McQueen home on Liberty Street. In very short order, Capt. Robert McQueen became a driving force in veterans' organizations and local politics. By the first decade of the twentieth century, the McQueen family had been able to overcome the hardships and deprivations of the Reconstruction period and was firmly established as one of Savannah's finest.

To the delight of Robert Bruce McQueen, Jr., James Edward McQueen was born on Saint Andrew's Feast Day in 1919. In keeping with the family tradition, James was enrolled at the Military College of South Carolina at Charleston in 1937, better known as The Citadel.

Jimmy had been an average student but a solid asset to The Citadel corps of cadets. He harbored no intentions of a military career upon his graduation in 1941, aspiring instead to learn the family business by working with his father at the shipyard.

Because it was the McQueen way to know shipbuilding from the keel up, Jimmy started as a laborer at his father's yard. When the Japanese struck at Pearl Harbor, Jimmy had worked his way up to an assistant shift foreman on the refitting crew. No one under or above him resented his position. They all knew Jimmy hadn't used his name to get past any of the hard work. After Pearl Harbor, Jimmy McQueen would have had a 1-A draft classification due to his age and military school degree, but his employment at McQueen Shipyard and his broad knowledge of the shipbuilding industry deferred him from immediate induction into military service. Jimmy was not happy with his classification and actively sought a commission in the navy, following in the footsteps of his great-grandfather Lt. William McQueen. It was by a twist of fate that Jimmy McQueen's life would be forever entangled with that of Francis Quinn.

Francis had been placed on Jimmy's work gang refitting an old four-stack destroyer from the First World War. Its boilers hadn't been fired in more than twenty years, and it was the job of Jimmy's men to bring them to life again. The years of neglect had taken their toll on the valves and fittings; and even though precautions had been taken before the boilers were fired, the effects of the rust and corrosion made themselves evident when the number two boiler exploded.

Although Jimmy had been in the boiler room when the explosion occurred, he had somehow escaped the scalding steam that killed three of his men. However, he was covered in debris and near death from suffocation and shock when Francis, risking his own life, entered the blackened boiler room in search of survivors. It was Francis who single-handedly pulled Jimmy from the boiler room and carried him to the deck above, where he was revived. While Francis had been trained by the Nazis to be obscure and inconspicuous as a spy, he had, on impulse, tossed that aside. There was something about the screams of the trapped men that he could not ignore.

After the explosion, Francis became a well-known figure at the McQueen Shipyard. Although he eschewed the notoriety for his own safety, the acceptance and trust it brought him at the yard afforded him unprecedented access to the plans and construction principles of the new Liberty ships. When Jimmy was made shift foreman for construction of the SS *General James Edward Oglethorpe,* McQueen's first Liberty ship, Francis was his right-hand man. Although Francis never forgot his mission as spy and saboteur, he grew to respect and admire Jimmy McQueen. He also knew his place as a laborer from Brooklyn in the social order of Deep South Savannah and never tried to be too friendly with the aristocratic McQueen. However, the war had leveled many of the old social barriers, and that became evident on a Sunday afternoon in late May at the Tybrisa Pavilion.

Grace had placed a copy of the puppies-for-sale ad in the *Savannah Morning Gazette.* The next day Francis was sitting at the bar of the Riptide looking for Grace when Jimmy McQueen walked in with an attractive young lady on his arm. The weather had been stunningly beautiful for the preceding week, and the beach was crowded, not only with the usual multitude of servicemen, but also with local Savannahians, some of whom lived at the beach during the summer months. Inside the Riptide it was shoulder to shoulder as Jimmy and his date worked their way to the bar. Grace had already spotted Francis and had just walked away after telling him to meet her at the cottage later that evening when Jimmy eased up next to him.

"Francis, can I buy you a beer?"

Francis was a little surprised to see Jimmy McQueen in the Riptide, since he considered it to be somewhat below McQueen's social standing. But Francis didn't yet understand Savannah. He wasn't aware that the rules changed some on Tybee Island, where all but a few of the rowdiest bars were frequented by a number of Savannah's social set, especially the young and daring.

"Why, Mr. McQueen, it's good to see you, sir, and you, too, ma'am," said Francis, as he rose from his bar stool. Jimmy's date smiled warmly at Francis as he said, "Here, ma'am, please take this seat." The slender brunette thanked him as Jimmy placed his hand on Francis's shoulder and said, "Meg, this is Francis Quinn. He's the one I told you about. He's the fella who pulled me out of the boiler room. Francis, this is Meg Reynolds."

When Francis smiled, dimples formed in his cheeks, and his eyes twinkled. They were large and bright; and when he set them on Meg, she could hardly keep from staring at him. A lock of Francis's hair had fallen across his forehead, and he reached up and brushed it back. When he did, he said, "Pleased to meet you, Miss Reynolds. May I order you something to drink?"

Meg was impressed by Francis's good looks and really wasn't paying much attention to what he said, but she did manage a smile and replied, "Uh, yes, I think I'd like a rum and Coke," then settled onto the stool, her legs demurely together, one hand clutching a small purse.

Jimmy turned to Francis and said, "I'm glad I ran into you. We only see each other at the yard."

"Thank you, Mr. McQueen. I'm glad to see you here too, I don't know many people in Savannah. It gets a little lonely, you know, working all the time and everything."

"Well, you found your way to the beach, Francis." Jimmy laughed as their drinks arrived.

"Where are you from, Francis?" asked Meg, sipping her drink through a straw, leaving lipstick on it.

"Brooklyn. Brooklyn, New York. I guess I'm one of those damn Yankees," answered Francis, smiling.

"You're no damn Yankee as far as I'm concerned," injected Jimmy, "not after you pulled me out of that boiler room."

"Oh, tell me about that, Francis," said Meg, her eyes getting large.

Francis dropped his head and said, "It wasn't anything that anybody else wouldn't have done." He watched as Meg pursed her red lips, remarking, "That's not what I heard." He caught the sensuous shape of her tanned legs, and his eyes traced her thighs to the hem of her yellow shorts just above where she stopped shaving her legs. Then he followed her exposed midriff to the knot where her white cotton shirt was tied off, and his eyes passed over the cleft between her breasts and noticed the sparkle of the single large diamond hanging from her neck. He caught a flash of red nail polish on the fingers wrapped around her glass and could see that the bright yellow headband holding back her hair perfectly framed Meg's unmistakable Anglo features. She was pretty, reeked of wealth and position, and was exactly the type of girlfriend he imagined Jimmy McQueen would have.

"It's like I said, Miss Reynolds, it wasn't anything that anybody else wouldn't have done."

"Phooey," answered Meg, "and stop calling me Miss Reynolds. Call me Meg."

Francis shot a quick look at Jimmy, who said, "Hey, it's smoky and crowded in here. Why don't you come on over to the beach house, Francis. Maybe grab a sandwich. Meet my father. You know, kinda enjoy yourself a little. I owe you one for what you did. Let me pay you back, OK?"

"Well, Mr. McQueen, I haven't eaten yet, so I suppose that'd be fine."

Later that evening, after Jimmy had dropped Francis off at the bus station on Sixteenth and Butler, Meg told him she thought Francis might be just the thing for her friend Helene Bowen. She said he seemed to be very nice, adding, "Even if he does work under you at the shipyard. Besides, it's just a date. We can all go to the party the Oldmans are having next weekend. Helene just broke up with Harry Moxely, and I think she's feeling kind of down. It'd make Harry realize what a nice girl he had in Helene if he heard about her dating such a handsome young fella. Maybe you can give him some kind of title that won't make it sound like he's a day laborer."

Y ou're late," was all Grace said to Francis as he slipped in the back door of her cottage.

"Couldn't help it. I've been gathering information."

"About what, that little thing you left the Riptide with?"

"No, not at all. About things like how long it takes to build a Liberty ship, or about where the bottleneck is in production and how many ships Mr. McQueen is supposed to turn out at his shipyard. And, by the way, that 'little thing' you saw me with is the girlfriend of Jimmy McQueen. I just spent the evening with him at his father's beach house, where I got the chance to meet the old man."

Grace took a long drag off her last Pall Mall and crushed it in an ashtray on the kitchen table. Not in the least rebuffed, she replied, "Good, then we've got something meaningful we can relay."

Reaching into the cabinet over the sink, Grace produced an unopened bottle of Dewar's and two glasses. Then she turned and handed Francis a glass. "Would you care for a drink?"

Francis followed Grace into the sunroom, sat across from her, and asked, "OK, what's so important?"

"Things are getting ready to happen, Francis," answered Grace, as she rummaged through her handbag in search of another cigarette.

"Such as?"

"We've got more agents being put ashore right now, some up on the Jersey coast and some down in Florida. The ones in Florida will be heading this way. They've got the explosives. I hope you've figured out where they can use them."

"Well, when do you expect them to be here?"

"Supposed to be a few days, maybe a week. They've got to be careful. Anyway, they know to find me at the Riptide just like you did. I'll run my ad in the paper when they're ready to meet up with you."

Grace raised her glass, drained it, then said, "OK, tell me about the Liberty ships."

For the next hour Francis recounted every detail he knew about the manufacture and structure of Liberty ships as Grace made careful notes. Then she left the room with her notepad, hid it, and returned to the porch with two more drinks. This time Grace sat next to Francis on the sofa and placed her feet up on the little wicker coffee table. She let out a long sigh and said, "Enough of this spy business for tonight, tell me about yourself."

Francis was reluctant and wary, but after so many months of no contact with a woman, he was stimulated by the looks, if not the charm, of Grace. While he felt the effects of his four ounces of Scotch, he was still able to spin a yarn for Grace that was false but believable. She was told nothing about his true identity nor the deal that had been made between the Nazis and the IRA. His life story was painful and pitiful enough to appeal to a woman's tender instincts, and soon Grace found herself attracted, not only to Francis's good looks, but also to the man who had been shaped by such a sad childhood.

As she sipped her third Dewar's, Grace began to talk about her own life. Her story, however, wasn't a fabrication. She had been born in Germany into an upper-middle-class family that had lost all its wealth in the postwar Germany of the Weimar Republic. The Boehmler family was from Munich and had had a grand home there before the war. Her father had had a managerial position with I. G. Farben Company, and her mother was descended from nobility, albeit poor nobility, but nobility nonetheless. She was a woman of obvious class and distinction, explained Grace, but had been forced into accepting the charity of strangers to feed her family. That last indignity had been too much for her unfortunate father, and he had taken his own life, but not before seeing to it that Grace was sent to Milwaukee, where she could live with her mother's relatives.

She had been educated in America and liked the States, but still, she'd never felt she was anything but German. When Hitler came to power in 1932 and things in Germany began to improve, Grace returned to her homeland. With great animation, Grace told of how she had seen Hitler himself at the Nueremberg party rally in '34. "He looked right into my eyes, and I felt as though he had touched my soul," she said. It was then and there, Grace explained, amid the miracles of National Socialism, that she decided to dedicate her life to the dream of a greater Germany.

Then Grace grew quiet. After a few moments she reached out and touched Francis's hand. In a soft voice, she said, "Do you have to go back to town tonight?"

Turning to face Grace, Francis whispered, "No, I'm off tomorrow." There was a stillness in the small house. Finally, Grace touched Francis's cheek and studied his face. Slowly, he leaned forward and kissed Grace softly, and as the kiss deepened, ran his hands through her hair and drew her to him.

Grace was breathing heavily as she kissed Francis on his cheek, his ear, and then his neck. She was almost frantic in the way she kissed him, as if she had to hurry. His body was solid and heavy on top of her, and she clawed at his back when she felt his full weight press against her. Her skirt was pushed above her panties, and Grace wrapped her legs around

Francis and thrust herself at him. When she felt she would burst with desire, Francis took Grace by the hand and led her to the bedroom.

A slight breeze lifted and ruffled the lace curtains on the windows, making the cut-glass ornaments on the old oil lamp next to the bed tinkle. A pale light from the moon cast the couple's shadow on the wall as Francis undressed Grace.

Francis lifted Grace's naked body in his arms and placed her gently on the bed. Her eyes never left him as he lay next to her and caressed her. She wanted to remember everything and kept her eyes open as they made love, closing them only in that deep reflex of her most passionate moment. Twice more that night Francis took Grace, and twice more she found herself wanting words of affection. She didn't know why—she thought herself silly and frivolous—but she really didn't care. It seemed such a natural and needful thing.

In the morning their lovemaking was as intense as the night before. When hunger for food finally overtook hunger for passion, Grace arose with an incredible sense of lightness. Her cottage was beautiful, and she felt as though she never wanted to leave it. She smiled broadly and hummed as she set the table. She could not take her eyes off Francis as he ate. Later that morning, while Francis was showering, Grace took his shirt, pressed it against her nose, and sucked in his scent. She had to force herself to remember what her mission was and several times reproached herself for all that had happened, only to find herself standing at the bedroom door, watching and wanting, as Francis dressed.

When Francis was ready to leave, Grace embraced him and said, "Maybe after all this is over, maybe then we could have something. Maybe we could make each other happy."

Francis smiled and answered, "I'll be looking for the ad," gave her a quick kiss, turned, went out the back door, slipped through the oleanders, and was gone over the dunes along the Back River. No one ever knew he'd been to Grace's cottage.

Later that day at the Riptide, Grace was happy and talkative. She smiled and joked with GIs who normally would have gotten on her nerves. She didn't grasp what had really happened until Maude, one of the waitresses, said, "What's up with you today, honey? You're acting like you're in love or something."

Francis caught the eleven o'clock bus to Savannah and sat in the back. At that time of day there weren't many passengers, only a few sailors who looked hungover and one young marine who definitely was. The motor was in the rear of the bus right under his seat, and Francis could feel it rumble and groan as the driver ground through the gears and bumped along Tybee Road. He watched the steel trusses of the Lazaretto Creek Bridge pass by and caught the scent of decayed seafood from the shrimp boats next to the bridge. He thought about what had happened as the bus rolled off the bridge and started across the long, straight causeway through the open marsh.

Grace was falling in love with him, that was obvious. It was also dangerous. They were both agents of a country at war with the United States. If caught, they would probably be executed. *But still,* thought Francis, *it could prove useful to have Grace in love with him.* She would certainly be more amenable to manipulation. Besides, she was a Nazi; and if she got too overbearing with her love, he would simply inform her that such emotions were interfering with their duty to führer and fatherland.

The next weekend Francis attended the Moxely party with Helene Bowen. It was a casual affair at the Moxely summer home on the Vernon River. The girls who had made their debuts with Sarina Moxely were there as well, as was a mixture of other Moxely friends. When Helene was able to get Meg alone in one of the bathrooms, all she could say was, "He's gorgeous. He has the most beautiful eyes. Oh, Meg, I just love you so much for this!"

"Just you watch yourself with him, Helene, he's a sweet boy. He may not have much, but he's a sweet boy. Don't hurt him," was Meg's only reply.

Jimmy and Meg waited in the car while Francis walked Helene to the door of her home on Victory Drive. The Bowen house had been built at the turn of the century, when the palm-lined Victory Drive had been called Colonel Estill Avenue. Large porches surrounded the house on three sides, and three sets of wide steps led from the street to the porch. Lights were burning on either side of the double front doors, and they illuminated a yard filled with a dozen enormous white azaleas in full bloom. When they got to the door, Helene quickly opened it, turned off the porch lights, then stepped back outside.

Helene was pretty but not beautiful. She had strong, well-defined features that reflected good breeding more than dashing beauty. Her eyes were pale blue, and she had a few freckles that turned into more than a few when she got in the sun. Her hair was fine in texture and blonde. She usually wore it in a ponytail tied off with a ribbon. She had an impish way about her, knew how to handle her father, had smoked cigarettes at fifteen, and had been drunk on bourbon at seventeen. She was not what Francis would have classified as unattractive, but he didn't care for her figure. She was what some of the ladies in the altar guild at Saint John's Episcopal Church might have described as "a little on the horsey side."

"Helene, it's been a pleasure meeting you. I had a wonderful time tonight. You have so many nice friends, and you're as lovely as Meg said you were. If you're not busy next weekend, would you like to go out again?"

Helene had trouble suppressing her excitement but managed to give a measured reply. "I'm not sure what next weekend looks like yet," she said, "but if you'll call me in a few days, I can let you know."

As the spring of '42 heated to summer, Savannah began to hum with the industry and activity of war. Singapore and the Philippines fell to the Japanese that spring, while the Germans advanced in North Africa and their U-boats wreaked havoc in the Atlantic. *Yankee Doodle Dandy,* starring James Cagney, played to record audiences at the Lucas, while around the corner at the Avon on Broughton Street, *Mrs. Miniver,* with Greer Garson, packed the house for every showing. Nylon stockings were rare, but "Kilroy was here" could be seen everywhere. In the summer of '41 there were 1.8 million active-duty U.S. military personnel. By the summer of '42, that number would grow to more than 3.5 million.

Activity at the McQueen Shipyard had also seen a dramatic increase. The SS *General James Edward Oglethorpe* was scheduled to be launched in September, and the keels for three additional Liberty ships had already been laid. The relationship between Jimmy McQueen and Francis Quinn became closer, both in and out of the shipyard. This was partially due to Francis's growing relationship with Helene.

While Helene may have been falling madly in love with Francis, her parents assumed a posture of subtle distance and a measured degree of aloofness in dealing with him. Percy Bowen, Helene's father, didn't care much for Irishmen and cared even less for Yankees. With the absence of suitable lineage, acceptable employment, and a proper education, Percy regarded Francis as nothing more than a temporary distraction for his only daughter. Still, Percy fancied himself as being somewhat progressive and egalitarian in his outlook and was, more than anything, happy that Helene was happy. He thought Helene regarded Francis as kind of a trophy boyfriend, noting that she derived much pleasure when her friends carried on about how "dreamy" he was. Percy fully expected the relationship to wither and die with the fall.

Sophia Wright Bowen was another story. Her main fear was that Helene might "do something rash," such as sleep with Francis and become pregnant. She believed that Helene was rebellious in nature and impulsive in behavior, a combination that could spell disaster for the Bowen name. Nevertheless, she was a firm advocate of the theory that good breeding would always manifest itself, and she, too, thought Helene would tire of Francis.

Helene showed no inclination that she would tire of her new boyfriend that summer. She saw him weekly, and the two often double-dated with Jimmy and Meg. At night the couples would frequently drive to the beach for dances at the Tybrisa and end up having drinks at Al Remler's Club Royale on Victory Drive. When they had time during the day and the weather permitted, they would go sailing on the McQueen family yacht, a thirty-eight footer named *Lost Cause*.

While Francis never let himself forget the real reason he was in Savannah, he often found himself thinking about what he would do once his mission was completed. Sometimes he caught himself thinking about staying in Savannah, about marrying into the Bowen family and living a life that few ever dreamed of in Ireland. It was on a bright Sunday afternoon aboard the *Lost Cause* that those daydreams came to a halt.

Francis and Jimmy were at the ship's helm guiding her across Wassaw Sound, with Meg and Helene in the cabin below, when Jimmy started talking about things at the shipyard.

"We had some FBI agents in the office today; they were asking a lot of questions."

"Questions about what?" asked Francis.

"Things about security. You know, guards at the gates, suspicious characters, stuff like that."

"Is there a problem?"

"Oh, I don't think there's a problem with our yard, but there have been with some up north."

"Like what?"

"Well, this is kinda confidential right now. The FBI said it'll be out in the papers soon but not to go blabbing it all around. So I gotta ask you to keep this under your hat, OK?"

Jimmy held the ship's wheel with his right hand and winched in the main sheet a little tighter with his left. When he settled back, he turned to Francis and said, "The feds captured six Germans in New Jersey a few days ago. They said the Jerries had been put ashore by a U-boat and had buried a big stash of explosives on the beach at Long Island where they came in. They said the Krauts had finally confessed to everything, and that part of their plan was to blow up shipyards. They also said they had caught some other Germans who had been put ashore close to Jacksonville. They got three of 'em there."

"Did the FBI say anything more?" asked Francis.

"Yeah, they said they think there could be some people right here in Savannah planning to blow something up. They want us to start reporting anything that looks suspicious. I remember a few months back when the rumor was that a sub had put some guys ashore near Savannah."

"I don't think I had come to Savannah yet when that happened," Francis responded casually.

"Well, whatever's going on, I think the feds are on to somebody around here," said Jimmy, as he scanned the western horizon.

"Looks like a thunderstorm is comin' up. We'd better take her back to the dock before it really starts blowing."

There weren't many people in the Riptide that evening when Francis slipped into one of the booths. Grace spotted him immediately and after a few minutes walked over and asked, "What'll ya have?"

"How 'bout a nice cold Blatz in a frosted glass?" replied Francis.

"Sure, buddy, anything else?"

"Naw, that oughta do me for a few minutes."

Then in a whisper, Francis said, "I need to see you."

Grace inconspicuously looked around and replied, "The cottage at ten."

At dark Francis set out for Grace's house. The moon was only a sliver in the sky, obscured by clouds, and the little tar road that led to the cottage had no streetlights. Francis moved along in the shadows; and when he got to Grace's, he found a hiding place among some palmettos across the street.

Francis had survived his service in Ireland by relying on his intelligence and training. But most of all, he had come to trust what his gut instincts told him. For the next hour he thought through everything with great care then balanced it against what he felt in his gut.

A little after ten, the sounds of a car jarred Francis from his thoughts. He could hear laughter as it approached; and amid the squeaking of the old Dodge's brakes, he heard Grace's voice say, "This is it, boys. I'll get out right here."

He could make out three sailors in various stages of intoxication and listened as Grace gently, but firmly, informed them that they were absolutely not coming in for "another one." He watched as the car pulled away and could see Grace fumbling with her keys at the front door. For another thirty minutes, Francis stayed in the bushes watching, listening, and thinking.

Francis decided Grace had been compromised by the capture of the German agents in New York and Florida. He reasoned that at least one of the nine would talk to save himself, and that Grace would be fingered. While no one but Grace knew his identity, he was aware from experience that she would eventually talk. Although the Americans liked to think their government did not resort to torture, Francis knew differently. He knew the rules changed when a spy was caught, especially one caught during wartime in the United States with radios and explosives. The FBI or the army or the State Department or somebody would wring every last syllable of information from their captives, and then they would quickly and secretly be tried before a military court and just as quickly executed. They wouldn't be shot, either; that was a death reserved for soldiers. These Germans, every last one of them, including beautiful Grace, would be hung by their necks until dead. Then their bodies would be buried in unmarked graves on the grounds of some federal penitentiary in Kansas or Nevada

Working his way down the side of the cottage, Francis eased the back door open and slipped inside. Grace was waiting in the sunroom when she heard him enter. The only lights on were two nautical lamps on the mantle. When Francis walked in, Grace was standing at the windows. The glow from her cigarette reflected off the glass, and Francis watched for a moment as she took a long drag. She had her back to him and was wearing a white terry-cloth robe and no shoes. She didn't turn to face Francis but only said, "You're late. I've been waiting thirty minutes."

Grace didn't sound irritated just disappointed when she turned and faced Francis. Her hair cascaded down her neck, framing a face with flawless skin. Her robe was parted at the top, loosely tied at the waist, and partially opened below, revealing a portion of her thighs.

"Well," Grace almost whispered, "what did you have to see me about?"

"This is crazy," said Francis, "but I can't stop thinking about things. About you, I mean. I haven't been able to get you out of my mind, what you said about how things might be when this is all over."

Francis moved to the window, stood next to Grace, and looked out over the river. On the windowpane he traced a heart with his finger then turned and faced Grace. They were inches apart.

"I care so much about you, Grace. I tried not to, but I do. I tried to stay away from you and only see you when we had business, but, damn it, I can't. I'm sorry. Please don't be angry with me, but I just had to see you and tell you how I feel and find out if you really meant what you said about us after the war."

Grace's eyes grew wide, then tears welled up and ran down her high Nordic cheekbones. Her lips, freshly adorned with a seductive color, trembled. She dropped her head slightly and looked into Francis's eyes.

"I haven't stopped thinking about you, either. That night was heaven for me. Never in my life did I ever dream that anyone could touch me as you did, that I'd ever love anybody, if love is what this is. This is silly, stupid, dangerous, all kinds of things, but I've got to have you, Francis. Germany, the führer, even victory itself don't mean as much to me as you do."

Without another word, Grace untied her robe, letting it fall open, revealing her naked body. Then she pulled Francis to her and pressed herself against him while kissing him. With great passion Francis returned her kiss, then he scooped Grace up in his arms as he had done that first night of love and carried her to the bedroom.

Francis started unbuttoning his shirt while Grace let her robe fall to her feet then turned to pull back the covers of her bed. As she bent over and smoothed the sheets, Francis stood behind her and admired the curve of her hips. Things began to stir in him as he moved behind Grace, put his arms around her waist, and forced himself against her. Grace was already breathing heavily and moaned as she held herself against Francis for several seconds, then she stood and rubbed her naked back against him and rested her head against his chest.

"You feel tense," said Francis, "let me rub your neck for you."

As Francis gently massaged her neck, Grace sighed and rolled her head from side to side, her heart pounding in anticipation.

"Oh, that feels so good," said Grace, as Francis put his left arm close to her neck. "Ummm," she moaned, as he moved his right hand up the right side of her head. "Oh," was all Grace could manage when Francis, with tremendous force, snapped her head to the left with his right hand while wedging her neck to the right with his left arm.

Grace's body fell limp against Francis, and he placed her on the floor, faceup. He looked into her eyes in the same way he had done with Nathan Eisenman and said, "I'm sorry, Grace. I had no choice. All of your friends have been caught by the FBI, and they're coming for you. I can't take the chance that you'd turn me in."

Francis could see tears in Grace's eyes just as he had in Nathan's and saw her blink just as Nathan had. Then he felt for the carotid artery in her neck. Her heart was still beating, and she was still conscious when Francis said, "It won't be much longer now, Grace. Darkness and peace are only moments away."

In the kitchen Francis poured himself a stiff Dewar's on the rocks and then set about wiping anything he could remember touching with a damp cloth. When he returned to the bedroom, he felt for Grace's pulse and found none. After he put her robe back on, he took her body in his arms and went to the back door. It was quite dark outside; and when he was certain no one could see, he carried Grace over the wooden walkway leading to the dock house. About halfway, he stopped and kicked out one side of the rickety handrail. At that point, there was only beach below; and Francis let Grace's body fall, headfirst, onto the hard packed sand. Then he went back into the cottage, fixed another, stronger Dewar's in the glass Grace had been drinking from, and carried it to the broken place in the railing. He placed the glass on the railing, complete with Grace's fingerprints and lipstick marks.

After returning to the cottage, Francis carefully walked through, looking for anything that might link him to Grace. When he was satisfied, he got a pair of Grace's shoes from the closet. He squeezed his feet into them as far as he could and left by the back door, leaving only women's shoe prints in the sand.

At ten o'clock the next morning, Grace's body was discovered by some children, but not before it had been found by a dozen crabs busy at work on her remains. The Tybee police report stated that Grace had been drinking and had fallen through the loose railing, hit the sand headfirst, and broken her neck. Three days later, the FBI appeared at her cottage with an arrest warrant. Later that day, they found the shortwave radio Francis had given her hidden under the floorboards of a little cedar closet next to her bedroom. The agents interviewed all of her neighbors and everyone who worked with her at the Riptide. Neither the name nor the description of Francis Quinn was ever mentioned.

During September of 1942, while the men of the First Marine Division fought desperate Japanese soldiers on Guadalcanal Island in the South Pacific, the men of the McQueen Shipyard worked under the punishing Savannah sun to launch their first Liberty ship. While the tide had begun to turn against the Nazis in Russia and the "Nips" in the Pacific, as far as people in Savannah were concerned, victory was still an uncertain and distant dream.

Jimmy McQueen had pressed hard for a commission in the navy when the war started but had been told that his knowledge and skills at shipbuilding were far more important to his country than a naval commission. By the same logic, Francis Quinn's draft status had also not changed, although he tried to stay out of the military rather than get in. Still, the enormous need for manpower eventually rendered a navy commission for Jimmy and an induction notice for Francis. Soon only women and those males under seventeen or over fifty were working on Liberty ships at the McQueen yard.

Jimmy McQueen was sworn in as navy ensign on September 14, 1942. The next day, "Miss Mit," the wife of Georgia governor Gene Talmadge, broke a bottle of champagne over the bow of the SS *General James Edward Oglethorpe,* and the ship slipped stern first into the Savannah River.

Three months later LTJG James McQueen was standing at the helm of PT 167. He and his crew were cruising the waters surrounding Guadalcanal in search of Japanese ships attempting to reinforce their starving island garrison. At the same time, half a world away, PFC Francis Quinn was riding on a transport in the Mediterranean Sea. He was part of Operation Torch and would land on the coast of North Africa in early November to fight Rommel's Afrika Korps.

Back in Savannah, rationing had made everything from sewing needles to car tires scarce, and sometimes impossible to acquire. Little things, such as the absence of elastic waistbands in underwear and scrap metal drives that collected the aluminum foil from candy and gum wrappers, served as constant reminders to everyone that America was in a fight for her life.

A lot had gone through Francis's mind since he'd visited Grace's cottage that last time. His feelings were quite different from what they'd been when U-123 had slipped him onto the Georgia coast. Then, he'd considered the Germans to be almost invincible and had been awed as he read of their victories in Russia and Africa. The swiftness of the Japanese takeover in the Pacific after Pearl Harbor had further served to convince Francis that America would have to settle for a negotiated peace with her Axis enemies. Now, the American victories at the Coral Sea, Midway, and Guadalcanal, as well as the blunting of the German offensive in Russia, gave Francis pause for thought.

With the Nazi spy network discovered and Grace dead, Francis realized his only hope for survival lay in becoming a real American in every way he could. To that end he accepted his fate and assumed the persona of Francis Quinn completely. He had no idea how long the war would last or if he would survive it. He also didn't know if he would ever see his parents and country again. What he did know was that if he were ever discovered, he would be hanged.

As the war progressed, Francis fought first in North Africa and then landed with Patton in Sicily in '43. He was with Gen. Mark Clark in Italy and was part of the assault on Monte Casino, where he was twice wounded and was awarded the Bronze Star as well as his sergeant's stripes. He also received weekly letters from Helene, who had fallen madly in love with him.

In the Pacific, Jimmy McQueen's PT boat had seen action at Guadalcanal, New Guinea, and New Caledonia. He had also been promoted and decorated for heroism, but he'd had to be sent back to the States in 1943 after sustaining a serious chest wound when his boat was attacked by a Japanese Zero. In early '44, because of these wounds, he was discharged from the navy and returned to Savannah. He married Meg that summer at Saint John's Church and two weeks later returned to the McQueen Shipyard and its Liberty ships.

5. Bolita

The great engine of change in the American South has always been war. First, it was the Civil War, which brought physical destruction as well as social and economic upheaval; then World War I took thousands of boys off the farms and out of the small towns that comprised the bulk of the South's population, sending them to faraway places in Europe. But the biggest change the South ever experienced was wrought by World War II.

For the first time ever, hundreds of thousands of men and women from all over the country converged on the cities and hamlets of the South in a peaceful manner to construct the implements of war. Among the things they brought were a different culture and a great deal of money, two things the South had not known before. Industries of all kinds sprang up everywhere. As a result, by the time MacArthur had accepted the Japanese surrender in September of 1945, the Old South and everything about her had been placed on a resolute course of profound change.

Even though change had certainly come to Savannah, it was considerably less than in other southern cities of similar size. To the north Charleston would emerge as a great naval base; to the south Jacksonville would become a trade center. Tucked between the two, Savannah would drift with the clouds over the Atlantic, sway with the moss, and float with the marsh grass. Savannah was content and happy in her isolation and enjoyed her special status in the state of Georgia. She was an aristocrat, secure in her family name, certain of her classical beauty.

By the time Francis Quinn and Jimmy McQueen had returned to Savannah, the high tide of change had begun to recede throughout the city. Some of the wartime workers stayed on, but most from the outside world went away and left Savannah to be herself again.

At the McQueen Shipyard, the end of the war meant contracts for a dozen ships had been canceled, forcing the layoff of hundreds of workers. Francis had hoped to step into his old position at the yard, and William Wallace McQueen V was in his office the day Francis came by the shipyard looking for a job. Mr. McQueen and Jimmy had been going over the figures together, both realizing that even more people would have to be laid off.

"We can give you a job as a welder, Francis," said Mr. McQueen, "but you know what that's all about. I don't have anything in a supervisory position now, and I don't know when, or really if, we will again for a long time."

"Yes, sir, I understand," said Francis, as he stood next to Jimmy in front of Mr. McQueen's desk.

"Francis," said Jimmy, "you know you've got a job here if you want it. We'll find something for you, but it won't be like it used to be."

"That's OK," said Francis, putting his hand on Jimmy's shoulder, "don't be upset. I'll find something; I'm not gonna starve."

Mr. McQueen pushed his chair back from his desk and stood up. He was a fine-looking man for his age, with a full head of gray hair neatly combed back from his forehead. He wore wire-rimmed glasses that gave him a scholarly appearance and spoke with the soft coastal accent of a Savannah aristocrat.

"Tell ya what," said Mr. McQueen, as he walked over to the large window that overlooked the Savannah River, "I know some folks who just might be interested in puttin' you on their payroll in a capacity that you might find most rewardin', Francis."

Two days later, Francis was at Tybee, sitting in a booth at a place called the Brass Rail. It was a Friday afternoon around five, and the last rays from an October sun shone through the windows, cutting long slices of light across the oak dance floor. From outside, the sounds of waves breaking against the seawall intermingled with "Ain't Misbe-havin'" playing on a big Wurlitzer jukebox. The smell of fried chicken drifted in from the kitchen; and while he waited, Francis watched as an overweight woman in a print dress fed quarters into one of four slot machines near the bar. Francis had been in the Brass Rail for about ten minutes when a well-dressed man in his late fifties came over and intro-duced himself.

"You must be Francis Quinn," said the man, as he extended his hand.

"Yes, sir, I am," said Francis.

"Well, I'm proud to know ya', son. I'm Willie Hart."

Almost immediately a waiter appeared at the table with a small, round tray tucked under his arm.

"Will you be havin' something now, Mr. Hart, or would you like to wait for a few minutes, sir?"

"I think I could go for a Manhattan, how about you, Francis?" asked Willie, as he looked over at his guest and smiled.

"That'll be fine, Mr. Hart."

Willie smiled once more and said, "Just call me Willie, son, every-body does; we're not much on formality down here at the beach." Then he turned to the waiter and said, "Tell Essie Mae we'll be havin' dinner here tonight. I want her to fix up some She Crab Soup special for Mr. Quinn here. Some fried oysters, too, Washington."

Willie sat back in the booth, took a long sip from his Manhattan, then placed it on the table. He looked at Francis thoughtfully for a moment and said, "Billy McQueen thinks a lot of you, son. He says you saved Jimmy's life."

Francis shifted in his seat and replied, "The McQueens have been good to me, Mr. Hart. Jimmy would have done the same for me or any-body else. He didn't get a medal at Guadalcanal for nothing."

"I agree," said Willie, "and I understand you're a combat veteran, too. North Africa and Italy, isn't it?"

"Yes, sir, some of it."

"You're from New York City, isn't that right?"

"Yes, sir, raised in an orphanage."

"Got a record?"

"No, sir. I'm clean."

Willie let out a sigh, took another sip, and said, "That's good." Then he leaned forward over the drink and said, "I need somebody I can trust, somebody who can take care of himself, too. I own this place, as well as several others down here, and I have a piece of the slot-machine action as well as the Bolita games back in town. I need a man who can tell me if somebody is stealin' from me and somebody who can take care of the problem for me, too. Do you drink?"

"A little," answered Francis. "I can take it or leave it. It's never been a problem for me."

"That's good too, Francis. How about the ladies? I understand you're involved with that Bowen girl. What's her name, Helene?"

"Yes, sir, we've been seeing each other since I came here in '42."

Willie studied Francis for a second and then said, "Don't misunderstand me, son, but isn't she a little out of your social league? How do her momma and daddy feel about you?"

Francis smiled and replied, "I understand, Mr. Hart. I don't think they're too happy about me, and I've tried to be real low-key about the whole thing. I'm taking it slow."

"Well, you must be a real charmer, son, 'cause the McQueens think you hung the moon, and they're right up there on top of Savannah society."

"I'm very flattered, sir. I hope I can live up to all that they've said about me, Mr. Hart."

"Goddammit, son, call me Willie, all my people call me Willie, I ain't nothing but a country boy from Screven County."

"Yes, sir."

"By the way," said Willie, after he had taken another sip of his Manhattan, "when can you start?"

"Right now."

"That's great," said Willie. "You'll get half a percent of what you take in each week. That should come out to something like three hundred a week. You'll also get a car. As a matter of fact, as soon as they start making new Caddies again, I'll let you have mine. It's a '42, but still a fine ride, Francis. I hope that'll suit ya'."

"Yes sir," said Francis. "But what about the police? I mean, I don't understand how all this works."

Willie smiled broadly and said, "Don't worry about a thing. You'll be right with me for several months and get to know them all. They're all our friends."

There were essentially two groups who controlled all the gambling in Chatham County. Willie Hart ran one, and tough local Irish-Catholic boy Snippy Flarity ran the other. While Willie had complete control at Tybee, back in Savannah, things were divided up by location. Slot machines were present in hotels, bars, and social clubs, such as the Moose, Elks, Knights of Columbus, and the various veterans' organizations that had proliferated after the war's end. They were divided about evenly between Willie and Snippy. Street gambling took place almost exclusively in the black areas on the west side of town, where Willie and Snippy each controlled certain neighborhoods. These were the numbers games collectively referred to as Bolita, named after a popular game of similar style played in Cuba.

Collecting and processing money earned from the slot machines were a simple chore that only required a key to the machine and a way to haul the coins to the basement of the Hotel DeSoto on Liberty Street, where it was counted. Bolita was another story.

With Bolita, players bet a nickel, dime, or quarter on a number from one to one hundred. On street corners and in convenience stores throughout black Savannah there were the "runners" with whom a player would place his bet. There were as many as a hundred runners collecting bets all day long. They turned over this money to another person who made the rounds daily, reporting to the collection room at the DeSoto in the afternoon. While highly profitable, it was a cumbersome operation fraught with problems of size and dishonesty. It was in this area that Francis's services were most needed.

For several weeks Willie ushered Francis all over Savannah. They went to every bar Willie owned at Tybee and visited every place in Savannah where he had slot machines, from the Marine Club on Drayton Street to the Drum Room in the Savannah Hotel on Johnson Square. After that they would direct their attention to the Bolita game and roll down West Broad Street meeting the various runners who worked for Willie. On Sunday mornings he and Francis would go calling on black churches, where Willie would make generous cash donations. On Sunday afternoons Willie and Francis would meet with the deacons from white churches, where Willie would dig deep again and make the deacon board smile.

The world that Helene knew had always been one of privilege. She enjoyed not only the material things her father's wealth provided but also the status of family lineage that could only be inherited, never purchased. Her pedigree ran through the bloodlines of Savannah aristocracy and coursed its way through those of Charleston and Richmond as well. The Bowen-Thompson house on Oglethorpe Square had been built by Helene's great-great-grandfather and designed by John Jay, the finest architect of the day. The building was considered to be the most superb example of Jay's splendid design work. After Percy Bowen had moved his family into their new home on Victory Drive, he donated the house to the Telfair museum. The *Savannah Morning Gazette* described this action as a "magnanimous gesture of civic pride and generosity unmatched in Savannah's history."

As she physically matured, Helene began to resemble her father in stature and her mother in complexion and facial features. Percy Bowen was an imposing man of six feet, three inches. When he was twenty-one he weighed 225 pounds, was broad of shoulder, and carried not an ounce of fat. By fifty he was close to 300 pounds with a forty-six-inch waist. On Helene's sixteenth birthday, she was two inches taller than her mother, weighed 130 pounds, and was the tallest girl in her class at Pape School. She was even taller than most of the boys. Yet there was something elegant and charming about Helene that made her popular in her circle of friends and not without interest from the boys. She was a spoiled romantic, who was unhappy that money could not buy her the looks she desperately wanted but was willing to accept the handsome prince she secretly knew it could. It was in this frame of mind that Helene pursued Francis.

By the summer of 1946, Francis was securely installed as Willie Hart's right-hand man. While everyone in Savannah knew Francis was involved in an illegal enterprise, most people did not look upon it as a criminal activity. Savannah was a tolerant town in which the vast majority of its residents viewed the slot machines, Bolita, moonshine, and Sunday liquor sales with a wink and a nod.

Although Francis was treated with respect and admiration by the lower and middle classes, the aristocracy was divided in its view of him. There was a kind of fascination with Francis in Savannah's upper classes that was a mixture of enchantment, fear, and jealousy. Some of the older ladies were offended that he had penetrated their ranks but could understand the attraction he held for Helene. The younger women all thought Francis was devilishly handsome. The more daring ones made passes at him, while those with retiring personalities harbored fantasies they dared not discuss, even with their best friends. Helene was simply content to bask in the limelight of her beautiful beau, while trying to convince her mother that he was "acceptable."

None of this deterred Jimmy in his admiration of Francis or in his growing friendship with him. Jimmy, as well as many of his friends, found Francis a fascinating person made all the more so by his association with Willie Hart.

Francis was, in a sense, Willie's ambassador of goodwill as well as his operations manager. In this capacity he would spend at least a few minutes a week in each of the establishments where Willie had his machines or where the Bolita runners were active. This could be the bars on Bay Street where sailors from around the world wandered in and out, black nightclubs on West Broad Street, or redneck hangouts in Garden City. Equally impressive was Francis's relationship with the owners of the black bars and businesses. He was well aware of their status in the South and took special care to show them unusual respect, kindness, and generosity. Because of this he gained not only financially but also politically.

Soon he would become known as the man who controlled the black vote in Savannah, and that was important to Willie Hart whenever some bluenose decided to try and reform Savannah's loose attitude toward liquor and gambling.

6. Politics and Religion

"Politics are almost as exciting as war, and quite as dangerous. In war you can only be killed once, but in politics many times."

—SIR WINSTON SPENCER CHURCHILL,
Remark, 1920

Nineteen forty-eight was the first four-year election cycle after the war. There were millions of newly minted veterans; and because of their growing power, Congress passed a series of very generous veterans' aid and assistance programs. In Georgia, as in many other states, veterans got everything from free drivers' licenses and scholastic aid to bonus points on state merit exams. In Savannah the veterans' organizations had become overnight kingmakers. They were well organized, young, and energetic. Most had their own social halls, complete with cocktail lounges.

The open gambling that took place all over Chatham County was possible only because the politicians who controlled the police made it so. It was natural, then, that the individuals who controlled the gambling and liquor businesses in Savannah were heavy contributors to the political process. Also, just as the business of vice had its interest in politics, so did all other forms of enterprise. Every industry in Savannah from papermaking to shipbuilding had a vested interest in how the city was run, and each usually had one of their best and brightest either serving on a government agency or holding some form of elected office.

From Savannah's beginnings, the McQueen family had been involved in state and local politics. Some members of the family had represented Chatham County in the state legislature, while others had been elected to the city council. But no McQueen had ever served as mayor of Savannah.

In 1946, Melvin Calhoun, then mayor of Savannah, let it be known he would not seek reelection. When word spread that Calhoun would not run again, the business community began to look for a successor. Although Jimmy McQueen had been interested in politics before the war, he had never considered seeking elective office. After the war he became active in various obligatory civic clubs, such as the Chamber of Commerce, the Rotary Club, the Propeller Club, and a half dozen others. But he was most active in the veterans' organizations and served as the chairman of the Chatham County Veterans Council. It wasn't long before Jimmy's friends on the veterans council were urging him to run for mayor.

Even though the majority of Savannah was willing to tolerate the gambling that went on in the city, there were those who were roundly opposed. Almost all were members of different Protestant churches in the city, and they had zero tolerance for alcohol and gambling of any kind, especially the kind that was out in the open for all to see. In 1947, a number of Protestant clergymen banded together and formed the Citizens' Progressive League. Its sole aim was to eradicate gambling in Chatham County. The CPL, as it became known, also targeted Tybee, which it considered to be an evil place of almost biblical proportions. When the CPL learned that Calhoun wouldn't be running, they seized on this as an opportunity to place someone in City Hall who had the fortitude to stand up to the liquor and gambling interests and clean up the city of Savannah.

The chairman of the Citizens Progressive League was Jesse Cooper Boatwright, pastor of the New Jerusalem Christian Church located in East Savannah just off Pennsylvania Avenue. Brother Boatwright, as he was called by the members of his congregation, was from Batesburg, South Carolina, a small town not far from Columbia. His father had worked all of his life in one of the cotton mills near there. His mother had been forced to take a part-time job at the Winn-Dixie store in town to make ends meet, but they were able to scrape together enough money to help send Jesse to nearby Bob Jones University, where he studied for the ministry.

Jesse arrived in Savannah in early 1947 with a year and a half of Bible studies under his belt and the burning fire of the Holy Ghost in his heart. He'd been drafted into the army during the war but had never left the States and had gotten an early discharge from the service when it was discovered he had diabetes.

Brother Boatwright had a natural cadence to his sermon delivery and a South Carolina sand-hill twang in his voice. His hair was jet black, parted on the right, and stood in stark contrast to a pasty white complexion marked by teenage acne scars. He had dark and piercing eyes that, from time to time, revealed the frightening intensity in Brother Boatwright's soul.

Six months after Boatwright took over at his church, the sanctuary couldn't hold the crowds that gathered every Sunday morning and Wednesday night to hear him preach the Gospel of the Lord Jesus Christ.

Preaching against the evils of whiskey and gambling was as natural for Brother Boatwright as preaching for the merits of salvation through faith in the Lord Jesus. Most members of his church already professed belief in total abstinence, so Brother Boatwright was on fertile ground when he started his campaign to remove gambling devices and flowing liquor from the Free State of Chatham. The only problem was that the New Jerusalem Christian Church was a working-class congregation made up of factory workers from the sugar refinery, paper mills, and shipyards. Other than votes, they didn't have much power in Savannah; but in a time when there were no television at all and only two radio stations in Savannah, Brother Boatwright was high-voltage entertainment mixed with old-time religion, and the people loved to hear him preach. It wasn't long before the pastors of Savannah's upper-crust Protestant churches were hearing about Brother Boatwright and the powerful message he was delivering about sin in River City. When members of their congregations began attending Brother Boatwright's Wednesday evening services just to hear him preach, there was a change in attitude among many of the downtown Protestant churches. It was then that the Citizens Progressive League began to gather strength and search for a slate of suitable candidates for the 1948 election.

At that time there was no real Republican presence in the South. This meant that winning the Democratic primary election was tantamount to winning the general election. In Savannah there were different organizations in the Democratic party that would place their candidates up for election in the primary. The most influential was the Chatham County Democratic Club, known as the CCDC. Its candidates could always be assured adequate financing and the delivery of the union and black vote. While blacks and union members didn't make up the majority of the electorate in Chatham County, they were dependable; and if a candidate could corral enough swing votes, he could win an election if backed by the CCDC. For a number of years, the CCDC had enjoyed financial support from the business community in Savannah as well as the liquor and gambling interests.

The day before Saint Patrick's Day, the leaders of the CCDC met at the Hotel DeSoto to pick their candidates. Many of the inner circle were veterans, and it didn't take long for the CCDC to choose Jimmy McQueen as their candidate for mayor. Over his wife's protests, he accepted the challenge.

Two weeks later, on Easter Sunday night, the Citizens Progressive League met to decide on their list of candidates. Brother Boatwright, along with the Reverend Billy Simms of the Savannah Christian Temple, had spent many long hours trying to find a candidate they thought could win against the CCDC. When Ernest Williams consented to run, both considered him an answer to their prayers.

Ernest Oliver Williams was an attorney who came from an upper-middle-class Savannah family, complete with Civil War ancestors and a summer home at the Isle of Hope. What was even better was that he was a Methodist and would be able to attract a much broader base of support. His only drawback, one that Jesse and Billy hadn't given that much thought to, was his lack of military service. He had been rejected because he had suffered from rheumatic fever as a child and had a heart murmur.

Ernie Williams had surprised everyone by being an energetic and resourceful candidate. Since he was a lawyer, he was able to schmooze regularly with the crowd down at the Chatham County Courthouse on Wright Square. He was pleasant and well liked by his colleagues, and saying nice things about Ernie wasn't hard for them to do.

Willie Hart had always been a heavy contributor to the CCDC, and 1948 was no exception. In fact, he considered this race so important he instructed Francis to give his full attention to helping get Jimmy elected. This meant that several nights a week Francis would make the rounds of the establishments that had Willie's slot machines and put the word out about voting for Jimmy.

While Francis was working the nightclubs for Jimmy, Brother Boatwright was working the churches for Ernie. He would be a guest preacher at different churches and never mention Ernie Williams by name but railed against the evils of drinking and gambling and what they were doing to the soul of Savannah. There would always be somebody at the church door handing out Citizens Progressive League flyers at the end of the evening.

Still, with all their hard work, Ernie, Brother Boatwright, and the Citizens Progressive League were behind, and they knew it. In mid-August, Brother Boatwright came to the conclusion that something drastic needed to be done.

It was no secret in the upper reaches of Savannah society that Jimmy and Francis were close friends. It was also no secret who Francis worked for, what he did for a living, and that he was making a lot of money doing it. However, Francis's friendship and support for Jimmy weren't something that was known by everyone in Savannah, and Brother Boatwright correctly sensed this could be used against Jimmy.

The Rotary Club of Savannah met every Monday for lunch in the ballroom of the Hotel DeSoto. Made of red-and-amber brick with a terra-cotta roof, it had a large porch running along the Bull Street side filled with rocking chairs and ferns. At the main entrance, a lion's head spewed water from its mouth into a pool of oversized goldfish.

Ernie was the scheduled speaker that day and had been fighting with himself over what to say. He wanted to tear into Jimmy McQueen and his buddies, Willie Hart and Francis Quinn, but he just didn't think it was wise for more reasons than one. As he rounded the corner of the lobby, he saw Brother Boatwright and another man.

"Brother Boatwright," said Ernie, as he extended his hand, "I'm surprised to see you here. Are you a member of the Rotary Club?" Ernie knew full well he wasn't, but he had a funny feeling when he saw the preacher and couldn't think of anything else to say.

"No, Ernie, I'm not. I'm here 'cause I want ya to meet this poor soul of a father and hear what he has to tell ya. Then I want ya to dig deep inside yourself, Ernie, real deep, and do what the Lord is expectin' of ya."

Brother Boatwright turned to the man and placed his hand on his shoulder.

"Ernie," said Brother Boatwright, "this here is Lester Bergeron, and he's got a story I want you to listen to before you go into that there Rotary Club meetin' and make your speech."

Then the preacher turned to the man and said, "Lester, why don't ya tell Mr. Williams here what ya told me last night? He's a friend of ours and can help put a stop to all that's goin' on in Savannah."

Lester looked at Ernie for a second or two and took a deep breath. "Well, it's like this, Mr. Williams. My baby girl, Darlene, she's sixteen now. Well, suh, I got a call last Saturday night from Candler Hospital. They said they had Darlene down there and that she'd been hurt in a car wreck. Well, I got her momma, and we both went down there lickety-split. When we got there, we found out she'd been throwed through a car winda' and had her face all cut to hell. Well, suh, she had to have 165 stitches in her face. The doctor said she'd be scarred for life probably, and she was my beautiful baby girl."

Ernie nervously shifted from one foot to the other and said, "I'm real sorry to hear about that, Mr. Bergeron. Do you want me to represent her in a civil action?"

"Well, suh, no, not exactly. Ya see, her and her boyfriend, his name is Jackie, they was at the Drum Room over in the Savannah Hotel that night, and they was both a-drinkin'. She ain't but sixteen, like I said, and me and her momma tried to raise her up better, but you know how kids is. Anyway, Jackie ain't no more than eighteen. Well, they was also playing them slot machines they got over there, and Jackie, he up and won a bunch. Then Darlene said he took to drinkin' a whole lot to sorta celebrate, if ya know what I mean. When they left and was riding back to home, that's when Jackie went'n piled his daddy's Ford into a oak tree along Bay Street. I ain't mad at the boy, not really. He wasn't hurt none, and he loves Darlene, I know that; and he's all broke up over what happened. What I am riled up over is that them kids could go into that place and buy liquor and play them machines, and them folks at the Drum Room, they had to know they was underage. I go to Brother Boatwright's church; and when I told him about Darlene and what all happened, he said you was the man who could put a stop to all this and would I come with him and tell you about what happened and maybe you'd try and stop it."

As lunch was being served, Ernie kept thinking about what he would do. He was lost in thought and startled when the club president rang the bell next to the podium to get everyone's attention. His heart was beating so strongly he could feel its murmur deep in his chest. When he got to the podium, he stood for several long moments looking out over the crowd; then Ernie began to speak.

"I guess in every man's life there comes a time when he has to do what he believes is the right thing. I've been fighting with myself for the past several days about doing the right thing today, about saying the right thing to this distinguished gathering. I had decided to do the easy thing today, to say the easy things to all of you. But then something happened, and something changed inside of me, and I think I now have the courage to do and say the right thing. What I'm going to tell you is hard to say, but it has to be said 'cause there are important things at stake in this election—more important than the businesses you own and the money you make. What's at stake is the welfare of our children.

"Not too long ago a distressed father told me about how his underage daughter and her boyfriend were served alcohol in a bar very close to here. He told me about how they gambled on the slot machines in this bar and about how the money they won from that machine got them drunker and drunker. He had tears in his eyes when he described how badly his little girl's face was cut up in the car wreck that was caused by that alcohol and those slot machines. It doesn't make any difference what the name of the joint is that served these children booze and let them gamble. It doesn't matter because it happens everywhere in Savannah and Chatham County, especially at the beach. There's not a person in this room who'll stand up and deny what I'm saying because you all know what I'm saying is the God's honest truth. Gambling is illegal in this state and most of the rest of the country because most sane and honest people recognize it for the evil it is and don't want their children being raised in an environment where they can see and learn the hypocrisy of having laws that are good but aren't enforced because they make money for a select few."

There wasn't a sound in the room now, and Ernie looked out over the audience, leaned close to the microphone as he had seen Brother Boatwright do, and continued.

"My opponent has some very close connections to the folks who are responsible for the pernicious influence of gambling in this town. I would daresay that one of the main contributors to the CCDC is none other than Willie Hart, owner of most of the slot machines in Chatham County. Is there anybody out there who would argue with me on that?"

The room was still, and not a soul spoke up. Then Ernie continued. "Everybody in town knows that Francis Quinn is Willie Hart's bagman, his right arm. They also know that Francis Quinn and Jimmy McQueen are tighter than ticks on a dog's backside. If Jimmy McQueen is elected your mayor, you may consider it a given fact that Willie Hart will be running City Hall from his little kingdom down on Tybee Island. Then, my friends, the innocent children and decent citizens of this town can forget about righting this terrible wrong and removing the embarrassing blemish on the reputation of this beautiful city. I know that today, before you all, I have crossed the Rubicon and there is no turning back. I am well aware that I have taken the battle to the heart of the enemy and that knives are being sharpened to use against me even as I speak. But I tell you all, I am a man at peace. It is the peace of a good conscience, and I throw my gauntlet at the foot of my opponent and challenge him to dispute what I have said to you this day. Furthermore, I pledge to you that I shall carry this message to every street and alley in Savannah. I shall shout it from the highest building until all have heard the truth and the truth sets them free from the addictions and depravity of gambling and alcohol abuse and until our precious children are no longer subject to the hypocrisy of Willie Hart, Francis Quinn, and Jimmy McQueen."

When Ernie finished, he didn't go back to his seat but rather walked off the dais and strode out of the ballroom, his shoulders back and a smile on his face. Some of the Rotarians attempted a polite applause as he walked out; most sat in stunned and embarrassed silence. In the back of the room, a reporter from the *Savannah Morning Gazette* finished scrawling the last of the notes he had taken on Ernie's speech and then hurriedly headed for the door.

"Wow," said Aubrey Thomas, as he listened to Perry Gnann read back his notes of Ernie's speech at the Rotary Club. When Perry finished and told him about Ernie's dramatic departure from the room after his speech, Aubrey leaned back in his chair and said, "Holy shit, you got one hell of a story there, Perry, my boy! I just want to know if ol' Ernie is crazy, or if he has the biggest set of balls in the Coastal Empire." Perry didn't say anything as he thumbed back through his steno pad, thinking of how he was going to write the story.

While Perry leafed through his notes, Aubrey picked up the phone and dialed furiously. "Tell Mr. Bradford that Aubrey Thomas is on the phone and needs to speak with him. Tell him it's important."

Aubrey covered the phone with his hand and said quietly to Perry, "Ol' Bradford is going to love this. He can't stand the McQueens. Goes way back. I'll bet he'll use this to tear Jimmy a new one."

"MCQUEEN LINKED TO GAMBLING KINGPINS," read the headline of the *Savannah Morning Gazette* the day after Ernie Williams's dramatic speech. The article then went on to give almost a full text of Ernie's speech, naming Willie Hart and Francis Quinn as "close confidants and contributors to the Chatham County Democratic Club in general and mayoral candidate James McQueen in particular." The final half of the article dealt with underage drinking in Chatham County and an estimation of how much money was being made on the slot machines in the city. It even had quotes from several members of the local clergy who also belonged to the Citizens Progressive League, including Brother Boatwright. But the final line was the one that had everybody talking. "Confidential sources in the FBI have linked local gambling activity with organized crime families in New York. These sources report that the Savannah economy is being drained of millions of dollars a year in payoffs to certain crime families in New York City."

The following Friday night, Jimmy met with Francis Quinn and Willie Hart at Willie's home on Ninth Street at the beach. Several other people who were active in the CCDC were also in attendance. They were what was known in Savannah as "ward heelers." These were political actives from the various voting districts in Savannah and Chatham County. Their job was to keep their fingers on the pulse of public opinion in their districts and report back to the party leaders.

Since it was hot, the meeting was held on the expansive screened porch of Willie's three-story "cottage," which looked out over the beach. The sun was almost down, and a breeze had picked up from the ocean. The group had formed itself into a circle of dark green wicker rocking chairs.

"Well, folks," said Willie, "as y'all know, we've encountered a little bump in the road this week following the actions of Mr. Williams and the *Savannah Morning Gazette*. What I'd like to do first is kinda go around the room and find out what's happened since the paper came out Tuesday mornin'."

As Willie went around the circle of rocking chairs, he heard the same tale. After each of the ward heelers had given his appraisal of the situation in his district, Willie leaned back in his chair, lit another cigar, and rocked for a few moments. Then he spoke.

"Y'all correct me if I'm wrong, now, but it seems to me that what I'm hearing is that the colored vote is OK, the Catholic vote is OK, and the Jewish vote is OK, too. But we got a big problem with the Cracker vote, especially the working-class Cracker vote. Are y'all all with me?" Willie looked around the circle, and everyone agreed. "OK, what do we do about it?"

Francis had been quiet all evening, sitting at Willie's right hand. He finally spoke up. "Willie, may I say something?"

"Of course."

"I think we need to play to Jimmy's strengths. As I see it, his biggest strength is with the veterans. If we can get them stirred up, we can cut into the CPL support in the Cracker districts. The veterans are the one group that cuts across all the economic, religious, and ethnic lines. It would be my suggestion that we go after that vote in a big way."

The following Sunday a full-page ad appeared in the *Savannah Morning Gazette* with the banner headline reading, "THE ONLY WAR VETERAN IN THE RACE," with a picture of Jimmy McQueen in his dress uniform, the Navy Cross and Purple Heart shining on his chest. Below the photo were the words, "He answered his country's call. He defended his nation's honor. He placed his life in harm's way. He is a product of all you hold dear and will serve you with distinction. Please elect Cmdr. James Edward McQueen mayor."

When the Democratic primary of 1948 was finally over, Jimmy had won 55 percent of the vote, with the rest of the CCDC ticket sweeping into office with him. The status quo in the Free State of Chatham would remain the same, but the seeds of discontent had been planted within the electorate.

With the election behind them, both Francis and Jimmy turned their attention to other, more important matters. For Francis it was his relationship with Helene, for Jimmy, his new son.

The way Francis saw it, there was really no pressing need for him to marry Helene. While he liked her, he didn't really love her. Francis had developed a philosophy, though, that did not preclude him from marrying Helene. He had analyzed his position in Savannah and had decided that marrying Helene would be the most prudent and beneficial thing he could do to ensure the lifestyle to which he had grown accustomed.

The following December Helene and Francis were married at Saint John's Episcopal Church, the same church where Jimmy and Meg McQueen had been married. Jimmy was best man and Meg matron of honor.

7. Metamorphosis

"Man is what he believes."

—Anton Chekhov

Fr. Michael Mulvaney did not fight in World War II. Although he had obtained his U.S. citizenship in the late thirties and volunteered for service, he was not selected. Instead, he remained at Blessed Sacrament Church to bury many of those who did fight, while comforting the ones they left behind. When some of the boys he'd watched leave for battle returned as men troubled by the ravages of what they'd endured, he was there for them through sleepless nights or simply listened as they sought to understand the cruelty of it all. One such casualty was Malachy O'Morgain.

Malachy was the last of four children born to Katlin and Ian O'Morgain in Savannah on the Feast of Saint Malachy in 1925. Three years later Ian died a painful death from prostate cancer, leaving Katlin to care for the children by herself. Although a typical boy in every sense, he was an obedient child and devoted to his mother. Upon graduation from Benedictine Military School in 1943, he enlisted in the army.

Malachy was not intensely religious before going to war; and while he never missed mass on Sundays, his thoughts were more worldly than spiritual. His life in Savannah was insular, tucked away from the rest of the world, a kingdom of long days and soft nights, of sweet springs and easy summers.

Perhaps Malachy's innocence was the reason he was so intensely affected by what he saw when he landed at Normandy on D day. After the first shock of Omaha Beach, that time of disbelief when only basic instinct rules the man, he changed inside. When he helped liberate the Dachau concentration camp, that change became even more profound.

When Malachy returned from the war, he started his life where he'd left off, at his mother's house. He accepted a job in the parts department at the local Ford dealership, attended mass daily, was home by five-thirty each evening, and gave his mother almost all of his salary.

Often his mother would find him kneeling in front of a statue of the Virgin Mary he kept on his dresser. On Saturdays and Sundays, Malachy attended morning mass at Blessed Sacrament and then stayed the rest of the day devoting himself to his rosary and the stations of the cross. It came as a surprise to no one when, in February of 1947, Malachy entered the Trappist monastery at Conyers, Georgia, a small town forty miles east of Atlanta.

The Trappists are a contemplative order whose lives essentially consist of work and prayer. They lead a spartan existence of simple foods and plain surroundings, and observe a rule of silence. At their monastery the monks support themselves by farming and baking. For the next year Malachy found peace and contentment in this life.

On the eighth of December, the Feast of the Immaculate Conception of Mary, Malachy was discovered prostrate in front of a statue of the Virgin Mary in a catatonic state. When revived, he offered no explanation. The next day he was on his way back to Savannah, deemed unfit for the rigors of monastic life.

Upon his return Malachy took up residence with his mother once more. He demonstrated no inclination for work, ate sparsely, prayed intensely, and seldom left his room. His mother's concern deepened for her son, and she sought help from the most reliable source she knew.

When Katlin O'Morgain began to tell Father Mulvaney about Malachy, she was soon in tears. Later that evening the father was sitting across the table from Malachy in the kitchen. Katlin had gone for a walk, purposefully leaving them alone.

Father Mulvaney sat for a few moments and toyed with a spoon while he studied Malachy. The young man was clean and well-groomed and had no tremors or ticks, and his eyes gave no hint of underlying insanity. To Father Mulvaney, in all outward appearances, Malachy seemed perfectly sane. But still, Malachy did not act normally. His mother was worried that he would not be able to support himself, that he would refuse to work, be judged insane, and end up at Central State Hospital in Milledgeville.

Father Mulvaney straightened himself in his chair, rested his elbows on the table, and clasped his hands under his chin. He hadn't lost a hint of his Irish brogue or his straightforward approach to problems in the nearly twenty years he'd been in Savannah. The priest cleared his throat and looked directly into Malachy's eyes.

"You know, Malachy, there are those who think you're a bit daft with all your prayin' and carryin' on."

"Yes, I understand, Father. It isn't normal; I know that."

"Your mother tells me you've no inclination for work. She says you stay in your room all day with your rosary and don't eat enough to keep a bird alive."

"I don't want to be a burden to my mother. I know money is tight, and I eat as little as possible so she won't have to spend so much on food for me."

"Speakin' of food, Malachy, just how do you plan to eat and keep a roof over your head when you're not hittin' a lick of work?"

"Our Lord will provide for me, Father."

"He takes care of those who care for themselves, Malachy."

"Our Lord will provide for my needs, Father. I'm certain of that."

"What makes you so sure, Malachy?"

"My faith."

Father Mulvaney shifted in his chair and took a sip of coffee; then he looked at Malachy again, who was absolutely serene and watched as the priest placed his cup back in its saucer.

"Malachy, I want you to tell me what happened up at the monastery and why you're moved to pray so much."

A few moments of silence grew to many as Father Mulvaney fixed his gaze on the man across the table.

"All right, I'll tell you; but what I'm going to say must be under the seal of the confessional. This mustn't be repeated to anyone."

"You have my word on that, Malachy."

"It all started on D day," said Malachy, as he told the priest about his combat experiences, including the liberation of Dachau.

"The reason that I prayed so much then was that I was afraid for my own sanity and was begging God to help me. When I prayed, this wonderful sensation came over me. Each time I was filled with immense joy and happiness. For me praying is like practicing the piano. The more I do it, the better I get. I feel as though Our Lord had singled me out, just as he has done with others all through history, and is preparing me spiritually to do his work. I decided to join the Trappists because I felt I'd be accepted as normal there."

Father Mulvaney didn't know what to think about Malachy's state of mind, but he certainly was interested in knowing what happened at the monastery.

"Well, Malachy, what happened to you at Conyers?"

"I was kneeling in front of a statue of Our Lady of Fatima. I don't know how long I was there when, suddenly, the smell of roses filled the chapel. When I looked around, I couldn't see a single rose, but the aroma was overpowering. When I looked back up at the statue, it wasn't a statue any longer. Our Lady stood before me, and all I could do was just stare at her. It was like I was standing by a fire and feeling the heat. I couldn't see the heat, but I could feel it. That's the way it was; I could feel her love for me."

"Did she speak to you?"

"Well, she spoke to me, but not with words. She just looked at me, and I seemed to know what she was thinking, and she knew what I was thinking, Father. She said that a time was coming soon that would be even worse than the last war. Then she told me that my purpose in life was to pray for all who would live through it."

The fact that Malachy had refused to speak of his visions and had placed Father Mulvaney under the seal of the confessional were two things that gave his claims a degree of credibility in the priest's mind.

But he wasn't in Kate O'Morgain's kitchen to decide whether Malachy's visions were real or not; he was there to try and help him snap out of his isolation, find a job, and support himself. The visions could sort themselves out later.

Father Mulvaney was searching for words when the sound of Kate returning from her walk put an end to the conversation. After telling Malachy good-bye, the priest spoke with his mother on her front porch.

"I think it's the stress of the war that's done this to him, Kate. He told me about some terrible things that he saw over there, and I'm sure it shook him to the foundations. I think he's had a kind of mental breakdown because of it."

"But, Father, what am I going to do with him? All he wants to do is pray. The money's running out, and all he tells me is that God will take care of his needs. Well, I'm not God, Father, and I'm at my wits' end."

"Kate, darlin', maybe Malachy's onto something. Just maybe the Good Lord will be watchin' out for him after all. I've an idea that just popped into my head that may be of some help for Malachy."

That evening Father Mulvaney paid a visit to his old friend Bishop Keyes. In the cathedral rectory on Harris Street, surrounded by antiques and religious art, Mulvaney gave his appraisal of Malachy.

"I think, after all is said and done, Bishop, that Malachy is a genuinely devout and pious man. I'm afraid his war experiences have rendered him a bit off-balance, and I don't know if he'll ever be right again. I'm no psychiatrist, but I'm thinkin', Bishop, that maybe we could be gettin' a veteran's disability check for Malachy. That's why I'm here. I thought you'd know the right ones to put me in touch with to get the ball rollin' and have some money comin' in for this young man."

The bishop settled back in his chair then said, "I'm not sure exactly who would be the best man to call, but I know where I can find out. This sounds like something our friend Mayor McQueen could help us with."

Two days later Father Mulvaney received a call at the Blessed Sacrament rectory.

"Father Mulvaney, this is Jimmy McQueen."

"Mr. Mayor, what a pleasure to be hearin' from you. What can I do for you?"

"Well, Father, it's really something I hope I'll be able to do for you. As you know, Bishop Keyes contacted me and filled me in on Sgt. Malachy O'Morgain and his problems. He knows how involved I am with veterans' affairs in Savannah and thought I'd be able to help Sergeant O'Morgain. Well, I just got off the phone with Congressman Preston in Washington, and I'm pleased to tell you that he's arranged for Sergeant O'Morgain to be examined by army doctors up at Fort Gordon in Augusta. Nobody can make any guarantees about what will happen, but at least we've managed to get things moving."

Several months after Mayor McQueen's appeal to Washington, Malachy was awarded a full disability pension by the Veterans Administration.

For Malachy O'Morgain, as well as Francis Quinn, the postwar years were times of growth and discovery. While Malachy intensified his life of prayer, Francis Quinn solidified his control over gambling operations in Chatham County. There were still the Citizens Progressive League and Brother Boatwright, but in the election of 1952, the CPL was unable to field a strong candidate for mayor, and the CCDC skated to an easy victory. Martin Bradford, publisher of the *Savannah Morning Gazette,* still used the paper in an attempt to link Jimmy McQueen and Francis Quinn in unscrupulous dealings; but the philanthropy of Willie Hart, combined with the charm of Francis Quinn and the connections of Jimmy McQueen, blunted their effectiveness. As in the past everyone knew what was happening but found no harm and saw no reason to change.

Less than a year after her marriage to Francis, Helene had her first child. Along with an eight-pound baby boy came twenty-five pounds of excess weight that she couldn't find the willpower to lose. Two years later came a little girl and another twenty-five pounds. As her weight grew, so did Helene's insecurity; and as her insecurity grew, so did her frustrations with the hours that Francis's job had him out of the house. Added to that, there were always the attractive women who frequented the nightclubs where Willie Hart's slot machines were.

Even though Francis eventually found little about his wife that attracted him, he still fought to maintain a respectable front for social consumption. He and Helene were the happily married couple at parties, but at home the acrimony grew. Helene was as miserable over her appearance as she was over her lack of affection and attention from Francis. In desperation she sought the quickest and most temporary cure for a broken heart.

In the beginning Helene drank only after the children were asleep. Later, because she had the luxury of a maid and a cook, she could postpone her sadness with a cocktail or two at noon and not feel guilty about neglecting the children. Toward the end Helene was tight when Francis arrived home for dinner and in a nasty mood when he left to make his rounds of Willie's operations. She had usually passed out by the time he came home.

Francis witnessed Helene's deterioration over a period of two years. He tried to help in a haphazard way, but his heart simply wasn't in the effort. He had grown disgusted with her and stayed in the marriage only for the sake of his children. He would have been willing to do that for many more years, but something happened one night in August of 1955.

Little Francis was seven, and his sister, Margaret, was five. Both children adored their father, and Francis relished their attention. Their bedtime was after the *Jackie Gleason Show,* which the whole family watched together. Helene had been drinking vodka since three that afternoon, and the whole sad affair started when Little Francis asked to stay up and watch the next television program. "It's summertime," said the child, "can't we stay up a little longer?"

Francis saw no harm in his son's request and gave his permission. Helene, resenting her husband's affection for his children and the lack of the same for her, overruled Francis and ordered the children off to bed in a particularly harsh tone. Francis responded in kind, and soon a full-blown argument was underway in the presence of the children. An alcoholic torrent of anger and pain came gushing from Helene. At first

Francis tried to quiet her because of the children, but this only served to fuel her rage.

"Helene," pleaded Francis, "let's put the children to bed and then talk, OK?"

"Hell no, you rotten bastard. I'm tired of them thinking how wonderful you are when you're not doing anything but whoring around in the bars your gangster friend Willie owns."

Both children were paralyzed and stood wide-eyed and speechless. Francis moved swiftly, picking Helene up and carrying her into the kitchen. The cook had stayed late that night, and in front of her he put his finger to Helene's face and shouted, "Never again! Do you hear me? Never again!"

During the ensuing months, both parties made attempts at reconciliation, but both knew the marriage was over. By the end of the year divorce proceedings were underway, and Francis was living full-time at Tybee.

When the divorce became final, Helene was awarded custody of the children. It was no surprise to Francis that the Bowen family had developed a deep-seated dislike for him, and this antipathy was passed along to his children, with less than subtle help from Helene. She and her parents spoiled the children, and his weekly court-ordered visitations became such a ritual of spitefulness that Francis eventually saw his son and daughter only on holidays and special occasions.

The end of the marriage was the highlight of Savannah's society gossip that year. Because he was essentially an outsider, and because he was engaged in a shady business, Francis was tagged as the offending party and roundly skewered by all who claimed to be in the know. Helene fared only a little better, since her drinking problem was as much common knowledge as was her weight problem. Even Jimmy and Meg McQueen suffered from the Quinn divorce.

When Savannah's upper crust had finally digested Helene Bowen's marital problems and had determined Francis to be the heavy, their ire was even brought to bear on his friends. Jimmy McQueen found himself criticized for his closeness to Francis, and Meg felt pressured by her friends to take Helene's side. Even at City Hall, Jimmy began to hear snide remarks about his "buddy," Francis Quinn. When the upper echelons of Savannah began to look at Francis differently, they also began to question the motives behind his close relationship with Mayor McQueen. None of this slipped by the members of the Citizens Progressive League, and they started gathering information and began making friends with those who now doubted the honesty of their mayor.

The CPL tried once more to unseat Jimmy in the election of 1956, but the old coalition of veterans, labor, blacks, and a respectable percentage of the upper-class white vote kept Jimmy in office. His margin of victory, however, wasn't as large as in the '52 election, and it gave the opposition hope for the next time.

As the latter half of the decade began, Francis's success continued; however, much of it was due to the magic of knowing Jimmy McQueen. Soon everyone came to realize that if a favor was desired from City Hall, Francis was the man to see. As his influence with city government increased, Francis started to put pressure on his competition to augment the expansion of Willie Hart's gambling empire, and the seeds of discontent began to flourish.

8. Tides of Men

*I loved you, so I drew these tides of men into my
hands and wrote my will across the sky in stars.*

—T. E. Lawrence, *Seven Pillars of Wisdom*

Most white southerners saw the change coming. Some
thought that change should be stopped, while others wel-
comed it. For black southerners, it was a dream passed down
for hundreds of years, finally to emerge into reality in the second half of
the twentieth century.

In Savannah the civil rights movement didn't foster the kind of strife
and violence that some southern cities experienced. There were some
demonstrations, but they were not marked by extreme violence, and
most occurred on a small scale. There was resistance to the change, but
Savannah was blessed with a tolerant attitude toward religion that
seemed to spill over into the area of race relations.

May or Jimmy McQueen was among the first of Savannah's leaders
to recognize the inevitable in the early fifties. World War II had sent
him to the opposite side of the globe; and when he returned, it was with
eyes and mind wide open. The changes the war had brought to Savannah were all around, and it was impossible to ignore them. He was the
first to sense the restlessness in the black community during his election

campaign of 1948 and used it to his advantage. After his victory, he appointed the first blacks to positions of responsibility in the municipal government. Because of that action, he lost some white votes but solidified his black constituency.

But the ending of an era, a way of life, the manner in which society itself was ordered and functioned can never come without a struggle, without resistance. The mechanisms, attitudes, and realities of a society that was totally segregated were deeply ingrained in each person. The mind-set of many white southerners, even in a place as gentle and refined as Savannah, would not die a swift and easy death.

M r. Bradford," intoned Brother Boatwright, "I'm tellin' ya Jimmy McQueen is a race mixer just as much as he is a promoter of gamblin' and whiskey drinkin'. He's done gone and had that nigger Robert Spencer made a member of the police department. Made him an officer of the law and put a gun in his hand. Gave him the power to arrest a white man! What's next, Mr. Bradford? Is he gonna join the NAACP or some other communist organization like that? Next thing ya know, he'll have them black bucks swimmin' in the pool down at the Hotel DeSoto with white girls!"

Martin Bradford eased back in his chair and looked out his office window. He watched the cars on Bay Street and followed them as they drove past City Hall only a block away. Then he leaned forward, clasped his hands together, and planted his elbows on the desktop.

"Well," drawled Martin, "what do you think about this, Ernie?"

"I'm not one bit surprised, Marty. It's typical McQueen arrogance. He's tryin' to shove this civil rights business down our throats. They vote for him; he kisses their black asses." Ernie looked over at Brother Boatwright and said, "Pardon my French, Preacher," and continued.

"Reverend Boatwright is slam on the money. What he failed to mention, though, is the increase in prostitution. There're whores hangin' all around downtown. It's just one more example of what a godless administration McQueen's running over at City Hall. Ask any member of the bar, and they'll tell ya that when one of those girls gets arrested, one of Willie Hart's runners shows up at the jailhouse with bail money. Cash on the barrelhead, and away she goes to spread some more filth on our streets. You gotta help us do something about this man, Marty."

"Like what, Ernie? Help get you and your friends elected?"

"Like exactly that, Marty. You got any problems with me being mayor?"

"Naw, none at all. Hell, we worked like a son of a bitch for you last time around, remember?" Marty looked over at Brother Boatwright and said, "'Scuse my language, Preacher." Brother Boatwright just nodded; he'd heard men cuss before.

"Well," continued Ernie, "there's a groundswell of people risin' up against this whole CCDC crowd. The paper can be a part of the change that's gonna take place in Savannah, or it can be on the outside lookin' in. Whatever you and the *Morning Gazette* decide to do, I want you to know that I'm in this thing to win."

Francis thought he had thoroughly hardened himself to the entanglements of romance. He was sure that what some knew as love was for him no more than affection, that lovemaking was nothing more than release of sexual energy. There were lots of pretty girls for this purpose in Savannah available to a man as handsome and charming as Francis, but they were only pretty and lacked the social status that Helene enjoyed.

After his divorce Francis began to get the cold shoulder from the attractive society girls who previously had fawned all over him. This stung Francis and wounded his pride, and he resolved to show his old set of friends a thing or two. He knew that nothing provoked more attention and jealousy from a woman than another woman more beautiful than her. It wasn't long after a particularly harsh public snubbing by one of Helene's friends that Francis was handed the opportunity to demonstrate that he dated only the finest when he met Margaret Mary Flannery at the Brass Rail one evening.

Margaret Mary was thought by many to be the most beautiful woman in Savannah. She was striking at five feet nine, with brown, flowing hair and eyes of deep mahogany that were large and full of passion. When she walked, her carriage was effortless and regal. While her figure was not robust in a movie star sense, she had all of the necessary curves to catch a man's eye. She radiated class without pretense and virtue without effort.

Margaret Mary came from an Irish-Catholic family of five children, where religion was so valued her only brother entered the priesthood and two of her sisters joined the convent. She had followed in the footsteps of her third sister and entered Saint Joseph's Hospital School of Nursing in Savannah and become a registered nurse. She was devoutly religious, still lived with her parents, and had never been in love.

The night Margaret Mary was at the beach was one of April perfection on Tybee Island. The tide was coming in, and an easterly wind carried the waves across the beach, where they crashed over the sand in the low rumble of surf thunder. It was seventy-six degrees, and the windows of the Brass Rail were open to the sound and smell of the ocean. On the jukebox "Come Softly to Me," by the Fleetwoods, was playing, while Margaret Mary's date worked on his third Bacardi and Coke.

As the evening wore on, his ability to speak and walk well was captured more and more by the rum. In an embarrassing moment for all involved, the newest member of Savannah's medical community experienced a fitful episode of profound emesis, during which he deposited the entire contents of his stomach on the dance floor and then fell into an unconscious stupor, leaving Margaret Mary to fend for herself amid a crowd of gasping onlookers.

Francis had one of the waiters pick Dr. Clark up off the floor and take him to the men's room while another quickly cleaned up the mess. Margaret Mary retreated to the booth where they had been sitting and hid her face in her hands.

"Miss Flannery, I'm Francis Quinn. I kind of manage this place for Mr. Hart. May I be of assistance to you?"

Margaret Mary didn't look up but only shook her head in the negative. Francis could tell she was sobbing and sat down quietly across the table from her. When he saw her tears hitting the tabletop, he pushed a napkin between her elbows and said softly, "Here, you might need this."

Margaret Mary used it to dry her eyes. She only glanced at Francis, but he could tell she was humiliated by the look on her face.

"Miss Flannery, wouldn't you like to go outside or something? Don't worry about your date; my boys are taking care of him right now. He'll be fine. Let's just get you outta here so you won't feel like people are staring at you."

Francis gently placed his hand on her shoulder. Without a word, she rose and walked out the door with him. When they reached the bottom of the steps, she hesitated, not knowing what to do or which way to turn. Francis said quietly, "Come on, let's walk over and watch the tide come in."

Margaret Mary placed her hands on the railing along the seawall and looked down at the beach eight feet below. She watched as a wave broke in the surf line, foamed white, then flattened and rushed up the beach to the great concrete wall. She listened to the waves hiss and fizzle as the sand drank them up. Still she didn't look at Francis and didn't speak.

Finally, Francis casually said, "They tell me this seawall was built during the Roosevelt administration. It was a WPA project. I think it was completed in the mid-thirties." Still nothing from Margaret Mary.

A larger wave began to roll in, and they both watched as it hit the pilings under the Tybrisa Pavilion. As the wave picked up speed, it slammed into the succession of pilings with a whoomp, sending a spray of water up and into the wind. When the wave hit the last of the pilings, Margaret Mary spoke, still not looking at Francis.

"Thank you for helping me. I'm so embarrassed I could die."

Then she turned and said, "He can't possibly drive home. What am I going to do?"

"I'll have one of my employees drive your friend back in his car and put him to bed," answered Francis. "I'll take you home whenever you're ready to go."

There was a spring tide that evening, and the high water crept up the shoulders of Tybee Road, almost covering it in places. After Lazaretto Creek, miles of open marsh lay between Tybee and the mainland. The tide covered all but the tops of the *Spartina* grass, and the moon's light bounced off the creeks that twisted through it and cut a path of reflected silver across the flooded marsh. The oleanders would not bloom for another month, but the sweet smell of marsh filled the big black Cadillac. Francis had driven the road a hundred times but could not recall a more beautiful ride back from the beach. Margaret Mary also found the ride enchanting and began to feel better. As they crossed the Bull River Bridge, they started to talk. The conversation lasted all the way into town.

By the time they arrived at her parents' home near Forty-first and Harmon Streets, Francis had decided Margaret Mary would be the perfect showpiece to flaunt in Savannah's face. As for Margaret Mary, she had found Francis to be a perfect gentleman, as personable as he was handsome.

During the ensuing weeks, Francis devoted a great deal of his time toward winning Margaret Mary's affection. That turned out to be the easy part. Margaret Mary was a virgin who would give herself to the man she loved only in marriage and refused to surrender those beliefs no matter how hard Francis tried.

This made Margaret Mary all the more desirable. He proposed marriage, but the Catholic Church and its doctrines concerning divorce and remarriage presented an almost insurmountable obstacle to overcome. Francis had chosen a woman who placed her religious convictions above her desire for him.

W ell, Father Mulvaney, it's been awhile since we've seen each other," said Francis, as he walked into the sacristy behind the altar at the Cathedral of Saint John the Baptist. Father Mulvaney had just finished saying the last mass that Sunday and was beginning to remove his vestments.

"Francis Quinn," answered the priest, with a hint of sarcasm, "what a surprise." Then he began to remove the chasuble, the first of six garments worn by a priest when celebrating mass.

"How have you been, Mike?" asked Francis. "What do you hear from Ireland?"

Father Mulvaney looked around quickly to see if the altar boys had left.

"They're all gone, Mike," said Francis. "We're by ourselves."

"I've been fine, Francis," replied Father Mulvaney, as he pulled the chasuble over his head. "But what I hear from Ireland is not as much concern as what I hear about you."

The priest reached up and removed the stole from around his neck, the symbol of his priestly duty. Then he said, "I understand you've become involved with the Flannery girl, Francis. How on earth did you manage that?"

"I'm more than involved with her, Mike. I'm in love with her, and I want to marry her."

Without looking up, Father Mulvaney slipped the maniple off his left arm, an ornamental vestment of silk that symbolized the labor and hardship a priest must expect. As he placed it on the countertop, he said, "Forget it, Francis. You know what the laws of the church are." Then he turned, faced Francis, and continued. "Margaret Mary is serious about her religion; she won't leave the church for you."

Francis moved in closer, leaned against the counter, and said, "I know she won't, Mike. Maybe that's one of the reasons I love her so much."

Mulvaney looked down and began to undue the cincture, a cord tied around his waist symbolizing the virtues of chastity and continence required of a priest.

"I take it, then, the reason you're here is to talk about Margaret Mary."

"That's right, Mike. I need your help."

Father Mulvaney laid the cincture on top of the chasuble and straightened the cords. Then he stopped and looked at Francis.

"This girl is special, Francis. Why don't you show a little respect for her and her family and just leave her alone? Surely you'd be able to find some other beautiful thing around town who'd suit your needs."

"I don't think you understand me, Mike. I know how special she is. That's why I'm in love with her. I've never felt this way before in my life."

Father Mulvaney began to remove the alb, a long, white linen garment that reached to his feet. It was the symbol of innocence and purity that should adorn the soul of the priest who ascends the altar.

"Look, Francis, I've known about this romance since it began last

April. Her father and I are close friends. The family's not happy at all about this. Believe me, she's not going to marry you outside the church. Why can't you just get that through your head, back off, and let the poor girl get on with her life?"

Francis folded his arms, thought for a moment, and answered. "We can't get married in the church because I've been married and divorced, right?"

"Well said," replied Father Mulvaney, as he began the removal of his last vestment, the amice.

Francis watched for a moment and then said, "I was married in the Episcopal Church, and I'm a Catholic. The church doesn't recognize the marriages of Catholics who weren't married by a priest. In the eyes of the church, I've never been married before, and there shouldn't be a problem."

Father Mulvaney let out a sigh as he pulled the amice off his shoulders and from around his neck. It was a square of white linen worn as a hood during the Middle Ages to protect the head in cold churches. In modern times it came to symbolize the "helmet of salvation," the virtue of hope that helps the priest overcome the attacks of Satan.

"I thought you might be coming up with that argument, Francis. In theory, you're correct. In reality, forget it. A ruling like that would have to come from Rome. They're few and far between and take years. Please, just forget about this girl." Then the priest lowered his voice to a whisper and continued. "Remember who you are, who you really are. What if all that came to the surface? How would Margaret Mary survive something like that? You're not for her, Francis. Please, I beg you, forget this thing."

Francis looked at the statue of Saint Patrick over in the corner, took a deep breath, and answered. "All I ask is that you talk with Margaret Mary yourself. If she doesn't tell you the exact same thing to your satisfaction, then I'll do what you advise. It'll be the hardest thing I've ever done, but I'll break it off. I promise."

Three days later Francis sat in Mulvaney's private office at the cathedral. "Did Margaret Mary confirm everything I told you, Mike?"

Father Mulvaney tapped a pen on his desk and then answered. "Unfortunately, she did."

"Mike, please. There's nothing unfortunate about it. I'm the perfect man for her. You've known me for a long time. What do you think I'll do to her?"

Father Mulvaney glanced over at the door to his office, instinctively checking to see if it was closed. Then he said in a low voice, "I think you're a man trained to be a cold-blooded killer, who lost his soul somewhere along the way and hasn't gotten it back. I think you'd do anything to survive, and I do mean anything. You're not the person I once knew. I don't think you're totally to blame, but that doesn't change the fact that an innocent girl could get caught up in something that could ruin her life. I think you've lost your belief in God, and that troubles me greatly, not so much for your soul, but for hers. In any event, this girl loves you desperately, and I promised her I'd help."

Then the priest leaned over his desk and motioned Francis to do the same. When their two heads were close, with a whisper he said, "On the soul of my dear mother, I swear a sacred oath before God Almighty that if you hurt this girl in any way, I will kill you myself."

Francis didn't move or blink but looked directly at the priest and said, "I believe you would, Mike."

While it took almost a year, the Catholic Church finally granted permission for Francis and Margaret Mary to be married in the church. His fascination with his new bride lasted for almost a year, and after that Francis slipped back into his old ways of having girlfriends on the side, some of whom he was less than discreet with. News of these indiscretions eventually made their way to Margaret Mary, but Francis was able to lie his way out of them all. Behind-the-back mutterings surmised that Margaret Mary must have been a bit dim-witted to believe Francis. In actuality, Margaret Mary truly loved her husband and was not completely fooled by him. True to her Cathoic upbringing, she was committed to her marriage, making divorce an impossibility.

In a particularly blatant episode of infidelity, Francis once appeared at a party on Tybee with a woman fifteen years his junior. Someone had a camera and took his picture with this woman, whereupon Francis seized the camera and removed the film, saying, "Gossip I can explain to my wife; a picture I can't."

Mayor McQueen was a regular at Johnny Harris's Restaurant and enjoyed sitting in booth No. 1 in the main dining room. It was one of twenty such intimate alcoves located all around the periphery of the large, circular room. They were made from heart pine and looked out onto an oak dance floor. Above, a domed ceiling of midnight blue, with hundreds of tiny lights twinkling like stars in the evening sky, gave a feeling a space and romance. Jimmy was close friends with the owner, Red Donaldson, a country boy from Bulloch County who had a knack for selling barbecue and making friends. Jimmy, Red, and Francis would sit in the No. 1 booth for hours some evenings, swapping stories. Jimmy knew that Red kept his finger on the political pulse of Savannah.

When Father Mulvaney arrived, Red was sitting with Jimmy and had just finished giving him his opinion on the upcoming election. The priest eased into the booth and sat next to Red.

"Mike," said Jimmy, as he sipped his second cup of black coffee, a habit he'd picked up in the navy, "election time is coming, and the word around town is that Ernie Williams and Brother Boatwright are teaming up again against me." Jimmy looked over at Red for confirmation.

"Yeah," said Red, "sorta looks that way. The CPL is making noises about a lot of things, and they're targeting Jimmy again this time around."

"I didn't want to bother the bishop with this sorta thing, Mike," said Jimmy. "Anyway, I knew you were his right-hand man when it comes to local politics, so I figured I'd just get a feel for things by talking directly with you."

"Well, Jimmy," replied the priest, "you and your administration have been most helpful to the church whenever she needed you; and although we can't make any official endorsement, I can assure you that I'll do all I can to see that you're reelected."

"What I need you to do, Mike," said Jimmy, "is just to keep an ear to the ground. Let me know what the Catholics are saying. We've always done well with them."

"I can tell you what the Crackers are saying right now," injected Red.

"What?"

"They're saying you're too soft with the coloreds. It's got a lot of them mad at you. Some of them have been calling you a nigger lover, Jimmy," said Red.

Jimmy thought for a moment, trying to suppress his anger, then said, "Maybe I am."

"I've heard that, too, Jimmy," said Father Mulvaney, as he stirred his iced tea.

Jimmy shook his head, looked down at the table and then back up. "What else have they said, Mike?"

"There's a lot of talk going around about you and Francis Quinn. Some people think you've been taking money from Francis or at least looking the other way with his gambling and liquor enterprises. It's talk that's been building over the years, ever since you first won back in '48, only now it's louder than ever."

"Father Mulvaney's right, Jimmy," said Red. "Ernie Williams and the preacher have been spreading that around a lot lately. I've even heard the Greeks talking about it. Word is, Pinky Masters is on your case, too."

Pinky Masters was the son of Greek immigrants and owned a popular bar on Drayton Street just across from the Hotel DeSoto. He was politically active, especially with the unions, and had been an ally of Jimmy's in the past. News that he wasn't so friendly anymore hurt Jimmy.

"Must be because of his nephew Andy. I heard he got his nose all out of joint when he didn't get that city job he wanted. It went to a colored fellow. He got it because he deserved it," said Jimmy, showing a trace of anger.

"That's not all," said Red. "Andy is working night and day now for Ernie and the CPL."

The conversation went on in that vein through lunch and for another hour after. The bottom line was that Jimmy had lost support in every segment of the voter population except with the blacks. By two that afternoon, all of the bad news had been delivered to Mayor McQueen. As he walked out to his car with Father Mulvaney, the priest said, "I'm sorry to be the one to tell you these things, Jimmy."

Jimmy looked over at the palm trees lined up in double rows in the center of Victory Drive. "I need to know the truth about where I stand, Mike. I knew I could count on you."

The mayoral election of 1960 turned out to be the nastiest in memory. Ernie Williams, Brother Boatwright, and the Citizens Progressive League used every trick they knew in their war against the Chatham County Democratic Club, Jimmy McQueen, Francis Quinn, and Willie Hart. They whispered to the white voters that Jimmy was soft on the "civil rights thing," implied to the Protestants that Jimmy was in Bishop Bourke's back pocket, and hinted to the Irish and Jews that Jimmy was a snooty Episcopalian blue blood who looked down his nose at them. Brother Boatwright was even able to agitate the union at McQueen Shipyard into a wildcat strike that didn't do anything but cost Jimmy most of his union support. But the worst blows came from Martin Bradford and the *Savannah Morning Gazette.*

Every other day there was a story in the paper about illegal drinking and gambling at the beach and other places. In every story Martin Bradford managed to link Jimmy's name with Francis Quinn and Willie Hart. Jimmy lost by four thousand votes. The only boxes he carried were in black neighborhoods.

By the end of the 1950s, the world of Malachy O'Morgain was measured by the beads on his rosary. He had become a legend in Savannah because of his devotion to prayer. Every morning Malachy attended seven o'clock mass at Blessed Sacrament Church. After that service, he would walk to the Cathedral of Saint John the Baptist miles away in downtown Savannah. As he walked, he prayed, his rosary beads dangling from his hands.

Many came to him with their petitions, asking him to remember in prayer a dying parent, a child in trouble, or a broken heart. Some claimed it was by simple chance, others were sure it was divine intervention; but whatever the reason, hundreds began to believe Malachy's prayers were ones for which God had a special ear. As a result, by 1960 Malachy no longer enjoyed the solitude and quiet contemplation he sought. The strain of so many people pressing their needs and burdens upon him began to take its toll. Father Mulvaney took notice and started to worry about the state of Malachy's emotional health.

Three days after the election, on the Feast of the Stigmata of Saint

Francis, Father Mulvaney called on Jimmy McQueen at his home. The mayor ushered him into the library then settled into one of the leather chairs across from the priest.

"What can I help you with, Father?" asked Jimmy.

"It's Malachy. I'm worried about him. People are after him all the time; and you know, Jimmy, he's a bit of a frail fellow when it comes to pressure like that. All he wants to do is pray. He doesn't want the spotlight and the attention he's getting now."

Jimmy nodded and said, "I see him almost every day walking down Victory Drive, saying his rosary and picking up trash."

Father Mulvaney shifted forward in his chair and continued. "He's happy with that, but people pester him all the time now, and he can't say no, especially when they come to him with such sorrowful tales. But I'm afraid he may have a nervous breakdown if this keeps up."

"How can I help, Mike?"

"Well, Jimmy, I recall you once saying that it would be nice to have somebody live in your place out on Jesus Island just to sort of look after things. Is that still open?"

"Father," said Jimmy, "anything for Malachy. And if you want my opinion, I think Malachy is kind of special."

II

Will's Story

9. The Only Son

She loosed the bar, she slid the bolt,
She opened the door anon,
And a grey bitch-wolf came out of the dark
And fawned on the Only Son!

—RUDYARD KIPLING, "The Only Son"

illiam Wallace McQueen VI was born in the spring of
1947. His mother's pregnancy had been a difficult one
since she suffered from preeclampsia, also known as tox-
emia of late pregnancy, a condition characterized by hypertension and
edema. This sometimes results in convulsions, which afflicted Meg and
petrified Jimmy. On two occasions, Meg was close to a miscarriage. It
was no surprise to Jimmy when Dr. Sharpley, Meg's obstetrician, told
him another pregnancy could take her life.

Dr. Sharpley was a close friend of Jimmy's and had delivered more
than a thousand Savannah children into the world, some healthy, some
sickly, some deformed. Telling parents that something was wrong with
their child was the most dreaded task of his profession.

"Jimmy, there's something else you need to know about the baby."

"What? Is something wrong?"

"Well, all of his organs seem to be working well. He looks like a
healthy little guy who'll grow up to be strong and normal, but he has a
type of facial deformity."

Jimmy felt as though he had been hit in the stomach. "What are you talking about?"

"Jimmy, your son has a cleft lip. A lot can be done these days with that, but it requires surgery."

"A cleft lip?"

"He has what most people call a harelip, Jimmy. Meg hasn't seen him yet, and she doesn't know. I wanted to tell you first and let you see him before she does so you could prepare her."

The home William Wallace McQueen VI came to know from infancy to manhood was located on Forty-sixth Street near Reynolds. It was a large, Tudor-style house built in the early twenties and purchased by Jimmy McQueen immediately following the war. It occupied a corner lot on a quiet street and was surrounded by cedars, elms, and magnolias. The sides were covered with ivy, and tall chimneys framed either end. The inside had a regal feel to it, with vaulted ceilings and exposed interior beams.

When Will was brought home from the hospital, family and friends came calling in order to admire and make over the new arrival. Often there were occasions when the gift-toting ladies of Savannah were taken aback and at a loss for appropriate words when they first viewed little Will McQueen. Many times his mother would be in tears following such visits.

The McQueen home was only a few blocks from Blessed Sacrament Church; and because Jimmy had developed a friendship with Father Mulvaney, the priest was a frequent guest. Jimmy enjoyed his conversations with Father Mulvaney and admired his vast knowledge of literature and world history. The McQueens were High Church Episcopalians, and Jimmy felt a natural affinity for Father Mulvaney's religious philosophy as well as his Irish wit.

Will had been through a series of plastic procedures at Barnes Hospital in Saint Louis, and Meg seemed to enjoy Father Mulvaney's visits more than Jimmy because she was always reassured by the priest's assertion that he could see an improvement in her son's appearance with each visit. On the day before Jimmy and Meg were scheduled to take their son back to Saint Louis for his most delicate surgical procedure yet, Father Mulvaney brought Malachy along on one of his visits.

Will was a year and a half at the time, already walking and trying to speak. It was near his bedtime, and he was cranky and crying when Father Mulvaney and Malachy were taken to the nursery by Meg. Will had never seen Malachy before and was usually shy around strangers, especially men.

When Malachy entered the room, Will was standing in his crib screaming and rattling the sides in frustration. When he saw Malachy, he immediately became quiet. He seemed to recognize Malachy and smiled, reaching out toward him. Malachy went to the child and picked him up. Will didn't utter a sound as Malachy placed the fingers of his right hand to Will's mouth, closed his eyes, and appeared to pray. When this happened, Will closed his eyes also, went limp, and fell into a deep sleep.

For the rest of the visit, Malachy held Will while the child slept soundly. When it was time to leave, Malachy said to Meg, "His operation will be a great success." A week later his prediction was borne out; and as Will matured, the investment his parents had made in his extensive plastic surgery began to pay dividends. By age four his lip deformity, while still present, was not so painfully obvious.

In the fall of 1956, Will McQueen was nine years old and starting the third grade at Charles Ellis Elementary School only a few blocks from his house. It was a handsome structure on Forty-ninth Street in the center of Ardsley Park.

While most of Will's schoolmates were kind and never did anything to hurt his feelings, there were those who routinely made cruel and deprecating remarks behind his back and even occasionally to his face. But what wounded Will the deepest were any statements that reflected poorly on his father's job as mayor. There was one such incident that had a dramatic and lasting effect on Will's self-esteem and corresponding behavior. It happened at a football game in Daffin Park.

Martin Bradford's son, Lane, was a year older than Will, a head taller, and twenty pounds heavier. He was a precocious child and somewhat of a bully, having inherited his father's disposition. Lane was a grade ahead of Will at Charles Ellis and belonged to the Panthers football team, the same team Will played for.

During the election of 1956, Martin often spoke of the mayor in the most disparaging terms, and Lane naturally adopted his father's views and manner of expression. Jimmy's victory had infuriated Martin; and the Thursday after the election, Lane decided to even the score at Will's expense.

Lane was all that Will was not on the football field. He was quick, coordinated, strong, aggressive, and full of himself. He played quarterback and was always the first player to be chosen when sides were picked, while Will was among the last. During the game, Lane began to taunt Will about his looks and repeat the things he'd heard from his father. Will was intimidated by the larger boy; but in an unexpected burst of fury, Will attacked Lane with his helmet, swinging it wildly at Lane's unprotected head. Lane was knocked to the ground and suffered a scalp laceration. Aside from teaching Lane a well-deserved lesson, what Will ultimately gained from this encounter was that in the future the other boys treated him with respect because they knew he was not afraid to stand and fight.

Even though Will McQueen lived a life of material as well as social privilege, sometimes this status was a burden he was not well suited to bear. Savannah was a relatively small town, and being the son of the mayor was a high-profile existence. He enjoyed his status, but often the boyish mischief he and his friends engaged in would be blown out of proportion when Will's name was mentioned. Will's father cast a long shadow; and even though he wanted desperately to please him, deep inside Will felt woefully inadequate. These feelings, combined with his sensitivity about his looks, sometimes drove Will to act out his anxiety with acts of defiance and bravado. One such incident occurred the summer of 1958.

For eleven-year-old boys, fireworks are a mesmerizing elixir of sound and fury. In Georgia they had been declared illegal in 1955, but there were still places around where they could be purchased. One such location was an establishment about twenty miles south of Savannah on U.S. Highway 17, the main route to Florida from the north.

The Monkey Jungle was a combination petting zoo and clip joint in Bryan County. It had a few monkeys, some alligators in a pit, and other assorted local wildlife, along with various forms of gambling that were all rigged. The Monkey Jungle also sold cherry bombs.

Fireworks were still legal just across the Savannah River in South Carolina, and on more than one occasion Will had implored his father to buy him some; but Jimmy had steadfastly refused, citing safety and his position as mayor. Not to be refused the devilish pleasure of explosions, Will and his friend John-Morgan Hartman decided to ride their bicycles to the Monkey Jungle and spend the money they had earned mowing lawns on firecrackers.

It took them almost four hot, humid, and frightening hours of pedaling down traffic-heavy Highway 17 to get to the Monkey Jungle; but when they did, their dreams of finding the powerful cherry bombs were realized. The ride back to Savannah was tiresome and harrowing, but Will and John-Morgan had enough fireworks for the rest of the summer. The only hitch was that Will had been recognized by several motorists, who'd called his mother to let her know he had been seen on the most dangerous road in Chatham County. In the end Will lost his cherry bombs forever and his bike for a month. It would have been worse had not "Uncle Francis" intervened with Jimmy on his behalf.

Francis and Margaret Mary were regular guests at Will's house, and Will sensed the close bond between Francis and his father. Francis had an irresistibly charming personality, and Will was naturally drawn to him. Perhaps the estrangement from his own children made Francis focus on Will more than he normally would have; but Francis felt genuine affection for Will, and those feelings were readily returned. Will admired Francis's savoir faire and noticed how, at social functions, his presence seemed to dominate the room. Christmas and birthday presents from Uncle Francis were always the best, and Will felt that he could tell Francis things he wouldn't dare tell his father.

10. Jesus Island

I will fly in the greatness of God as the marsh
hen flies
In the freedom that fills all the space 'twixt the
marsh and the skies . . .

— SIDNEY LANIER, "The Marshes of Glynn"

Jimmy McQueen nudged the throttles of the *Miss Geechee* forward, and the thirty-eight-foot Chris Craft Constellation pulled away from the dock at the Savannah Yacht Club on the Wilmington River. Its twin V-8s rumbled from deep within the stern, and the passengers could feel the power of the engines through the deck. It was a Friday afternoon, and twenty-four Scouts from Troop 16 stood along the railing and watched as a pod of porpoises swam near the boat.

A lot of stories about Jesus Island circulated in Savannah. There were tales of Indian ghosts and the spirits of slaves who roamed the island at night and stories about Dr. Divine, Sister Mystery, and their voodoo.

The scariest story of all was about the big alligator who had come to be called the Devil Himself. He lived in the freshwater pond named Salvation Lake, where the slave descendants who lived on Jesus Island were baptized. The story was that the Devil Himself had snatched up a twelve-year-old girl during her baptism in the pond. As the tale went, the big gator pulled the screaming little girl into the deep water and ate her in two gulps while her parents looked on in horror.

September is a hot month in Savannah; the vegetation is still vibrant, and the animals are still actively feeding. Water moccasins and alligators sun themselves at the water's edge on Salvation Lake, and bull frogs snatch juicy mosquitos down by the water hyacinth and yellow lotus near the stand of cypress trees. Fall weather is at least six weeks away, slowly seeping into Jesus Island with the night air of late October.

When the *Miss Geechee* pulled next to the dock on Doomsday Creek, Uncle Moses was waiting. His full name was Moses Leviticus McQueen, and he had been born on the island a few years after World War I. Both of his grandparents had been slaves who had lived and worked on the island and were some of the thirty or so who had chosen to stay after the Civil War. He was the superintendent of the island, knowing and loving it more than anyone else. All of his ancestors were buried in the rich black soil of the graveyard behind Saint Andrew's Chapel.

All of his life Moses had eaten the collards, tomatoes, and onions that his mother had grown on the island. He had hunted, killed, and eaten the deer, hogs, and coons there and caught the fish in its creeks. As far as Moses was concerned, he and Jesus Island were one.

"Uncle Moses, proud to see ya again," said Jimmy McQueen. "I got a buncha boys with me who're gonna be spendin' the weekend out here."

When Moses answered, he spoke in the thick Gullah accent of the blacks who lived on the sea islands of Georgia and South Carolina.

"Proud ta see you too, Mr. Jimmy. Looks like them young fellas is ready to have a good time. They be stayin' in the big house?"

"No suh, we're gonna be hikin' to the dock down by Williamson Island and then takin' the bateaus over to Williamson and stay for the weekend. Tomorrow I'd like you to show the boys the rest of the island."

John-Morgan Hartman was in the troop, and his father was an adult leader who had come along on the camping trip. He worked at the *Savannah Morning Gazette,* where his job was to cover the political action in Savannah. Although his boss, Martin Bradford, thoroughly disliked Mayor McQueen, John Hartman's opinion was considerably less critical. He knew Bradford answered to Chauncey Spencer, the president and principal stockholder of the Coastal Empire Savings and Trust Company.

Chauncey Wellington Spencer, whose nickname was "Snooks" because of his affinity for the pool game snooker, was a heavy advertiser at the paper. He had developed a dislike for the McQueens when Jimmy's father had withdrawn the McQueen Shipyard money from deposit at Snooks's bank. To the McQueens it was a simple matter of better interest. Snooks could have matched those rates but had refused to, thinking the McQueens were bluffing. When they left and didn't return, he was incensed.

The hike to Williamson Island took the boys past the old slave huts and then the chapel and its graveyard, where the long limbs of the oaks were so heavy they brushed against the ground. Cedar trees grew among the headstones, pushing some askew with their creeping, hungry roots.

The McQueen family plot had a rusting iron fence surrounding it, and thorny rosebush runners wrapped themselves through the bars. Within its confines were the graves of six generations. Outside the fence were the simple graves of the McQueen slaves and their descendants. At the edge of the churchyard was a forbidding wall of dense forest.

The trail to the dock at McQueen Creek began in a tight growth of palmettos. A covering of live oaks blocked out all but slivers of sunlight along the narrow path. After a few hundred feet, the palmettos gave way to an area of smaller scrub oaks, cedars, and sweet gums, tangled with vines that clung to the high branches of the larger oaks then drooped to the ground. Overhead, turkey buzzards circled, riding the thermal updrafts from the afternoon heat. The troop was growing weary when it finally reached the old shack at McQueen's Creek and the short boat ride to their campsite.

When the inky dark of full night settled in on Williamson Island, everyone gathered around the campfire to hear the stories of long-gone Indians and pirates who roamed the islands around Savannah. After ghost stories about the Banjo Man and the Blue Light Lady, Jimmy McQueen explained how Jesus Island got its name.

"The island used to be called Guale," said Jimmy, "until just after the

Civil War. Back then, most of the black people who worked the planta-tion left. Things kind of fell apart and started to run down out here. My great-granddaddy got concerned that the big house would fall in and the church and cemetery would be grown over by the woods. He was friends with the Catholic bishop of Savannah, who told him there were some priests who were interested in starting a monastery on one of the islands. He asked my great-granddaddy if he knew of a place where they could do something like that. Well, ol' Willie McQueen said they could come out here if they wanted; all they had to do was watch after the place. He told the bishop they could live in the big house and use the lit-tle chapel, too. So in 1871, fifteen monks from the Order of Saint Bene-dict arrived on the island and established their monastery. There were a few of the old slaves still living here, but thay had moved deep into the woods down by Salvation Lake."

"Mr. McQueen," asked John-Morgan, "why is this called Jesus Island?"

Jimmy drew a breath and said, "Well, all the monks did was work during the day on the crops and then pray at night. They prayed for all sorts of things, like sick people and people who were in trouble. After a while, folks in Savannah started sending letters asking them to pray for certain things, like a sick child. Well, some things started happening in town to the people who had asked for the prayers. A little girl who was about to die got better, and a man who had fallen overboard out in the ocean was found alive when everybody thought he had drowned. Pretty soon folks were bringing sick people out to the island for the monks to pray for them. A lot of them got better, or seemed to, and that really got folks to talking back in town. The black people who still lived here believed in Jesus, but they also believed in some of the old ways their ancestors had brought over from Africa. It's kind of like voodoo, and they believed in magical potions made from roots and the casting of spells."

The wind picked up a little off the ocean and made a whistling sound as it moved through the branches of the red cedars down by the creek. A burst of burning embers swirled up from the fire, climbing high into the night, and the circle of boys grew a little tighter.

"After a while," continued Jimmy, "the people in town who believed in voodoo were coming out here, too, so they could visit the root doctor and get his magic potions. Pretty soon people started saying that God was working miracles out on Guale Island. After a while they just started referring to Guale as that island where Jesus worked miracles. Then it started just being called Jesus Island. The monks left in 1898, but the new name stayed on."

Nicky, a small boy with black curly hair and a Swiss Army knife on his belt, asked, "What's a root doctor, Mr. McQueen?"

"It's like a witch doctor only not quite as scary," answered Jimmy. "Root doctors make up all sorts of magical potions, mostly from roots they dig up. The different mixtures are supposed to cure sickness or put a spell on a person."

Nicky gazed into the fire and thought for a moment; then he looked up at Jimmy and cautiously asked, "Do the potions really work?"

"Only if you believe they do, Nicky. The root doctors have power because people really and truly believe they do."

One of the older boys then asked, "Is Dr. Divine a root doctor?"

Jimmy rubbed his hands across his jeans and replied, "Yep, Dr. Divine is a root doctor, and his wife helps him. But you don't have anything to be afraid of."

The next morning, Uncle Moses drove the boys all over the island. After lunch they were given permission to wander the island, with instructions to be back at the campsite by five. Will and John-Morgan decided to explore together.

"Do you know where Dr. Divine and Sister Mystery's cabin is?" asked John-Morgan. "Have you ever seen the Devil Himself?"

"I've seen some alligators on the island, but they weren't all that big. The Devil Himself is supposed to be fifteen feet long. You want to go find Dr. Divine's house, John-Morgan?"

"Yeah," answered John-Morgan with enthusiasm, "and I want to go to Salvation Lake, too, and look at the alligator."

The trail that led to Dr. Divine's cabin followed along the banks of Doomsday Creek. It was a sandy road well worn by Dr. Divine's pickup truck. After a mile and a half, the road took an abrupt turn away from the river and started into the thickest and deepest part of the island.

When they finally came upon a clearing, Will and John-Morgan quietly slipped into the underbrush and surveyed Dr. Divine's cabin.

The one-story structure was made from weathered cypress harvested from the wetlands around Salvation Lake. It had a chimney at one end, and a covered porch ran the entire length of the cabin, with a door in the center and two windows on either side painted blue to ward off evil spirits. In front of the house was a massive live oak that was three hundred years old. It spread its limbs over the cabin and all of the front yard.

"Looks spooky, doesn't it?" whispered Will.

"Yeah, real spooky," replied John-Morgan.

"Do you think anybody's there?" asked Will.

"I can't see anybody, Will."

"Let's slip up to the side of the house and peek in the window," suggested John-Morgan.

The boys could feel their hearts pounding as they ran across the clearing then flattened themselves against the side of the cabin and looked into the open window. A stuffed owl with its wings widespread and claws outstretched hung from the far wall. Mason jars filled with all kinds of dried things sat on shelves, and a large portrait of Jesus with a big halo around his head hung on one wall. On the low table in front of a sofa were two big jars. One had a small alligator curled up and preserved in alcohol. The other had a two-headed baby pig about the size of a puppy. Instinctively, the boys turned and looked at each other, their eyes wide with excitement.

Lucifer had been sleeping most of the morning under the front porch steps. Will and John-Morgan hadn't seen him when they hid in the woods, and Lucifer hadn't heard them as they'd crept up. When a slight breeze carried their scent past his nose, Lucifer's eyes popped open, and his head jerked up.

With an awful howl Lucifer came tearing out from under the steps, around the side of the cabin, and straight for Will's legs. He was able to grab his walking stick in time to poke at the dog and make him fight with it. But that lasted only a second because Lucifer was an eighty-pound bluetick hound who'd fought with every big raccoon on the island and hadn't lost to one.

"What are we gonna' do?" screamed Will, in desperation.

"I don't know. Just keep fightin', Will. Don't let him get in close!" yelled John-Morgan.

Then from out of nowhere, a high, shrill voice filled the air. "Come here to me, Lucifer, right now, or I'll bust you up side the head, so help me God!"

From around the corner of the cabin came a middle-aged black woman in a long, full dress with a bandanna tied around her head. She had a switch in her hand and started swinging at Lucifer when he didn't move fast enough to suit her. The dog let out a yelp when she landed a strong blow over his hindquarters, and backed off.

The woman followed the dog and yelled, "Now git yoself outta here right now!" then swung at him again. Lucifer cowered, whined, and finally slunk off under the porch steps. Then she turned to face John-Morgan and Will.

"Who you two boys is anyway, and whatcha doin' snoopin' round my house?"

Will was shaking and scared. After he wiped his nose with the cuff of his shirt, he managed to say, "I'm Will, and this is my friend John-Morgan. We were just lookin' around. We weren't doin' anything wrong, I promise."

"That's right," said John-Morgan, maintaining a tight grip on his walking stick, "we're here on a campin' trip with the Boy Scouts at the other end of the island. We were just lookin' around, really. We don't mean any harm."

The woman looked closely at Will, first his eyes and mouth. She cocked her head to the side then reached out and took his cap off.

"Lawd have mercy," she said, almost in a laugh, "ain't you Mista Jimmy McQueen's boy?"

"Yes, ma'am," replied Will.

The woman smiled broadly and said, "Lawd, if you ain't the spittin' image a dat man hisself. Mista Jimmy on the island with y'all?"

"Yes, ma'am," said Will politely.

"Um-um," cooed the woman, "such nice manners, too. You can tell you is raised up to be a McQueen."

"Are you Sister Mystery?" asked Will.

"In da flesh, chile." Then she turned to John-Morgan and said, "Who all's youngin' is you?"

"I'm John-Morgan Hartman. My daddy works for the *Savannah Morning Gazette*. He's a writer," answered John-Morgan proudly.

"Sho nuff," said Sister Mystery, "dat's mighty fine."

Sister Mystery grew quiet for a moment while she looked at Will. It had been a long time since she had been to the southern end of the island, where the dock and the big house were. She'd known Jimmy McQueen had a son but had never seen him.

For the most part Sister Mystery kept close to her cabin, tending to her garden and chickens. She was a palm reader and fortune-teller with a large following among a lot of the blacks and some of the whites who lived in Savannah. She was a wise and perceptive woman, well versed in reading expressions on people's faces and the desires of their hearts. After a moment her gaze fell on Will's lip and then into his eyes.

She reached out to Will, put her arm around him, and in a soft voice said, "Come on here, lamb. You and your little friend come with Sister Mystery. She gonna' show you da inside a her house. Y'all like dat?"

Will was thrilled and replied, "Oh yes, ma'am. We'd really like that."

Sister Mystery took the boys into the room with the stuffed owl and took a seat in the red chair next to a small table with half a dozen thick candles on it. A box of kitchen matches was next to the candles, and Sister Mystery struck a match off the sole of her shoe and lit all the candles.

Will and John-Morgan sat next to each other; and while the boys looked around in wonder, Sister Mystery studied Will.

"Mista Will, let ol' Sister Mystery see yo hand for a minute. She gonna tell you your fortune."

Will looked at John-Morgan, smiled, and said, "OK," eagerly thrusting his hand forward. The woman placed Will's hand in hers, waved an eagle feather over it, and mumbled with her eyes closed, while her nostrils flared when she took a deep breath. Then she looked down and straightened out his fingers, making the lines in his palm more distinct. What she saw startled her, and she almost looked up at Will but kept her head down, not saying a word. Finally Will asked, "What does it say, Sister Mystery?"

Sister Mystery thought for a few more seconds. "It says you is a strong boy who done been through a whole lot in his life already. It says you is gonna be a great man who grows up to lead other mens. You gonna' take a long trip one day, and that trip gonna change your life."

Then Sister Mystery stopped talking and looked up at Will. He searched her eyes, and finally Sister Mystery began to speak again.

"Ol' Sister Mystery know how you done hurt sometimes, but she see how it made you stronger than all the rest. What I see is that you gonna need that strength one day 'cause God gonna test you and you is gonna win, just like he tested ol' Job in the Bible and he won. You ain't got nothin' but greatness ahead a you, boy." Then she let Will's hand go.

Will was confused. She was nothing like the gypsy who read palms at the Coastal Empire Fair.

"Thank you, Sister," said Will, as he settled back against the sofa with his fist tightly clenched.

The woman looked over at John-Morgan and said, "Your turn now, lamb." He was a little hesitant but got up anyway and traded places with Will. Sister Mystery went through the same ritual then looked down at John-Morgan's palm. She realized she had frightened Will and now sought to repair the damage.

"Oh my," she whispered, "I got two great men here with me in my house."

"Lemme see here," said the woman, as she stroked John-Morgan's palm. "This here lifeline of yours is long, jus' like Mista Will's. You both is gonna live a long time. Mista John, I see here where you is good with the book learning and how much you loves Jesus. Is that right, lamb?" John-Morgan's eyes grew wide, and he simply nodded his head. Then Sister Mystery continued. "I seen this on Mista Will's hand, and now I sees it on yours. You two is gonna be good friends all your life and do things together when y'all growed up. I sees lots of happiness for both a y'all."

Then Sister Mystery placed her hand over John-Morgan's and said, "All this here fortune-tellin' done gone and wore ol' Sister Mystery out." Sister Mystery settled into the chair and let her head rest against the high back.

"Well, I guess we'd better be goin' now," said Will, as he stood up.

"It was nice to meet you, Sister Mystery, and thank you for telling our fortunes."

Sister Mystery went over to a chest of drawers at the other end of the room. She rummaged around and pulled out two cloth bags about the size of tobacco pouches. They had something in them and were tied tightly at the tops. Both bags were attached to a long piece of string. She shuffled back over to the boys and said, "Dis here is strong medicine," then hung them around their necks.

"What is it?" asked Will.

"Dis here is an asafetida bag. Dr. Divine done filled them up with powerful roots."

John-Morgan fingered the bag around his neck and asked, "What do they do?"

With a serious look on her face, Sister Mystery answered, "Dey wards off evil spirits dat roams da woods on da island." Then from under her blouse she produced a similar bag. "See here, I don't never leave da house without one hangin' 'round my neck. Da woods is full a spirits."

On the front porch, Will asked Sister Mystery how to get to Salvation Lake from the cabin. She pointed to a path on the other side of the big oak and said, "Down dat way fer a piece."

The path to Salvation Lake was narrow. Yaupon holly shrubs and wax myrtles crowded the trail, and sometimes the boys had to push the branches out of their way. As they drew closer to the lake, whitetop sedge plants and smartweed, with their spherical pink and white flowers, lined the ground along the path. Water and laurel oaks filled the woods, and their dark brown acorns were everywhere. The path led through a chest-high growth of palmettos and then down a slight incline to the edge of Salvation Lake.

The oval lake was covered about a hundred acres with the overflow running off to the north, where it fed a large stand of cypress trees. Cattails crowded the edge of the lake, and water lilies floated everywhere. A short dock was at the end of the path with a small rowboat tied to it. John-Morgan and Will walked out to the end and surveyed Salvation Lake.

The water was dark and still and reflected the moving clouds overhead. The boys watched as a half-dozen wood storks took flight from their resting place on the branches of a dead oak and soared over the tops of the cypress trees. The still air was scented with a light aroma of pine and cedar, and the only sound was the buzzing of a dragonfly darting in and out from under the dock. The two Scouts sat at the end of the dock with their legs almost touching the water and looked in.

The air was cool, and the September sun on their backs relaxed them. For a long while they said nothing as they watched cloud formations puff and roll through the azure sky. Will's eyes grew heavy, and he lay back on the dock. John-Morgan was sleepy but forced himself to watch a ripple in the water down by the cypress trees. His eyes narrowed and focused on the center of the V-shaped wake moving their way. When whatever it was on the lake was about a hundred yards away, John-Morgan stood up to get a better look. Behind the point of the wake, perhaps ten feet, he could see something moving slowly from side to side. At fifty yards he could see a knob at the point of the wake and two smaller knobs about two feet back. Then it increased its speed.

"God Amighty, Will, get up. There's an alligator coming after us!" Will had fallen asleep and was a little dazed. When he sat up, he wasn't quite sure what was happening; but when John-Morgan screamed, "Run, Will, run," he hopped up and chased after John-Morgan, who was already off the dock and running up the path. The boys could hear thrashing in the water down by the dock and then the ominous sound of something crushing the cattails behind them.

"He's coming after us, Will," John-Morgan cried out. Will screamed as the sound of the breaking cattails and the thumping of thick feet on the wet ground grew closer. "Oh God, no!" cried Will, when he looked over his shoulder and saw the tops of the cattails wobble and then collapse as they were pushed aside.

John-Morgan spotted an oak with some low branches close to the path and cut off toward it, Will right behind. In an instant, both boys were up the tree as far as they could go.

The Devil Himself had been hatched from a clutch of eggs deep within the cypress forest in 1945. He was one of only three from a nest of twenty eggs to survive that first year. When he was younger, he had dined off the big frogs and fat water moccasins that lived around the lake. As he grew, he became swift enough to catch the large trout and bass in the lake. However, his favorite meats came from the raccoons, feral pigs, and deer who drank from the waters of Salvation Lake.

The story about the Devil Himself eating the little girl at her baptism was only partly true. While he did grab the child by her leg as she was being immersed in the water, her father was able to pull her free from the alligator's jaws. The wounds were so extensive, though, that the child's leg was ultimately amputated below the knee. The reason the gator was never hunted down and killed was that Dr. Divine and Sister Mystery would not allow it, so powerful was their influence on the island.

Once, when Dr. Divine was fishing from a rowboat on Salvation Lake, he saw a young alligator snatch a pig off the lake bank and was impressed with his aggressiveness. He could see the gator was missing part of his tail, probably from a fight with an older bull, and made note of it. Whenever he went to the lake, he would look for that alligator and mark his growth. As he marked its growth, Dr. Divine began to realize that he and Sister Mystery could use the alligator as a kind of prop in their root medicine and fortune-telling business. With this idea in mind, Dr. Divine set about to train the alligator.

Alligators are, by nature, shy animals. They are not at all like their aggressive and hostile cousins, the crocodiles. Indeed, the only reports of humans being attacked by alligators in the Southeast always involve those animals who live close to humans and have been repeatedly fed by them.

Dr. Divine was a keen observer of wild animals and quite aware of an alligator's habits and temperament. With this knowledge in mind, he began killing raccoons, possums, and rabbits and taking them to the dock on Salvation Lake. At first he would row out in his boat and find the gator with the chunk out of his tail. Then he would toss one of the dead animals to him. Later, as time progressed, he would stand at the end of the dock, knock on it with a stick, wait for the gator to appear, and throw him the kill of the day. Soon the alligator would swim up to the dock whenever Dr. Divine appeared. With time, nurtured by the meals Dr. Divine provided, the reptile grew big, strong, and obedient.

Whenever Dr. Divine or Sister Mystery had a particularly difficult case, they would call upon the persuasive powers of the big alligator in Salvation Lake. Since the crux of their power lay in the belief that supernatural forces were at their command, a dramatic demonstration of such abilities was a very effective tool of the trade in voodoo.

When the situation merited, Dr. Divine would lead his supplicant, with great fanfare and incantations, down the path to Salvation Lake. As he walked, he would speak of the evil forces that had taken control of that person's life. In dramatic tones Dr. Divine would tell his patient how he would thrust into the jaws of the devil the evil spirits that plagued him, thus ending his misery. When they arrived at the lake, Dr. Divine would stand at the end of the dock and go into a trance. When the alligator appeared in the water awaiting his dead raccoon, Dr. Divine would ceremoniously toss a bag filled with the appropriate symbols of the offending evil spirits. Without fail, the big gator would lunge at the bag, jaws wide open, catch it in midair, and disappear into the depths of Salvation Lake. It was powerful, impressive, and expensive medicine that always succeeded. Soon, Dr. Divine's alligator became know as the Devil Himself all over Savannah.

There was only one problem. The alligator was not discriminating. Whenever someone appeared on the dock, the big gator would swim over ready to eat. Dr. Divine failed to realize this, and that was why the little girl, as well as Will and John-Morgan, were attacked.

"Oh God," cried Will, "what are we gonna do?"

"Just stay here 'til he leaves," answered John-Morgan.

"We can't, John-Morgan. This branch is starting to lean over. What if we fall out? What if it breaks? He'll grab us!"

At the base of the tree rested the Devil Himself. He was now twelve years old, twelve feet long, and two and a half feet wide, and weighed close to one thousand pounds. With unblinking eyes he watched the boys as they clung to life eight feet above.

As the sun slipped below the tree line and the light lavender sky above Salvation Lake turned deep purple then black, the frogs began to croak, and the boys began to pray.

In the deep woods, where starlight does not penetrate, the darkness is absolute. By six-thirty the boys could hardly see each other. The ground below was inky black, and the Devil Himself was invisible. But they could smell him. They could smell the moldy, organic humus that rose from the great body and filtered up through the leaves and moss. They could hear the air pass through the alligator's nostrils as he sucked in and feel the humid vapors of his expirations drifting up in the darkness.

Back at the campsite, the anger felt by Jimmy McQueen and John Hartman at seven o'clock had turned to fear by nine. At ten they had organized a search party. Jimmy and John took the Jeep and started down the road that led to Dr. Divine's cabin. When they reached the cabin, Dr. Divine was on the porch with Sister Mystery.

"Somethin' wrong, Mista Jimmy?"

"Our boys are missin', Dr. Divine. They were supposed to be back at the camp on Williamson Island by five."

"Lawd have mercy," said Sister Mystery, "dey was here dis afternoon. We had us a nice sit-down visit, and den dey take off down da path ta Salvation Lake."

Dr. Divine stood up. "Come on with me, Mista Jimmy. I take ya down dat trail. Jus lemme get my light."

Clinging to life in the branches above the great body of the Devil Himself, the boys were discussing the merits of jumping and running for their lives. Their plans were cut short when the big gator opened his jaws and groaned the long, low, guttural noise of territorial dominance, telling all the females on Salvation Lake that they were his for the taking, while giving a stern warning to any adventurous male.

"I don't think I can hold on much longer, Will," sobbed John-Morgan.

"I don't either," answered Will.

A stillness settled over the boys as they each faced the distinct possibility of falling and landing in the grips of the alligator. Then Will said, "Did you hear something?"

John-Morgan cocked his head slightly and listened.

"No."

"There it is again. I think I hear somebody calling for us!"

"I'm over here, Daddy," cried out Will. "We're hiding up a tree.

There's an alligator on the ground underneath us. Watch out; he's real big!"

The three men stood still. In the glow from their flashlights they looked into each other's faces. Jimmy turned to Dr. Divine and said, "Go get your shotgun."

"Mista Jimmy, it's aways back to my place and aways back up here. Lemme try sumpin' an' see can I get that gator away from da tree. Anyways, all I got is bird shot for my gun. It ain't gonna do nuttin' but make dat big gator mad if 'in I hits him wid it." Then Dr. Divine dropped his voice and said, "He big, Mista Jimmy; he real big."

"OK, do your best."

As the men came closer, they shined their flashlights up at the tree. It was in a small clearing; and when they were fewer than fifty feet away, they stopped and concentrated their beams at its base. Lying by the trunk was the long body of the Devil Himself. In the harsh artificial light, the alligator's eyes reflected a dark red color. They were almost the size of baseballs, and the big gator was the most frightening thing John Hartman had ever seen.

"Mista Jimmy," whispered Dr. Divine, "I'm gonna circle 'round the other side a dat tree and try ta draw da gator toward me. I think he know my voice, an' he jes might come after me if I calls out to 'em."

Dr. Divine moved silently off the path and through the woods. Minutes later there was a loud ruckus in the woods on the other side of the tree.

"Yo, you devil," cried out Dr. Divine, "come here to me. I is what you wants. Come on here to me, Satan. Come here, I say!"

The alligator shifted his head in the direction of the noise and seemed to sniff the air. Dr. Divine moved in a little closer, beating the ground with a branch and yelling. The alligator moved toward the sound, clearly interested. Then Dr. Divine appeared on the edge of the clearing no more that a dozen feet from the gator. When Dr. Divine switched on his flashlight and shined it into the alligator's eyes, it became confounded and disoriented. Then Dr. Divine threw the biggest limb he had been able to find at the alligator and hit him between the eyes. The animal reeled to his left and snapped at the air. Dr. Divine hit him again with another log, and the gator began to move back from the light. When Dr. Divine was sure he had the alligator confused, he kept the flashlight focused on the alligator's eyes and moved in, holding a long branch in his right hand. At six feet he began to beat the alligator in the face with the branch. It was something that even the Devil Himself had never encountered, and his reaction was to seek safety in the dark waters of Salvation Lake.

That night the boys fell asleep huddled next to their fathers. Both men cradled their son's heads in their arms and watched the boys throughout the night. Occasionally, one would wake with a startle only to be comforted by a weary but thankful father. Neither boy removed the asafetida bag Sister Mystery had hung around their necks. It was powerful medicine.

11. Friends and Enemies

Keep your friends close,
and your enemies closer.

—An Italian proverb

In 1961, Will McQueen started at Savannah High School, a massive, dignified brick structure, built on stately Washington Avenue in the mid 1930s. He tried to play football, but his performance on the Blue Jackets's junior varsity was as unimpressive as his football career had been with the Panthers in Daffin Park.

While Will was greatly attracted to girls, he was self-conscious around them and lacked the confidence to initiate conversation. He despised his looks and stood for long periods in front of the mirror, imagining what he would look like were it not for his upper lip. He knew he was a child of privilege, and there was no denying he enjoyed his status, but he often vowed to himself that he would trade it all to be without this blemish.

Even though fear of rejection was still with Will during his sophomore year in high school, turning sixteen and getting his driver's license seemed to be the boost he needed. His father gave him a white 1955 Mercury convertible that summer, and a whole new world opened up for Will. He wasn't about to let the social benefits of his new car go to waste; and even though he was afraid, Will began asking girls for dates. He was pleasantly surprised how many said yes.

Will often double-dated with John-Morgan, and Tybee Island was a frequent destination. The ride to the beach with the top down was irresistibly romantic. At night there was a palpable throb of lustiness about Tybee that seemed to have a disarming influence on even the most cautious and correct young ladies. Most of all the bars and liquor stores on Tybee exercised little restraint when it came to underage drinking. Will and his friends were in perfect harmony with the laid-back, carefree posture of the island and indulged themselves in it all summer long.

John-Morgan's parents had a house at the south end of Tybee Island; and one evening in late August of '64, he and Will took it upon themselves to host an unchaperoned party there. Later that evening, on the ride back to town, Will was stopped by the Tybee police.

"You Will McQueen?" asked the officer, as he shined his flashlight in Will's bloodshot eyes.

"Yes, sir."

"Your daddy used to be mayor, didn't he?"

"Yes, sir," said Will hopefully.

"Well, I don't care who you are," shot back the cop, "you're under arrest for speeding, DUI, and underage drinking. Follow me back to the station."

Will, John-Morgan, and their dates were taken to the Tybee jail located in the old stockade at Fort Screven and placed in a holding cell. Both girls were crying, and Will felt like doing the same as he watched the deputy who had his driver's license make a phone call. He couldn't hear what was being said, but he saw the officer looking at the license as he spoke and girded himself for the imminent arrival of his father and the wrath that was sure to follow.

Ten minutes later Francis Quinn appeared and spoke briefly and cordially with the deputy, who then unlocked the cell door and said, "All right, y'all can go now. I'm releasin' y'all into the custody of Mr. Quinn."

As the deputy handed Will his driver's license, he said, "Take it easy down here and don't go gettin' into any more trouble." Then he looked over at Francis, winked, and finished with, "If there's a next time, I ain't sure Mr. Quinn'll have enough juice to get y'all out."

As soon as they were outside, Will asked, "How did you know we were here, Uncle Francis? Did my father call you?"

"They know to call me whenever somebody like you gets in trouble," answered Francis, as he opened the door to his new Cadillac.

"Look, I know you want to have a good time, Will," continued Francis, "but these guys are just sittin' out there waitin' for kids like you to come whizzin' by with the radio up and the top down. Watch yourself from now on, OK?"

"Yes, sir."

Just before he closed the door, Francis leaned in close to Will so no one else could hear and quietly said, "This is our little secret, Will. Your old man doesn't know a thing about this."

"Thanks, Uncle Francis," replied Will in a relieved voice. "Thanks a lot!"

One of the first tricks Willie Hart had taught Francis was to give the desk sergeants at the Tybee, Savannah, and Chatham County Police Departments a list of names. If anyone on that list happened to get himself arrested, Francis was to be called before any formal charges were made. The list contained the names of enemies as well as friends; and for their trouble, the sergeants received a generous cash donation each year to what Willie euphemistically called "the charity of their choice."

If the charges weren't too severe, and often they weren't, Francis could usually persuade the authorities to forget about the unfortunate incident and release their prisoner. Over the years he ran up a healthy list of payback favors from both friends and enemies. In police circles the list was cynically referred to as "the social register"; and during Jimmy's reign as mayor, Francis used it several times to neutralize critics who strayed from the straight and narrow.

12. Bubbas, Bums, and Lambs

Question: "How is the cow?"
Answer: "Sir, she walks she talks, she's full of
chalk, the lacteal fluid extracted from the
female of the bovine species is highly prolific to
the nth degree."

—From *The Guidon*, a publication of the Military
College of South Carolina, The Citadel

As a child Will's favorite toys were his soldiers, and he played with them for hours under the sweet gum tree in his backyard. He had read *Gaudalunal Diary* at nine and Winston Churchill's *The Gathering Storm* by eleven, and had devoured *Lee's Lieutenants* the summer of 1960. At Savannah High he was the outstanding freshman in the ROTC program and earmarked for a commission in his senior year.

When it was time to think about college, there was only one thought in Will's mind; and in March of 1965, while serving as cadet major at Savannah High, he received word from the Military College of South Carolina in Charleston, The Citadel, that he had been accepted for the fall term. He was ready to leave that day.

The Citadel has always prided itself on having the toughest plebe system of any military academy. There are few who would argue with that claim, while there are many who find fault with its harshness. Some claim the school breeds a culture of violence and intolerance that is without merit in the modern world. However, the ones who have endured The Citadel's plebe system believe the bonds formed with their fellow cadets, and all that ensues from that kinship, are the precise result of what they survived together during the hell of their freshman or "knob" year. Whatever the reason, anyone who graduates from the Military College of South Carolina knows he has been tempered by the hottest part of the fire.

Will was one of four boys from Savannah who entered The Citadel that year, and there were others in the upper classes. One was Lane Bradford. Lane was a year ahead of Will, and he had been waiting for Will to arrive.

There are no fraternities at The Citadel because the school itself *is* a fraternity. The knobs are the pledges, and the first year at The Citadel is one long initiation period designed to weed out those who don't fit the fraternity's standard, which is to endure what seems to be the unendurable. When that is accomplished, the next three years are considerably less stressful. But until then life at the school is an unrelenting litany of tortures, large and small, meted out by upperclassmen.

Jimmy McQueen had made sure that Will was well prepared for his knob experience. When his son was still a junior at Savannah High, Jimmy had given him a copy of *The Guidon,* a little book that contains all sorts of things a new cadet must know. Most new cadets receive their copy of *The Guidon* six weeks before they enroll and haven't soundly committed to memory all that they should. What's in the book is referred to as "knob knowledge," and it's "God help the knob who doesn't know the right answers."

Will's knob year began in the quadrangle of Padgett-Thomas Barracks, home of the Second Battalion and the oldest barracks on the campus. Built to resemble a Moorish fort, the dominant feature is a tower that rises above the fourth story and overlooks the parade ground to the east. In keeping with the fortlike structure, the middle of the building is an open area onto which each room opens. The floor of the quadrangle is painted in a red-and-white checkerboard pattern, and it is where the cadets assemble each morning. It is also where Will had his first encounter with Lane Bradford at The Citadel.

Lane had not forgotten the beating administered to him by Will. His animosity toward the McQueen name had been fueled by his father's running battle with Mayor McQueen. Cadet Bradford had prepared well for his chance to break Will and deny him entrance into The Citadel's brotherhood of cadets.

On a hot morning in August, on the checkerboard quadrangle, hell on earth started for Cadet Will McQueen with a question. "What are your orders, Knob?"

Without hesitation, Will replied, "Sir, my orders are of two classes: general and special. My general orders are, number one: I will guard everything within the limits of my post and quit only when properly relieved." He continued with the others, not missing a word. Charlie Williams, a friend of Lane's, had asked the question and looked over at Lane when Will finished. With a sly look he said to Lane, "Well, looks like we got us a knob who thinks he knows his shit. Let's just see how really good he knows it. You better not fuck up, Mister Smart-Ass. What's the significance of the brass buttons, Knob?"

"Sir," Will shouted out, "over a period of more than 150 years, a comradeship has developed between the Washington Light Infantry and the Corps of Cadets of The Citadel. As a result the brass buttons worn on The Citadel hats, full-dress uniform blouses, and overcoats are exact replicas of those worn on the Washington Light Infantry dress uniform, sir."

"Well, Mr. Bradford," sneered Charlie Williams, "this piece of shit really is a smart-ass. What is honor?"

"Sir, honor is the most cherished principal of the cadet's life, sir."

"What is duty, Scumbag?"

"Sir, duty is the sublimest word in the English language, sir."

"Who said it, Shit Face?"

"Sir, Gen. Robert E. Lee, sir."

"Well, now, mister," snarled his inquisitor, "because you're such a smart-ass, get down and give me a hundred."

Will gave out at fifty-five push-ups, but by that time, the upperclassmen had lost interest in him for the day. This type of harassment continued for the next several months, only growing worse as Lane tried to break Will.

Not much escaped the eyes and ears of Lt. Col. Thomas Nugent Courvoise, assistant commandant of cadets at The Citadel. His nickname was "the Boo," and it was his job to enforce discipline at the school. The Boo had been born in Savannah and had graduated from Benedictine Military School there. He was also a Citadel graduate and knew Jimmy McQueen. He also knew about Lane Bradford's efforts to break Will.

The Boo was a combat veteran who had retired from the army and taken on his job at The Citadel in 1961. He was a larger-than-life character with an uncanny ability to understand the mind of The Citadel cadet. According to the Boo, there were three types of cadets at The Citadel: Bubbas, Bums, and Lambs. The Boo thought of the cadet corps as his flock and of himself as the good shepherd, referring to the cadets as his "Lambs." If a cadet were in the Boo's good graces, he was addressed as "Lamb." If the opposite were true, that cadet was referred to as a "Bum." Somewhere in between came the "Bubba," a term he had picked up at Benedictine, where the universal nickname was "Bubba."

Will had been called to the Boo's office in October of his knob year. By that time he and the rest of the survivors were in a state of perpetual shock, and not much fazed them. However, a summons to the Boo's office was always cause for special concern. When Will knocked on the door, a lion's roar called out, "Enter!" Will stood at attention in front of the Boo's desk, expecting a world-class chewing out. Then the Boo said those special words. "Sit down, Lamb, I want to talk to you for a minute."

Will let out a sigh and almost fell into the chair next to the Boo's desk.

"I want you to know, Lamb, that I'm well aware of all the grief you've been catching. I also want you to know that you're gonna make it, too. Just don't take any of this personally. Sometimes my Lambs begin to think they've been singled out for a hard time because of who they are or something like that, but it ain't the case. Just hang in there, son. If you need me, I'm always ready to listen to my Lambs. Now go on and get."

Will sat dumbfounded for a moment as he looked at the Boo.

"Got something you want to tell me, Lamb?" asked the Boo.

Will quickly stood up, said, "Sir, no sir," and waited to be dismissed. The Boo put a cigar in his mouth and lit it with a lighter shaped like a cannon. He puffed on the cigar until a cloud of blue smoke filled the air over his head; then he leaned back in his chair and said, "Dismissed."

"Racking" is the term applied to the harassment and intimidation poured upon the knob by his seniors. Lane had tried to avoid any direct racking of Will, since everyone knew he personally had it in for him. That finally changed the week before the Christmas break.

Will's platoon was standing at attention in the quad for morning formation when Lane and several of his friends approached. Will was fully "braced" with his chin and stomach pulled in and his shoulders back and down.

"What the fuck did you say, Doo-Willy?" sneered Lane, as he put his face directly into Will's after he answered a question about knob knowledge.

"Sir," shouted Will, "discipline is the state of order or obedience derived from training that makes punishment unnecessary, sir."

Lane stood back with his arms folded and cast a glance at those around him. "This smack thinks he knows his shit, but I can't understand a thing he says because of his deformity."

Lane moved in close once again and pointed to Will's lip. "Do you see this harelip the knob has here, Mr. Williams?"

Williams snickered a little, mostly for Lane's consumption, but felt Lane was going a little over the line. A few other upperclassmen had gathered around to watch the fun, and there was silence in the Second Platoon.

In an exaggerated imitation of the way Will talked, Lane said, "Well, this here knob-ass piece of shit has a deformity with his lip, and he can't talk right, can you, Knob?"

Will was taken aback for a moment and didn't respond immediately. Lane put his mouth next to Will's ear and said, in mocking imitation, "You can't talk right, can you, Knob. You also look like a damn freak, don't you, Smack?"

Will shouted out, "Sir, yes sir."

Lane slowly came around to the front of Will and studied his eyes. He thought he saw, for the first time, the signs that Will was going to lose emotional control.

"Couldn't get a date with a good-looking broad in high school because of that lip and the fucked-up way you talk, could you, Smack?"

"Sir, no sir."

"You know what the girls at Savannah High School have to say about you, McQueen?"

"Sir, no sir."

"The cute ones said you're a freak. The ugly ones said kissing you was like kissing a fucking pancake."

It had been a long time since August, and even Will was beginning to get a little frayed around the edges. The night before, Will and about forty other knobs had been given what was referred to as a sweat party. They were made to put on all their rain gear and were packed into the showers, where the water was turned on as hot as it could get. Then they were taken on a three-mile forced march. It had been a hard night.

"I even know one little girl who said she kissed you good night because she felt sorry for you, but that she'd never do it again. Do you know who that was, Dumb head?"

"Sir, no sir."

"It was Kathy Broadmore, Knob-ass, and she laughed about it because she said you had a crush on her. Did you have a crush on Miss Broadmore, Harelip?"

Will had taken Kathy to his senior prom. She was cute and popular, and it had taken all the courage he could muster to ask her out. He had kissed her good night, their only kiss, and she had never accepted another date with him. He was never sure why. The fact was that he had, indeed, had a crush on Kathy and had had trouble hiding it when he was around her at school. None of Lane's taunts had really gotten to him until Kathy Broadmore's name was brought up. Will was hurt and humiliated. Then tears formed in Will's eyes and began to roll down his cheeks.

"Look at this, gentlemen," said Lane, "our knob-harelip is starting to cry. Look like Citadel material to you, Mr. Williams?"

Charlie was looking at the ground in embarrassment and just mumbled, "Come on, Lane, let's get some breakfast. He's had enough."

Lane got in Will's ear once more and whispered, "You ain't seen nothing yet, Willy Boy. Enjoy your Christmas because I've got some more presents for you when you come back. Now assume the position and give me twenty-five good ones."

Will tried to control himself, but the sobs burst forth as he did his push-ups. Before he turned to walk away, Lane snarled out, "Not as tough as you thought you were, are you, Knob? Must run in the family."

Later that day Lane Bradford stood at attention in the Boo's office. "Mr. Bradford," spit out the Boo, "you're a Bum. I don't generally interfere with what goes on with the knobs, but if I ever hear about you pulling another stunt like the one you pulled today with McQueen, I'll ream you a new one so big it'd take the Ashley and the Cooper River up it. Now get out of my sight, Bum." The Boo had spoken.

When Will came back from Christmas break, he never had any more problems with Lane Bradford. In his sophomore year he participated in the training of the incoming cadets. While he administered his share of harassment, he didn't forget what it was like to be a knob and approached his job with less intensity than other members of the cadre.

13. Thunderstorms

Beauty can pierce one like a pin.

—THOMAS MANN, *Buddenbrooks,* Part XI

While it was harsh and unrelenting, the plebe system at The Citadel had given Will McQueen something he'd never had. When he arrived in Savannah for the summer before his junior year, he had gone through a noticeable change. He was two inches taller and thirty pounds heavier than when he'd first walked under the arch at Lesesne Gate. The extra weight was all lean muscle, but an internal metamorphosis had also occurred. The Citadel had given Will McQueen confidence in himself.

Charlotte Drayton was considered by many to be one of the prettiest girls in Savannah. Will knew her but had never approached Charlotte, fearing rejection. That, too, had changed at The Citadel.

When Cadet Corporal McQueen arrived home the first week in June of 1967, it was still a relatively cool eighty-five degrees in Savannah. That Saturday evening he pulled his father's new Jaguar S-Type up to the curb at Francine Simpson's house on Washington Avenue. She was Charlotte's roommate at Emory, and her parents were friends of Will's. Francine was having what she called a "beginning of summer" party and had invited Will. Miss Simpson was attractive and popular in her own right and considered Will somewhat "nerdy" but was polite to him because of his family's position in the community. Naturally, Charlotte Drayton was there.

Charlotte had dated John-Morgan Hartman in high school. On a number of occasions, they had gone with Will and his dates on excursions to the beach at Jesus Island. She had easily captured Will's attention with her looks, but it was his impression that Charlotte didn't find him the least bit attractive, and it bruised his ego. At that time he would never have had the nerve to ask her out.

When Will walked into the Simpsons' game room, Charlotte was standing at the pool table with Francine and several other girls. She was pretending to be serious about shooting pool, and Sam Espy, Francine's date, was trying to show her how to hold the cue stick. She was wearing white cotton slacks that were tasteful but demonstrated, with close perfection, the tight shape of her anatomy; and no one failed to notice the faint outline of her bikini panties. Her long, sandy blonde hair hung past her shoulders, and she had already acquired a tan that served to highlight her pale pink lipstick, the popular color that year.

There were no sharp, chiseled features on Charlotte. Just as her lips were rounded and full, her nose was dainty, with a soft ridge that carried perfectly onto cheeks with dimples that formed whenever she smiled. But it was her eyes that were the most captivating. They were bright emerald, with delicately expressive brows and long, sweeping lashes.

When Will entered the room, at first Charlotte ignored his presence, but then she noticed the change in him. At six feet, he was taller than the last time she had seen him, and the 195 pounds he now carried were in his arms and chest and neck. His shoulders had broadened, and they tapered to a slender waist and hard, flat stomach. Charlotte had always admired boys with what she and Francine liked to call a "tight butt," and Will could thank The Citadel for that, too.

Sipping from a bottle of Budweiser, Will stood nonchalantly next to the wet bar, pretending to ignore Charlotte. After a few minutes of small talk with other guests, he noticed Charlotte working her way through the crowd toward him. When she finally approached, she greeted him warmly, and for a while they spoke of their trips to Jesus Island. For the first time Charlotte seemed interested in him.

Eventually the conversation turned to college, and Charlotte acted impressed with Will's stories about The Citadel. For the next thirty minutes Charlotte focused her attention on Will, asking him questions about everything from Charleston to the war in Vietnam.

As the room began to fill, it became stuffy and uncomfortable. The number-one record on the charts that week was "Respect," by Aretha Franklin, and it was pounding from the speakers of the Simpsons' new Sony stereo system when Charlotte leaned over and shouted into Will's ear, "Let's go outside where we can hear ourselves talk."

They sat in the Simpsons' garden on a swing that hung from an oak tree and continued their conversation. The swing was in a far corner of the garden, away from the party, and they spent the rest of the evening moving in a slow arc through the settling night air while they talked and listened to the music. Toward the end of the evening Charlotte turned the conversation back to Jesus Island.

"That's the prettiest beach I've ever seen," said Charlotte, "it's much nicer than Tybee. Not so many people."

It couldn't really be called courage since Will had waited until he was sure she would say yes, but it did take a little nerve when he finally asked, "Would you like to go there with me tomorrow?"

Charlotte turned to him and said, "Oh, yes, I'd love to go."

The service boat for Jesus Island was a 1947 Gar Wood open-style sedan hardtop named *Little Feats*. Even Charlotte, who knew nothing about boats, was impressed by the deep red luster of the mahogany hull and the shine of the chrome-and-brass fittings.

Charlotte wore a pair of red short shorts over a one-piece, black bathing suit cut low in the back and sat close to Will on the ride to Jesus Island. When they hit choppy water, sometimes her bare thigh would brush against Will's. Once, when they were forced to cross the wake of a larger boat, Charlotte grabbed his arm and held on through the rough water. Each time she touched him, Will smiled to himself.

It was just after eleven in the morning when Will pressed the throttle of his boat forward and brought it onto a plane. Soon a cool wind coursed through the vent windows, carrying with it the welcome smell of salt air. The boat rose and fell with the tender rhythm of the swells as they passed Skidaway Island and pointed the boat toward the Tybee Cut.

Inside the cut the water was calm, and the boat skimmed across the creek. The tide was low, and above the exposed creek banks stood walls of fresh green marsh grass, new from the spring. Armies of fiddler crabs marched across the mud. Charlotte watched as snowy egrets, festooned in their springtime nuptial plumes, hunted along the water's edge. She nudged Will and pointed to a great blue heron perched in stately seclusion on an oyster bed and smiled when she spied a cormorant dive under the water, swim for several yards, then emerge with a fish in its beak.

The Tybee Cut opened into the Half Moon River; and when Will eased his boat into the sweeping starboard turn, the outline of Jesus Island began to appear. Charlotte screamed with excitement when a porpoise rocketed out of the water up onto the bank. It had forced several fish to beach themselves and quickly gobbled them down before sliding back into the river.

Soon they were in Wassaw Sound, circling the southern tip of Jesus Island, heading into the Atlantic. They cruised along the ocean side of the island then turned into McQueen's Inlet. Will nudged the bow onto the beach, where he and Charlotte unloaded the cooler. Then he dropped the anchor onto the sand, pushed the boat into deeper water, and pulled a beer from the cooler.

"I hope you brought enough for two," said Charlotte.

Like most kids from Savannah, Charlotte had led the way in party life at Emory and could hold her own with just about any boy when it came to drinking beer. Will gave her a can, and she held it up to him in a toast.

"Here's to a glorious day and a wonderful summer, Will. I can't tell you how glad I am we ran into each other and how much I appreciate you asking me out to your island."

The rest of the day was spent swimming, sitting on the beach, but most of all talking. While there had been ample bodily contact in the water as Will let Charlotte dive off his shoulders or held her hand as they waded out to the sandbar where the pelicans liked to gather, Will had not tried to be romantic in any way. He had wanted to but was held back by his old fears of rejection.

That night, when their date ended, Charlotte was a little tipsy. When Will told her good night, she pulled him toward her. Just before their lips were about to meet, she stopped and whispered, "It was a wonderful day. I hope we can do this again." Then she gave Will a kiss that lasted several seconds, whirled around, and opened the door. As she stepped inside, she looked over her shoulder and said, almost as an order, "Call me in the morning."

The second kiss came the next night. Actually, there were scores of kisses; and as the summer of '67 rolled through the rest of June, Will's wildest dream came true. He and Charlotte Drayton were going together; they were an item. Some people even said they were in love.

Will and Charlotte visited Jesus Island frequently that summer. On the weekends they usually had friends with them, and their days were spent at McQueen's Inlet waterskiing or on Driftwood Beach bodysurfing. The weekday trips often involved only Charlotte and Will. Those were the days he liked most of all.

By the middle of July, Charlotte had become a solid presence in the deepest recesses of Will's emotions. He thought of her constantly, ached for her when they were apart, and could not take his eyes off of her when they were together. This kind of infatuation was nothing new to Charlotte. Many boys had fallen in love with her, and she was well acquainted with all the signs. What was surprising to Charlotte, though, was how much she had come to like Will. She confided in Francine one day when they went shopping together. Over lunch at the Pink House on Reynolds Square, Charlotte explained her feelings for Will.

"You know why I went out with him in the first place, don't you?" asked Charlotte, as she wiped her mouth, taking care not to smear her lipstick.

"Of course I do, silly," replied Francine, leaning in close to Charlotte and speaking in a tone of confidentiality. "It was because you had broken up with Stevie Breckenridge, or he had broken up with you, the week before we came back home from Atlanta. You were bored and wanted something to take your mind off Stevie. I know you loved the beach at Jesus Island—you raved enough about it up at Emory when it was so cold and dreary—and you just saw your chance to get back out there again, even if it was with Will McQueen, right?"

Charlotte looked out at the square and thought for a moment. Her hair was held back with a yellow silk band that matched the bows on the straps of the white sundress she was wearing. She smiled and pushed back a strand of hair that had fallen out of place then answered.

"I was the one who broke it off with Steve, not the other way around, Fran honey," said Charlotte, in a sarcastic tone. "But yeah, I guess you're right. The only thing is Will is so much more than I thought he was. I mean, when we talk, he just knows so much. He's so smart and just has a way with words. I know he's not the greatest-looking thing I've ever been out with, but I don't really even notice his lip anymore. When we're in Savannah, everybody knows who Will is, and I don't care; I'm not embarrassed to be with him around here."

Francine grew quiet for a moment and then looked at Charlotte with a probing eye. "OK, you like him a lot, he's interesting, he's been a lot of fun, and you've gotten your fangs into a boy from one of the nicest families in Savannah. That's fine, but are you in love with Will?"

Charlotte smiled cunningly and then shook her head from side to side. "No, I'm not, but I still think he's sweet; and at least for the rest of the summer, Jesus Island is Drayton family property."

Puffs of cumulus mediocris clouds slipped eastward at two thousand feet over the dock at Jesus Island as Uncle Moses helped Will tie up the boat.

"Is Malachy at the house, Uncle Moses?" asked Will as he placed the cooler with his and Charlotte's lunch in it on the backseat of the Jeep.

"He ought to be at the chapel right about now," replied Moses. "Ol' Malachy, he a prayin' man, and every single mornin' he be down ta da chapel, kneeling at da altar, working dem beads like there ain't gonna' be no tomorrow."

"Do many people come out here to see him?" asked Will.

Moses chuckled a little as he took off the old baseball cap he wore and wiped the sweat from his forehead.

"Oh, yes suh, dey comes out here to see Ol' Malachy near 'bout as much as dey comes out to see Sister Mystery and Dr. Divine."

The Jeep bounced along the road that crossed through an oak forest that had been open fields of cotton a hundred years before. In some places, seven or eight separate trunks rose from the same spot like great flower cuttings stuffed together into a vase. The soft, dark ground was covered with leaves, and small groups of short palmettos were scattered among the oaks. Moss hung heavy from every limb, and thick vines wrapped themselves around the trunks and climbed through the trees. Red, white, and sometimes orange lichens stuck to the trunks like splattered paint.

At Saint Andrew's Chapel, Will quietly pushed open the heavy front door and peeked in. Malachy was on his knees at the front of the chapel praying. Will put his finger to his lips then motioned in silence for Charlotte to look into the chapel. Malachy was motionless, kneeling in a trancelike state. Every few seconds the rosary beads moved slightly as he finished one Hail Mary and moved to the next bead. Charlotte pulled back from the door and looked at Will, mouthing a silent, "Wow," before looking back into the chapel. Then she saw Malachy slowly make the sign of the cross, stand, bow deeply to the altar, and walk toward the door.

Outside the chapel, Malachy embraced Will and said, "I've been expecting you."

Then he turned toward Charlotte as Will said, "This is my friend Charlotte Drayton, Malachy. She wanted to meet you."

Malachy extended his hand, saying, "I'm very happy to know you, Charlotte," as he looked into her eyes.

"I'm pleased to meet you, Malachy," answered Charlotte. For a brief moment Malachy held onto Charlotte's hand; and as he did, she felt a peculiar yet relaxing warmth in his touch.

The three walked over to the old cemetery and sat on the stone bench outside the iron fence surrounding the McQueen graves. A pair of yellow butterflies darted around the headstones, and Charlotte brushed away an occasional mosquito as Will told Malachy about his life at The Citadel. While Will talked, Malachy studied him closely.

After a few minutes, Malachy turned to Charlotte and said, "Tell me about yourself."

Charlotte was surprised at how comfortable she felt with Malachy and enjoyed telling him about the courses she was taking at Emory. Malachy listened as the two talked and would often look over at Will while Charlotte was talking and catch the unmistakable countenance of a boy in love. He did not sense the same thing in Charlotte.

It was just past noon when Will and Charlotte reached the cabin on McQueen Creek. They sat in front of it and watched as tall, flat-based clouds hung over the Atlantic. They drank from a bottle of chilled Johannesburg Riesling and fed each other cold slices of cantaloupe and watermelon.

Miles to the west, in Bryan and Effingham Counties, a low-pressure cell had formed and was moving at twenty-five miles an hour toward Savannah and the barrier islands. Towering cumulonimbus clouds with slate-colored bottoms sucked up moisture from Georgia's farmlands then dropped torrents of water on everything in their path, while strong gusts toppled power lines and lightning strikes shot down tall pines.

On Jesus Island the wind had picked up from the ocean as the low pressure of the thunderstorm pulled in the air. Will and Charlotte could see the storm building while it was still twenty miles away. The anvil-shaped cloud formation reached thirty-five thousand feet into the heavens and covered the entire western horizon. Will stood with his arm around Charlotte as they watched the storm close in on the island. Soon the sky was dark purple, then almost black, as the wind began gusting and the temperature dropped from ninety-five to seventy-five degrees in a matter of minutes. When dime-size hail started falling, Will took Charlotte into the cabin.

The rain came down in sheets across the marsh and blew inside. The couple could not avoid getting wet and began to shiver when the cool wind whipped through the old building. They nestled together in a corner, and Will pulled Charlotte close to him to keep her warm.

Outside, lightning flashed, striking the tallest trees on the island. Will counted off the seconds between the flash of the lightning and the bang of the thunder as the storm moved toward the ocean.

Shivering, Charlotte buried her head in Will's chest and wrapped her arms around his back, pulling herself as close to him as she could, pressing her cheek against his chest. Will looked down and saw that the top of her bathing suit had pulled away, revealing her breasts. Charlotte's eyes were squeezed shut, and she could not see him staring at her while the tempest raged outside.

When the rain began to slacken and the wind no longer cut through the cracks in the cabin walls, Charlotte looked up at Will. Without a word she took his face in her hands and pulled him to her. She covered his lips with hers and searched his mouth with her tongue. Will reached for the small of her back and pulled Charlotte close. He remembered there were a couple of old army blankets tucked away in a footlocker and said, "I think I know how we can get more comfortable."

A light rain still tapped on the tin roof, and tiny waterfalls ran off the eaves. The air was cool and clean, and in the distance, they could hear waves breaking on Driftwood Beach as they lay together on the blankets. Charlotte was on her back and Will on his side as he kissed her on her neck and shoulders. Charlotte was breathing heavily when she pushed Will back and looked at him. "I think I'm in love with you, Will," she said.

"I know I'm in love with you," was Will's reply, and Charlotte pulled him on top of her.

There had been no passion like this passion for Will. Feelings of great intensity arose within him and swirled around in his head. Everything was alive inside, and he could feel rushes of emotion passing through him. Impulsively, he pulled down the top of Charlotte's bathing suit and immersed himself in her soft charms as she responded with sighs and moans. She slipped her hands down the back of his bathing suit and clutched his buttocks, forcing him to her while she rose to meet him. It wasn't long before Will and Charlotte lay completely naked, bonded in the motions of physical love.

Out over the ocean, in the far distance, the storm still rumbled and the clouds glowed with hot pink tops that gave way to shades of lavender. Will looked at Charlotte and followed her tanned thigh to the point where her skin was pale from her bathing suit. He drank in every curve on her body, every landmark of distinction, each shape that thrilled him for future reference in his daydreams.

"I had always hoped it would be like this, Will," whispered Charlotte. "I'm so glad I waited for somebody like you." Then she took his hand and kissed it.

"I'm glad I waited, too, Charlotte. I'm so in love with you; I never dreamed anything could be this wonderful."

When Will spoke, he was being sincere. It was his first time, and it had been all that he'd imagined it would be and more. But Charlotte had simply given way to the wants and demands of the flesh. Not only had she lied about her feelings, she'd also lied about her virginity. Charlotte was experienced, and Will was willing to believe anything about the girl he loved.

In the weeks that followed, Charlotte would surrender herself to Will many times. And he, dazed and infatuated, exulted in his belief that she craved his touch as much as he did hers. When it was time for him to return to The Citadel, Will briefly entertained thoughts of enrolling at Emory just to be close to Charlotte. However, on the fourteenth of August, he broke himself away from something that had become as sweet and precious as life itself and returned to Charleston for his junior year.

14. The Ring Hop

And a woman is only a woman, but a good
cigar is a smoke.

—RUDYARD KIPLING, "The Betrothed"

Upon his return to The Citadel, Will signed on as a Bond Volunteer. This also signaled to the rest of the corps his intentions to be a member of the elite Summerall Guards drill team when he entered his senior year. He also became a "roach," or one of the fifty-four cadets allowed to try out for the Junior Sword Drill.

The Junior Sword Drill, or JSD as it was known, was composed of fourteen members of the junior class and was considered to be the elite within the elite at The Citadel. The only time they performed their intricate precision drill with flashing swords was in October at the senior ring hop. It was a festive, yet formal, function, with proud parents and desirable young ladies in ball gowns and long, white gloves. The highlight of the evening was when the seniors walked under an arc of steel formed by the swords of the JSD. When Will was selected for the JSD, he considered it his greatest achievement and looked forward to having Charlotte come to Charleston for the ring hop and share in his triumph.

Will had been completely immersed in his activities and had not seen

Charlotte since leaving Savannah. They had written frequently, and there were occasional long-distance calls. At first Charlotte was as affectionate as always; however, as September gave way to October, Will began to sense a distance forming between them.

Initially Charlotte denied any change in her feelings, but frequently when Will called, she was not at the dorm, and Francine made excuses for her. On the second day of October, Will was finally able to catch Charlotte in her room. She told him she had been feeling smothered by their relationship and wanted to see other people. She assured him she still cared for him but wasn't sure if love was the right word to describe her feelings. When Will tried to find out more, she was evasive. Before Charlotte hung up, she dropped a bomb on him.

"I can't come to Charleston for the ring hop, Will. I just don't feel right about it. I care for you and want to be friends, but I want to back away for a while, have my own space. I hope you understand. You'll always be one of the sweetest boys I've ever known, Will, and I'll never forget last summer; but, well, things change, and I just can't come to the dance."

"But Charlotte," sputtered Will, "we were talking about getting engaged and everything. Is there somebody else? Have you been going out with that Stevie creep behind my back?"

"Don't call him a creep," said Charlotte sharply, "he's a KA and comes from a nicer family than yours. Anyway, you don't own me, and I can do whatever I want."

The rest of the conversation was downhill, but Will's love for Charlotte would not let him give up without a fight. The next day he was standing at attention in the Boo's office.

"Stand at ease, Bubba," said the Boo, as he reached into his desk and fished out a Double Corona, "and tell me whatcha' want."

"Colonel, I need a pass for tonight and tomorrow and maybe the next day. It's an emergency."

The Boo cut off the end of the cigar with a penknife, then said, "An emergency. What kind of an emergency, Bubba?"

"It's personal, sir. I gotta go to Atlanta on personal business."

The Boo knew exactly what was troubling Will. He had seen pictures of Charlotte in Will's room and had heard the Savannah boys talking about what a knockout she was. He'd also heard Lane Bradford had been snickering about Will's girlfriend, saying she was only using the "harelip" because she had been dumped by her real boyfriend and wanted something to do for the summer.

"Sit down, Lamb," said the Boo, "and tell me about this girl you're all worked up about in Atlanta."

Will respected and trusted the Boo and told him the whole story. When he finished, the Boo leaned back in his chair, puffed on his cigar, and studied the ceiling for a few seconds.

"Now look here, Lamb," said the Boo, "I ain't gonna give you that pass 'cause I'm not gonna let one of my Lambs go up to Atlanta and make a fool of himself over a gal that don't give a hoot about him."

"But Colonel, I just want to see her and talk to her; maybe it'll change things."

"That's a lot'a bunk, Bubba, and you know it. If I thought this Charlotte gal could be changed, I'd drive you up there myself. But it isn't gonna make one bit of a difference. She's got her old boyfriend back now, and she's not interested in you anymore. That's the bottom line, Lamb, and you know the Boo wouldn't put you on."

Will sighed and looked down at the floor. He felt like crying, he hurt so badly. The Boo could tell and felt sorry for him. Will had been a good cadet, tried his heart out. Failed sometimes, but he always tried, and that was what the Boo considered the most important thing about a man, that he didn't give up. *A kid like this,* thought the Boo, *just doesn't know that romance is different.*

"Look here, Lamb," said the Boo softly, "I know you at least want to try and get her back. But girls are different from other things. Sometimes the harder you try and the more attention you pay to 'em, well, it just drives 'em farther away. You might have a shot at her, but you don't take it by chasing her. I promise you that. Plus, you lose her respect."

Then the Boo reached into his pocket, pulled out a ten-dollar bill, and said, "Here, take this and go on down to the Ark tonight. Cry in your beer a little. Take a couple of your buddies with you. It'll do you good. If anybody gives you any static, tell 'em to see me about it."

Will looked at the money. Quietly and without emotion he said, "Yes, sir, and thank you." Then he stood and waited for permission to leave. The Boo thought for a moment and then said, "Come on back here tomorrow. I might have a little surprise for you. Can't promise anything, but we'll see."

The Ark was a dingy pool hall not far from The Citadel. It was the place Citadel boys slipped away in order to unwind from the pressures of school. Will went there that night with his roommate, and the two drank up all of the Boo's money plus a little more. The last thing Will said to his roommate before he passed out was, "Kennickell, she's so beautiful, I'd throw myself into a cotton gin if I thought I'd come out the crotch to her panties."

The next afternoon Will was sitting in the Boo's office with the remnants of a hangover.

"Your head hurt, Bubba?" asked the Boo.

"Not as much as it did this morning, sir."

"Look here, Bubba, you got any replacement plans for a date to the ring hop?"

"No, sir."

"Well, would you like to have a date with a real nice Charleston girl if I could arrange it?"

Will looked at the Boo in surprise. He thought for a few seconds and then said, "Yeah, I guess so. Who is she?"

"This young lady is the daughter of a Citadel man, a classmate of mine. She's kinda in the same boat you are right now. Just broke it off with her boyfriend. Here's her name and number; give her a call. She's expecting to hear from you."

Laura Lee Moultrie was no Charlotte Drayton, but her class and breeding were unmistakable. Her father's side of the family were French Huguenots who'd come to Charleston fleeing religious persecution in Canada during the early 1700s. Her mother was descended from cotton planters of an English line, who had owned a large plantation in Hampton County before the Civil War. Laura Lee was in her sophomore year at the College of Charleston and had been dropped by her boyfriend of three years for another girl who had been her best friend in high school.

The Moultrie family lived near the battery in old Charleston in a house her late grandmother Hampton had owned. Her father, Wade, was a member of The Citadel class of 1938 and had been a moderately successful investment banker. The Moultries could not be considered wealthy, but they were financially comfortable and socially connected. When Laura Lee made her debut into Charleston society, the *Post and Courier* described her as "an attractive brunette with fetching brown eyes and a winning smile."

Laura Lee was a slender five feet, six inches tall, with chestnut hair parted down the middle and curled under at the ends. Her complexion was almost flawless, and her mother considered it her greatest asset. Ellen Hampton Moultrie insisted that Laura Lee had inherited it from her grandmother Hampton.

While Laura Lee's figure was certainly acceptable, it was in no way voluptuous. She thought she was skinny and dreamed of being able to fill out the bust of a bathing suit like her cousin Elizabeth Ann in Beaufort. In response, her mother kept reminding her to be grateful she wasn't overweight. Her eyes were large and brown and matched to a nose that she thought much too big but that really wasn't. She had expressive lips and a strong chin that demonstrated a slight cleft inherited from her father.

Laura Lee's biggest asset was her personality, not her complexion. She was a kind and humble person of compassion and caring. Even though she was sensitive in nature, she was not emotionally high-strung and disliked the pettiness and backstabbing that often punctuated social functions in the upper echelons of Charleston society. While her behavior had always been that of a lady, she still enjoyed off-color jokes, had gotten a little tipsy at Myrtle Beach more than once, thought her father was the greatest man alive, and longed for the day she would meet someone who would return—with equal intensity—the love she knew she was capable of giving.

The night Will picked up Laura Lee for the ring hop, she was apprehensive about him liking her. Both had never been on a blind date before and worried frightfully about what the other would think. Will was perhaps the more self-conscious, fearing what Laura Lee would think the first time she saw him. He had properly surmised that the Boo had told the Moultries about his lip; but when he appeared on their front porch in his full-dress uniform, with brass gleaming and his sword hanging by his side, any apprehensions the Moultries might have had about the Boo's recommendation evaporated instantly.

The performance that night of the Junior Sword Drill was awe inspiring. When Laura Lee stood in the darkened gallery and watched as the JSD went through their silent moves under the bright beam of a single spotlight, she was overwhelmed. It was the first time she had really understood her father's devotion to the school, and later that evening she told Will. It was the best thing he had heard in two weeks.

After the dance Will and Laura Lee went to a private posthop party at the home of another Citadel alumnus. The house was located directly on the battery, with Fort Sumter visible in the distance illuminated by the light of a full moon. The couple took a position on the second-story balcony that afforded a spectacular view of Charleston Harbor, where they spent the rest of the evening sipping punch and getting to know each other. It surprised Will how much he enjoyed talking with Laura Lee. There was none of the tension he had often felt when he had been with Charlotte. Conversation with Laura Lee was relaxing for Will; and although he didn't know it, she felt the same about him.

Through the balance of his junior year, Will and Laura Lee continued to see each other. When he received his Citadel ring in his senior year, it was Laura Lee who was on his arm as they walked under the crossed swords of the JSD at his ring hop. Even though she was not as beautiful as Charlotte, Will had grown to appreciate Laura Lee's virtues and, because of her, had begun to see beauty in a different way. He found her to be lacking in the self-absorption that Charlotte often demonstrated and that he'd always ignored because of her physical beauty.

By graduation day in May of 1969, Will had achieved every goal he had set for himself at The Citadel. He had been selected for membership in the prestigious Summerall Guards and had been commissioned to command Second Battalion. By that time he and Laura Lee had been seeing each other exclusively for almost two years. They had spoken of love and even marriage, but it was Laura Lee's level head that offered a cautionary note to their relationship. She was more mature than Will; and though she was sure she loved him and that he loved her, she wasn't sure he was ready for such a commitment. Will had an obligation to the navy upon graduation and had told her he would volunteer for service in Vietnam. All of this troubled her, so when Will left for training at Coronado, California, her only promise was that she would be waiting for him when he returned.

15. Walking Wounded

At times he regarded the wounded soldiers in an envious way. He conceived persons with torn bodies to be peculiarly happy. He wished that he, too, had a wound, a red badge of courage.

—STEPHEN CRANE, *The Red Badge of Courage*

D amn, Mr. McQueen," complained Jay (the Jaybird) Abramovitz, "it's so fuckin' hot here, I don't know how the Dinks stand it. Must be in their genes, I guess." Jaybird cut another quick look over to LTJG Will McQueen standing at the wheel of PBR 196, the wind blowing back his helmet straps while he grinned, as Alonzo (Zippo) Pinkney was fond of saying, "like a possum eatin' shit." Jaybird cursed again then went back to his job of watching the riverbank. In a few seconds he looked back at Will and said, "Shit, Skipper, I don't understand it. I'm standing here sweating my ass off, and you're just as cool as a cucumber, acting like the heat and humidity don't bother you a bit. How's that, sir?"

Will looked over his shoulder at Jaybird. He had a three-day beard, and Jaybird could see his reflection in Will's Ray•Ban Aviator sunglasses. Zippo really dug Will's sunglasses and called them his "Cool Hand Luke reflectors," resolving to get himself a pair at the PX. After a second, Will gave Jaybird one of his sneaky grins and said, "Ever been to Savannah, Georgia, in the summertime, Birdman?"

"Shit, Mr. McQueen, the farthest south I've ever been was when my aunt Sophie died and we had to go to the funeral. That was in Baltimore, and it was January."

Will looked out over the bow of his boat and checked their position in the river. They were cutting through the muddy waters of the Mekong Delta at twenty-five knots. He corrected slightly to port then looked back at Jaybird.

"Well, if you had, Bird, then you'd know why this weather doesn't get me down like it does you Yankees."

Jaybird shook his head and looked back at the passing nipa palms on the riverbank. He tilted his M-60 machine gun up a few degrees, estimating how much a round would drop if he had to fire at the tree line. Then, for the twentieth time, he looked warily at the size of the splinter shield fitted around the weapon; it was all that stood between him and incoming fire. As always, the shield appeared woefully inadequate.

Will scanned the river once more then turned and spoke to Jaybird again.

"Look at Zippo there, Jaybird. He isn't a bit bothered by this weather either, are you, Zip?"

Zippo was at his battle station on the port side of the boat, both hands on the trigger housing of his grenade launcher. He turned toward Will and flashed a smile. Then he looked over his shoulder toward Jaybird standing at the starboard gunwale and said, "Mr. McQueen thinks it gets hot in Savannah. Likes to think he's a badass or something. Shit, Bird, the skipper ain't never picked cotton in Jasper County, South Carolina, in the middle of the day. That's hot, Birdman."

Two of Will's crew had been with him since his first days "in country." His port-side gunner and machinist mate was a twenty-year-old draftee named Alonzo Pinkney who went by the nickname Zippo. He was a black farm boy from just outside the little town of Ridgeland, South Carolina. Ridgeland was on U.S. Highway 17, about twenty miles across the Talmadge Bridge from Savannah. Zippo had been homesick from his first day in the Navy; and when he found out where Will was from, it made him feel a little closer to home and a little safer.

The seaman who manned the twin fifty-caliber M-2 machine guns, also referred to as a "Maw Duce," in the bow of Will's PBR was a twenty-two-year-old Italian kid from Cherry Hill, New Jersey. Santino "Sandy" D'Angelo had been a history major at Rutgers when he dropped a course, lost his student deferment, and was drafted in December of 1968. Although somewhat bitter about having to serve, Sandy had become philosophical about Vietnam and rationalized that shooting up the Mekong Delta with his twin fifties was at least a whole lot more exciting than teaching history at Cherry Hill High.

The "newbie" on board PBR 196 was "the Jaybird" from Long Island, New York. He was the nineteen-year-old son of an Orthodox Jew who was in the garment or *schmata* business. Sandy had pinned the nickname Jaybird on the newbie not only for the obvious name play, but also because of his skinny "bird" legs.

Jaybird was a free spirit, who had totally rebelled against what he felt was the repressive atmosphere of his parents' home and the life they had planned out for him in complete detail. His enlistment in the navy was an assertion of his independence and something that prompted his father to almost stop speaking to him.

Sandy and Zippo had been part of Will's crew from the time he'd been a "shake 'n' bake," a term applied by the enlisted ranks to a newly commissioned officer with no combat experience. They had already been veterans of the river war for six months when Will arrived and took command of the 196 as an ensign. Sandy and Zippo both had had other boats shot out from under them when they were assigned to the 196 and brought a great deal of valuable combat experience to Will's new command.

Jaybird had been aboard the 196 for only a week when Will was ordered to Saigon for a special briefing. It was the first prolonged period of time he and the other two crew members had been together without Will around. Sandy had scored an ounce of Thai marijuana known as *koon sa* from a Vietnamese dockworker, and Zippo had gotten a whole case of Ba-Ma-Ba, which was Vietnamese Tiger Beer. The 196 was tied to a dock in the safety of their base, and its crew had decided a little R and R was in order during Will's absence. The three were crouched in the boat's cabin drinking beer and smoking pot when the discussion of Will McQueen started.

"So what's McQueen like in a firefight?" asked Jaybird, before he inhaled deeply from Sandy's bong. It had been fashioned from a spent forty-millimeter shell casing, and Jaybird thought it was the coolest bong he'd ever seen.

"Cool, real cool," answered Zippo, as Jaybird passed the bong to him.

"Yeah?" said Jaybird. "Well, what else about him? I mean, what kind of a dude is he when the shit's not hitting the fan?"

"He's OK," said Sandy, who was stretched out in the bow under his gun turret sipping from a bottle of "Tiger Piss" while he fiddled with his new radio.

"He don't take no shit, though," said Sandy, "I can promise you that. He's OK, but you better by-god jump to when he tells you something. Still, he's reasonable. Hasn't let his new rank get to his head. Kind of a pussy hound, too, from what I can gather. There's so much poontang running around in this fucked-up place, who couldn't be?"

The geostrategic center of the Republic of Vietnam was the Mekong Delta. It is an alluvial plain created by the Mekong River and constitutes almost one-fourth of the country's territory. It also held nearly half the population and was the center of agricultural production for the entire region. The delta had twenty-four hundred kilometers of navigable waterways, which were interconnected by another four thousand kilometers of man-made canals. The military importance of the delta was that it had become a major Vietcong infiltration route from Cambodia as well as a sanctuary. As a result, in early 1965, the American military decided to put an end to communist operations in the delta region.

In December of 1966, the lead elements of what became known as the Mobile Riverine Force, or MRF, arrived in the Mekong Delta. The MRF was a joint army-navy operation, with the navy component being given the name Task Force 117 or the Riverine Assault Force. In October of 1968, TF 117 had further evolved into the Southeast Asia Lake Ocean River Delta Strategy, or SEALORDS, under the overall command of Vice Adm. Elmo R. Zumwalt, Jr.

To implement Operation SEALORDS, the navy called on its small, shallow-draft, heavily armed vessels knows as PBRs for Patrol Boats River. Designed in 1965 by Willis Slane of the Hatteras Yacht Company and built by United Boatbuilders, the PBR had a fiberglass hull and was driven by a Jacuzzi water-jet propulsion system powered by two General Motors truck diesels. The Mark II model was thirty-two feet long and almost twelve feet wide. It could make better than twenty-eight knots and was armed with twin fifty-caliber machine guns fitted into a turret on the bow and a single fifty-caliber machine gun in the stern. In addition, an M-60 machine gun and a forty-millimeter automatic grenade launcher were mounted amidships. It drew only two feet of water and was highly maneuverable.

Carrying an all-volunteer crew of five, sometimes only four, the PBR was the spiritual descendent of the PT boats of World War II fame. The sailors who crewed the PBRs liked to say those initials really stood for proud, brave, and reliable.

Will McQueen had arrived in Vietnam in November of 1969 after completing his training. By that time the Mobile Riverine Force had been operational in one form or another for three years. The navy component of the MRF reached its peak in the fall of 1968. After that President Nixon's "Vietnamization" policy was starting to take effect under the direction of Gen. Creighton Abrams, and the U.S. Navy began to turn their boats over to the Vietnamese.

The Americans did, however, retain some of these vessels for special operations in the Mekong Delta. From 1970 to 1972, the navy executed Operation Brightlight, which was an attempt to resuce prisoners of war held by the Vietcong in the delta. This was primarily a Navy SEAL operation, and Will's boat was frequently employed on these missions.

Seven miles south of Saigon is a thick mangrove swamp that was known as the Rung Sat Special Zone, or RSSZ. This had been a safe haven for the Vietcong until mid-1966, when SEAL operations began denying the VC their uncontested use of this sanctuary. By late 1969, U.S. intelligence indicated that American soldiers were being held in small prison camps within the RSSZ. A number of missions were carried out by SEAL rescue teams, but they had only found Vietnamese POWs or deserted camps. In May of 1970, the U.S. Military Assistance Command, Vietnam's Studies and Observations Group (MACV-SOG), the organization responsible for all covert operations conducted in the Republic of Vietnam, had learned that American POWs were again being held within the confines of the Rung Sat Special Zone. They ordered a SEAL team in, and it was Will's job to get them there.

What's up, Skipper?" asked Sandy, as Will stepped off the dock and into the cockpit of the 196, with a map tucked under his arm.

"It's another laugh a minute," answered Will, "and it ain't gonna be no ten, that's for sure. Might be *bookoo bok-bok.* Here," said Will, as he unfolded the map, "let's take a look at the funnies."

As a newbie Jaybird was unfamiliar with a lot of the slang used in country and looked at Will with a confused expression. Will noticed, smiled, and said, "Explain for the cherry, Zippo," as he opened the map and spread it out on the stern.

"Skipper said we're goin' upriver again, and there might be a lot of fightin', Bird."

The crew gathered around Will as he looked the map over and said, "We shove off from here with three SEALS at 0600 tomorrow. We then proceed along this river here," said Will, as he pointed to a place on the map, "and into the Rung Sat Special Zone right here. Then we drop our SEAL boys off and fall back to this little spot, where we lay chilly 'til extraction time. At 1600 hours, we fire up to meet our guys right back where we left 'em for pickup at 1645 hours. Comprendez-vous?"

"Yeah, Skipper. I think everybody's got the lay of the land," answered Sandy, as he looked up at Zippo and Jaybird. They both nodded their heads in approval.

"Good," said Will. Then he looked around the boat and spied Sandy's bong lying on the deck inside the cabin along with several empty bottles of beer.

"Y'all party down last night, D'Angelo?"

"Yes, sir."

"Well, looks like you used your artillery piece again. Score any good hits?"

Sandy cracked a very small smile then answered, "Yes, sir."

"Well, I don't want any of that shit goin' on tonight, hear me. I want everybody straight and in good form tomorrow, you understand?"

"Don't worry, Skipper. We'll all be on our toes. No more bullshit 'til we get back, sir."

"There better not be," shot back Will. Then he looked around the boat again and said, "Somebody get me a beer, I could use one."

As soon as Will was out of earshot, Zippo slipped over to Jaybird and whispered, "See, I told ya' he ain't so bad but just don't cross his ass."

That night Will slept on the boat while the crew bedded down in their barracks. He felt the need to be alone, to have some private time to himself and just think. It had been almost a year since he'd seen Laura Lee. She had been faithful in writing, and Will looked forward to her letters. He could tell from them that she was the same girl he had known when he left the States. There was still that quality of innocence and sweetness about Laura Lee that came through in her letters, and it made Will long for those times before the war when they had both been sweet and innocent.

All Laura Lee knew about the world had been run through the filter of Charleston's moss draped, cut-crystal gentility. While she knew that misery, poverty, and cruelty existed, she had no real sense of what it was like to be miserable or poor or senselessly abused. The only dead body she had ever seen was that of her grandmother Moultrie lying in her coffin at the funeral home. The foulest odor she had ever come in contact with was spoiled fish. She had never slept on anything but clean sheets, changed her underwear every day, sometimes twice, and had never been spoken to harshly in her entire life. Every Sunday without fail, Laura Lee would make her way to the corner of Meeting and Broad Streets, where she attended services at Saint Michael's Episcopal, the church in which she had been baptised and confirmed. There she knelt and prayed for Will's safe return and their lasting happiness together.

There was comfort for Will in knowing that Laura Lee was the same. But, then, why shouldn't she be? After all, she was half a world away, in another place, in another time. And what of Will? Well, Will had changed.

Stretched out in the cabin, with a fifth of Jack Daniel's and a pack of Marlboros, Will began to think about what he would do when he got back to the "world," back to that "big PX," back to America. A smile creased his lips when he thought about the night before when he was in Saigon. She was half-French, half-Vietnamese, and all beautiful. He really hadn't paid for it, just dinner and a few drinks, although he would have had it been required. She'd been a friend of a friend who'd been seeing one of those "rear echelon motherfuckers" who'd briefed him at Mack-vee headquarters. He'd tagged along "just for shits," and it had turned out to be quite a night.

After a long pull from the Jack Daniel's, Will lit another cigarette and settled into some deep thinking. But rather than think about the future, he thought about the past. He hadn't smoked until he'd gotten to 'Nam, nor had he ever enjoyed drinking whiskey straight from the bottle. The only girl he'd ever had sex with was Charlotte Drayton. He and Laura Lee had engaged in some heavy petting, but she had always said no and he'd respected that. Will wondered what she'd say if she knew about the girl last night.

The engines of the 196 had been warming at idle for ten minutes when the SEALs arrived. There were only three, comprising what was known as a "light" team. All were dressed in tiger-stripe camos with black bandannas tied on their heads. One carried a Stoner light machine gun while the other two had carbine versions of M-16s slung over their shoulders. Their faces were painted in dark green-and-black stripes that matched those on their fatigues. It gave them a menacing, animal-like appearance. Various accoutrements of war were wrapped, attached, or hung over their uniforms, such as ammunition belts, knives, ropes, canteens, and extra ammo magazines. All three had been with Will at the Saigon briefing and knew exactly where they were going and what to do when they got there. As Will pulled the 196 away from the dock and then up onto a plane out in the river, the members of the SEAL team moved to the stern and kept to themselves. Occasionally, one would check a piece of equipment or nervously finger the trigger of his weapon. They said very little to each other and nothing at all to the crew. Their eyes had a cold look about them, and their jaws were set hard. Jaybird was thoroughly impressed with the appearance and demeanor of the SEALs and told Zippo that they looked dead serious. "They'd better be dead serious if they don't want to be just dead," replied Zippo.

In the middle of a chocolate-colored river, Will advanced the throttles and brought his boat up to cruising speed. The 196's engines were situated side by side on the deck and amidships about two-thirds of the way back from the bow. They were quite loud, and the harmony of their vibration could be felt throughout the entire vessel, while the smell of diesel fuel and exhaust fumes swirled around in the cockpit.

Will liked what he was doing and sometimes marveled at how much at home he felt in the delta. The waterways there reminded him of those around Savannah, and he wondered if that was one of the reasons he liked his job.

After two hours of twisting and turning along the rivers of the RSSZ, the 196 neared her destination. Everyone was at battle stations as Will eased his boat to the riverbank. The lieutenant in charge of the operation pointed at a tree that had fallen into the water and told him to put in there. "Remember that tree, Mr. McQueen. That's where we'll be waiting on you to pick us up."

Everyone involved at Mac-vee had been impressed with the quality of intelligence information the operation was based on. They believed it had come from reliable sources and were sure no one, except those involved, was aware a rescue mission had been planned. Unfortunately, the people at Mac-vee were wrong.

The VC had planted the story about GIs being held in the RSSZ in hopes of staging an ambush when the Americans came searching for their comrades. They had also been informed of the impending rescue attempt; and when they observed the 196 making its way through the rivers of the RSSZ, they put their plan in motion.

The VC had watched the 196 all along its journey and had noted where the SEALs had been dropped off. As soon as the SEALs had moved away from the area, the Vietcong planted a series of Claymore mines along the riverbank and settled back to wait.

The Claymore is an antipersonnel mine that sprays a wide area with hundreds of projectiles. It is exploded by a remote detonator attached to the mine by a wire. The VC had planted their Claymores about ten feet from the bank, facing toward the river. They planned to detonate the mines just as the SEALs boarded the 196. They felt they could kill the SEALs before they were able to get in the boat and then, in the surprise of the attack, lob hand grenades into the 196 while spraying it with automatic fire.

At precisely 1645 hours, the waiting SEALs saw the 196 come around the bend and head for the fallen tree. The SEALS had found the prison camp, but it had been empty.

When the 196 was a boat's length from the riverbank, Will cut the wheel hard to port and presented the starboard side to the bank. All the SEALs had to do was step off the bank and into the boat. D'Angelo was in the bow turret covering the riverbank forward, Zippo had it amidships with his M-60, while Jaybird swept the jungle from the stern with his fifty caliber.

The SEALs stepped out of their hiding place and moved toward the boat. Just when the lieutenant put his foot on the 196, he and his two men were blown forward by the explosions of two well-placed Claymores. The SEALs weren't wearing flack jackets, and from head to toe, the backs of their bodies were shredded and deeply punctured by scores of hits from marble-size pieces of metal.

The lieutenant was blown into the boat. Rendered unconscious by the blast, he would bleed out and die in a matter of minutes. The other two SEALs were both collapsed in a heap on the riverbank, one unconscious, both severely wounded.

When the Claymores went off, all guns on the 196 opened up. No one could identify a target, so they sprayed everything except the area where the two SEALs had fallen. Will was able to quickly pull the 196 away from the bank and out of immediate danger. When the boat was a hundred yards from the ambush point, Will cut back on the throttles and did a quick casualty and damage assessment.

Up in the bow, D'Angelo had been protected by the splinter shield and the armor around the gun tub. He didn't have a scratch. Zippo had taken pieces of the Claymore in his shoulder and arm, but otherwise was OK and at his battle station. Jaybird's flack jacket had saved him from two hits that would have been lethal, but metal from the Claymore had sailed through the fiberglass side of the boat and hit him in the left thigh. He hurt like hell, but he could still fight. The SEAL lieutenant was piled up right outside the passageway to the wheelhouse. His blood covered the deck, and Will couldn't find a pulse.

There were small holes all through the hull of the 196, but none were below the waterline. In the Mark II PBR, the dead spaces in the double hull had been filled with foam, so there was little chance the 196 would sink. Because the helmsman is surrounded by armor, Will had not been injured.

"What're we gonna' do, Skipper?" shouted Zippo, while he pressed a dressing against his wounds. "I think them other two is still alive. Shit, I know one was; I seen him move!"

Will looked at the riverbank and thought for a moment; then he shouted to D'Angelo. "What'dya think, Sandy? Did we run 'em off?"

"Shit, Skip, I don't know, but we can't leave those poor fuckers there, sir."

"Damn straight!" shouted Zippo.

"OK," yelled Will, "we're going back in. Sandy, you light up that riverbank on both sides of the tree, and I'll run in just like before and come up against the bank sideways. Zippo, you think you can jump off and get those two guys into the boat by yourself?"

"I'll try, sir."

"Birdman," yelled Will, "if Zip needs any help, jump to it. Otherwise, pour what you got into the riverbank."

"OK," shouted Will, "let's do it." Then he pushed the throttles all the way forward, and the 196 leapt out of the water and raced toward the riverbank.

Double lines of tracers flowed from the barrels of D'Angelo's guns in an orange stream that arced across the river and into the tree line. Will could see limbs falling from the nipa palms as the big fifty-caliber projectiles cut the jungle to pieces. The heavy smell of gunpowder blew over the front of the cabin and into Will's face as he steered his boat straight for the fallen tree.

When the 196 was fifty feet from the bank, Will cut the wheel to port and jammed the boat into reverse. She slid sideways and hit the riverbank hard. Zippo was almost thrown overboard but managed to keep his balance and grab a line before he jumped onto the bank. With two loops, he tied the 196 to a tree, then ran directly to the downed men.

The conscious SEAL was able to help Zippo with his buddy, and they'd both started dragging him toward the boat when another Claymore went off. They all went down, but the Claymore hadn't been as well placed, and, after a few moments, the men struggled to their feet and were able to make it to the boat.

While Zippo cut the mooring line, Will got set to pull the 196 away from the riverbank. Just when he reached for the throttles, two VC popped from their hiding places near the boat and tossed grenades at the 196. Somehow one landed in Sandy D'Angelo's lap. The instant Sandy heard the grenade bang off the housing of his port-side gun and watched it fall between his legs, he knew he was finished. He had enough time to say, "Sweet Jesus, take me in your arms," before the captured American M-33 "baseball" grenade detonated, blowing the lower half of gunner's Mate1C Santino Carmine D'Angelo into the cabin below while his upper torso was propelled out of the gun tub and into the river.

The other grenade hit near Zippo's battle station then rolled next to the wheelhouse. The wheelhouse on a PBR looks like a bathroom stall in a public restroom and is about the same size. The protective wall around the wheelhouse doesn't extend all the way to the deck, and the lower legs of the helmsman are completely exposed. When the second grenade exploded, Will's legs absorbed most of its destructive power.

For several seconds total confusion reigned aboard the 196. Screams and smoke filled the cockpit of the boat, and everyone but Jaybird was either dead, unconscious, or stunned. Jaybird was standing at his machine gun screaming, "Skipper! Skipper!" and trying to see through the smoke when the two VC responsible for the entire ambush began firing at the 196 with their AK-47s.

When Jaybird heard the AKs open up, he swung his weapon toward the sound of their fire. Amid the deep foliage, a pair of star-burst muzzle flashes caught his attention, and Jaybird depressed his trigger and tore the jungle apart. There wasn't a tree in the whole Mekong Delta thick enough to stop a fifty-caliber round at that range, and the VC who had planned and executed such a brilliant ambush would never get to exercise their bragging rights.

By the time Jaybird had stopped firing, Will had managed to pull himself to a standing position, throw the boat into reverse, and get the 196 away from the riverbank. Once in midstream he popped the boat into forward and took off.

"Holy shit, Skipper," said Jaybird, when he got to Will, "you're pumping blood from an artery in your leg." Jaybird wheeled around and shouted to Zippo, "Zip, you gotta take the wheel; Skipper's bleeding from an artery. I gotta get a tourniquet around his leg."

As soon as Zippo took the wheel, Will collapsed into Jaybird's arms. Jaybird laid Will down on the engine decking. Fashioning a tourniquet from a length of rope, he tied it around Will's left thigh and stopped the pulse of blood that had been spurting from the severed artery in Will's lower leg. Then the Birdman started cutting away his fatigues to get a better look at his wounds.

"Aw man," said Jaybird when he finished and was able to examine Will's wounds more closely. With tears streaming down his cheeks, Jaybird did what he could to help Will.

It took three days at a military hospital in Saigon to stabilize Will before he could be evacuated to Yokahama, Japan. When his parents were notified of his injuries, the tone of the communication from the Department of the Navy was blunt and to the point: "Lt. J. G. McQueen has injuries that are serious and life threatening." Will's mother lost her composure and became so hysterical that Jimmy had to call a neighbor to help with her.

Externally, Jimmy was stoic and in control. On the inside there was a deep and frightening pain he knew could only be relieved by being with his son. After he was sure Meg was calm, Jimmy called the only man he knew who would understand his agony.

"Francis?"

"What's the matter, Jimmy? You sound like something is wrong."

Jimmy tried to maintain his composure but began to sob as he told his friend about Will.

"I'll be right there," said Francis. Relieved, Jimmy pulled back the kitchen chair, sat down, and rested his head on the table. There he cried as he had never done before, remembering everything about Will: all the operations he had endured, all the pain he had seen in his son's young eyes, all the humility and frustration he knew Will had felt by being so different from the other children. He thought about his triumphs and how proud and strong Will had been the day he'd left for Vietnam. The thought that death might take his only child descended upon Jimmy. His mouth became dry, and there was a tightness in his throat and chest, while his fingers tingled and his toes grew cold. He had never known such fear, and in desperation a cry came from deep within Jimmy, "Oh, God, don't take my boy."

Arriving at the McQueens', Francis found the street lined with cars and the house filled with people. When he walked through the door, what he saw reminded him of a wake. Men stood in the living room speaking in subdued tones, while the women were in the kitchen fussing over the trays of food from McQueen friends.

Francis found Jimmy in Will's room sitting on his bed. He sat next to his friend and placed his arm around him. Not a word was said as Jimmy struggled to gain control of himself. Finally, Jimmy was able to say, "I want to go to my boy. He's in Japan, Francis. I checked, and, with connections and layovers, it'll take almost three days for me to get out there on a commercial flight. He might be dead by then." Francis thought for a moment, then reached for the phone.

"Operator, I want Sen. Richard Russell's office in Washington."

Francis put his hand over the receiver and said, "I'll bet our old buddy Dick Russell can help us out."

When the senator's office answered, Francis said, "Gladys, this is Francis Quinn in Savannah. Is the senator there? I have something of the utmost importance, and I need to speak with him immediately if it's possible."

A pause, then, "He is! That's great."

At six o'clock that evening, Jimmy and Francis boarded a C-140 military transport at Hunter Army Airfield in Savannah bound nonstop for San Francisco, where it would be refueled. Eight hours later they landed in Yokahama and were greeted by a navy commander, who escorted them to the hospital.

Will was heavily sedated and sleeping when his father was led to his bedside. An IV was in his right arm carrying antibiotics; in his left, he received whole blood. He labored to suck air down a steel tube inserted through a dime-size incision in his trachea. A five-day growth of beard sprouted on Will's swollen face, and his hair was greasy and matted with blood. A sheet covered Will to the waist, exposing his chest and arms, which were festooned with bruises and abrasions. EKG leads were stuck to his chest, and a monitor over the bed beeped with each heartbeat.

Will's left leg was elevated in a sling. A metal pin had been driven through his heel and connected to a traction device. An eight-inch gash in his calf was packed with a yellow-colored gauze, as were several smaller wounds. The foot was tense with swelling, and each toe was the diameter and color of a boiled hot dog. Will's right leg had been amputated below the knee that first day in Saigon.

Jimmy said nothing as he stood at his son's bedside and surveyed his wounds. After a moment he reached out, carressed Will's swollen cheek, then leaned over and whispered into his ear. After that he slipped to his knees. Francis was standing slightly behind Jimmy. As tough and self-centered as he was, Francis was still moved by what he saw and found himself wiping away tears.

For the longest time, Jimmy knelt with his elbows resting on Will's bed, his hands clasped in prayer. Finally, Jimmy uttered a short, simple prayer. "Oh, God, please don't take my son."

The surgeon responsible for Will's care had been standing in the back of the room. After Jimmy said his prayer, the doctor came forward and placed his hand on Jimmy's shoulder, saying, "Let's go outside and talk.

"Mr. McQueen, may I be frank with you?"

"I don't want you to be any other way, Dr. Lewis."

"OK, here's the whole story. Your son has multiple injuries that have been compounded by a number of problems, not the least of which is a serious infection in his left leg that has caused him to become septic. That means the infection isn't just confined to his leg but has gotten into his bloodstream and is affecting his whole body. He's had problems with his kidneys, and that's one reason he's so swollen. We've got him on the strongest drugs we have, and so far there's been no improvement. He also lost a lot of blood, but that's being replaced."

Captain Lewis, the surgeon, stopped and let that sink in. Then he said, "He may lose his left leg, too. When that grenade went off, it drove pieces of clothing deep into the flesh. The cloth was covered with bacteria of all types. That's how the infection got started. The bad part is that pieces of metal hit the tibia bone and broke it in several places. That's the reason for the traction device. Worse than that, the metal also carried infection into the bone; and believe me, bone infections, especially mixed infections, are extremely hard to treat. So far all we've been able to do is cut away infected flesh and bone in that leg. The antibiotics aren't working yet, but we've got a few more tricks up our sleeve."

Jimmy looked down at the floor and then into the eyes of Dr. Lewis. "So what are you telling me, Dr. Lewis?"

"Mr. McQueen, your son is a very, very sick boy. If we can get the infection under control, he's got a chance of living. I don't know about that leg. It may eventually have to come off. That may be the only way we can control the infection process."

"If you do take the other leg off, can he walk with no legs?" asked Jimmy plaintively.

"If it's below the knee like the other one, sure. He won't be a long-distance runner, but he'll walk—if the stumps he's left with aren't so scarred up he can't wear a prosthesis."

"Is there anything I can do?" asked Jimmy.

"Mr. McQueen," answered the captain, "if you're a praying man, you can pray like you've never prayed before. Other than that, it's up to God and this medical staff."

That night when Jimmy called Meg and explained the extent of Will's injuries, especially the amputations, she became hysterical once more. Luckily Michael Mulvaney was there when the call came.

Father Mulvaney was now Monsignor Mulvaney, the title having been bestowed upon him in gratitude for decades of dedicated work in the Diocese of Savannah. He had also been transferred back to Blessed Sacrament Church, where he would be pastor until his retirement.

"Monsignor," said Jimmy, "I'm so glad you're there with Meg; she's become totally unhinged by this whole thing. Will is everything to her, Mike."

"I know, Jimmy, I know. I just happened to be here when you called. She's got plenty of help though. Fr. Dan Whittaker from your church is coming over, and the ladies at Saint John's have arranged to have somebody from the altar guild stay with her at night so she won't be by herself. It's always tough to be alone during a time like this, particularly at night."

"Has Malachy been told about Will?" asked Jimmy.

"I don't believe so. Come to think of it, he's still out on Jesus Island and hasn't been in town for weeks, but I'll get word to him tonight."

Over the next two days, Will's infection raged out of control, and his condition deteriorated. On the third day it was apparent that a clostridium infection, known as gas gangrene, had taken hold along the tissue planes in Will's leg. It was a disastrous and life-threatening complication, and that same night Will's left leg was amputated below the knee. Thirty-six hours later, Will's fever began to drop, his kidneys regained normal function, and Dr. Lewis was able to tell Jimmy he thought his son would live.

Another call from Francis to Senator Russell's office resulted in Will's transfer to the U.S. Navy hospital in Beaufort, South Carolina, only forty-five minutes from Savannah. His father and Francis were with him when the giant C-5A transport lifted off the runway in Yokahama, bound for Charleston.

In Beaufort Will began the task of confronting and living with his injuries. It was not an easy undertaking, but there were those who were eager to help. His mother visited every day, Laura Lee every weekend. There was a steady stream of cards, calls, and friends. Even Charlotte Drayton came to see him. She tried to act cheerful and ignore the obvious loss of Will's legs, but her eyes gave her away. Will noticed how she refused to let them wander to the foot of his bed.

Charlotte was more beautiful than she'd ever been; and when she bent over and kissed him on his forehead, Will inhaled her scent, and a cascade of memories came raining down. When she smiled, he watched the dimples appear in her cheeks; and he remembered the time they'd made love in the cabin on the marsh. Her attentions then had made him feel attractive for the first time in his life; her actions now only served to hurt him more.

He could tell by the tenseness in her voice and the uneasiness in her eyes that Charlotte was repulsed by what she saw. He knew the visit would be construed as an act of kindness by Charlotte's friends and wondered if she were visiting him more out of concern for her social standing than his state of health.

Charlotte forced herself to stay for an hour. The time was filled with her chatter about life in Atlanta and trips to the North Georgia mountains with Stevie.

When Charlotte decided she'd stayed long enough, she came to Will's bedside and held his hand. She put her head back, struck a defiant pose, and spoke to him as if she were lecturing a child.

"Now, Will McQueen," said Charlotte, "I know you're going to overcome everything. You're the strongest person I've ever known and . . . and if anybody can learn to walk on, um, on artificial legs, it's you. I know you can do it, and I've told everybody in Savannah you can. So, um, so just keep your chin up, and you'll be walking again in no time."

Then Charlotte bent over, kissed Will on his forehead once more, and said, "See you when I'm in Savannah again." Will knew she'd never come back.

After the echo of Charlotte's high heels clicking against the polished linoleum had faded down the hall, Will's roommate said, "Holy shit, she's a knockout. Is that a girlfriend of yours?"

"Used to be," said Will. Then he rolled to the wall, pulled a pillow over his head, and quietly wept for all he'd lost.

The emotions a person experiences after the loss of a major body part are quite similar to those caused by the death of a loved one. First, there is denial, then the stark, profound realization that what was once perhaps taken lightly is now irretrievably lost.

Next is the mourning process. This sometimes lasts only months; usually it's years, occasionally a lifetime. When the heart is freshly wounded, a person constantly remembers the deceased and responds to life's vagaries, good and bad, as if that person were still present. An amputation causes the same emotions. There is a chained response to stimuli that, before the loss, terminated in emotional or physical satisfaction. Only now these deeply cut neural pathways lead, not to satisfaction, but rather frustration and renewed pain. The magnitude of the loss determines the length of the mourning process.

The final phase in recovering from a catastrophic loss is acceptance. It is learning to circumvent the loss rather than being overwhelmed by it. Just as a young widow takes on another life with a new and different partner, likewise will the amputee take on a different partner in his life. Sometimes it is a wheelchair, sometimes an artificial arm or leg. Unfortunately, for the amputee, his partner will always be less than what it replaces.

There is also a unique and additional burden placed on a person who suffers such a mutilating injury, one not borne by those who lose a part of themselves to death. The physical appearance of an amputee is altered. Where there once was a muscular arm or leg, with sinuous curves and powerful movements, there hangs a stump of bone covered by scarred and flabby flesh. There is nothing appealing about the stump of a missing limb.

Ten years earlier, in her cabin on Jesus Island, Sister Mystery had seen the torment Will would be forced to endure when she took his hand and read his fortune. She could not discern exactly what or how, but she had seen a life that would confront pain and dismemberment and had been frightened for young Will. The day Malachy came to her cabin and told her about Will, Sister Mystery fell to the floor, thrashed about, and screamed in torment.

"Oh, Lawd God, why didn't I tell that boy? Why didn't I tell his daddy what I seen?" wailed Sister Mystery, as Malachy and Dr. Divine gently restrained her flailing arms.

"If I'd done that, then that sweet, precious chile might be whole now!" screamed Sister Mystery. "Oh, Jesus, I was scared, and I didn't tell nobody. I fooled myself by thinkin' maybe I was wrong, but I knowed I wasn't. Oh, Sweet Jesus, have mercy on me!"

Later, as Sister Mystery sat sobbing in the same corner chair where she had read Will's fortune, she intoned, "Brother Malachy, I seen more than just bad things for Will. I seen good things, too. I seen he was a strong chile who got somethin' deep down inside him that gonna help him get through all this. I seen great things for him. I seen that God is got plans for Mr. Will. They's plans that's bigger than he is, plans for him doin' great things."

Malachy glanced at the faded picture of Jesus hanging on the wall above Sister Mystery then slipped his glasses off. He thought for a moment, looked into her eyes, and said, "Sister, you're puttin' too much on yourself. You know as well as anybody that God's plans can't be changed, even if we do know beforehand what they are. Don't go beatin' yourself to death over this."

Sister Mystery tilted her head a little and listened intently as Malachy continued.

"God knows what he's doin'. He's passin' Will through the hottest part of the fire to temper him, to make him stronger. You're right about Will. He does have that sign, that special something about him. I've seen it in him myself. So I don't want to hear anything more from you about how you could have saved him from what happened; it's not your fault."

Sister Mystery dabbed the corners of her eyes with a wad of tissue then blew her nose. "Thank you, Brother Malachy. Ol' Sister Mystery ain't looked at it like that. Imagine me thinkin' I could change the will of God! Why that's a sin itself, ain't it?"

Malachy smiled, "No, not for somebody who has your gift, Sister. You're different."

On the way out, Malachy turned and spoke to Sister Mystery and Dr. Divine.

"I'm going to Savannah tomorrow. I'll get word to Mr. and Mrs. McQueen that you've foreseen greatness for their son. I think it'll make them feel better."

That night Malachy stayed in the chapel, on his knees, saying his rosary.

When Will arrived at the Beaufort Naval Hospital the last weekend in May, he'd lost sixty pounds. Forty-five of those pounds were from the amputation of his legs, the other fifteen were from general muscle atrophy due to inactivity and appetite loss. He'd drop another twelve pounds over the next few weeks, wouldn't have enough strength to sit up in bed, and would undergo weekly surgical debridements of the nonviable tissue on his stumps. The pain from the surgical procedures was compounded by phantom nerve pain, a common complication following amputations.

Emotionally Will put up a brave front, especially when his mother was around; but his days were tedious, and his long nights were filled with the same fears and self-doubt that had plagued him as child. He was apt to have mood swings, partly as a result of the drugs he existed on, but mostly from his overwhelming sense of helplessness. He occupied himself by following the progress of the war and clung to the hope that America could eventually triumph if only the politicians in Washington would let the military dictate how the war would be fought.

As for Laura Lee, she was genuinely in love with Will and could sense, as his mother did, the depth of his torment. She was patient and affectionate; and on Will's bad days, she understood his sullenness and withdrawal. While there had been no discussion of their future relationship, Meg McQueen had grown quite fond of Laura Lee and was grateful for her loyalty to Will.

Even with all the support Will had, his emotional status deteriorated. On the Fourth of July weekend, he tearfully told Laura Lee that accepting the loss of his legs would be easy if only his sacrifice had not been in vain.

Will felt the steady decline of popular support for the war as well; what he considered Washington's no-win policy could only result in defeat for America. He reasoned that, if there were no victory, then all he'd been through would be for nothing. When Laura Lee told him that answering his country's call and bravely doing his duty were enough justification for his sacrifice, he exploded.

"Haven't you seen the pictures of those stinkin' hippies spittin' on combat veterans when they get off the planes from 'Nam?" Will shouted.

Then he looked out the window of his room and said, "Can you imagine that happening after World War Two? Can you imagine people like my father being called "baby killers" when they came back home?

Can you possibly imagine sending people like me to fight a war where the enemy can cross a line and you can't go after him but he can come after you?"

Will went silent and looked at Laura Lee from his wheelchair. She had tears in her eyes and pleaded with him, saying, "Please, Will, please, please don't do this to yourself again."

But Will's anger could not be controlled, and he pointed to his missing legs and shouted, "You see these. I gave these for my country; they were a living part of me, I loved them, I enjoyed them, I needed them, and now they're gone for fucking nothing! I'm crippled for the rest of my life for fucking nothing, Laura Lee! Do you understand that? It was for fucking nothing! Is there anybody who understands?"

By September Will's legs were healed well enough for him to be sent home. Plastic surgery would be required to revise and repair the scars on his stumps before he could be fitted for prosthetic legs, but that would be done later. When a person suffers injuries of the magnitude that Will had, the most effective balm that can be applied to those wounds is the tincture of time. Scars must mature, swelling must subside, nerve endings must forget their severance, and emotions must be allowed to cool.

On the day of his discharge, Will's doctors told his father the most important thing for Will was to simply "get his head together." Jimmy McQueen could think of no better place for such an undertaking than Jesus Island.

By mid-October, summer had fled from Jesus Island. It was chased away by cool Canadian air that had slipped down over the Appalachians and the Piedmont Plateau then pressed its way to the Georgia coast. With the air less humid, the sky was a brighter blue, and tree lines on distant islands were a sharper green. In the dense, cool air, the smells of Jesus Island seemed stronger to Will as he sat with Malachy and inhaled the breeze that drifted through the cedars on the high bluffs in front of Driftwood Beach.

Will had been with Malachy since the end of September, and the island's seclusion and beauty soothed his painful heart. They had ridden to the beach in the old Jeep and parked it near the point where Wassaw

Sound and the Atlantic Ocean came together. They could see the big house above the dunes, standing tall on the high ground that dominated the south end of Jesus Island. The oaks and cedars surrounding the house were brushed back in a westerly direction, the result of two centuries of ocean winds.

Will's eyes wandered to the marsh. With October's end, it had become a dull and faded brown. Now it shone like gold in the autumn sun. He watched terns near the water's edge pick at the sand, while a flock of gulls stood into the wind and a flight of pelicans glided over the sound searching for their last catch of the day.

With his hands resting on the steering wheel, Malachy leaned back and let the sun warm his face and watched as waves rolled in and splashed off the tree trunks that littered Driftwood Beach. Will had been silent most of the day, and Malachy sensed something was on his mind.

"Why do you think people like to be by the ocean so much, Malachy?" asked Will, as he reached into the back of the Jeep for his jacket.

"For the sounds, Will," replied Malachy.

"Whatdaya mean, 'the sounds'?"

"Well," said Malachy, "you know, babies can hear before they're born. I mean when they're inside their mother's womb."

"I never really thought about it before," said Will, "but I guess it's so."

"Well, anyway," continued Malachy, "there's no place a human will ever feel safer than in his mother's womb. The womb is filled with fluid, and the baby just floats around in the stuff until it's born. That means the first sound it ever hears is the fluid sloshing around inside the womb. I think the ocean waves sound like the inside of a mother's womb, and that's why people like it so much at the beach."

Will thought for a moment then said, "I remember reading about some psychiatric theory that said people really wanted to crawl back into the womb because it was safe. Maybe they were onto something."

Malachy turned to Will and asked, "Do you feel safe now, Will?"

Will sighed. "No, and I don't think I've ever really felt safe, at least not since I was big enough to think for myself and know about the world around me. There was a time when I think I felt that way, but now I don't know. Maybe it was when I got out of The Citadel and I was so physically strong and fit. I think I felt safe then 'cause I could take care of myself. It was a wonderful feeling. When I was little, I always felt like I wasn't quite good enough, like I wouldn't be able to do what my father had done. Then I went and got blown all to hell, and now I don't know what's up and what's down."

"How do you feel inside?" asked Malachy. "I mean, what do you think about when you're trying to fall asleep at night?"

Will clenched his jaw and looked out over Wassaw Sound. The sun had dipped low over the water. Its reflection had turned the waves to platinum, and the light bounced into his eyes, making him squint.

"I think about what my life would have been if I hadn't gone to 'Nam and lost my legs. I think about it over and over and over again. It's just such a waste. I'd put all the bullshit about my lip and all the pain attached to it behind me. Then it was literally gone in a flash. I play that scene over and over in my mind. I'm just pissed off about everything, and I have trouble falling asleep."

"Are you pissed off at God?" asked Malachy.

"Pissed off at God?" asked Will in surprise. "How could I be pissed off at God? I can't be pissed off at somebody or something I don't even know if I believe in!"

Malachy shifted in his seat then put his right hand on the gearshift. "It's getting close to dark. We'd better be getting back up to the house, but I was just wondering, what kind of plans do you have with Laura Lee?"

"She's OK," said Will, "I don't know. I just want to walk, that's all, I just want to walk."

Will took his first steps in the summer of 1971. They were few, short, and painful. At first, the stumps of his legs frequently broke down and ulcerated, especially where there was scar tissue, but he refused to be discouraged. All during the summer and fall of that year he struggled to walk in spite of the pain. Finally, by Christmas, the swelling was gone from his stumps, the scars had toughened, and Will was walking again. He was still in considerable pain, but he was walking, and that was all that mattered to him.

After the first of the year, Will started working for his father at the shipyard. In the spring of '72, he moved out of his parents' house and into his own apartment in Savannah's Historic District. He and Laura Lee became engaged the following June and were married the week before Christmas at Saint Michael's in Charleston. While walking was occasionally uncomfortable and sometimes cumbersome, Will had mastered the problem; and unless people knew him, there was little indication he was missing both legs.

Laura Lee blended into Savannah's social life seamlessly and became an instant asset to Will. A year after their marriage, they purchased a home on East Bryan Street, right across from Warren Square and only two blocks from the Savannah River. It was a three-story, postcolonial house with hints of federal styling. Both Will and Laura Lee delighted in entertaining their friends, and soon an invitation to a party at the McQueen home became one of the most sought-after social perks in the city.

16. Divine Interventions

I am the man that hath seen
affliction by the rod of His wrath.
He hath led me, and brought
me into darkness, but not into light.
Surely against me is He turned;
He turneth His hand against me all the day.

—King James Version, Lamentations 3:1–3

You could do one hell of a job for us up in Atlanta, Will," said
Francis, over lunch at the Chatham Club.

"I agree with Francis," injected Art Thomas, new editor of
the *Savannah Morning Gazette*. "You can win this thing, Will. I know,
I've been checking around," he continued.

"I think it'd be good for you, son," added his father, while he tore
open a packet of Sweet 'n Low and added it to his tea.

"I don't know, Daddy. What about the shipyard?" asked Will.
"Who'll do my work for me when the legislature's in session?"

"I'll take care of that," said Jimmy. "What we and the rest of Savannah need more than anything right now is somebody in the Georgia
State Senate who understands how important this port is."

The Chatham Club is on the fourteenth floor of the DeSoto Hilton
and has a commanding view of Savannah's skyline. Will sat back in his
chair and looked out the windows toward South Carolina. The Savannah River was a wide ribbon of brown that wandered to the Atlantic.
Beyond that, the Savannah National Wildlife Refuge and the marshes of

Carolina stretched for miles. He watched as a tremendous ship, its decks stacked high with freight containers, inched its way under the Eugene Talmadge Bridge on the way to the Georgia Ports Authority docks at Garden City.

Will took a breath and said, "Well, I've got to talk this over with Laura Lee. I don't want to do anything unless she's for it."

That evening Will and his wife discussed what running for the Georgia State Senate would mean for him. Politics had always interested Will, and he had inherited all the natural inclinations and political talents for it from his father. Although Jimmy McQueen had acquired a long list of political enemies responsible for his defeat back in 1960, that was now considered ancient history. Besides, the paper had changed hands since that time, and the new owner had nothing against the McQueens. Martin Bradford had taken a job with a Tallahassee paper, and all the bad blood from the past didn't mean a thing anymore.

"Will, if you want to do this, it's fine with me," said Laura Lee, as she walked out of the bathroom in her nightgown and crawled into bed next to Will. "I think you'd make the best senator the great state of Georgia ever had."

Will lay on the bed wearing only his shorts. Laura Lee snuggled next to him, ran her hand over his chest, then kissed him. In moments they were making love, and nothing else existed for Will and Laura Lee.

W̲ill ran as a Republican in the election of 1976 and won easily. Georgia had been slipping into the Republican column since Barry Goldwater first carried the state for his party in the presidential election of 1964. After that, the policies of the Johnson administration only served to push the conservative, formerly Democratic white voters toward the Republicans, and the McQueens flowed with this tide. In '68 and '72, Georgia figured prominently in Nixon's successful "Southern Strategy," which helped him win the White House both times.

Although native son Jimmy Carter carried Georgia in the '76 presidential election, it was essentially a hollow victory for the state Democratic party, which watched helplessly as the Republicans took big bites out of both the Georgia State House and Senate, even losing seats to the

Republicans in the U.S. House of Representatives. Almost overnight Will had become the star of Georgia's Republican party and was closely watched by the Republican National Committee for his Washington potential. By 1978, anybody who knew anything about politics in Georgia was familiar with William Wallace McQueen from Savannah.

Will had all of his father's natural charm and speaking ability. When he delivered an address, he started slowly in a soft-spoken and humble manner. He appeared vulnerable but not weak, educated but not arrogant. His diction was tailored to the tastes of the audience, and he spoke with the distinct accent of Savannah's aristocracy, which was southern but not country. The effect of Will's body language and eye contact on a crowd were electric.

In addition to his natural speaking talents, Will brought with him the aura of a war hero who had given both legs in the unselfish service of his country. When he spoke of Vietnam, he spoke with reverence about the valor of the soldiers who fought there, not of America's humiliation. Finally, Will began to see how good life truly could be.

On the weekend before Thanksgiving of 1979, Will boarded *Little Feats* at the Savannah Yacht Club and headed for Jesus Island. It was a crisp and clear Friday morning, and he looked forward to seeing the island again. Ever since being elected to state office, the time he'd spent on the island had steadily decreased, and he missed it greatly. He wanted to stand on the bluffs in front of the big house and feel the wind from the ocean, smell the salt air, and hear the surf pounding in the distance. He yearned for the solitude of the marsh and the great expanse of the ocean and sky. He was drawn to the stillness of the deep woods and the elegance of its vines and moss-covered trees. While there was always something pulling Will to Jesus Island, that sensation had seemed stronger over the last few weeks whenever he thought about Malachy.

Late that night the wind picked up from the northeast and moaned as it passed around the chimneys and through the gables on the main house. Will stood at one of the tall windows on either side of the mammoth fireplace that dominated the east end of the ground floor and sipped Benedictine from a brandy sniffer. He watched as the tops of the oaks swayed in the wind and the flame-shaped cedars bowed with each gust, while out on Wassaw Sound the wind-whipped tops of whitecaps shone brightly in the moonlight. When Will returned to his chair by the fireplace, Malachy dropped another log on the fire, causing a fountain of orange sparks to swirl up the chimney. He punched the logs with a poker, gazed into the fire, then turned and spoke to Will.

"How is Laura Lee, Will?"

"She's fine. She didn't come because she had a doctor's appointment this afternoon and is going to see her parents in Charleston tomorrow. She insisted that I come by myself because she knew how badly I wanted to be here."

Malachy warmed his hands for a few seconds then sat in the chair across from Will. He watched as the light from the fire painted Will's face in a flickering amber and sent long, dark shadows across the room's tabby walls. Malachy thought back to an earlier time Will had spent with him on the island and remembered how hurt and disoriented he'd been then.

"Are you happy now, Will?" asked Malachy.

"Yes, very happy. But there was a time when I thought I'd never feel this way again."

"Laura Lee has been good for you," said Malachy. "I could tell she truly loved you the first time I met her. I had a different feeling that time I met Charlotte."

Will shrugged and snorted. "Yeah, I'm glad now that Charlotte dumped me. If she hadn't, I'd never have met Laura Lee."

"I've often felt," said Malachy, "that a man is inclined to marry a woman who is just like his mother. If a man has a good mother, he will instinctively seek out and marry a woman who is like her and will probably have a happy marriage. But if the opposite is true, the man will seek out a similar woman, and the results will be disastrous."

"I guess I was fortunate in that I had a good mother, because I certainly sought out a good wife," replied Will.

"You are fortunate in so many ways, Will," said Malachy, who momentarily grew silent, then continued.

"Tell me, how is your faith now?"

"Well, as you know, there was a time when I didn't believe," said Will, "but that's past now."

Malachy shifted in his chair and said, "Those were terrible times for you, and you were angry with God, weren't you?"

"I had been robbed of my legs for no good reason, was in pain, and I was very, very angry and very, very unhappy, Malachy. I had believed in a loving God but had seen and been through so much torment, I couldn't believe that a God of love would do something like that to me," answered Will.

"Do you think you could be like Job and love God even when terrible things befall you and those you love?" asked Malachy.

"I hope so," said Will, "but I also hope I don't have to find out. I've been through so much, I think God is going to let up on me for a while."

Malachy stared into the fire and looked between the logs where the fire was the hottest. He watched as blue flames turned white then orange and listened to the hissing of a damp log. Then he turned to Will and said, "It's always easy to believe in God when times are good. True faith in God comes only when we accept Him in bad times."

Will nodded his head then rubbed his legs. Sometimes they hurt just as much as before.

At noon the following Monday, Laura Lee had desperately wanted to call Will but decided she needed time to think. While she sat in the living room of the home she and Will had decorated together, she watched children playing across the street in Warren Square. She wanted to cry but couldn't. It was all so sudden and unexpected, the call from her doctor and the words that still rang in her head. "I'm sorry to have to tell you this, Laura Lee, but your PAP smear came back, and the results are very bad."

"'Very bad?'"

"Yes, Laura Lee. You have an aggressive form of uterine cancer, and I must tell you now, the best chances for survival are a hysterectomy followed by several weeks of radiation therapy."

"What are my chances for survival?"

"If the cancer hasn't spread to other organs already, pretty good."

Laura Lee watched as two little girls whispered secrets to each other then giggled. She turned away from the window, and her eyes fell on the picture of Will and her standing in front of the altar on their wedding day. She wondered what their children would have looked like. If the first child had been a boy, would he have been named for Will? She had wanted to give children to Will so badly, but now there would be no baby of her very own to hold in her arms, no small lips to press against her breast, and no joyful feeling as they suckled life from her.

"Dear God in Heaven!" cried out Laura Lee. "I'm only thirty years old. Why?"

A torrent of tears followed, but Laura Lee felt no better when, finally, there were no more. She was cold inside, and fear began to creep in. She was not afraid of dying but rather of the life she would have to live. For Will and her there would be no little girl dresses to buy, no little boy scratches to kiss and make well. On Christmas morning no screams of joy, no sunburned backs in the summertime. "Why did we have to wait to build this house then furnish it?" She sobbed. "I could have had at least one child by now."

Two weeks later, after confirming consultations and a trip to Emory University Hospital in Atlanta just to make sure, Laura Lee's uterus and ovaries were removed. Six weeks after that she began radiation therapy. None of it was easy. Even though things were not going well at the shipyard, Will rarely left his wife's side.

The incisions on Laura Lee's abdomen healed, and her doctor said she'd tolerated the radiation better than any patient he'd ever had; but Laura Lee's health seemed to decline. Over the following months, she lost weight and strength. Then her follow-up CAT scans began showing nodules in her liver, and her blood work indicated the cancer had spread to her bone marrow. Laura Lee had sensed early on that her prognosis was poor but had remained brave and fought hard for Will's sake. He was so sweet to her, and she loved him so dearly.

There came that time when Laura Lee accepted the fact that the fight was lost; and when she did, her only concern was for Will. He was strong in many ways but fragile in so many others, and she feared that her death would embitter him and break his spirit. *He's been through so much,* thought Laura Lee, *and there is only so much he can take.*

On a Sunday in the early spring of 1980, when the mornings were cool and the azalea buds ready to burst forth with the first warm day, Laura Lee called Will to her bed. She had spent the morning fixing her hair and makeup, then dressed herself in the nightgown she had worn on her wedding night. She had been unusually tired the whole week before, but that morning, she had awakened with some energy. It was obvious she was ill, but the dark circles under her eyes were hidden, and there was color in her cheeks. Will sat next to her, caressed her hair, then kissed her tenderly.

"Lie with me, Will," whispered Laura Lee, "and make love to me."

Will took his wife into his arms; and when Laura Lee cried out in ecstasy, "I love you, Will," he opened his eyes, and in that moment Laura Lee appeared to be nineteen again.

Two weeks later, on that same bed, with Will by her side, Laura Lee slipped into a deep and peaceful sleep from which she would not awake.

For months there was no comfort for Will. No one could console him, not even Malachy. Monsignor Mulvaney called him regularly, but Will was nothing more than brief and polite. He wasn't a tearful wreck but, rather, just the opposite. He told his father that when Laura Lee died, she'd taken part of his soul; and he would be forever missing that piece of himself just as he was forever missing his legs. Once Malachy made a special trip into town to speak with Will. The conversation got no further than Will saying he felt as though he had been cursed by God.

"I've had my legs taken from me for no good reason," Will lamented; "then the only woman I ever truly loved and who ever truly loved me was taken. I'm not Job from the Bible. There is no God who speaks to me from the clouds. I'm not Noah either, nor am I Saint Peter. I'm Will McQueen, simple, weak, and devastated. If there is a God, then I want that God to leave me alone because I certainly intend to leave Him alone." After that Malachy returned to Jesus Island and did not see Will again for months.

It was ironic, but what may have been most helpful in getting Will's mind off the death of Laura Lee were the serious problems the shipyard was having. During the mid 1960s, Will's father had mortgaged the yard heavily and used the money to invest in much-needed new equipment in anticipation of government contracts. The banks were to be paid over a fifteen-year period, and for a while, everything hummed along as planned. Then, in the early 1970s, the refitting work being done for the navy began to decline. It disappeared completely after the Vietnam War ended and the nation's military posture was allowed to depreciate. Two months after Laura Lee's funeral, Jimmy McQueen was forced to tell his son that the banks holding the notes on the McQueen Shipyard were calling them in and the 162-year-old family business had been lost.

When the McQueen Shipyard and its assets were liquidated and the banks satisfied, a healthy portion still remained of what had once been a substantial family fortune. Most of Jesus Island had been donated to the state of Georgia in the 1960s in exchange for the tax-free status of certain parcels of land on the island. The big house, chapel, slave huts, and some of the surrounding acreage remained with the McQueens. Part of the deal also included provisions for Uncle Moses, Dr. Divine, and several other descendants of the original slave families. They were allowed to keep the small plots where their houses stood. The rest of the island was declared a state wildlife sanctuary, and further development was forbidden.

Just as the problems with the shipyard had helped Will deal with the loss of Laura Lee, they also gave him the ability to focus more completely on his political career. After the yard closed, Will threw himself into his work in Atlanta. He became deeply involved with the Georgia Republican party and traveled the state extensively on party business. It wasn't long before Will's name was being circulated as a candidate for U.S. Congress in the First Congressional District.

Next to his father, Will's biggest supporter and closest political adviser was Francis Quinn, who had come to care for Will almost as a substitute son. Francis enjoyed helping Will with his political connections and was lavish with his campaign contributions. There were still whispers and snide remarks about Francis's past, but the slot machines were long gone, and Francis had no further overt connection with gambling or liquor in Chatham County. He had invested his earnings from his days with Willie Hart in various real-estate deals that had paid healthy dividends over the years and was still a silent and little-known partner in several bars at Tybee. The beach had remained his favorite haunt, and he maintained a splendidly large cottage there overlooking the ocean.

Francis had been generous with a large number of local and state politicians as well as charitable organizations of all stripes, effectively blunting or silencing any serious questions about his honesty or the ultimate source of his money. As Will's political fame and stature grew, the Republican National Committee had quietly checked into his background. Those in the know were satisfied his association with his "Uncle Francis" would survive media scrutiny.

W ill was thirty-three when Laura Lee was taken from him, and more than a year passed before he even thought about dating. When he finally did begin going out, every girl was compared to Laura Lee, and every one was found wanting.

While Will didn't realize it, in many ways the years had actually been kind to him. All that he had endured had matured him and added character to his looks and personality, and women were very attracted to him. As a single man in his thirties, with a family name and political power, Will McQueen had become prey for a number of lovely young women from the finest families in Savannah and Atlanta.

Whenever the legislature was in session, at both public and private functions, Will was always in the company of an attractive lady. A frequent guest at the Piedmont Driving Club and the Capitol City Club, he was introduced to scores of mothers, all of whom had eligible daughters. When in Atlanta, seldom did a week pass that he was not a dinner guest at one of these mothers' homes.

Will enjoyed his frequent romances and all the pleasures associated with them, but he was not looking for love. He tried to have feelings that went deeper than physical attraction, but a void had been left where Laura Lee once resided, and it seemed that no one could fill it. Will was also fearful that if he did allow himself to fall in love, something would happen, and he would be hurt once again.

Then there was what Will referred to as "the fun factor." After watching Laura Lee wither and die, then enduring the loneliness and heartache of her absence, he was finally enjoying himself again and had no desire to stop. He found beautiful women enchanting and was intoxicated by their attention and affection.

In the summer of 1983, Will's name again floated to the top of the candidate list for the First Congressional District seat. There had not been a Republican or a resident of Savannah elected to that office since Reconstruction, but demographics and party affiliations were changing in southeast Georgia. Wealthy retired northerners were now moving to the Savannah area and its environs in large numbers, and they tended to vote Republican. Their largest enclave was on Skidaway Island, an upscale retirement community just outside Savannah. While in the Georgia State Senate, Will had been a frequent guest speaker at numerous functions there, and the transplanted Democrats as well as Republicans were charmed by him.

His father's treatment of the black community while he was mayor, as well as his long association with black ministers and other community leaders, was a great asset to his son. Will had also been responsive and compassionate when dealing with various black politicians at the state and local levels and even though it was a given that his Democratic opponent would receive the bulk of their vote, there was no burning reason for them to turn out in heavy numbers against him.

The McQueens also enjoyed cordial, if not close, relations with organized labor in much the same manner, and any opposition to Will's candidacy was muted and perfunctory at best. But it was Will's standing with women that quickly caught the eyes of the national Republican party when they surveyed the First District's voters and began handicapping potential candidates.

Will had a 70 percent approval rating with women voters; and when they were questioned about why they liked Will, the leading responses were trust, truthfulness, and affability. Several respondents even said his class and style reminded them of John Kennedy.

In an address to the American Association of University Women (AAUW) in Atlanta, Will recounted in vivid detail his Vietnam days and gave such an emotional narrative about the wounds he'd received and his struggle to recover, the room was left quiet and still. But it was his tribute to Laura Lee and her fight against cancer that moved most in the audience to tears. A high-ranking member of the Republican National Committee was with his wife at the banquet. When Will had finished speaking and received a thunderous ovation, he whispered to her, "This guy is so smooth, he's the best natural speaker I've ever seen. I'm telling you, if bullshit were electricity, Lib, he'd be the president of Georgia Power. Watch him; he could go places."

On election night of 1984, Will's hard work and the Reagan landslide assured him a comfortable margin of victory. During the ensuing years, he was reelected with only token opposition and rose through the House ranks to obtain several important committee seats. Because he didn't have serious opposition, he was able to spend time campaigning and raising money for other Republicans. When the Republican revolution of 1994 gave that party control of both the House and Senate, Will's efforts on behalf of Republican candidates did not go unnoticed, and the buzz in Washington was that he would be the nominee for the Senate seat to be vacated in 1996 by the retirement of Sam Nunn.

III

In the Fullness
of Time

17. Coming Home

"Where lies that final harbor,
Whence we unmoor no more?"

—HERMAN MELVILLE, *Moby-Dick*

I never feel like I'm home until I smell the marsh." Inhaling deeply, Will smiled and said, "I know I'm home now, Uncle Moses."

"It's good to have ya back, Mista Will," replied Moses as he helped tie off the old Gar Wood. "Brother Malachy waitin' to the big house. He say he really miss seein' ya, Mista Will, jes like we all do. Ya know, suh, since ya done got elected to Washington, ain't nobody sees much of ya out here on the island."

"I know, Uncle Moses, and I miss this place more than you can imagine," said Will, as he looked at the other boats tied to the dock.

"Looks like Malachy has a few visitors this weekend," remarked Will.

"Yes, suh," said Moses. "People be comin' out all the time just to hear Brother Malachy talk. Lots a rich folks, too. Seems like dey got more trouble than po' folks do."

"I can promise you that, Uncle Moses." Will chuckled.

Moses nodded his head, smiled, and pushed back his old baseball cap, exposing nothing but gray hair. He had watched Will grow up and had broken down and cried the day he was told about Will's legs. He was there on the dock to help lift Will out of the boat when he returned to the island in a wheelchair. Moses had a long memory and good intuition, so as he and Will walked up the dock, he chose his next words carefully.

"There's somebody here you know from a while back, Mista Will."

"Really? Who's that?"

"Well, suh, kinda like an old friend I guess ya might say."

"An old friend?"

"Yes, suh. She used ta come out here with ya a long time ago, back when you was at The Citadel."

Will stopped and turned to face Moses.

"It's Miss Charlotte Drayton," said Moses quietly. "She been out here with a camera crew since yesterday. They doin' a TV story 'bout Brother Malachy. I told her you was comin' today, and she acted like she really wanted to see ya, suh. I hope I ain't gone and done nothin' wrong."

Will was silent for a moment, then he let out a sigh.

"Naw, you haven't done anything wrong, Uncle Moses. Where are they now?"

"At the cabins talkin' with some of the folks that's here to see Brother Malachy. Want me to go fetch her for ya?"

"That's all right, Uncle Moses. I want to go by Laura Lee's grave first, then see Malachy. After that I'll find Miss Drayton. Just tell her I'm here and looking forward to seeing her."

Over the years Malachy's reputation as a holy man and mystic had flourished. Many people from all walks of life journeyed to Jesus Island seeking his prayers and advice for a myriad of spiritual and physical aliments. In the early seventies, Jimmy McQueen had restored the old slave cabins and allowed Malachy's visitors to stay in them.

There was something about Malachy that eluded definition, and many people refused to accept him as only a simple teacher, and eventually miraculous cures were once again reported to have occurred on Jesus Island.

Charlotte Drayton had come to the island because some credible people claimed to have experienced visions of the Virgin Mary while praying with Malachy. She was aware that, only a few years earlier, millions had flocked to Majagoria in Yugoslavia when a group of peasant children claimed to have seen the Virgin. Even in Georgia during the early nineties, tens of thousands of believers had descended on the town of Conyers, Georgia, where a woman who lived on a farm asserted she had had visions of Mary and had even received messages from her. At both sites some pilgrims maintained they had also seen signs in the sky or had experienced a miracle of some type. Although the reports of visions on Jesus Island had been kept quiet, the Cable News Channel had somehow learned of them and wanted to be the first to break the story. Because Charlotte was from Savannah and was familiar with Jesus Island, she was given the job.

In 1998, Charlotte had left WTOC-TV in Savannah and moved to Atlanta, where she had accepted a position with the Cable News Corporation (CNC). It was Lane Bradford who was responsible for her hiring. He'd known Charlotte when they were at Savannah High together and in a casual way had followed her TV career. After The Citadel, Lane had become a career army officer, serving with military intelligence in Vietnam and later at the Pentagon as press officer for the Joint Chiefs of Staff. After retiring as a colonel from the army in 1994, he'd gone with CNC, where he was in charge of regional news. Even after more than thirty years, Lane still harbored a grudge against Will and saw this story as a way of discrediting him.

It's so good to see you again, Congressman McQueen," said Charlotte, as she extended her hand.

"It's nice to see you, too, Charlotte. By the way, you can call me Will."

Charlotte laughed then said, "Well then, come here, Will, and let me give you a hug."

When she put her arms around Will's neck, she pressed her cheek against his and said, "I'm so proud of you."

From the minute Uncle Moses had told Will about Charlotte being on the island, Will had been uneasy. He'd really never quite gotten over her. After all, she was his first love, and he'd fallen so hard for her. For a long time after she'd broken it off with him, whenever he saw her or heard her name, there was a smattering of that funny twinge he used to get whenever he kissed her. Only that twinge had turned from pleasure to pain. He began to get it again as he watched her approach and was surprised how hard it hit when she touched him.

Awkwardly, Will returned Charlotte's hug; then she stood back to admire him.

"You look wonderful, Will!"

There was sincerity in Charlotte's voice, and Will thought he noticed her eyes moisten when she spoke.

"I was watching you when you walked up, and I can't get over how well you do. If I didn't know, I swear I'd think there was nothing at all wrong."

Will had heard that remark before and mumbled his stock reply. "Thank you. I've been very fortunate."

Smiling, Charlotte took Will by the arm and said, "Come on, Congressman, take me for a walk. It's been a long time since I've been on the island. I want you to tell me all about what you've been up to."

Will had seen Charlotte on TV when she did the news in Savannah and had caught her face on the tube a few times after she had gone with CNC; but somehow they hadn't been face-to-face in maybe twenty-five years. Secretly, and with some guilt, Will had envisioned that justice would be served on Charlotte. He'd decided that as she aged, she would gain weight, wrinkles, and bags under her eyes. *That will humble her,* he'd thought; and if he ever did run into her again, that old pop in the gut she used to give him would never come back again. It hadn't worked out that way. Charlotte was still a gorgeous woman who looked a good decade younger than she really was.

While they walked, Charlotte held on to Will's arm and told him about her life.

"Well, after Steve and I got divorced in '86," said Charlotte, "little Steve and I moved back to Savannah. I sold real estate for a while and got tired of that. Then I went to work selling advertising for WTOC. That was kind of boring, too, and I almost quit. Then Doug Weathers asked me if I'd like to try my hand on the broadcasting side. I did, and thank God, I was able to do real well. Then Lane Bradford called me from CNC and offered me this job. I had to move back to Atlanta, which I hated to do; but I've got a child to put through college, so off I went."

"What about his father? Doesn't he help out?"

"Steve had a real drinking problem. I don't know where he is or what he's doing. He hasn't seen or spoken to his son in over five years and had stopped his child support a long time before that. It really hurt the boy. A child like that needs a father figure, and I worry about him, but I'm doing the best I can."

Will and Charlotte followed the path to the high bluffs that overlooked the Atlantic. They sat under the shade of a knurled oak and watched as a flight of brown pelicans skimmed low over the ocean searching for fish. A mile out a shrimp boat strained to pull its nets.

"You've never considered marrying again?" asked Will.

"Not really. I've dated some, but I just haven't met anybody I care to be with all the time. I know I used to be kind of an airhead, Will, but I've changed. Maybe it's having a child to worry about, or maybe it's just getting older, but my priorities are different now. I look for things in people I never cared about before."

Will nodded in understanding while the wind brushed back the sea oats on top of the dunes. There was silence for several minutes before Charlotte turned to Will and asked, "What about you, Will? Has there been anybody else since Laura Lee?"

Will gave a little shrug and said, "Yeah, there've been a few I was interested in but nobody I was ready to make a long-term commitment to. Bein' in Congress is sorta like bein' married. It's a major demand on me, and I just don't think I could devote the time necessary for the success of a new marriage. Right now I'm not involved with anybody in particular."

He was telling the truth but not the whole truth, and Charlotte knew it. After his election to Congress, Will had developed into somewhat of a ladies' man, and his romantic involvements with a number of high-profile political celebrities on the Washington social scene had provided ample grist for rumor mills from Washington to Atlanta. More than once Charlotte had heard the term *playboy* associated with Will's name, and the word around the CNC newsroom was that Congressman McQueen was a bit of a Lothario who thoroughly enjoyed the female turnover rate in Washington.

There was a thunderhead building out over the ocean. Its flat bottom was heavy, dark, and pregnant with water. A low-hanging sun blistered the cloud tops, turning them into flaming coral. Will watched as the cloud grew and boiled and spilled its rain into the sea. Charlotte was watching the storm, too, and occasionally Will would glance at her. Each time he did, she'd sense it and turn to look at him; and each time she'd smile that same luxurious, intoxicating smile he'd fallen for a lifetime ago, and that tiny twinge grew just a little bit more.

Damn, he thought to himself, *I don't believe this is happening!*

All the alarm bells and whistles that should have been going off in his head were functioning properly, but something else was working, too. It had been a long, long time since he'd felt this way, too damn long, and it felt good, real good. It made Will feel alive; it made him feel like he had that summer he and Charlotte had dated. Besides, he was on vacation, and he decided that this was all a gift from the gods of summer.

Will checked his watch then said, "It's close to four. Are you planning on spending the night?"

"Well," answered Charlotte, "actually we got about all the footage we need, and I was planning on going back with the camera crew around six."

"Could you stay overnight again?" asked Will. "I think you might enjoy dinner, and I'd be honored if you would accept an invitation to come as my guest."

Charlotte smiled, pulled out her cell phone, and replied, "With an invitation like that, Congressman, I think it can be arranged."

On the beach later that evening a lemon-colored moon rose over the Atlantic, while Will and Charlotte listened to the breaking waves. There were few nights more beautiful than this.

"What do you think about Malachy's after-dinner conversation?" asked Will.

"I've never heard anybody quite like him," replied Charlotte. "Before I came out here, I thought Brother Malachy was just another dime-a-dozen religious fanatic. But this man is well-read and is obviously no dummy. He seems to have one foot in the physical world and one foot in the spiritual world. There's something else about him, too."

"Like what?" asked Will.

"The only word that seems to fit is kind of trite and well-worn, but it's the only one I can think of that describes him."

"Well, at the expense of seeming trite, Charlotte, what is that word?"

Charlotte turned to face Will, then she smiled and said, "Vibes, Congressman. Brother Malachy is sending out some heavy vibes."

Will laughed and said, "I understand what you're saying. He's got a way with animals, too. Sister Mystery has two of the meanest dogs down at her cabin. They don't like anybody, but they love Malachy. I know they've never been trained, but he can tell them to sit or be quiet, and they obey instantly. Even Sister Mystery is impressed with what Malachy can do with Lucifer and Jezebel."

"Who?"

"The dogs. Sister Mystery calls them Lucifer and Jezebel. I guess she thinks that impresses her clientele."

Charlotte and Will started laughing and continued until tears filled their eyes. They were sitting side by side on the trunk of one of the downed trees littering the beach; and when the laughing finally stopped, they found themselves face-to-face, only inches apart. Will was the first to speak.

"You're exactly as I remember you, Charlotte. You're still beautiful."

Everything about the evening was perfect for romance. The beach, the moon and stars, the return to Jesus Island, Will, the way he looked, who he was, what he was, just everything. But Charlotte was frightened because the Will McQueen sitting next to her wasn't the same insecure boy she had once abruptly dismissed from her life.

Charlotte smiled and said, "You're just as sweet as you were when we were teenagers," then looked out over the ocean.

Will's mind filled with the images of the first time he and Charlotte had made love. He wondered if he could ever go back to that time again, recapture a part of it . . . feel like he had when he was young and strong and complete, back to those days before the war.

"Do you think you could manage to stay for a little longer?" asked Will.

L ane Bradford was sitting in his office at the CNC broadcast studios in Atlanta when Charlotte called. She'd been cleared for three days in Savannah, and now she wanted three more. He couldn't understand why. He'd already seen the video she'd shot of the island with the slave cabins and the imposing main house on the old cotton plantation. He'd liked the segment that had Brother Malachy kneeling in the chapel, appearing to be in a trance. The interview with Dr. Divine and Sister Mystery at their cabin was great, and the piece with the kooky-looking woman describing how she'd seen the Virgin Mary in the clouds over Jesus Island was perfect. But the best had to be the bit where Charlotte interviewed an old black lady who lived in Savannah.

The video of Rosa Mae (Sweet Rose) Bostic talking about how the Devil Himself had grabbed her daughter and bit off her leg was a real showstopper. Charlotte had served up a piece that made Congressman McQueen's favorite place on earth look like a mixture of voodoo and fundamentalism, with the smell of slavery times. It couldn't be run on the air until Charlotte had done the editing; and after the time she'd spent with Will, she'd decided she didn't want the piece to have the negative connotations Lane was insisting on.

"So why do you want to stay longer, Charlotte? I need you to get back to Atlanta, write the copy, and get this thing on the air. We've got some jerks running around up here talking about electing McQueen to fill Senator Coverdell's seat. Besides, I miss you."

"Look, Lane," said Charlotte, "I've done what you asked. You wanted a trash job on the congressman, and you got it, but I'm not proud of myself at all. I don't want to put the spin on it that you and Ed want. We can talk this over when I get back. Besides, I'm worn-out and just need a few days to myself."

"But, Charlotte, honey, I miss you. I need to see you again just so we can talk. Give me another chance, OK? Come on back tonight. I promise that if you do, I'll tell Cindy I want a divorce when she gets back from LA."

Charlotte drew in a deep breath then let it out. "Look, Lane, I don't know what it takes to get it across to you, but it's over. I told you that last week, and I'm telling you that now. It's over. Go find somebody else to screw; I'm tired of your bullshit."

"Baby, I know you're upset, but give me a chance to get my finances straight with Cindy where she can't take everything," pleaded Lane. "Then we can get married, I promise."

Charlotte pushed her hair back then changed the phone to her other ear. "Lane, it's over. I don't want to live like that anymore. It makes me feel like dirt. But more than that, I've been doing a lot of thinking down here, and I've decided I don't want to be around you even if you get divorced tomorrow."

"What are you trying to tell me, Charlotte?" asked Lane sarcastically, "that you've gone and found religion on Jesus Island. What a hoot!"

"I'm telling you that I've decided you suck as a human being, and I don't want anything more to do with you. Is that clear enough?"

Lane was silent for a few seconds then said, "All right, have it your way, but get your bleached-blonde ass up here right now and finish this story and do it the way I tell you to."

"In case you failed to notice, Mr. Bradford, I'm a natural blonde," answered Charlotte; "maybe you're just too stupid to know how to tell. In any event I'm staying here for three more days whether you like it or not. I've got some sick leave coming, and I'm taking it right now because I'm damn sick of you."

"Now you listen to me, you little screwtail bitch, you either be up here in six hours, or you're history at CNC!"

Charlotte smiled to herself and in a falsely sweet voice said, "Lane, sugar darlin', if you're even thinkin' about firin' me, you've got fewer brains in your bald little head than I thought you had. You fuck with me or my job, and I'll personally perform your castration live and in front of a national audience of millions. That's after I've entered suit against you and CNC for sexual harassment but not before I've gone to Cindy and spilled my guts about how you've been using the both of us. Do I make myself clear, darlin' heart?"

"Come on, Charlotte, don't act this way. What happened between us?"

"Nothing, Lane, absolutely nothing, and that's what I've discovered. So if you don't have anything more to say, I'll see you maybe Sunday night, maybe Monday morning. You'll just have to wait to find out. Till then, 'bye."

The next morning Will and Charlotte met for breakfast on the second-floor balcony of the main house overlooking the ocean. They'd talked through most of night, and both were a little sleepy, but they enjoyed a delicious sense of lightness about the morning as the sun crept up the sides of the house and spilled onto the breakfast table.

In some delightful, unexplainable way a connection had been made between them the night before, and Charlotte marveled at how good it felt just to be around Will, just to watch him and hear him talk. It had been a long time for her, too, and she was leery of these emotions but drawn to them because of their . . . well, sweetness.

Will had always been a sweet guy, and Charlotte really hadn't wanted to hurt him way back when; but Steve had been the most gorgeous thing she'd ever laid eyes on, just as gorgeous as she was, and she was used to nothing but the best. Steve had lots more qualities, but sweetness wasn't one of them. Charlotte had never known exactly what had been missing from her life until she realized it was the tenderness she'd sensed in Will. He wasn't physically perfect, but in his imperfection there was kindness, gentleness, and need.

Why have I never wanted that before? thought Charlotte, as she watched Will drink his coffee.

A copy of the *Atlanta Journal-Constitution* rested on the table next to Will. On the bottom of the front page was a story with the headline, "STATE GOP EYES MCQUEEN IN SENATE RUN."

"Well, whatdaya think, Will? Are you interested in running?" asked Charlotte.

"Are you asking me as a reporter or as a friend?"

"It's off the record, Congressman. I'm asking you as a friend."

"If the stars line up right," said Will, "I'll probably do it. Naturally, the whole thing revolves around money. It takes a whole lot of money to get elected to the Senate now. Probably about ten million."

Charlotte shook her head, smiled, and asked, "Where do you come up with ten million dollars to spend on an election?"

"Mostly from rich people and powerful organizations who want something in return. You should know that by now."

"Come on, Will, of course I know that. What I'm talking about is how do you approach these people and how do they approach you? It must get pretty disgusting to have to walk around with your hand out all the time."

"Trust me, Charlotte, it does," said Will, "but that's how the game is played. As a matter of fact, I've got to go into town this morning and meet with some folks who're interested in getting my attention, if you know what I mean. They're friends of Francis Quinn's."

"I've heard about Francis," said Charlotte. "He's been a big supporter of yours, hasn't he?"

"He's been like a father to me. He's been a great help in raising money and introducing me to some real heavyweights around the country."

In Savannah the Jewish Educational Alliance (JEA) is, in many ways, an ecumenical organization. While it primarily serves the varied needs of Savannah's Jewish population, the JEA's health club is also a popular place with gentiles. It offers a number of amenities from indoor handball courts to steam and dry saunas, but the most celebrated aspect of the men's locker room is the socializing and camaraderie. Jimmy McQueen had been a long-standing member of the JEA, as had Francis Quinn. For years the two would meet there during lunch for a steam bath and a rubdown. The health club was kind of a social intersection where successful Jews shared gossip and news with their Christian counterparts, and it was still a part of Francis's daily routine.

"So," said Charlie Gross, as he kneaded the muscles along Francis's left arm, "how's Will doing?"

"He's doing fine, Charlie. As a matter of fact, he's supposed to meet me down here at noon."

"Will's a good boy," said Charlie, squirting more oil on Francis's shoulders. "His daddy was a prince of a man." Charlie reached up, pushed his glasses back on his nose, then continued.

"He's just like Myron Kornblat, though, always got schmooie on his mind."

"He's single, Charlie; he can afford to." Francis laughed.

"I'll swear," Charlie said, "he'd schtup a butterfly if somebody would hold the wings."

"Will's a good-looking guy who happens to be a congressman, Charlie. The women are chasing after him. What do you want him to do?"

"Well," replied Charlie, "I'll tell you what I told Myron when he was seeing that little shiksa on the side. I said, 'Myron, no man is stronger than that hairy one-eyed monster. It's stronger than the hydrogen bomb.'"

Francis let out a howl then said, "Charlie, let me up; I want to get in a few laps in the pool before Will gets here."

While Charlie wiped the oil off Francis's back, he again noticed the birthmark on his neck and said, "I tell ya', every time I see this thing back here, I can't get over how much it looks like Italy."

Francis rolled over and slipped off the table, saying, "That's because I'm an Italian, Charlie."

"Yeah," said Charlie, "and I'm the pope!"

Francis was in good shape for a man his age. He'd had a heart attack at sixty, followed by a quadruple bypass, but since then he'd had no more problems. He exercised daily and particularly enjoyed swimming laps in the JEA's pool. He'd been alone when he started swimming and hadn't noticed the elderly woman in the shallow end accompanied by her nephew.

When he finished his laps, Francis pulled himself out of the water and sat resting on the edge of the pool. His hair had thinned as he'd grown older; and when it was wet, his birthmark was plainly visible. After a few minutes, the old lady slowly climbed up the ladder and out of the pool. As she walked past Francis, she glanced at him, did a double take, and stopped.

For several seconds Gretchen Meyer stood and stared at the mark on Francis's neck. Hesitantly she reached down and touched his shoulder.

When Francis turned around, Gretchen stared into his eyes then drew back in horror and cried, *"Oy gevalt!"* She pointed at Francis and screamed with a heavy German accent, "He is a killer! I know this man from the camps; he is a killer! I saw him murder a man with his own hands!"

The pool was indoors, and the sound echoed and bounced off the walls. A group of ladies sitting at a table nearby looked up in surprise, and the lifeguard dropped her clipboard on the deck. Francis struggled to his feet as Gretchen backed away, continuing to yell, "This man is a killer! I saw him kill a man in the camps!"

Francis stood speechless as Gretchen's nephew hurried over and wrapped a towel around her shoulders, saying, "Aunt Gretchen, this man is from here; he's never even been in Germany. I've known him all my life; he's no killer from the camps. You're just a little confused, sweetheart."

"No, I recognize him! He was there! He is a killer!" she wailed.

Bubba Silverman looked at Francis with pained eyes and said, "I'm sorry, Francis," while he helped his aunt Gretchen to the women's locker room. When he got to the door, the lifeguard and some of the ladies who were in the pool area took Gretchen into the locker room, and Bubba hurried back over to Francis.

"Francis, I don't know what to say. Gretchen has Alzheimer's, and she gets a little meshuga every now and then. She's never done anything like this before, though. She was at Bergen-Belsen, so I guess something just set her off. Sometimes she'll just start crying about things that happened there. Please forgive her. Five minutes from now she won't even remember what happened."

Shaken, Francis replied, "It must be hell on earth to have a disease that makes you slip in and out of reality. Good Lord, Bubba, it breaks my heart just to see somebody like that."

"She's not really my aunt," said Bubba, "she's my mother's cousin. I just call her Aunt Gretchen. She used to live in New York, but after her husband died, she was all alone. My parents brought her down here so she could be around somebody close. About a year ago she developed Alzheimer's and has really started to slide since then. She's at the Savannah Nursing Center, and I thought it might do her some good if she could get out a little. I sure am sorry for what happened."

Francis put his arm around Bubba and told him not to worry then said, "You know, Will's supposed to be here in a little while."

"Yes, sir," replied Bubba, "I'm supposed to meet him here, too. We're planning to go diving for some wrecks off the coast next week, and we need to get things worked out."

Francis had been a member of the JEA for close to forty years. For Bubba, the Alliance was like a second home, and he'd grown up watching Charlie Gross give Francis rubdowns and listening as the two bantered with each other. It seemed to Bubba that just about everybody in Savannah knew Francis and liked him. More than once, after Francis was gone, Bubba had heard his different business ventures discussed in the locker room at the health club. Several times he'd heard Francis described as a man who had "the looks of a goy and the brains of a Jew."

"What did you say your aunt's name was, Bubba?" asked Francis.

"Gretchen, Gretchen Meyer. She was the only one from her family who made it through the Holocaust. She's still got her number tattooed on her forearm. I memorized it as a little child. It's 97803."

"I've got good friends with Alzheimer's," said Francis. "They were strong and happy people once. Now when I see them, it's pitiful. It breaks my heart. Judge Davis has it, and he's a shell of what he used to be. He looked at me one time and told me he wished God would take him. I can understand why."

"So can I," said Bubba. "I don't want to see Gretchen suffer anymore. It's almost like she's back at Bergen-Belsen again the way she carries on sometimes. I hope God'll take her before she goes back there in her mind and can't come back."

Francis was quiet for a moment then sadly shook his head and said, "If there's anything I can do to help you with her, anything at all, let me know, OK?"

"You're a mensch, Francis, but I don't know what can be done. I'll just take her back to the nursing home and hope for the best."

In the women's locker room, Gretchen was frantic and couldn't be consoled. As several women dried her hair and dressed her, Gretchen babbled on, sometimes in English, sometimes in German.

"He is the one, I tell you. He has the mark on his neck. I remember it. He is the Irishman with the beautiful eyes. We talked about him. You think I'm *meshugeneh;* I tell you I am not," cried Gretchen.

"*Ich vais, ich vais,*" said Esther Lasky tenderly, as she helped the old lady to her feet and walked her to the door.

"Your nephew will take you back to the home now, Gretchen. You need to get some rest. Bubba is such a *haimish* boy; you're lucky to have him," said the rabbi's wife.

After Gretchen had left, Esther, who was not from Savannah, looked at the rabbi's wife and asked, "What do you know about this man Francis Quinn?"

"Francis has been in Savannah all his life, as far as I know. He's been a member of the Alliance as far back as I can remember, too. Why do you ask, Esther?"

"I don't know," replied Esther, "it was just the look in her eyes. She seemed so sane, so sure."

Then Esther shrugged and added, "What a terrible way to be in your old age. God have mercy on her."

Hey, Miz Linton," said Francis, "how're things goin' today? Been keepin' busy?"

"Lawd God, yes," replied Daisy Linton, the three-to-eleven charge nurse at the Savannah nursing center.

"Is Judge Davis in his room," asked Francis, as he scanned the chart rack for Gretchen Meyer's name.

"I reckon so, Mr. Quinn. If he ain't, then check the TV room," replied Nurse Linton, who then buried her head in a chart and started writing.

"Room 209-A," Francis said to himself when he spotted Gretchen's name on one of the charts hanging in the rack. The B-bed chart was in the rack also, but had no name on it, indicating the bed was empty.

It was 7:15; meals had been served and trays collected. Meds wouldn't be out until around nine, maybe later. It was a quiet time at the nursing home. Unless there was a problem, all the nursing staff would be gathered at the nursing station, filling out charts and gossiping.

Francis walked past Room 209 and noticed the door slightly ajar. He looked in and saw Gretchen sleeping on the bed. She'd been in an aggravated state ever since returning from the outing with her nephew the day before and had been medicated with an increased dosage of Haldol.

Francis continued on to Judge Davis's room, where he found him staring at the television with his mouth open. The judge didn't know where he was, and Francis took a pair of exam gloves from the bathroom and stepped back into the hall.

No one saw Francis slip into Room 209. Once inside, he quickly put the gloves on and eased next to Gretchen's bed. Carefully and quietly he lowered the bed's railing and looked at her. For a moment he hesitated. Then in one swift movement, Francis bent over, placed his left arm around the right side of Gretchen's neck to act as a fulcrum, put his right hand against her left ear, and pushed her head to the right. He could feel and hear cervical vertebrae three and four dislocate and knew her spinal cord had been crushed. Gretchen never made a sound and never knew what had happened.

Throwing back the covers, Francis lifted the woman from her bed and dragged her to the bathroom. Once there, he slammed the side of Gretchen's head into the sink, fracturing her skull, then let her body drop to the floor. He hadn't been in Room 209 more than thirty seconds.

"You leavin' already, Mr. Quinn?" asked Nurse Linton.

"Yes, ma'am," said Francis, "the judge is out of it. I don't think he knows where he is; he sure doesn't know who I am."

"I know it," said Nurse Linton, "he don't even recognize his wife no more. It's a terrible shame. Such a fine, smart man to be that way. Miz Davis done said she hopes the Lord will just go on and take the judge."

"That would be a merciful thing," replied Francis.

Gretchen's body was discovered at the beginning of the eleven-to-seven shift. Her doctor told the Silvermans that Gretchen would have died from the skull fracture if she hadn't broken her neck when her head hit the sink. "Either way," said Dr. Schwarz, "she's at rest now."

18. The *Sword of Lee*

> *Forth from its scabbard! all in vain,*
> *Bright flashed the sword of Lee;*
> *'Tis shrouded now in its sheath again,*
> *It sleeps the sleep of our noble slain;*
> *Defeated yet without stain,*
> *Proudly and peacefully.*
>
> —The reverend Father Abram Ryan, Poet
> Laureate, Confederate States of
> America, "The Sword of Robert Lee"

On May 3rd, 1995, after years of searching, Clive Cussler's dive team discovered the wreck of the CSS *Hunley* off the South Carolina coast near Charleston. The *Hunley* had been one of the most elusive wrecks Cussler had ever tried to find, and he'd almost abandoned the search he'd started in July of 1980.

The CSS *Hunley* was a Confederate secret weapon of devastating potential and innovative design, and years ahead of anything else. Just over thirty-five feet long and fashioned from an old boiler, the *Hunley* was a human-powered submarine. On the evening of February 17th, 1864, the *Hunley* had attacked and sank the USS *Housatonic* with a spar torpedo near the mouth of Charleston Harbor. It was the first submarine to sink a warship and a feat that would not be repeated until U-21 torpedoed the British cruiser HMS *Pathfinder* during World War I.

The *Hunley*'s discovery sparked renewed interest in the Confederate navy, especially those vessels of ingenious design employed against the federal blockade. In Alabama there was talk of finding another Confederate submarine that had gone down in Mobile Bay. Meanwhile, Civil

War enthusiasts in Savannah showed renewed interest in the story of the CSS *Sword of Lee.*

In the fall of 1864, Savannah was struggling for breath, fighting for her life. She was firmly caught in the ironclad stranglehold of the federal fleet, as monitor-class and other warships kept a constant vigil over all the water approaches to the city.

At the beginning of the war, the blockade had been porous at best; but with the growth of the federal navy, blockade running had become risky business. The weapons of war and the implements of destruction the Confederacy depended upon from the factories of England and France had fallen off to a trickle.

Commodore Josiah Tattnall, former captain of the CSS *Virginia,* had been given command of Savannah's riverboat squadron and charged with defending the port of Savannah as well as breaking the blockade. His ships numbered so few he dubbed his command "the Mosquito Fleet." The only ships at his disposal with a chance of standing up to the Union Fleet were the ironclads *Atlanta* and *Savannah.*

In June of 1863, out of desperation, the CSS *Atlanta* sailed down the Wilmington River and into Wassaw Sound in an attempt to break the blockade. But just as the *Atlanta* was passing through the sound on her way into the Atlantic, she struck a sandbar and was unable to free herself. The monitors, *Weehawken* and *Nahunt,* moved in and circled her as jackals might a wounded lion, staying just out of range. As the tide went out, the *Atlanta* settled at an angle that precluded bringing her guns to bear. With five quick shots, the defenseless *Atlanta* was so mauled that she was forced to surrender.

When the CSS *Savannah* was finally ready for action, it was found that the obstructions placed in the rivers to keep the Union warships out could not be removed. The last great hope of breaking the blockade of Savannah was bottled up in her own port.

Still, Commodore Tattnall would not give up, but with the defeat of the CSS *Atlanta,* and paralysis of the CSS *Savannah,* it became apparent to Tattnall that some other way of breaking the blockade had to be found.

Deficient in everything from raw materials to manpower, Confederate naval designers turned to innovative solutions in their fight and achieved some success with the use of floating mines, then known as torpedoes. But this was a haphazard and clumsy means of attack, quite dependent on chance. However, from this success, the idea of using small, swift boats to deliver the torpedoes to the target was born.

Most torpedo boats were steam-powered screws about thirty to forty feet long. The payload was a keg of black powder lashed to the end of a long spar jutting out from the bow. The method of attack was simple. The torpedo boat aimed herself at the target and sailed headlong until the keg of powder was impaled under the waterline of the federal ship. With this accomplished, the torpedo boat would back away and detonate the warhead with a lanyard pull.

There were encouraging successes in Hampton Road using ships such as the CSS *Squib,* and in Charleston with boats known as "Davids," a play on the diminutive David of biblical fame.

In order to overcome the defensive screen of fire, Confederate naval engineers decided to construct a torpedo boat that could approach its target underwater, and thus the CSS *Hunley* was born.

After news of the *Hunley*'s success, Commodore Tattnall turned to McQueen Shipyard in Savannah, builders of both the *Atlanta* and *Savannah*.

The foremost designer at the McQueen yard was Christian Jensen Deitz, an immigrant to Savannah from Bavaria whose trade in Germany had been clock making. As Deitz saw it, the solution to the problem was to deliver the warhead in an unmanned vessel, preferably submerged. This torpedo would be carried as close as possible to the target in a swift craft, where it would be loosed against the enemy ship, driven to the target by its own means of propulsion, and detonated with a contact fuse. Since he envisioned a run of no more than a thousand feet for his weapon, he designed a spring-driven motor as his power plant.

The payload and spring motor were fitted, one behind the other, into a cylinder made from copper, shaped like a bullet, and ballasted to float inches beneath the water's surface. Stabilizing fins were attached to the stern; and when it was finished, its shape and design were remarkably like that of a modern-day torpedo. By April of 1864, the McQueen yard had a boat ready for trial and christened it the CSS *Sword of Lee* in honor of the Confederacy's most successful general.

The two torpedoes that Christian Deitz had built were mounted on either side of the hull. When the *Sword of Lee* came within range of its target, the spring motors would be engaged and the torpedo rolled over the side.

During the late summer of 1864, as Sherman pounded Atlanta, the crew of the *Sword of Lee* secretly practiced their torpedo attack in the Herb River near Dutch Island. When news came that Sherman was leaving Atlanta intent on a march to the sea, Commodore Tattnall decided the time had come for the *Sword of Lee* to make her attack. At six in the evening, on October 15th, 1864, the CSS *Sword of Lee* steamed out the Herb River and down the Wilmington toward Wassaw Sound and three Union ironclads on blockade duty.

The captain of the torpedo boat was twenty-year-old Lt. William Wallace McQueen IV, youngest son of Robert Bruce McQueen, owner of the shipyard. With him was a crew of five that included Isaiah McQueen, a former McQueen slave given his freedom in exchange for serving in the Confederate States Navy.

The night was moonless and cloudy, perfect conditions for a surprise attack. Presenting a low silhouette, the Confederate ship had been undetected when she launched her starboard torpedo at the USS *Weehawken* from seven hundred feet. Thirty seconds later, the *Weehawken* shuddered from an explosion. *Sword of Lee* then turned her attention to the USS *Unadilla,* but the element of surprise had been lost and *Unadilla* commenced an attack of her own.

Heavy gunfire from *Unadilla* forced the Confederates to abandon their second torpedo run and seek refuge in the open Atlantic. The *Sword of Lee* was faster than her pursuers, but the long-range federal guns damaged the boat. *Unadilla* stayed with the chase for two hours, breaking off the pursuit when they lost sight of the ship in a fog bank.

Nearly out of coal, taking on water, and with four of her six crew members mortally wounded, *Sword of Lee* was doomed. When she finally went down, the only crew member who survived was Isaiah McQueen. He pulled himself onto a piece of decking and drifted for almost a day until he was rescued by the USS *Nipsic,* five miles from the mouth of the Savannah River.

When interrogated, Isaiah concealed the fact that he was a Confed-

erate sailor. His vague descriptions of the torpedo led the Union officers to believe the Confederates had launched a floating mine and that
the swift current had carried it to the *Weehawken*. Isaiah developed
pneumonia and died two weeks later at the federal coaling station on
Hilton Head, taking the fate of the CSS *Sword of Lee* and her crew to his
grave.

In mid-December of 1864, when it became apparent that Sherman
would soon take Savannah, all equipment and munitions that could not
be evacuated across the Savannah River with General Hardee's command were destroyed. This included the burning of the still uncom-
pleted CSS *Macon* along with her blueprints at the McQueen yard.

Christian Deitz, the designer and builder of the torpedoes, reluc-
tantly tossed all of his plans into the same fire except one sketch of the
overall torpedo design. Upon returning home, Deitz put the sketch
between the pages of his family Bible for safekeeping then assumed a
commission in the Savannah Republican Guards.

During the pandemonium surrounding the evacuation of Savannah,
Deitz neglected to tell his wife about the sketch. Three weeks after cross-
ing the Savannah River with Hardee's Corps, Capt. Christian Jensen
Deitz died of pneumonia in Charleston. He had said very little to his
wife, Helen Louise, about the torpedoes; and since the entire operation
was secret, when the war ended, all that survived of the *Sword of Lee* and
her torpedoes were rumors and hearsay.

After the war, Helen Deitz told her children what little she knew of
their father's secret war project. The other men who had direct knowledge of Christian Deitz's torpedo were either dead or scattered by the
winds of war. So the story of the remarkable torpedoes designed by an
immigrant German clock maker faded into the shadows of Savannah's
memory.

However, in the Deitz family, the story of the *Sword of Lee* was kept
alive and passed from one generation to the next, more as legend than
fact, until John-Morgan Hartman discovered his great-grandfather's
sketch while flipping through the old Deitz family Bible. That was three
years before the remains of the CSS *Hunley* were discovered.

John-Morgan was an avid Civil War historian and president of the
Savannah Grays Civil War Roundtable, which was a discussion group

composed of amateur historians. When he presented his paper on the *Sword of Lee* along with Christian Deitz's sketch to the group, it energized them.

There were retired generals and admirals in the Savannah Grays, and soon the logs from the federal vessels blockading the port of Savannah in November of 1864 were located and copied. When the logs of the USS *Weehawken, Unadilla, Pocahontas,* and *Nipsic* were scrutinized, it led John-Morgan and his friends to believe the damage done to *Weehawken* wasn't caused by floating mines set adrift by the Confederates but rather by Deitz's torpedoes.

John-Morgan's next step was to contact his old friend Will McQueen. With the help of the congressman's office and the expertise of a Savannah Gray member, retired Adm. Raphael Semmes, Citadel Class of '43, John-Morgan was able to acquire charts listing all known wrecks off the Georgia–South Carolina coast. In addition, Admiral Semmes was able to obtain declassified U.S. Navy charts detailing the locations of repeated sonar contacts on the ocean floor in these same areas. These charts had been developed by the navy at the advent of sonar during World War II for the purpose of identifying old wrecks. The coordinates were carefully plotted and used both during and after the war to distinguish between old and new sonar findings. Knowing the locations of previous sonar contacts helped the navy distinguish between sunken freighters and lurking submarines.

When the log of the USS *Nipsic* was reviewed, the entries concerning the rescue of Julius Caesar McQueen were discovered. After his name was cross-checked with the records of the Confederate States Navy, the Savannah Grays knew they were on to something. Swearing all members to secrecy, John-Morgan began quietly planning a search for the *Sword of Lee* the next summer.

Will McQueen was the first person John-Morgan invited to be a part of that expedition. When he received John-Morgan's invitation, Will accepted without hesitation.

With the help of Admiral Semmes and several other members of the Savannah Grays, John-Morgan had been able to narrow down the number of possible wreck sites for the *Sword of Lee*. Because the vessel was designed to operate in coastal waters not far from port, it was decided that the little ship carried only enough coal to give it a range of no more than fifty miles. Then the old navy charts showing the sonar findings from World War II were studied. Using the mouth of Wassaw Sound as the center, John-Morgan drew an arc extending fifty miles out into the Atlantic.

Three possible sites were chosen for the initial search. One location was forty miles due east from Wassaw Sound. There were Coast Guard notations at this place on the chart indicating an old sea buoy had been replaced in 1941 with a newer model then towed farther out to sea and sunk. During the war, the navy thought the sunken buoy was what they kept detecting with their primitive echo-location devices and noted it as such in their reports.

John-Morgan knew that in June of 1981, when Clive Cussler had been searching for the *Hunley,* an object the approximate size and shape of the submarine had been located using a magnetometer. Initial investigation at the time indicated an old Coast Guard buoy had been found. Fourteen years later, on a hunch, the site was explored again, and the CSS *Hunley* was discovered. On a similar hunch, John-Morgan decided to check out the old buoy site first.

I've had a wonderful time," said Charlotte, as she rode with Will to the Jesus Island dock. Will looked at Charlotte, smiled, and replied, "Seeing you was the last thing on earth I expected. To be perfectly honest, when Uncle Moses told me you were here, I wasn't very happy. Then things just sorta' melted away, and I kinda' feel the same way you do."

Other than the time she had spent talking with Brother Malachy, Charlotte had been with Will. They had traveled all over the island and had done everything from visiting with Sister Mystery and Dr. Divine to crabbing in McQueen Inlet. While there had not even been a good-night kiss between them, Charlotte felt drawn to Will. The emotions she had experienced on Driftwood Beach were still with her, but they weren't quite the same. She found him physically attractive, but there was something else about Will, something she'd never felt about a man before.

Charlotte was well acquainted with the initial thrill of a fresh romance and knew what it was like to have a handsome man hold and want her. Charlotte knew she was beautiful and understood why men pursued her; and for most of her life, that had been enough. But her time on Jesus Island had altered her perspective.

The ride from the main house to the dock was over an oyster-shell road lined on both sides with two-hundred-year-old oak trees forming a moss-draped tunnel through the forest. About halfway to the dock, Will stopped the Jeep and turned to Charlotte.

"Do you think you could manage to come back next weekend? I'd love to see you again," he said.

Charlotte looked up at the long strands of moss hanging from the branches then down at her hands. For several seconds she gave no reply, then she turned to Will and said, "The short answer is yes, I'd love to come back. The long answer is that I have neither the time nor the desire to be the object of another Will McQueen conquest."

Will started to speak, but Charlotte put her finger to his lips and said, "Just let me finish, OK?"

Will nodded, sat back, and listened as Charlotte continued, "I guess you could say you've already conquered me during that thunderstorm at the crab shack, Will."

Will shook his head and said, "Come on, Charlotte, I . . ."

"Let me finish, OK."

"All right, go ahead."

"You were so much better than I was back then, I mean as a person. I just used people, especially vulnerable people like you. I thought I was hot stuff then, and I thought I was hot stuff for a long time after that, Will. But something has changed in me, and this trip has made me see that change even more."

Charlotte stopped, drew a deep breath, looked Will in the eyes, and continued, "Will, I don't have time for games anymore." Charlotte studied Will's eyes. They were kind and always appeared to possess a hint of melancholy that made him seem sweet and accessible. She'd never seen that with Steve or Lane. Then she continued. "I like you, Will. I like you a lot, and it's a feeling I've never known before. I promise I won't mislead you, but I want the same thing out of you. I'll come back if you'll be honest with me."

Will and Moses watched as John-Morgan steered the *Admiral Graf Spee* out of Wassaw Sound and into Doomsday Creek. They listened while he throttled back on his engines and slowed as he came near. Moses remarked quietly, "Miss Charlotte done come back, Mista Will. I can see her sittin' on the side of the boat."

Will squinted and said, "Yeah, I see her, too. Come on and help me with their lines." Moses noted Will's smile as he caught the *Graf Spee*'s bowline from Michael Sullivan, another of his friends.

"Uncle Moses," shouted Bubba Silverman, "good to see ya' again!"

"Yes, suh, good to see you, too. It's been a long while," said Moses. Then he reached down and helped a slender brunette woman step off the boat.

"Uncle Moses, this is my wife, Ann-Marie," said John-Morgan, "I don't think y'all have ever met before."

Next Moses helped Charlotte step from the boat. "Welcome back, Miss Charlotte."

Charlotte smiled and said, "It's good to be back, Uncle Moses," then went to Will, gave him a hug, and simply said, "Hey, I missed you."

"OK, folks," said Will, "we've got the Jeep and the pickup here, so let's load your stuff and head on up to the cabins and get y'all settled in. Cocktails this evening will be in the main house at seven, dinner somewhere around eight. Malachy, Monsignor Mulvaney, and Francis will be eating with us tonight so be ready for some good conversation. We'll be shoving off in the morning."

May I fix you another, Monsignor?" asked Bubba Silverman.

"I believe so," replied Monsignor Mulvaney.

"It was Jameson, wasn't it? Monsignor."

The monsignor laughed and said, "Well, it should be, but I've grown fond of vodka over the years. Strange drink for an Irishman perhaps, but not when you consider vodka is made from potatoes. Maybe that's the attraction in it for me."

When he returned with the monsignor's vodka and tonic, Bubba felt compelled to apologize to Francis once more for his aunt Gretchen's behavior at the JEA.

"Francis, I want to tell you again how horrified I was by Aunt Gretchen's outburst and apologize for her and the whole family. I hope you understand what a sick, confused, and tortured person she was."

"I do completely, Bubba, and don't ever think I was angry with the poor soul. Only God knows what hell she suffered in her own mind."

Monsignor Mulvaney was unaware of the incident at the JEA and asked, "What are you two talking about?"

Bubba gave a sigh then recounted the story for the monsignor.

"Of all the people in the world," said Bubba, "I just for the life of me don't know why Gretchen would decide to fixate on Francis. In any event she's gone now, Monsignor, died the very next night. Fell in her bathroom at the nursing home and broke her neck when she hit her head on the side of the sink."

"May she rest in peace," said the monsignor, as he looked at Francis.

There was silence for a moment, then Bubba said, "Y'all please excuse me, I've got to get with John-Morgan and Will about tomorrow."

The cocktail party was on the same second-floor patio where Will and Charlotte had eaten breakfast the weekend before. It would be another hour before the sun went down, but a steady breeze from the sound kept everyone comfortable. Monsignor Mulvaney and Francis moved to the edge of the patio, placed their drinks on the low wall that surrounded it, and looked out into the vastness of the Atlantic Ocean. The monsignor was the first to speak.

"She recognized you, Francis."

"Yeah, she sure did. Thank God she'd been diagnosed with Alzheimer's; it could have gotten sticky. You know how Jews are about that concentration camp business."

"Yes, I do," responded the monsignor, who then looked sideways at Francis and said, "Seems like a stroke of incredible luck when she died the very next day, doesn't it?"

Francis didn't take his eyes off the darkening horizon when he replied, "It certainly does, Monsignor Mulvaney. One thing is for certain, though."

"And what might that be?"

"Dead Jews are like other dead people; they tell no tales."

Monsignor Mulvaney was staggered by Francis's response and placed his hand on the railing to steady himself as he felt the blood drain from his head. Francis noticed and started to brace him with a helping hand when the monsignor hissed, "Don't you dare touch me," then turned away and walked to the other side of the balcony, where he stood in stunned silence.

Later that evening, after the meal had ended and everyone had retired to the patio, Francis raised his glass and tapped it with a spoon. "May I have everyone's attention?" said Francis. "I have an announcement to make."

"I invited myself to the island this weekend because I had something to discuss with Will and was thrilled to find some of his close friends would also be here. So I decided to let you all in on a little secret that won't be a secret too much longer. As you all know, Will's name has been bandied about as a candidate for the seat of our late senator Coverdell. I serve in an advisory capacity to the Republican National Committee and was in Washington last week for a meeting. I'm authorized to tell you now that the committee feels Will is its best bet to keep that seat and will be throwing their significant financial muscle behind Congressman McQueen if he should choose to run."

"Bravo," said Bubba, as he slapped Will on the back and the others applauded.

"So as I said in the beginning, this is a secret right now but won't be too much longer. I ask that you all keep this to yourselves for the next couple of weeks while Will decides what he wants to do." Francis then raised his glass toward Will and said, "Congratulations, Congressman McQueen. You deserve it."

In the early morning of the next day, the sun colored the sand dunes on Jesus Island with a delicate brush. As it rose, pinks gave way to golden hues, while the cool night air still hung over the creeks that wandered through the marsh. Next to the dock on Doomsday Creek, a pair of porpoises broke through the calm water and breathed in the new day.

As they walked down the dock toward John-Morgan's boat, Will and Charlotte could hear waves breaking on Driftwood Beach.

"I was a little uneasy," confided Charlotte, "about how Ann-Marie would feel being around me."

"She's not like that," said Will. "What happened between you and John-Morgan was back when y'all were in high school. That was a long time ago; I'm sure she's over it now."

Charlotte took Will's hand as they walked and said, "I know, but I was kind of in the middle and well . . ."

"Listen," said Will, "Ann-Marie has John-Morgan, and that's all she ever wanted, I promise."

Charlotte was silent for a few steps then asked, "What about Mike Sullivan? Didn't he get divorced?"

"Yeah, twice," replied Will. "Mike still carries around some pretty heavy baggage from 'Nam. What he went through in the war still eats at him pretty bad. I think he feels guilty about getting the Medal of Honor. Guys like Mike know they're just like everybody else, but everybody else doesn't know that. He gets judged by a different and higher standard. It's like when he got busted for a DUI. It made the paper 'cause he was a Medal of Honor recipient and for no other reason. It's hard on him."

"He's helped you a lot, hasn't he?"

"Couldn't ask for a stronger supporter. He's been my point man with the veterans' organizations. When I can't show up at some function, I know I can always count on Mike to fill in for me."

"What about Bubba?" asked Charlotte. "I thought he lived in Atlanta and was married to some rich Christian girl?"

"He was," said Will, "but that's changed, too. Bubba rejected everything he was raised with to marry Gail. Things worked for a long time, but then his father got sick, and he started coming back to Savannah a lot. I don't exactly know what happened between Bubba and Gail, but I kinda think she turned out to be a spoiled pain in the butt. Anyway, they got divorced a few years ago, and Bubba moved back to be closer to his parents."

19. To the Bottom of the Sea

*He goes a great voyage that goes
to the bottom of the sea.*

—GEORGE HERBERT,
"Jacula Prudentum,"
1651

The *Admiral Graf Spee* pushed with great strength against the incoming tide in Wassaw Sound. Her new twin 225-hp Yamahas easily drove the Grady White's twenty-six-foot hull through the gentle swells that rolled in off the Atlantic.

Out over the ocean, the June sun tinted wisps of clouds with coral, and the early light turned the *Graf Spee*'s hull a light rose color. At the helm John-Morgan pressed the throttles forward and brought the engines to forty-two hundred rpms. The Grady White was a heavy, robust craft, considered by many to be the Mercedes-Benz of boats, and she rode well as she left the confines of Wassaw Sound, pressing away from the Georgia Coast.

Scattered about the boat were all the accoutrements of scuba diving, along with maps bearing the location of half a dozen suspected shipwrecks. This was the glue that held her crew together. That, their love of history, and their determination to find the final resting place of the CSS *Sword of Lee*.

The *Graf Spee* churned her way through the Atlantic until the murky, olive-drab waters of the sound and adjacent coastal area gave way to the clear emerald green waters a dozen or so miles out at sea.

It took almost two hours for the *Graf Spee* to reach the *Sword of Lee* search site. It was a cloudless sky, and the Atlantic was calm with a three-knot wind from the southwest. For an hour John-Morgan guided his boat over a square mile area where the old navy charts indicated a sea buoy had been sunk in 1941. The ocean floor was sandy and flat, and any objects projecting above the seabed would be detected by the *Graf Spee*'s sonar. Will, Mike, and Bubba watched the sonar screen and made notations with the GPS (global-positioning system) whenever an interesting outline appeared. At the completion of the search, the desired sonar findings were reviewed and the GPS coordinates checked, and a determination was made about where to dive. To conserve air only three divers went into the water to examine what was on the bottom. This routine continued until two in the afternoon, when Mike climbed aboard the *Graf Spee* and announced, "I think we've found an old submarine!"

"Unbelievable," was the first thing Bubba said, after he had pulled himself onto the *Graf Spee*'s swim platform and removed his face mask. Mike was already in the cockpit getting two more tanks of air ready.

"It's a Nazi sub, John-Morgan, I swear," blurted out Mike, as he pulled a tank out of the rack and began hooking up his regulator.

"It's leaning to the side a little and about halfway covered in silt. Looks like part of the stern is missing, probably blown away. Some of the bow is gone, too. But it's a sub, man, it's a Nazi sub!"

"Did y'all try to get inside or anything?" asked John-Morgan.

"Naw, we were at the end of our air," said Mike. "I was so excited I was afraid I'd forget to decompress. It's the wildest thing you ever saw, John-Morgan. It's covered with growth, plates buckled in on the side, and there's a periscope sticking up from the conning tower."

As Will started getting himself ready to dive, he asked, "How do you know it's a Nazi sub?"

"'Cause there's a swastika painted on the control tower," said Bubba. "It made my skin crawl, but I want to go back down."

While John-Morgan wrestled with his weight belt, he said, "We've got enough air for fifteen minutes on the bottom, and that's all, but I just gotta see if I can get inside."

At eighty-five feet down, artificial light was necessary. But even with limited illumination, it was clear the remains of a submarine had been discovered.

Will and John-Morgan swam to the conning tower and inspected the insignia painted on it. John-Morgan rubbed away nearly sixty years of growth to reveal the painting of a wreath surrounding a Nazi helmet crossed by swords. John-Morgan didn't need this to identify the ship, though. He was well versed in the history of submarine warfare off the Atlantic Coast and knew they had found a Type-IX U-boat.

While Will and John-Morgan were inspecting the conning tower, Bubba and Mike were poking around for openings in the sub's hull. They found one where the stern had been damaged.

Entering the engine room through a large tear in its bulkhead, Mike and Bubba carefully swam between the two nine-cylinder diesel engines. Their flashlights cut beams of light through the water, while particles stirred up by their movements floated in and out of view. Lying on the narrow walkway between the engines, Bubba saw a large wrench, then a china plate, followed by another tool of some kind. When his light fell on an empty shoe, an eerie feeling came over him. Mike's light found an array of dials, gauges, and levers, all partially encrusted with growth but seemingly well preserved and ready to respond to the engines.

After inspecting the sub's exterior, Will and John-Morgan swam to the ship's bow and began probing for a way in. What they found was a jungle of twisted pipes and wires where the forward torpedo room and crews' quarters had been. Will caught his air hose on the pipes several times as he maneuvered through this maze toward the relative order of the ship's galley and officers' wardroom. John-Morgan had the same thing happen to him and became concerned they both might sever their air lines entangled on the jagged metal that was everywhere.

John-Morgan and Will were finally able to pick their way into the relatively intact galley that opened into the officers' wardroom. In the galley the remains of a three-burner electric stove stood next to a small refrigerator. Overhead, scores of pipes ran fore and aft, with valves and knobs sprouting out like metal mushrooms. There was sediment on the deck, but the black-and-white checkerboard pattern of linoleum tile was still visible. In the officers' quarters, Will shined his light on a set of storage compartments with half a dozen coffee mugs piled up in one corner. A double-stacked row of bunks, their bedding long ago rotted away, lined either side of the passageway leading to a closed bulkhead door. John-Morgan knew that past this door was the radio room and captain's quarters.

Together, John-Morgan and Will strained to turn the wheel on the door, but it wouldn't budge. Looking at his watch, John-Morgan motioned to Will that their time on the bottom was over, and they started back through the twisted pipes and out of U-123. At the other end of the wreck, Bubba and Mike were doing the same thing.

"I've dreamed all my life of finding something like this," said John-Morgan, as Ann-Marie helped him remove his air tanks.

Will sat on the gunnels and gazed out over the ocean. Then he turned to Charlotte and remarked, "I've never seen anything like this. It's incredible. It's like finding an open grave. I kept expecting to see a skeleton or something, but we didn't find any."

On the trip back to Jesus Island, everyone agreed to keep what they had found a secret. Mike summed it up best when he said, "If this gets out, there'll be a hundred people bugging us about where the sub is. When we leave to come back out here, they'll find a way to follow us. This sub is a big, big deal. It'll be picked apart before we have a chance to go over it. Trust me, y'all, treasure hunters are a cutthroat bunch. Let's do our thing first, haul out what we want, then quietly turn our information over to the Georgia Historical Society and let them figure out what to do with the rest of it."

Francis had been right when he'd said the news about Will would get out quickly; he'd just been wrong about how it would happen. He failed to consider the possibility that one of the servants at the main house might let the story slip.

It was Tyrone Polite, Uncle Moses's nephew and part-time employee on the island, who'd overheard Francis's grand announcement and had called his friend Shenika Gadsen. Shenika did the late-night news for WSAV-TV and didn't waste any time letting her boss at the station know about Tyrone's gossip. That set off a whole series of phone calls to Atlanta and Washington; and by the time the *Graf Spee* had reached the dock at Jesus Island, Lane Bradford had been calling Charlotte's cell phone for two hours.

"Goddamnit, Charlotte, where the hell have you been?" snarled Lane, when he finally reached her.

"Out on a boat in the middle of the Atlantic Ocean. I didn't take my phone with me because they don't have relay towers at sea, Lane," replied Charlotte sarcastically.

"Well," snapped Lane, "I've heard all about Will's endorsement by the Republican party, and I want you to find out more. Were you at that little shindig last night where Francis Quinn made the announcement?"

"Who told you about that, Lane?"

"So you were there," shot back Lane. "Lemme tell ya', Charlotte, regardless of all the other bullshit between you and me, you still work for CNC, and they pay your salary, lady. When you fail to report something like this, you're cheating the network out of their money, and that makes Ed very, very angry. Follow me?"

"Look, Lane, I was asked not to say anything. So was everybody else. You ought to know better than anybody what the rules are when something's off the record."

"Forget that bullshit 'cause the cat's way out the bag now. You owe the network a scoop on this thing, and I don't want some puff piece like you did last week. Are you going soft on McQueen or something?" asked Lane.

"I'll do what I can," responded Charlotte.

"Have something good for me when I get there," replied Lane.

Charlotte stiffened and said, "Don't tell me you're coming down here."

"As soon as I can get things straight up here."

The *Graf Spee* was anchored over the U-123 by ten o'clock the next morning. It had been decided that all four men would dive together in a group effort to gain entry to the control room and captain's quarters. Everyone thought either the bulkhead door from the engine room or the one from the officers' wardroom could be forced open. They decided to try the door from the engine room first. With this in mind, Mike had scrounged around the island and found a three-foot section of steel pipe he planned to wedge in the sprockets of the wheel that locked and unlocked the watertight door.

Once inside the stern, Will and his friends glided past the twenty-foot-long diesels again to the control room door. Air from the previous dive was trapped along the top of the compartment and shone like globs of mercury in the glow from their lanterns. Will cast his light across an array of dials and gauges and spotted the ship's telegraph, its needle pointing to "halt."

While Will and John-Morgan held the lights, Mike and Bubba swam to the door and wedged the bar in the spokes of the wheel. Mike was the strongest and tried to turn the wheel by himself but couldn't; then with hand signals he indicated to Bubba that he needed help, and they both pulled on the bar.

Sound travels very well through water, and everyone heard the creak and scrape of metal on metal as the wheel started to slowly turn. In the harsh light, the divers watched the metal rods securing the door begin to slide out of their slots in the bulkhead. Mike was excited and held up one finger to Bubba, indicating that one more try would do it.

When engaging in hazardous activities such as diving on sunken wrecks, it's a good idea not to make assumptions; but one had been made about U-123. The previous night, during the discussion of the wreck that carried through dinner and late into the evening, everyone agreed that all compartments on the sub were flooded.

The first hint that something serious was about to happen was when Will saw bits of debris suspended in the water start to move to the edges of the door. An instant later his eyes grew wide as he watched sediment on the deck being sucked through an invisible crack at the door's bottom. He wanted to scream but knew he couldn't. Instead, he reached out in panic and tried to grab Mike just as the door gave way. Then thousands of gallons of seawater under tons of pressure blew the door open and rushed into the control room, carrying Mike with it.

Bubba and John-Morgan had realized what was about to happen only a split second after Will, and all three were able to grab on to something just before the door swung open. Their lanterns were sucked into the control room with the water, and Bubba had his mouthpiece pulled out, but all three were able to hold on until the pressure had equalized.

In less than five seconds the two dry compartments were filled with water. Will and his two friends swam into the control room toward the light from their lanterns. Inside the compartment, all sorts of debris had been stirred up by the rush of the water. In horror, John-Morgan watched as the mummified remains of a corpse floated past and recoiled as another bumped against him in the swirl of the current.

Will found Mike pressed against the periscope in the center of the control room. His face mask had been torn away, but Mike was still clutching his mouthpiece between his teeth and still breathing. His eyes were tightly closed, and Will shook Mike to let him know he was there. When he did, Mike opened his eyes, blinked several times from the sting of the saltwater, then gave a thumbs-up. John-Morgan found Mike's face mask caught on the conning tower ladder and brought it to him. He put it on, blew air into it through his nose, and was able to see again. For almost a minute, all four men floated motionless in the flooded control room and by the light from their lanterns beheld a most incredible sight.

Everything buoyant had floated to the top of the compartment, and pieces of dried corpses were pressed against the overhead pipes. When the water rushed in, its force had broken off the remains of arms, legs, and skulls from the dead, and these all lay scattered about the deck. Shreds of cloth from their uniforms drifted amid the silt, while the remains of an officer's cap began to settle back to the decking.

John-Morgan tapped Will and motioned for him to follow. Together they swam past the periscope and two large steering wheels that operated the hydroplanes. They were in the sub's nerve center, and all around was a maze of valves, gauges, handwheels, and pipes. John-Morgan turned his light on a series of speaking tubes used to communicate with the rest of the ship. Some of the tubes bore labels that said, *SPRECHEN KUCHE,* or *SPRECHEN MASCHINEN.* Others said *SPRECHEN DIESELMOTRAM* and *ANPFEIFEN BUGTORPEDORAUM.* John-Morgan knew this sub's first officer had stood at this spot during her last hours and relayed the captain's orders to his dying ship.

John-Morgan and Will glided through the open bulkhead door that led from the control room into the captain's quarters and radio room. Once in the radio room, their lights revealed a black typewriter sitting on a desktop attached to the ship's hull. Next to the typewriter was an old-fashioned wind-up phonograph with a record sitting on the turntable. Next to that was a pair of earphones plugged into a large, overhead radio set. On a separate shelf Will found what he thought was a smaller typewriter in a wooden box. John-Morgan recognized it immediately as the Enigma cipher machine used so extensively by the Germans.

Across the passageway from the radio room was the captain's quarters. It was small, and the only privacy afforded to the ship's master came from a simple draw curtain that had long ago rotted away. The contents of the captain's quarters and radio room had not been badly disturbed by the rushing water, so when John-Morgan and Will played their lights on the captain's bunk, they found his remains still lying there.

Most of Captain Hardeman's uniform had rotted away, revealing dark, leathery skin stretched tightly over his skeleton. In a way it appeared that some of the body had melted into the bunk. Will shined his light at the nickel-plated Walther P-38 pistol lying askew between the captain's legs, nudged John-Morgan, and pointed to the pistol. John-Morgan nodded his head in reply then shined his light around the rest of the cabin. When he noticed a small safe welded to the bulkhead, he swam over.

The safe was about a foot square, with a standard combination dial and locking handle. When John-Morgan tried the handle, it moved. When he pulled against it, the door opened and a small rush of seawater poured in, filling the little safe. Inside were several stacks of papers and a rubberized pouch. John-Morgan reached in to retrieve the papers, and they started to disintegrate, but the pouch stayed intact.

Bubba and Mike swam into the captain's quarters and looked around. Then Bubba tapped on his watch and motioned that it was time to head for the surface. On the way out, John-Morgan took the pouch with him while Will picked up the captain's pistol.

Back on the *Graf Spee,* the four could hardly contain themselves. John-Morgan's hand trembled as he removed the contents of the pouch and spread them out on the galley table. The papers were in remarkably good shape, legible for the most part, and there was even a photo among them. He read and spoke some German and would try to interpret them later; but for the present, there was plenty of air and much more booty to haul out of U-123.

There were two more dives that day, but Mike didn't go down. He said he felt OK, but he had been badly bruised when he was thrown against the periscope and thought it best if he stayed topside and kept the girls company. By three that afternoon, several large bruises had formed on Mike's chest, back, and his right leg. His thigh was swollen and painful to touch, and he told John-Morgan it hurt to breathe, adding that he'd probably broken a couple of ribs. John-Morgan and the others could tell Mike was in more pain than he was admitting and canceled the last dive for the day. With a load of trophies from the wreck of U-123, the *Graf Spee* pointed her bow toward the setting sun and Jesus Island.

At supper that evening, everyone tried to be discreet about the discovery of the U-boat and not discuss it in front of Moses or his nephew Tyrone. Uncle Moses had been around the McQueens long enough to have heard hundreds of confidential conversations and knew not to repeat anything. Besides, he was loyal to Will and the memory of his father and considered himself to be part of the McQueen family. He reasoned that what happened to the McQueens happened to him. His great-nephew had another point of view.

Tyrone had never lived on Jesus Island. His grandmother Minnie was Moses's sister, but she'd left the island as a teenager, and Tyrone had never developed an attachment for the island or the McQueens. He had never known his father, and his mother had drifted in and out of his life. By forfeiture, responsibility for Tyrone fell to his grandmother.

Minnie had done the best she could; but when Tyrone became too much to handle, Minnie often called upon Uncle Moses to act as disciplinarian. Because of this Tyrone grew to resent Moses, but it was

Moses who insisted that Tyrone receive a college education, even pay-ing his tuition.

Tyrone was in his last year at Savannah State University; and in addi-tion to his resentment for Moses, he had come to regard him as an Uncle Tom. He was also offended by the fact that his ancestors had once worked as slaves in the cotton fields of Jesus Island and that the family who had originally enslaved his people still owned it. While he had no particular dislike for Will and had never been mistreated by him, the fact was that Tyrone was an angry young man who worked at Jesus Island only because of the pay and benefits.

While Moses let what he heard slip in one ear and out the other, Tyrone soaked up every bit of conversation. When Lane Bradford learned from Tyrone's girlfriend at the TV station that he was the source of her information, it wasn't difficult for Lane to persuade Tyrone to share any further stories with him, especially when Lane paid so well.

"This is fabulous stuff," said John-Morgan, as he spread out the doc-uments from the sub on the library conference table. Tyrone was in the room delivering after-dinner drinks and was hardly noticed as everyone crowded around to examine the papers. It wasn't difficult to see the Nazi eagle and swastika that adorned the tops of many of the pages; and from bits of conversation, Tyrone was able to piece together the fact that Will and his friends had discovered a Nazi submarine. He wasn't sure how important this was but thought it was something Lane Brad-ford might find interesting.

20. The Fifth Commandment

Q: What is the fifth Commandment?
A: "You shall not kill."

— *The Baltimore Catechism*, 1948

John-Morgan and Will watched the weather channel as they sipped coffee in the solarium of the main house. At nine o'clock the sun cascaded through the room's stained-glass windows, pouring reds and oranges across the white tablecloth. Outside, the pointed spears of yucca plants rustled in a northeast wind, while on the TV a pretty brunette in a yellow pants suit explained the movement of a low-pressure area that had formed off the coast near Jacksonville.

"Looks like you were right last night, John-Morgan," said Will. "We aren't going out today or probably even tomorrow. It won't be bad here, but out where the wreck is, they'll probably have eight-foot seas and forty-knot gusts."

"Is the trip canceled?" asked Charlotte, when she walked in with Ann-Marie.

"Yeah, looks like it," said Will.

John-Morgan lowered the paper he had his head buried in and said, "You know, not being able to go out today is really just fine with me. I know somebody who can translate all that German in those papers."

Bubba took a bite of his toast, thanked Tyrone for the coffee refill, then watched to make sure he was out of the room before saying in a jocular tone, "I wish that picture weren't so faded; I'd swear that guy looks familiar."

Will chuckled, saying, "I think he looks like Clark Gable sans the stick-out ears and mustache."

"It looks like he has pretty eyes," remarked Ann-Marie, while she admired the freshly cut daisies sitting in the center of the breakfast table, "but it's hard to tell. John-Morgan, were you and Bubba able to translate any of that German last night before you went to bed?"

"Some," replied John-Morgan, "but most of it was over our heads. One thing is for certain, though."

"What?" asked Ann-Marie.

"I did recognize a name and signature at the end of what appears to be a set of orders," said John-Morgan.

"Whose name was that?" asked Charlotte.

"None other than Adm. Wilhelm Canaris," said John-Morgan, "the head of the Abwehr, which was the German War Ministry's intelligence and counterintelligence service. I'd be willing to bet the guy in that picture was a spy who was to be put ashore by that sub. We were able to read the dates on those papers, and they coincide perfectly with Operation Pastorius, which took place during that time and was the same operation where the Germans slipped people into New Jersey and Florida. That sub just got sunk before they were able to get him ashore."

"Where's Mike?" asked Ann-Marie.

"Still in bed," said Bubba. "I don't think he was feeling too good this morning."

"I tell ya," injected John-Morgan, "I think he was hurting a lot more than he said he was. Y'all should have seen those bruises by the end of the day. I told him last night I was worried about phlebitis in his right leg. I've treated him for it before, and I thought it might be a good idea to evaluate him further; but everybody knows how hardheaded he is. I just hope he at least took the aspirin I recommended."

Sonny Weiler's office was on Bull Street close to Forsyth Park. Not only was he John-Morgan's friend and lawyer, he also spoke German, and Will had agreed to let Sonny translate the papers from the submarine. After they'd left the papers with his secretary, John-Morgan and Bubba went to the headquarters of the Georgia Historical Society. The society had an excellent research library, and Bubba and John-Morgan pored over their microfilm copies of the *Savannah Morning Gazette*. Several dates appeared in the text of the documents, and they decided to check through the old newspapers around those dates for anything that might relate to German submarine activity. It didn't take long to find something.

"Wow," whispered John-Morgan, when the April 9, 1942, *Gazette* front page scrolled into view.

"Whatcha got?" asked Bubba.

"Listen to this headline. It says, 'U-boat sinks *Esso Baton Rouge* and SS *Oklahoma* twelve miles off St. Simons.' You think this could be our sub?"

Their suspicions were heightened when they read the *Gazette* headlines of April 10th, which said, "Nazi Sub Bombed Off Coast." The body of the story told about a sub that had been chased by a destroyer and bombed by planes, but said that a confirmed kill had not been established. An hour later they were sitting in Sonny Weiler's office listening to his translation.

"I had some problems with some of these terms," said Sonny, "and parts of it were illegible, but here's the body of the text."

Sonny leaned back in his chair and read, while occasionally glancing at John-Morgan and Bubba over the reading glasses perched on his nose.

"You will accept on your warship the individual here identified by these accompanying documents as code name Sea Lion. On March 2, you will depart Lorient and take a direct course to the U.S. East Coast. Make your descent through naval quadrant CB opposite Norfolk and steer for the Georgia coast in quadrant CA. On April 7, you will proceed to quadrant 6475 DB off Ossabaw Island, where you will rendezvous with an American shrimping boat named *Dixie Warrior*. You will place Sea Lion on this vessel and depart immediately. On April 8, you will, at your discretion, engage and sink any enemy vessels you encounter."

Sonny looked up and said, "It's signed by Wilhelm Canaris, a big shot in the spy business if I recall correctly."

"What do the ID papers on this Sea Lion say, Sonny?" asked John-Morgan.

"The usual stuff." Then Sonny rattled off Sea Lion's height, weight, hair, and eye color. When he got to the line that said, "distinguishing marks and characteristics," he looked up.

"I can't make out the whole thing, but it says, 'Port-wine stain, back of neck, 3.5cm by 1cm, shaped like,' and then the rest is smudged."

John-Morgan thanked Sonny; and when he stood to leave, the lawyer asked, "What in the hell is this all about? Y'all chasing Nazi spies or something. A little late for that, isn't it?"

"Yeah, real late." John-Morgan laughed. "They're just some old papers we got hold of and were wondering what they said. Thanks for the help."

"My pleasure," replied Sonny. Then he asked, "Have y'all heard all that stuff about Will McQueen running for the Senate?"

"Yeah," said John-Morgan, "pretty hard to miss."

"Well, the word is he's got it in the bag," said Sonny, as he walked John-Morgan and Bubba to the door.

Out on the street Bubba turned to John-Morgan and said, "Those orders say for that sub to put Sea Lion on a shrimp boat on April 7th and then go hunting for ships the next day. The *Baton Rouge* and *Oklahoma* were torpedoed on the eighth. On the tenth, the *Gazette* has a piece about a sub being bombed. By my way of thinking, we've found the sub that sank those two ships; and if her captain followed his orders, which I'm sure he did, then this Sea Lion did not go down with the sub we found. He got put ashore somewhere around here."

"Yeah," said John-Morgan, "and something else seems funny to me."

"What?"

"When I was going over those newspapers, I think I remember reading something about a shrimp boat named *Dixie Warrior*. Let's go back over there and check it out."

It didn't take ten minutes for John-Morgan to locate the April 8th copy of the *Savannah Evening News* that carried a story about the murder of the *Dixie Warrior*'s crew.

I was wondering when you'd be coming by," said Monsignor Mulvaney when Francis appeared in the sacristy door at Blessed Sacrament Church. The monsignor had just finished saying the eight o'clock mass. Without saying anything else, he took a seat in the pew next to the altar of the Blessed Virgin Mary. Francis followed and sat next to him.

For several minutes neither man said anything as Francis stared at the stained-glass window on the other side of the church and the monsignor fiddled with his rosary beads, occasionally glancing at the Virgin's statue. Francis was the first to speak.

"I had to Mike," whispered Francis, "she recognized me."

"I understand why," replied the Monsignor. "I just don't understand how."

Then Monsignor Mulvaney turned and said, "For so long I was able to live with myself and the knowledge of what you were because I saw you as a soldier. But killing that old woman . . . it's just more than I can fathom."

Monsignor Mulvaney stopped for a moment, drew a breath, then continued. "As I said, Francis, I understand your motivation. I don't say that it's right, but I understand your instincts for self-preservation. I just don't know how a man your age could find it in himself to do such a thing. It calls into question all that I've believed we were fighting for. What kind of a monster did our people create? Why did you kill people in that concentration camp, Francis? Just how did you bring yourself to it?"

In hushed tones Francis explained why he'd felt compelled to kill Nathan Eisenman at Bergen-Belsen then rationalized the murder of Gretchen Meyer by saying that his exposure would ruin the lives of many innocent people, including that of Will McQueen. "Besides," whispered Francis, "it wasn't like she was a kid or something. She was old and suffering with Alzheimer's."

"Dear God," said the monsignor, as he shook his head; then he asked, "Are you here for me to listen to your confession and grant you absolution, Francis? Is that what this is all about?"

Francis sighed, looked at the blue votive candles burning before Mary's statue, and said, "I really came just to explain to you so you'd maybe understand why, but yeah, Mike, maybe you can call this a confession of sorts. But I'm not asking for absolution from you or anybody else; I did what I had to do to survive. I simply never dreamed that after all these years something like this would happen. I just couldn't see another way out. As far as I'm concerned, the circumstances are the same as when I killed that prisoner at the camp."

"We're both old now, Francis," said Monsignor Mulvaney. "I can't imagine what it's like to be faced with killing someone when you're as old as we are. You don't seem the least bit sorry for what you've done. You still look at this like you're in combat and that old lady you killed was a soldier out to shoot you. For the love of God, you even think that what you did was less evil because she was old and demented. You disgust me."

Tears formed in Francis's eyes, and he wouldn't look at the monsignor when he said, "I would imagine a man like you welcomes death, Michael. You've killed; and if that was a sin, you've certainly redeemed yourself in the years since then. I was a soldier, too; but in a way I never got to stop being one. All I care about is Will McQueen, and I'm not going to let anybody or anything stand in that boy's way."

Both men were silent for several minutes. Then Monsignor Mulvaney raised his head toward the altar and looked at the crucified Christ hanging above it.

"Do you believe in God anymore, Francis?" asked the monsignor.

"I'm an old man now, Michael, I have to."

Still not feeling so hot, are you?" asked John-Morgan, when he saw Mike at supper that evening.

"Naw, I'm not. My leg is really swollen and hurts like hell. So does my chest."

"You're going back into town in the morning, Mike," said John-Morgan. "The last thing we want is for you to have a pulmonary embolism, and that's what could happen. I think you need to go into the hospital."

"Aw, man," said Mike, "I don't want to go into the hospital. I want to go back out to that sub."

"People in hell want ice water, too," said Will. "We can't go tomorrow anyway 'cause the weather out at the wreck will still be too rough. So just go on and do what John-Morgan says, OK?"

The old General Oglethorpe Hotel on the Wilmington River had been empty for a number of years before a private investor group purchased the building and converted it into upscale condominiums. Francis was one of the first to purchase a unit and lived there by himself.

In a way moving to the old hotel was a sentimental gesture, an attempt to be around reminders of his younger years and happier times. It was almost like a homecoming, too, since Francis had been one of the silent, almost invisible financiers who'd had a hand in running the General Oglethorpe when the mob owned it. During that time a number of underworld figures had been guests there, some stopping over on their way to fancier digs in South Florida, some hiding out, and Francis knew them all. Frankie Carbo was one of those Francis knew best.

Frankie had a long history of involvement with the Mafia and its related activities. When Francis first met him, Frankie was in the fight-promotion business and was in Savannah to organize the first nationally televised, closed-circuit boxing match. It was the 1955 Marciano-Moore fight at Yankee Stadium and was televised to a capacity crowd at the old City Auditorium in Savannah. At the time Francis was still involved with Willie Hart and his gambling ventures. As it turned out, Willie had garnered a piece of the action; and after the fight was over, everybody, including Frankie Carbo, had done well. Over the years Frankie had returned to the General Oglethorpe, and from those visits, a business relationship with Francis had developed.

Francis was a source of funding for Carbo and often made large cash loans to him on the basis of only a handshake. Frankie was always good for the money, but the relationship was cut short when Frankie was sentenced to twenty-five years for conspiring to extort money from welterweight boxing champion Don Jordan. After that, Francis dealt with Frankie's friends.

The last loan Francis had made was to Vincent Magesto in 1990. It wasn't terribly large, only two hundred thousand, but things went sour, and Francis wasn't repaid. This loan was also sealed with a handshake, and only Francis and Vinnie knew about it. For a long time Francis was patient, but in the last year he had begun to press for his money.

I'm tellin' ya, Mr. Bradford," said Tyrone, "I think the congressman and his friends have found a German submarine."

Lane got up from his chair and walked over to the wet bar. "You want another one, Tyrone?"

"Yes, sir."

Lane fixed another Crown Royal and ginger ale for Tyrone and returned to his chair by the window, where he watched for a moment as a fully loaded container ship glided past on its way up the Savannah River.

"Look, Tyrone, what McQueen does with his buddies doesn't really interest me unless he's breaking the law or something, know what I mean?"

"Yeah, Mr. Bradford, you're looking for dirt."

"You can call it what you want, Tyrone, but I'm looking for a story, whatever it turns out to be; and if you can help me, there's a nice piece of change in it for you."

Lane fished an envelope with five hundred dollars in it out of his coat pocket and pushed it across the table.

"Thanks, Mr. Bradford," said Tyrone, as he stuffed the money into his jeans pocket.

"It's Lane, Tyrone, you can call me Lane. Now tell me what else is happening on Jesus Island."

Tyrone smiled and said, "OK, Lane," then proceeded to tell him everything he knew. When he got to the part about Charlotte and Will, Lane let out a grunt and said, "I knew that little bitch was getting sweet on him."

Lane sat back and thought for a moment then asked, "Did you say they have some papers from this sub?"

"Yes, sir."

"Do you know where they're kept? I mean could you get to 'em and read 'em if you wanted to?"

"Yeah, Will keeps 'em in the drawer of his father's old desk. He doesn't know it, but I saw him put 'em in there last night."

Lane scratched his head and said, "Well, it might not be anything like what I really want, but you think you could take a peek at those papers, you know, read over 'em and kinda' fill me in on what they're all about?"

"No problem at all."

Mike Sullivan was so uncomfortable he registered just a mild protest when John-Morgan insisted on admitting him to Memorial Health University Medical Center in Savannah. About the only comment he made on the boat trip back to the mainland was, "Being in the hospital is a hell of a way to spend my vacation."

As a younger man, Mike had been large and powerfully built. In middle age he'd gained weight, exercised little, and drank too much. He had a family history of hypertension and heart disease, with his father succumbing to a heart attack at fifty-five. With prior episodes of deep-vein thrombosis in his legs, the injuries he had received aboard U-123 put him at risk for having a clot form in one of those veins. If that happened, the clot could break off and travel to his lungs. Once there, it could block a pulmonary artery, perhaps resulting in death.

Mike seemed to be responding to treatment the first day of his hospitalization; but on the second day, John-Morgan's worst fears were realized when he got a call from the nurses' station that Mike was beginning to demonstrate signs that multiple small clots, known as "shower emboli," were forming in his lungs. Before John-Morgan was able to reach the hospital, Mike had succumbed to a pulmonary embolism.

Mike's funeral mass was held at the Cathedral of Saint John the Baptist in downtown Savannah. Even though it was the largest Catholic

Church in the city, the crowd was so great it spilled out onto the street. It was a military funeral, and the casket was carried on the shoulders of marines from Parris Island. Will, John-Morgan, and Bubba were listed as honorary pallbearers and followed behind as Mike's remains were carried into the church.

Bubba had been upset by the death of his friend; but as he sat in the first pew and studied the stained-glass windows above the main altar, he wasn't thinking of Mike. Something had been troubling him ever since the papers from the sub had been found. In his mind he kept mulling over the description of Sea Lion, but what troubled Bubba the most was the unsettling feeling that he knew the man in the photograph.

At the end of the service, Mike's coffin was again shouldered by the marines for the solemn procession out of the church. When a lone bagpiper high in the choir loft started to play "Amazing Grace," Mike and his friends began their long walk down the center aisle. As he walked behind the coffin, Bubba recognized a score of faces. About halfway down the aisle he observed Francis and watched as Francis's head turned to follow the flag-draped casket as it passed. He noticed the dark red birthmark on the back of Francis's neck and remembered his aunt Gretchen and the incident at the JEA pool. It was then that Bubba realized the man in the faded picture looked like Francis Quinn.

His aunt Gretchen's screams tore at Bubba as he walked past Francis. "Port-wine stain, back of neck, left side," echoed in his head. On the way to Bonaventure Cemetery, every time Bubba closed his eyes, all he could see was the newspaper headline about the murders on the *Dixie Warrior*. At the cemetery, Francis was standing on the other side of Mike's open grave across from Bubba. While the bugler played taps and Mike's coffin was slowly lowered into the ground, Bubba stared at Francis, trying to convince himself that he was wrong. When the service was over and people started leaving, Bubba got Will aside.

"I need to talk to you privately," said Bubba.

"About what?"

"Not here, Will. We need to go back out to the island right away. I've got to see those papers again. It's about Sea Lion. I think I know who he is."

At the same time the seven-man firing squad from Parris Island was touching off its last volley in honor of Mike Sullivan, Tyrone was by himself in the big house back on Jesus Island. Even Moses had gone to Savannah for the funeral, so Tyrone felt safe as he crept up the stairs to the library. He sat behind Jimmy McQueen's old desk and opened the bottom right-hand drawer. He removed the black rubber pouch and placed it on the top of the desk. On the outside of the pouch, embossed in flaking silver, was the word KREIGSMARINE. Tyrone's hands trembled a little as he opened the pouch and removed the papers. On the top of the stack was Sonny Weiler's translation and the photograph of Sea Lion. The rest of the papers were all originals and all in German. When he read the translation, Tyrone whistled and said to himself, "Lane's gonna like this."

H oly shit," whispered Will, when he looked at the photo of Sea Lion, "I see what you mean. This does favor Francis, but it can't be, it just can't be."

Bubba was standing next to the desk holding Sea Lion's identity papers in his hands, looking at the line that said, distinguishing marks." The smudged word Sonny Weiler couldn't read looked like it started with an "I" and had six or seven letters. Bubba thought one of the letters was maybe a "T" or an "L." He laid the paper in front of Will and said, "You know, this word could be 'Italien.'"

"This just can't be Francis," said Will. "He went to Europe during the war and fought with the army there. He worked with my father at the shipyard before that. There's just no way."

Bubba pulled a chair up next to the desk and sat down. He rubbed his brow, sighed, and asked, "Is Francis from Savannah? I mean, how long did your parents know him?"

"He's from New York," said Will. "The story I got was that he was raised in a Catholic orphanage and never knew who his mother or father were."

"Do you know when he came to Savannah?" asked Bubba.

"I'm not sure," said Will, "but it was during the war. Since he was working at the yard with my father, it had to be at the beginning of the war."

"Is there any way you can find out for sure?"

"I can call my mother; she'd probably know," replied Will.

Bubba sat by the desk and listened while Will talked with his mother. When he hung up, Will shook his head and let out a sigh.

"Well," asked Bubba.

"She says he came here about April of 1942. She remembers because that was the month he pulled my father out of an old ship that blew up and saved his life. That means it's possible that he was the one who was put aboard the *Dixie Warrior* on April 7, 1942."

"Then it's possible he really could be Sea Lion."

Will shook his head in amazement and said, "This is all just too much. I've known Francis all my life. He fought in Italy during the Second World War. Hell, he was awarded the damn Bronze Star for valor. This man isn't some Nazi spy put in Savannah from a submarine! This is just too far-fetched, Bubba."

"Yeah, damn far-fetched, Will, but what if it's true?"

Picking up the photo, Bubba said, "You've got to admit this picture sure looks like a young Francis Quinn, and the physical description fits him to a tee. But the real kicker is the birthmark."

Bubba put the photo down, held up the identity paper, pointed to the illegible word, and said, "Francis has a birthmark that's shaped like Italy exactly where this paper says it is; and if this smudged word says, 'Italien,' that seals it for me."

Will shifted in his chair and replied, "OK, let's assume that Sea Lion is really Francis. What do we do about it?"

Bubba hadn't really thought about that yet and wasn't sure what to say; but after a moment he blurted out, "For God's sake, man, he's a fucking war criminal if you can believe what my aunt Gretchen said. If you don't buy that, then, at the very least he's a Nazi spy! What do you mean, 'What do we do about it?' We turn the bastard in!"

Will leaned forward, rested his elbows on the desk, and ran his fingers through his hair. Then he looked at Bubba and quietly said, "We gotta know more, Bubba. We also gotta think about everything that could happen if this gets out, all the people it could involve."

Bubba leaned back and looked at Will in shock, then he said, "Yeah, we gotta be sure, but what's all this bullshit about thinking about what might happen to other people? The fucker killed innocent people in a Nazi concentration camp!"

Bubba pointed at his chest and said, "He helped kill *my* people, Congressman, *my* people. Isn't that enough for you? If that's not, then how about being a spy for a foreign power that was at war with your country, Congressman? It sounds like you're telling me you're worried about what this might do to you politically. Is that what you mean?"

"I mean give me a fucking chance to digest all this stuff," said Will angrily. "This is just too preposterous to understand, OK? One minute Francis Quinn is a lifelong friend, and in the next second, he's a Nazi spy. Just settle back for a second and let me think, OK?"

When Tyrone heard Moses's truck pull up, he quietly stepped away from the library door and slipped down the stairs. He'd heard everything Will and Bubba had talked about; and as soon as he was able, he called Lane Bradford and told him about the papers he'd read, the photo he'd seen, and the conversation he'd overheard. He'd also hand copied Sonny Weiler's translation and read it to him over the phone.

After he finished talking to Tyrone, Lane sat on the edge of his bed and dialed his office. He told his secretary he'd be in Savannah for at least another week, then accessed his voice mail. The message from Charlotte really riled him, but there was nothing he could do about it.

"Hello, Mr. Bradford. This is Charlotte Drayton calling to tell you that I'll be taking some sick-and-tired leave, perhaps two weeks. If a doctor's note is required, please let me know because I'll be happy to have my doctor put in writing how all the pressure I've been under lately has just gotten my nerves in a frazzle. He's been so helpful and cooperative. I've been able to tell him all about everything that's been bothering me. I'll call Becky and tell her I won't be back on Monday so she can get somebody to fill in for me. Well, so long, and thanks for understanding. Oh, I think I was supposed to remind you that your anniversary is on the twenty-ninth and you need to get Cindy a present. 'Bye."

Under his breath Lane muttered, "Fuckin' bitch," then got out his Palm Pilot and started looking up numbers. The first call went to an old friend in McClean, Virginia, he'd worked with at the Pentagon. The second was to a buddy at the FBI offices in Washington. They both owed Lane big favors, and he intended to call in his debts. He knew that millions of pages of documents had been declassified in both the Departments of Defense and Justice, especially files from the fifties and earlier. He also called a source at the Department of State.

What Lane asked for was anything that could be found regarding the insertion of spies on the Georgia coast during World War II, and all they had on Francis Joseph Quinn. His sources told him it would take a day or so to get the information together.

It had been unbearably hot at the cemetery, and everyone at supper that night was grateful for the early evening storm that cooled the island. The rain came heavy at times, and the wind was so gusty several small limbs were torn from the trees surrounding the big house. Out over the ocean the sky still flickered with lightning, sending a gentle rumble of faraway thunder across Jesus Island.

After supper everyone gathered in the library. The conversation was mostly about Mike until around ten-thirty when Bubba pulled Will aside and said, "I think we ought to tell them. Lay it all out and see what they have to say, Will. It wouldn't hurt to have some other opinions."

Will removed the papers from his desk, placed them on the long, cherry wood table in the center of the room, and announced that what they were about to hear must he held in the strictest confidence. For the next thirty minutes, Bubba used the papers to explain why he thought Sea Lion and Francis Quinn were the same person. In the hallway, lingering in the shadows, was Tyrone. He had heard every word.

The following day, on Lane's instructions, his office contacted Charlotte and told her to call him at his hotel. She was reluctant and angry but made the call anyway.

"Now I understand how you feel, Charlotte," answered Lane, "and I've been thinking things over. I've decided you're right about us, and I apologize for the way I talked to you. You've got your own life to live; and I understand that what was between us can't go anywhere for you, and I sincerely wish you the best. But we still have jobs to do with the network, and I want to call a truce with you so we can both protect our positions there. You've got a son to raise, and I've got a wife . . . well, you know what I mean, so how's about let's smoke the peace pipe and put the other stuff aside so we can get on with business, OK?"

Charlotte hesitated and almost told Lane to shove it, but she realized he was right about protecting her job and decided to take him up on his offer.

"OK, Lane," replied Charlotte, "I'll bury the hatchet, but I still want to stay here a little longer. I like it here on this island; it's given me a chance to decompress and unwind."

"Hey," said Lane, "go ahead and take the full two weeks; you've earned it. Just do me one favor, though."

"What?"

"You know I'm down here for this McQueen political stuff, and I'd really like to be able to talk to Will. He's been pretty removed from the press, and I was hoping you'd be able to help with it."

Charlotte was silent for a moment, then said, "All you want to do is trash him."

"All I want to do is talk to him, Charlotte. He's going to have to talk sooner or later. I don't care one way or the other about his politics; I just want a good story for our—and I want to emphasize the word *our*—network. Will you help me on this?"

That Friday began gently on Jesus Island. The tide was out, exposing the beaches to the morning sun; and at the water's edge sandpipers picked their way through foam left by the waves. The breeze hardly rippled the waters of Doomsday Creek, and John-Morgan paused to watch as a great blue heron took to its wings and flew away. He was wiping the morning dew off the windshield of the *Graf Spee* when Bubba arrived with his bag and tossed it into the boat.

"Sleep all right?" asked John-Morgan.

"Not really," answered Bubba. "I kept waking up thinking about Francis Quinn and then looking at that empty bed next to me and thinking about Mike. It's been one hell of a week. I wish we'd never found that U-boat."

"Me, too," said John-Morgan, as he went to the stern to check his engines.

"I appreciate you taking me back to town, John-Morgan. I wish I could stay; but the Sabbath starts at sundown, and I'd just as soon go back now as later in the day."

"Actually," said John-Morgan, "this works out just fine, 'cause I needed to go back in and take care of some things at the office. I think Ann-Marie is looking forward to some time by herself out here while I'm gone."

John-Morgan guided the *Graf Spee* into the middle of Doomsday Creek, startling a pair of egrets feeding by the marsh and causing them to flap their large, white wings in alarm. Thousands of mud fiddlers scurried into their holes along the creek bank as the boat moved into Wassaw Sound. Just before he brought his boat to cruising speed, John-Morgan turned to Bubba and asked, "What do you think is going to happen with this Francis Quinn thing, Bubba?"

"I don't know," was Bubba's only reply.

Lane had come over later in the morning from Priest's Landing in a borrowed thirty-foot Sea Ray; and just when he and Moses finished tying off his boat, Will and Charlotte arrived at the dock.

Lane stuck out his hand and said, "Congressman, it's been a long time."

When they got in the Jeep, Will told Lane they'd first ride to the beach then go by the old slave cabins. After that they'd drive across the island to see Sister Mystery and Dr. Divine, then stop by Saint Andrew's Chapel so Lane could meet Brother Malachy.

"We'll wind it up with lunch at the main house, where we can talk about whatever's on your mind," said Will.

It was close to eleven when Will pulled up at Sister Mystery's cabin. Nothing much had changed with the old place over the years. There was still a Lucifer and a Jezebel, probably ten generations removed from the originals. They came running out from under the porch and menacingly circled the Jeep, snapping and howling until Dr. Divine appeared at the front door and with a booming voice ordered them back under the house.

"Dr. Divine," said Will, "this is Mr. Bradford, the man I told you about yesterday. He was interested in meeting you and Sister Mystery."

Dr. Divine was tall and thin and wore an old, black, double-breasted suit and a white shirt with the collar buttoned at the top but no tie. Instead, a cross of silver inlaid with topaz hung from his neck on a heavy chain. He was past seventy now but spry in his walk and looked much younger than his years. His voice was deep, and he occasionally sang bass with one of the church choirs in Savannah. A scraggly goatee sprouted from his chin, and his eyes were hidden by a pair of expensive Aviator sunglasses. He wore rings on three fingers of both hands and bowed with a flourish to Charlotte when she got out of the Jeep. Then he turned to Lane and said, "How'd do, suh."

"Sista inside," said Dr. Divine. "She don't get out much anymore 'cause a health so come on in."

Dr. Divine led his guests into the same room where Sister Mystery had read Will's palm years before. Little had changed there too; and over in the corner, sitting in the same chair, was Sister Mystery. Her skin was leathery now with deep wrinkles. A large, black candle burned on the table next to her; and when Lane walked into the room, she didn't move or say a word. But when Will came in behind him, she sat up straight and exclaimed, "Lawd God in Heaven, come here, Mista Will, and give ol' Sista Mystery a hug 'round her neck."

After Will hugged Sister Mystery, he stepped back, motioned toward Lane, and said, "Sister, this is Lane Bradford. He works for a big TV station in Atlanta and is doing a story on the island. He wanted to meet you and the doctor and maybe have you look at his palm and read his fortune."

Sister Mystery cackled and said, "Well, come on over here and sit next to Sister Mystery, boy, and lemme see your hand.

"Uh huh," was the only sound Sister Mystery uttered as she took Lane's hand in hers. Several times she stretched the skin on his palm to make the lines stand out more, and several times she looked into Lane's eyes. After a minute she folded his fingers into his palm and pushed his hand away.

Lane didn't believe in anything but himself and had difficulty hiding the smirk on his lips. He was impressed with the show but saw it as nothing more than theatrics and didn't think for a minute Sister Mystery had the slightest ability to decipher his future or that of anyone else.

While it was debatable that Sister Mystery had the ability to see into the future, she was without peer in her ability to read all of the subtle signs of body language, eye contact, and voice inflection. She could even smell changes in body odor brought on by stress and fear and recognized the changes in pupil diameter caused by the same emotions. She was also well versed in the vagaries of human nature and could spot a phony in a New York minute.

"Well," asked Lane, in a voice that Sister Mystery recognized as being laced with disdain, "what did you see, Sister Mystery?"

"You right with your maker?" asked Sister Mystery.

Lane thought that was all bullshit, too, and felt like saying so, but instead he chuckled a little and answered, "Yes, ma'am, right as I'm gonna be."

"Ain't no laughin' matter if a man ain't right with God," said Sister Mystery. "Ya never know when the Master of the House come callin' for ya."

"I'll go along with that, Sister Mystery, but what did you see about my future?"

Sister Mystery sat in silence for a moment then said, "I seen you is gonna come to know a great truth right shortly, suh."

"Whatdaya mean by that?" asked Lane, barely hiding the amusement in his voice.

"Sista don't know that, mista, she only know you is gonna find out about somethin' that few mens ever knowed." Then she grew silent, indicating the session was over.

Out on the porch, Lane handed Dr. Divine a hundred-dollar bill, saying, "Please accept this as an offering to Sister Mystery. I can't tell you how interesting it was to meet her."

Dr. Divine took the money, held it up to the light and inspected it to make sure it wasn't counterfeit, then said, "Thank you, suh," and slipped it into his pocket.

On the way down the steps, Lane turned to Dr. Divine and said, "You know, I've heard that you could summon up spirits from a lake out here on the island. Is there any chance I could see you do something like that?"

"Yes suh," said Dr. Divine, "but I can't promise you nothin', and tryin' to call up a spirit from da lake don't come cheap."

"Well, how about tomorrow afternoon and another donation like today?" asked Lane.

"Best to go at dark," said Dr. Divine, "spirits like to roam at night."

Placing his glass back on the table, Lane said, "I didn't bring a camera with me today, Will, because I wanted this to be informal and relaxed. Tomorrow I'd like to come back with a camera and get some stuff on tape, but I don't have anybody to shoot for me."

Lane looked over at Charlotte, who was sitting across from Will, and asked, "You think you could handle that for me, Charlotte?"

"Yes, sir, I think I can."

"Great," said Lane, then turned to Will and started asking all the usual questions Will had come to expect. There were no curveballs or trick questions; and when it looked like the interview was winding down, Charlotte relaxed and started to watch a pair of squirrels chase each other through the trees.

Then Lane leaned forward in his chair and said, "The real reason I don't have a crew with me today is that I've uncovered some information I'd like to ask you about; and out of respect for you and your office, Will, I didn't want to spring it on you *Sixty Minutes* style, if you know what I mean."

Charlotte could feel the blood draining out of her face and a knot forming in her stomach. Will didn't know what to expect but prayed Lane wasn't talking about Francis Quinn.

"Well, fire away, Lane," said Will. "What's the big question?"

"It concerns the death of Mike Sullivan, Will."

Will let out a deep sigh and looked over at Charlotte, who was holding her breath.

"OK, what about it?"

"Well, I've been told that he was hurt diving on a Nazi submarine that you and your friends found."

"Where did you hear that?" asked Will.

"From hospital personnel who took care of Mike," replied Lane. "They said he got delusional a couple of times and started talking about finding a Nazi sub with you and John-Morgan. Is there any truth in that?"

Will sat back in his chair, more relieved than anything else.

"OK, Lane, I'll make a deal with you."

"Like what?" asked Lane.

"I'll give you an exclusive on the best story of your life if you promise me you won't release it until I say so."

Lane cocked his head to one side and asked, "Why and when?"

"Because I haven't made up my mind yet on whether or not I'm going to run for the Senate, that's why. When I've decided what I want to do, and I've made my announcement, then you can release the story, OK?"

"You've got a deal, Congressman."

"One more thing, Lane. I don't want you to tell a living soul anything that you're about to hear and see until I've said you can, nobody, not anybody at the network, not even Ed. Is that clear?"

"Yeah, I understand. You've got a deal on that," said Lane, trying to suppress his excitement.

It took Will almost an hour to tell the story of how he and his friends had started out to find the *Sword of Lee* and ended up stumbling over the wreck of the U-123 and how Mike had been hurt. He even took Lane up to the library and into a closet where he'd stored the artifacts removed from the wreck.

Charlotte drove Lane back to the dock while Will stayed in the library and returned his calls. When they got to the dock, Lane thanked Charlotte for her help and added, "You know, this story could be really big for both of us. Ed's been talking about somebody new for the Washington bureau; and if this works out like I think it will, you could have that job on a platter. He's acting like a single guy again, too, Charlotte; and take it from me, he's noticed you more than once."

Charlotte was sitting in the driver's seat with both hands resting on the steering wheel and looked away from Lane when he told her about

Ed's interests. After a moment she looked back at him and said, "Isn't that Ed's boat you're using today?"

"Yep, sure is," replied Lane.

"Well, tell Ed I appreciate his interest; and as for Washington, tell him seeing is believing." Then she revved the engine and said, "Time to go, Lane darlin'. See you tomorrow."

Tyrone was working on the dock when Lane walked down the gangway and started toward Ed's Sea Ray. Behind it was the *Miss Geechee,* and Moses was aboard making repairs. Tyrone didn't know his uncle was watching through a porthole when Lane approached and spoke to him.

"How ya' doin', Tyrone?" asked Lane.

"OK. Did you get what you wanted today?"

"Some of it," said Lane. "I'll be back tomorrow with a camera for the rest."

Lane drew in closer to Tyrone and said in a low voice, "I was in the library today. That big desk in front of the window, is that where those papers are?"

"Yeah, in the bottom right-hand drawer. Will's got a bunch of things from the sub stacked in the closet off to the side."

"I know, he showed me; but he didn't say a word about the papers. I just played along. You think you could swipe them for me? All I need is that picture and the stuff about that Sea Lion guy."

"Tellin' tales is one thing, man," said Tyrone. "Going into Will's desk and takin' something is another. That's stealin, and what if I get caught? There ain't exactly a whole lot of people out here who could get in there and take something. They'd suspect me just by a process of elimination."

Lane smiled and said, "I understand that; but after I get this story together, the last thing in the world Will McQueen will be worrying about is who took those papers."

"I don't know, man, that's some heavy shit," said Tyrone.

Lane reached into his pocket, pulled out a roll, peeled off two bills, and said, "Here're a couple of hundreds just for considering it. There'll be another three if you put the papers in my hand before I leave here tomorrow."

Tyrone looked for Moses; and when he didn't see him, he took the money, stuffed it in his pants, and said, "I'll think about it."

While he couldn't hear what Tyrone and Lane were saying, Moses had seen money change hands, and it made him suspicious. After Lane had pulled away from the dock, he confronted Tyrone.

"Mighty tight with the TV man, ain't ya'?" said Moses, after he closed the door to the dock house.

"Anything wrong with being nice to folks?" asked Tyrone, as he washed his hands.

"Bein' nice is one thing; bein' chummy with some slick, white fella' is another."

"Lane's an important guy in Atlanta, Moses, and he said he'd be glad to help me out when I finish up at State."

"Lane!" said Moses. "Who you to be callin' some big-shot white fella by his first name?"

"He's a cool guy, and he's different from Will McQueen and his friends. He doesn't expect us to go around bowing and scraping to whites like you do, Moses. When are you going to see that you ain't nothing but an Uncle Tom?"

"Is he where you been gettin' the money to buy them fancy shoes and dat gold chain you been sportin' 'round in?"

"I ain't got shit from him, old man," said Tyrone, in a contemptuous tone.

Moses had worked with his hands all of his life, and they were large and strong. Even at seventy-three, he was an exceptional specimen of a man, weighing 225 pounds and standing six feet, two inches tall. Tyrone was a scrawny 140 pounds, barely five feet nine, and even at twenty-two he was no match for Moses McQueen.

Before Tyrone could even try to move, Moses had him pinned against the wall with his left arm across his chest, while he reached into Tyrone's pocket with his right hand and pulled out the money. He held it up to Tyrone's face and said, "I seen your buddy Lane give you this here cash, an' I got a feelin' it was for somethin' that ain't no good. Now are you gonna tell your ol' uncle Moses what you been takin' money from dat man for, or do you want me to beat your scrawny little ass, Mr. College Man?"

Tyrone tried to struggle, but Moses only leaned against him harder, grabbed his crotch, and lifted him off the ground. Tyrone's eyes popped wide open, and he screamed in pain, but Moses didn't let go.

"I can hold you here all day long if you want me to, boy, and I'll do just dat lessin you tell me what dat man givin' you money for," said Uncle Moses, before he squeezed Tyrone's testicles a little harder.

When Tyrone screamed as loud as he could, Moses said, "Yell all you want, boy, there ain't nary a soul around to hear you. Now what was dis here money for?"

"I'll tell ya'; I'll tell ya'," cried Tyrone, "jes lemme down, lemme down!"

Moses lowered Tyrone until his feet were on the floor but kept him pinned against the wall and didn't let go of his crotch.

"Well," growled Moses, "what was the money for?"

"Gettin' him girls," blurted out Tyrone.

"That's bullshit," said Moses, "he don't need some wet-behind-the-ears colored boy to round up pussy for him. Who you think you talkin' to?" Then Moses clamped down on Tyrone's testicles once more and Tyrone screamed, "All right, all right, it was to tell him about Will."

"Tell him what about Will?"

"Everything I know."

"Like what?"

"Like about that German submarine he done found and who calls and what all I hear 'em talkin' 'bout when I'm around," said a sobbing Tyrone.

"Anything else?"

"That's all. I done told you all I know, now lemme go."

Moses squeezed Tyrone's crotch one more time, put his face against Tyrone's, and whispered, "It damn well better be."

Tyrone dropped to the floor crying and curled into a fetal position, holding his crotch. Moses stood over him and said, "I ain't gonna tell your momma 'bout this 'cause it'd kill her. I also ain't sure what I'm gonna do with you," then he looked at the two one-hundred-dollar bills in his hand and tossed them on the floor next to Tyrone.

"Here's your money. I hopes dat you enjoys it, but I kinda thinks it's like them thirty pieces a silver that the chief priests gived to Judas when he went and sold out Jesus. Ain't no good gonna come from money like that."

A lengthy fax was waiting for Lane when he got back to the Marriott, and another came while he was taking a shower. The first was from his friend at the FBI, and it detailed all the suspicions the Bureau had about Francis Quinn's connections to organized crime.

The second fax was from Lane's contact in the Department of Defense. This report briefly described the capture of Nazi spies inserted into Maine, New Jersey, and Florida, as well as suspicions that "a German agent had been active in the Savannah, Georgia, area during the month of April 1942. This suspicion is heightened by the murder of two shrimpers found on their boat in the town of Thunderbolt, a fishing village just outside of Savannah. They had both been dispatched by a point-blank gunshot to the head with a 4-mm bullet. This is an extremely unusual projectile of the same caliber known to have been employed by German agents." The report further stated it was the belief of army intelligence that if there had been an agent in Savannah, he had survived the war and could still be living in the area.

Lane didn't get a fax from his friend at the State Department, but she did call at four stating she preferred not to send anything in writing.

"Look, Lane," she said, "here's the way it is. When we enter into treaties with other nations, there are all these little confidential sidebar agreements that don't appear on the document the diplomats sign. These agreements can be about all kinds of things. Take England and the United States, for example. You know both nations are involved with the peace talks in Northern Ireland, and even before that we had arrangements with the Republic of Ireland during World War II. One of the little side agreements we made with the Irish—and the English weren't too happy about it—was that the Brits would take the heat off some of the IRA boys who had popped some English soldiers and come over here to hide."

"So what are you trying to tell me?" asked Lane.

"Well," said the voice from Washington, "we didn't have anything on a Francis Joseph Quinn; but since you're down there in Savannah, I thought I'd tell you what I did come across."

"OK," replied Lane, "shoot."

"This was done back in 1940 when we were engaged in the lend-lease negotiations with the Brits. They were upset because they had discovered the IRA was cutting deals with the Germans for guns and munitions that involved IRA members becoming spies for the Nazis. Their MI-5 unit claimed an IRA member had been trained in Germany and had been inserted into the States by a sub. I also found some stuff that's been declassified that involves a Catholic priest who was stationed in Savannah during that time. His name was Michael Mulvaney. It seems that the British suspected him of killing two of their boys over in Ireland. They never could prove it, but this Mulvaney character sort of took refuge in the priesthood and was sent to America. The British kept pestering us for permission to interrogate him, maybe even deport him, but some congressman from Boston with deep Irish roots insisted that part of the deal had to include the Brits taking the heat off of Mulvaney. There were several other priests named, too, but he was the only one down your way."

"OK," said Lane, "I appreciate the help."

"Are we square now?" asked the lady from State.

21. When the Master Cometh

*"Watch ye therefore: for ye
know not when the master of the
house cometh, at even, or at midnight,
or at the cockcrowing, or in the morning."*

—King James Version, Mark, 13:35

Monsignor Mulvancy had just finished saying the eight o'clock mass Saturday morning and was on his way to the rectory when a stranger approached.

"Monsignor Mulvaney?"

"Yes."

"I'm Lane Bradford of the Cable News Channel, would you mind if I asked you a few questions about some church history?"

"Well," said the monsignor, "I'm hardly an expert on such things, but I'll do my best. I've got a luncheon engagement at twelve-thirty, but if you're not talkin' about more than half an hour or so, I think I can spare the time."

Monsignor Mulvaney led Lane into one of the consultation rooms on the first floor of Blessed Sacrament's rectory. A statue of the Infant Jesus of Prague rested on a small table next to Lane's chair, and on the opposite wall was a cross with a very lifelike and tortured figure of Jesus nailed to it. The monsignor settled into a chair below the crucifix.

Sitting upright and strong, Michael Mulvaney was a vibrant man for his age who looked as though he had been born to wear the Roman collar around his neck. He was almost completely bald and wore wire-rimmed glasses and a hearing aid. His hands were large, like those of a farmer, and they perfectly matched the broadness of his shoulders. While he had the body of a yeoman, his face was that of a scholar; and Lane almost regretted what he was about to do.

"Are you aware, Monsignor," asked Lane, "that Congressman McQueen, Mike Sullivan, and some other friends of his have located the wreck of a Nazi submarine off the coast?"

The monsignor looked surprised and replied, "Why no, I'm not. That's incredible. I haven't heard a word. They never said anything about that to me. Is this the wreck they were diving for when Mike Sullivan was injured?"

"Yes, it is."

Monsignor Mulvaney thought for a moment, then said, "I'd love to hear more about it, but you said you had some questions on church history, didn't you?"

Lane leaned forward and said, "Well, you see, Monsignor, I think that sub has something to do with you and Francis Quinn."

The monsignor set his jaw firm and said, "What is your question, Mr. Bradford?"

"I'll cut to the chase for you, Monsignor. I have evidence that indicates you were a former member of the IRA and were suspected of killing two British soldiers when you lived in Ireland."

Monsignor Mulvaney sat stone faced and didn't take his eyes off Lane.

"This evidence indicates you entered the seminary to avoid suspicion and that later you were sent to this country when the British began to close in on you."

Lane stopped and waited for the monsignor's to reply; and when there was none, he continued. However, he decided to employ the trick of stating as fact something he wasn't sure really was the truth, in addition to throwing in what Tyrone had told him about Francis.

"What was then called the Department of War, now Defense, as well as the FBI and army counterintelligence, came to believe that a Nazi sub put a spy ashore here at Savannah in 1942. They also believe there was some connection to the IRA and that Quinn was involved in this, too. Do you have any comment on that, Monsignor?"

"I don't, not a word," replied the monsignor in an icy tone. Then he continued. "I'm an old man now," said the monsignor, "and I've heard thousands of stories in the confessional about any subject you might care to mention. I've also been told some pretty fantastic tales over a good glass of Jameson, Mr. Bradford, but none of them can match the one you've told me here today. Good day to you, sir, and the house-keeper will show you out."

M oses was standing on the dock when Lane nudged Ed's big Sea Ray into the spot behind *Miss Geechee*. As he passed a line to Moses, he asked, "Where's Tyrone? He was supposed to drive me around the island."

"Da rascal, he ain't showed up," said Moses. "I jes don't understand how these young folks today expects to make a living when they goes and lays out anytime dey takes a notion to."

"Tyrone's not here?" asked Lane.

"Naw suh, but don't worry, Mr. Will done told me to carry you up to the house, so come on and I'll help ya with ya things, Mr. Bradford. Hope ya' don't mind ridin' in my ol' pickup."

Lane was decidedly upset that Tyrone was not on the island. The documents and photograph pulled from the U-123 were an integral part of his story, the only hard evidence he had that might link Francis to the German sub, and he had to have them. All the way to the McQueen House, he was thinking of a way to get his hand on the papers. When Moses stopped at the front entrance to the house, Lane had decided on a plan.

"Where would you like to shoot the video?" asked Will, as he helped Lane carry the camera and tripod inside.

"Well," said Lane, "I thought the library was just about the most interesting room in the whole house, and the light coming through those tall widows would be perfect. Could we do it there?"

Will agreed and told Lane to go to the library and start setting up his equipment while he got Charlotte from her cabin. When Lane got to the library, he went immediately to the big desk and opened the lower right drawer. The rubber pouch was sitting right where Tyrone said it would be; and when Lane opened it, the first thing he saw was the picture of Sea Lion, his identity papers, Captain Hardegen's orders, and Sonny Weiler's translation. When he looked at the picture of Sea Lion, he had no problem seeing the resemblance to Francis, especially in the eyes. He smiled, said, "Thank you, Tyrone" under his breath, then stuffed the papers, along with the photograph, into one of the large pockets of his cargo pants. By the time Will returned with Charlotte, Lane was waiting patiently on the veranda.

Lane had chosen the full-length portrait of the original William Wallace McQueen, first owner of Jesus Island, as the backdrop for his video. William was dressed in the Scots Highlander's kilt he'd worn when he was with Oglethorpe at Bloody Marsh, and Will bore a striking resemblance to his ancestor. Lane thought it was just the right touch he needed to emphasize Will's aristocratic ancestry and one that would play well into his scheme since he believed most people had no sympathy for the rich and well established.

Charlotte was good with the camera and was actually happy Lane had asked her to handle it because she was able to select angles that were flattering to Will. Will was straightforward, just as he'd promised, and his description of the sub and how Mike Sullivan had been fatally injured was so vivid, Lane knew he had a winner of a story even without the Francis Quinn tie-in. Toward the end of the interview, Lane sprang his trap, even though Will didn't realize it.

"Now, Congressman," said Lane, "everyone knows about your relationship with Francis Quinn. As a matter of fact, you're already quoted as saying that Mr. Quinn has been like a father to you, and you don't deny his financial support of your campaigns going all the way back to your first run for the Georgia State Senate. Is that correct?"

Will thought for a moment. Although he was uncomfortable with the question because of what had been found in the sub, he assumed that no one other than those involved in the discovery knew about Francis and Sea Lion. He was also acutely aware that his long association with Francis was well-known and documented. Any attempt at evasion or equivocation at this point would only raise suspicions.

"Mr. Bradford, you've stated my feelings correctly," said Will. "I know that many years ago Francis Quinn was involved in some local gambling operations. There was no great stigma to that then. As a matter of fact, at the time, Savannah was known as the Free and Independent State of Chatham. You see, Mr. Bradford, I want to be straight with the voters. I want them to know that I don't turn my back on people who have been good to me just because they might have been involved with something like gambling that was illegal years ago but that the state of Georgia now openly promotes with the lottery. I'm not going to run from the truth or try to twist or spin it. In all my dealings with him, Francis Quinn has been aboveboard." Then Will looked into the camera and continued, "Francis Quinn was a friend of my late father. He saved my father's life once. Francis was with my father when he went to Japan after I was wounded in Vietnam. My father later told me that he didn't know what he would have done without Francis to lean on while I was fighting for my life. I've represented the people of the First District for a long time now, and they know me. I guess all I can say is that if it bothers somebody that I'm friends with Francis, then they don't have to vote for me."

Lane leaned forward in his chair, extended his hand, and said, "I guess that about says it all, Congressman. Thank you for taking the time to be with our viewers and for sharing your thoughts and feelings with them. This has truly been an extraordinary interview."

Will had already planned to have Charlotte drive Lane around the island to shoot some more video while he took care of some business. After some small talk about The Citadel, Lane said good-bye to Will, and he and Charlotte headed for the beach. They were almost to the dunes overlooking Driftwood Beach when Lane decided to tell Charlotte what he knew about Francis and Monsignor Mulvaney, but he thought it best not to tell her about stealing the papers from Will's desk.

"Look, Charlotte," said Lane, "this is going to be a huge story. I know you kind of like Will, and he's not a bad guy, but he's going down and going down hard. Do you think he could even be elected dog-catcher after I break this story about Quinn and Mulvaney?"

Charlotte turned to Lane and said, "Do you have to do this? You just set the guy up. Why?"

"Because it's my job, that's why," said Lane, "and it's your job, too.

Listen, remember I told you about that slot in Washington? Well, I talked to Ed yesterday after I left here, and he asked about you specifically. I told him you were in on this story with me. I'm telling you this is gonna be bigger than you can imagine. Holy shit, Charlotte, a Nazi submarine, a dead Medal of Honor winner, a priest who was in the IRA, the friend of a congressman who might be a German spy, and the congressman lies about it right on camera. There're reporters who dream all their lives about having a story like this. They'd give anything just to be a part of it, and I'm asking you to help me with it. Just substantiate what I already know. You're the inside source. This will make the cover of *TIME, Newsweek,* you name it. I've got enough to go with now; but if you help, hell, it's airtight. You can name your number with Ed. The two of us will be like Woodward and Bernstein for God's sake."

Charlotte stopped the Jeep on the sandy meadow just before the dunes and thought for a moment. She knew he had more than enough without her, and he was right; it would be a story of colossal proportions, and it would bury Will five minutes after it hit. So Charlotte decided to buy time while she tried to think of something, anything, to stop Lane Bradford.

"All right," said Charlotte, "this whole thing sucks, and you especially suck, Lane, but if you can promise me a byline and that job in DC, I'll help. But don't you dare try to screw me, you little bastard."

Lane threw his hands up and said, "Hey, you don't need to say anymore. I'm being straight with you on this. Ed says we come through with something big, we write our own tickets."

"How much does he know about the specifics of this story?" asked Charlotte.

"Nada, nothing. I'm saving the whole thing to drop in his lap when I get back to Atlanta," replied Lane.

"Anybody else know anything?"

"Not a soul. You think I'm stupid enough to let this out. No, ma'am, this is my baby one hundred percent. I wouldn't trust that bunch of sharks we work with for a minute. You're the only one who knows what I know."

It was almost six, and Charlotte was in the Jeep waiting for Lane to finish with the camera. He was at the end of the dock shooting a video of porpoises playing in Doomsday Creek when Moses and Malachy approached Charlotte.

"Miss Charlotte, I need to speak with ya'."

"What's wrong, Uncle Moses?"

"I ain't told nobody 'bout this but Malachy. It's been eatin' at me, and I thought 'cause you and Mr. Will was so close, and 'cause you knows that Lane fella, I could tell you and see what'cha thinks about it before I goes and tells Mista Will and he takes to worrying 'bout it."

Charlotte glanced over at Malachy, who remained silent, then said, "All right, Uncle Moses. What's the matter?"

"It's Tyrone, Miss Charlotte."

Charlotte wrinkled her brow and said, "I noticed he wasn't here today, Uncle Moses. What's wrong?"

"He ain't here 'cause I done run him off."

"For what?"

Moses looked over his shoulder at Lane to make sure he was out of hearing range then said, "It's him, Miss Charlotte. I seen him givin' Tyrone money yesterday; and when I got that boy aside and called him on it, he told me that Mr. Bradford done been payin' him money to spy on Mr. Will and tell him what all Will been sayin' to folks and what happens out here an' just everything. I show nuf been upset, Miss Charlotte, and thought maybe you might know what to do."

Charlotte took a quick look down the dock at Lane then Malachy and said, "Oh God, Uncle Moses, almost the same thing has happened to me, and I don't know what to do either. Mr. Bradford just told me he's going to do a story on Will that will probably finish him. He's going to use Will's friendship with Francis Quinn and some other stuff from a long time ago to destroy him. It's too involved to tell you about right now, but I'm playing along with him while I try to think of something that I can do to stop him. I haven't said anything to Will about it yet 'cause I just found out a little while ago."

Tears started to form in Charlotte's eyes when she looked at Moses, and he took her hand and said, "Now, Miss Charlotte, don't be lettin' go with your feelin's right now; that ain't gonna help us at all."

Charlotte held on to Moses's hand and stole another look down the dock at Lane. He was talking to John-Morgan and hadn't noticed Moses standing by the Jeep.

"Who else know 'bout this, Miss Charlotte?" asked Moses.

"Nobody except you and me and now Malachy."

"When he leavin' da island?"

Charlotte quickly wiped her eyes and said, "Probably after he finishes up with shooting some pictures down at Dr. Divine's house this evening. He asked Dr. Divine about calling up some spirits or something, and he's supposed to go down there after dark. I'm gonna' work the camera for him. I guess he'll go back to town when that's done."

Moses thought for a moment then said, "He goin' to Dr. Divine's place tonight for a callin' up a da spirits?"

"Uh huh."

"Well, chile," said Uncle Moses gently, "don't go sayin' nothin' to Mr. Will right yet. You is gotta have faith and pray for help, ain't dat right, Malachy?"

Malachy nodded his head and quietly said, "Prayer is a powerful weapon, Charlotte."

"Put it in da Lawd's hands, honey," continued Moses, "an' He'll take care of it."

As Charlotte and Lane were pulling away, Moses looked at Malachy, and their eyes locked. Neither man said a word. After a few moments, Malachy turned and quickly headed for Saint Andrew's Chapel.

Because Dr. Divine wasn't inclined to call up the spirits until after dark, Will invited Lane to have dinner with him and his friends. The crabs John-Morgan and Ann-Marie had caught the day before had found their way into Uncle Moses's crab cake recipe, and he was standing at the stove browning them in a large frying pan when Charlotte and Lane walked in.

"Mr. Bradford," said Moses, "you in for a treat tonight. These here is crab cakes my momma taught me how to make. Everything in 'em is from right here on the island, from the crabs and vegetables to the spices."

"I can't wait to taste 'em," replied Lane, as he looked over at Charlotte.

"Miss Charlotte told me the two of you was goin' down to Dr. Divine's place for a visit tonight," said Moses, as he gently nudged the golden brown cakes in his favorite iron skillet.

"That's right," answered Lane, "she's going to be my cameraman."

"Ain't no place for a lady down there tonight," said Moses, without taking his eyes off the skillet.

"Whatcha' mean by that?" asked Lane.

"Hot and nasty down there. Bugs be carryin' Miss Charlotte away," said Moses, as he glanced over his shoulder at Charlotte.

"Lots of snakes down by the lake, too. Water moccasins goin' after all them fat frogs and things. Just not a place where a lady like Miss Charlotte would be comfortable," said Uncle Moses, as he started slipping a spatula under the crab cakes and lifting them out of the frying pan.

She didn't want to, but Charlotte felt compelled to protest.

"Oh, Uncle Moses, I think I can take a little heat and humidity. I won't melt, and I've got plenty of bug spray."

Lane had already downed two well-oiled vodka martinis and was feeling chivalrous as well as hoping to win some points toward renewed affection from Charlotte, and said, "Uncle Moses is right, Charlotte. You don't need to be going down to that hot, nasty little cabin tonight. I'll use the tripod and do just fine by myself."

"I don't mind going," said Charlotte weakly. "I'm not afraid of anything down there."

"Naw, sweet thing," replied Lane, with a cocky wink. "I can handle it just fine. You stay here and relax. When I get back, we can go over the video. Maybe start putting a story together tonight."

"You want me to see if Will can help you?" asked Charlotte.

"Leave the congressman alone; he's got other things he needs to do. I'll be just fine," Lane said, as he sniffed the crab cakes.

Just as dinner was ending, Uncle Moses came to the table and told Will he had a phone call. Less than two minutes later, Will returned and said to John-Morgan, "You might know it would happen during our vacation, but there's some business that sorta' needs attention from you and me. Can I speak to you in the kitchen, John-Morgan?"

Will made sure the door was closed then in a low voice said, "That was Bubba on the phone. He's in a semiballistic state right now. Seems like he's been brooding all day long over Francis and wants to go over to his place tonight and confront him. He sounds really worked up. I'm concerned about what he might do when he gets face-to-face with him. He sounds like he's pissed enough to hurt the old man. I told him to meet us at the yacht club in an hour, and the three of us would go over to Francis's together."

A few minutes after Will and John-Morgan returned to the dining room. Lane announced it was getting dark, said his good-byes, then climbed into Will's old Jeep and headed for his meeting with Dr. Divine and the spirits of Salvation Lake.

The *Graf Spee* roared down Doomsday Creek and out into Wassaw Sound. The tide was high and the water calm as John-Morgan pointed his bow toward Half Moon Creek, trimmed out his engines, then advanced to full throttle. Less than ten minutes later they were in the Tybee Cut, screaming through at 5,500 rpm's, with only three feet of the *Graf Spee*'s stern touching the water. They shot out of the cut and made a wide, sweeping power turn into the Wilmington River. What was left of the sun was slipping down the far side of the earth, boiling the river to a copper glare and heating the sky over Savannah to a hot glow.

While the *Graf Spee* had been cutting its way through creeks and rivers, Monsignor Mulvaney was standing in the living room of Francis's condo at the old General Oglethorpe, watching the sun drop out of sight over the shrimp boats at Thunderbolt. He said very little to Francis when he was ushered in and remained silent for several moments; then, finally, he turned and spoke.

"I had this fella from CNC come by the rectory after mass today, and he knows a lot about me and my ties to our people back home. What's worse, he asked questions about you and the Nazis."

Francis moved close to the window. Puffy clouds drifted over the marsh, and he followed the course of the Wilmington River as it curved south toward Priest's Landing. He noticed a boat in the distance, moving very fast, and admired the way it sliced across the water, leaving a widening wake in its path. Then he took another sip of Glennfiddich from a tumbler with the green seal of the Hibernian Society on it and looked at the monsignor.

"Francis," said Mulvaney, "I never thought I'd come to despise you as much as I do now."

"Why? Because I killed that old Jew who was going to give me away?" asked Francis, as he took another sip of whiskey.

"That and a lot of other things," shot back the monsignor.

"It was self-preservation, Michael," responded Francis in a heightened tone.

"Were all the affairs you had while Margaret Mary was alive self-preservation, too? Were all the pain and humilation you caused her and all the lies you told her also in the name of self-preservation? Do you remember the conversation we had when you told me you wanted to marry her and how much you loved her?" asked the monsignor, as he glared at Francis.

"Yeah, you told me you'd kill me with your own hands if I hurt her."

"Did you ever wonder why I didn't come after you, Francis?"

"Not for a minute, Mike, because I knew you didn't have the nerve or the stomach to do it."

Monsignor Mulvaney dropped his head and sighed. "That's right, I didn't, because I'd grown to hate violence, and I couldn't bring myself to harm anybody again, even a person as evil as you."

Francis threw his head back, gave a quick, sarcastic laugh, and said, "You pious bastard! You're full of more shit than a Christmas turkey. Perhaps you've chosen to forget, but you blew the heads off those two British soldier boys. Get serious, Monsignor! What kind of a fool do you take me for?"

"That was war," replied Mulvaney, before Francis put his hands up and said, "Please, spare me the fuckin' sermon, Mike. I've been at war for over sixty years now. I'm the one who's supposed to be dead, drowned back in the old country, remember. I'm the one who got on that damn German sub and put his ass on the line for our country and lived in fear ever since, so don't start preaching to me, OK? Especially about some nasty old Jew who didn't even know where she was. I did everybody concerned, including her, a favor. Knowing Jews, I'll bet the Silvermans are counting their inheritance right now. They don't give a shit if their loonie aunt Gretchen is dead. I've put up with you trying to tell me what's right and wrong for years. So if you don't intend to turn me in, then just stuff it, Monsignor."

Monsignor Mulvaney shook his head and said, "I never got to the point where I was that cold, Francis. I couldn't turn away from the way I was raised."

Francis looked out the window and said, "So what are you here for, Michael? If you're not going to rat me out, then are you here to save my soul or something?"

Monsignor Mulvaney sighed again and responded, "I'm afraid saving your soul is a task that far exceeds my powers. I just came to tell you that something was brewing. I guess I also wanted to see if there was any remorse at all in you. It looks like there isn't."

The monsignor was starting to leave when there was a knock on the door. Seconds later Will stood in Francis's living room with a somber look on his face.

Will looked at Monsignor Mulvaney and said, "If you don't want to hear this, you'd better leave."

Monsignor Mulvaney started for the door but was stopped by Francis when he said, "Stay, Michael, by all means"; then he turned to Will and said, "Now, what's all this about?"

Will took a deep breath and said, "We found the wreck of a Nazi submarine. Its secret papers were locked in a watertight safe, and we were able to get them out and read them. There was a picture of a man who I believe could be you along with orders from the head of the Nazi spy apparatus directing his insertion onto the Georgia coast back in 1942. The identity papers for this character say he has a birthmark on the back of his neck with the same exact dimensions and location as yours, shaped like Italy."

"Are you out of your mind?" asked Francis.

"Unfortunately, no," replied Will. "As a matter of fact, Bubba Silverman was on the way up here to confront you with this, but I was able to convince him to let me speak with you alone."

"Then he's the one who put you up to this?"

"I had to almost physically restrain him from coming up here, Francis. What he wants to know, what I want to know, is whether or not this spy referred to in those papers as Sea Lion is actually you."

Francis stood with a look of complete surprise on his face; then he said in an astonished voice, "Good Lord, Will, are you being serious with me? I've never even been on a submarine, much less a Nazi sub. Have you boys been smoking some of those funny cigarettes, or have you just lost your minds?"

"You remember his aunt Gretchen, don't you?" asked Will.

Francis's acting abilities had served him well over the years, and he assummed the most convincing wounded look on his face and said, "Of course I remember her."

"Well," responded Will, "Bubba did a little checking and discovered that you were at the nursing home the night she died, and he thinks you had something do with her death."

Francis straightened up, poked his jaw forward, and spit out, "He's a damn fool and a raving lunatic! Are you and John-Morgan part of this, too?"

"Look, Francis," said Will, "the picture is faded, and it was taken sixty years ago, but it does bear a resemblance to you. And the birthmark thing, you gotta admit that it's a real unusual circumstance, probably a one-in-a-million chance of somebody else having a mark the same size and location as yours. Can't you give me some idea, some proof that it wasn't you on that sub? I want to believe you, Francis, you know that, but . . ."

"Well, where is this picture and those documents?" asked Francis. "Don't I at least get to look at the evidence that's supposed to make me a Nazi spy as well as a murderer?"

"They're back on the island in a safe place," replied Will. "I'll bring 'em in the morning."

There was something about the way Francis looked when Will told him about Bubba's suspicions concerning the death of Gretchen Meyer, and it gave Will a very uncomfortable feeling.

Monsignor Mulvaney stood by the window with his head down and a grave look on his face. Will approached him and said, "By the way you're acting, Monsignor, it appears to me that you know something about this and that it's not good news."

There is an unwritten law in the Irish Republican Army that says, "Once in, never out," and it was as real at this time as it was six decades prior when Mike took the oath of allegiance to the cause. He had sworn to never, under any circumstances, betray his fellow comrades in arms, and Mike Mulvaney was a man of his word.

For several seconds the monsignor said nothing, then he looked at Will and answered, "Don't go readin' things into my actions that aren't there. Before you came, Francis and I were talkin' about something very serious but something between just the two of us."

Monsignor Mulvaney wasn't half the actor Francis was; and even though Will wanted to believe him, his suspicions had been raised, and more convincing evidence would be needed now. Will didn't know what to do and instinctively started for the door. Just as he put his hand on the doorknob, he turned to Francis and said, "Ever heard of Simon Weisenthal?"

"Yeah," replied Francis, "he's that old Jew from Austria who fancies himself a Nazi hunter."

Will was surprised at the way Francis spit out the word "Jew." He'd never heard him speak like that before. Then he shook his head and said, "That's right. Bubba says he's going to contact Weisenthal and send him copies of the papers we found." After he said that, Will dropped his head and let out a sigh.

Francis walked over to the door, put his hand on Will's shoulder, and looked directly into his eyes.

"Look, Will, I've known you since you were born. I've treated you like you were my son, and there's nothing you ever needed or asked for that I haven't done for you. I'm not a Nazi spy, I'm Francis Quinn, an orphan from New York City. I fought for this country and was wounded. I was by your father's side when he went to get you in Japan, remember? I've worked my ass off for you to get you where you are today. If that little jerk Silverman decides to go public with this, you're gonna take a big hit, don't kid yourself. This is all absolute and pure bullshit, but just the accusations! God Almighty, the press will start dredging up all that stuff about me back when I was with Willie Hart, and they'll hang that on you, too! You let that stupid little bastard go runnin' around spewin' all this cock-and-bull about me and the

Nazis . . . hell, it won't hurt me, I can take the heat, but your little goose is cooked . . . well-done, too."

Will knew Francis was right, but there was just something about him that was different. It was almost as if the man talking to him wasn't the same man he'd always known.

Will shrugged, nodded, and said, "OK, I'll get the papers and come back in the morning. Maybe you can straighten this out then."

Francis looked at Will and said in a plaintive voice, "You sound as if you doubt me, Will?"

"Look, Francis, this is all just a little too much for me to digest right now. I can never pay you back for all that you've done; and like I said, I want to believe you, but that photograph, the birthmark, Bubba's aunt saying you were at the concentration camp . . . I don't know what to think."

Will opened the door and started to leave but turned to Francis and said, "I'll talk to Bubba, and then I'll be back around nine tomorrow."

Francis reached out and stopped Will from closing the door. Then he drew in close to Will. There was a frightening look of hard steel and absolute coldness in his eyes as he zeroed in on him and in a low, menacing voice said, "Now you tell that little smart-ass son of a bitch that if he does anything to injure my reputation, I'll bring to bear upon his stinking little head all of my assets. I'll call in every favor that's ever been owed to me, and they are legion, and I'll use them to crush him like the nasty little worm he is. He won't have a window or a pot when my lawyers have finished with Mr. Silverman. So tell him to go right ahead and contact Simon Weisenthal because Weisenthal hasn't got a thing to lose, but Bubba Silverman sure as hell does."

Will was stunned. He'd never seen Francis look or speak that way. It was almost surreal and reinforced his unease about Francis's truthfulness. Then, just as Will was going out the door, Francis looked at him and said, "I can't believe you let crackpots like Silverman around you. This nut is going to ruin you. Dump him."

When Francis closed the door, Monsignor Mulvaney was again standing by the window. The sun was all the way down, and the sky had turned from light magenta to deep purple. The moon was starting to creep up over the tree line at the southern tip of Wilmington Island,

and in the distance over Wassaw, the monsignor could see a storm gathering.

"Well," said the monsignor, "who do you plan to kill now, the whole lot of them?"

Francis just shrugged, poured himself another drink, and replied, "At least you kept your word; you didn't rat me out."

"It's ironic," said Monsignor Mulvaney, "that Silverman has this whole thing figured out and I know enough to send you to prison, but I'm bound by a seal that I've got to respect. I hope God is more forgiving of me than Bubba Silverman is of you."

As he was leaving, Monsignor Mulvaney turned to Francis and with the saddest of looks said, "I think you went wrong when you quit believing you'd be held accountable for the evil you've done in your life."

After he left Francis's, Will drove to the yacht club, where he met with Bubba and John-Morgan in the Quarterdeck Lounge. Bubba had cooled off considerably; and as they sat at the bar, he said, "I'm sorry, Will. I lost my cool tonight, and I'm glad you wouldn't let me confront Francis, but I'm just certain that he's Sea Lion, and I'm frustrated that I might not be able to prove it."

Will nodded and replied, "I understand. All I ask is that we take it easy with this thing. I want the truth as much as you do. Let's not go crashing around. You can come back with me tomorrow and ask Francis anything you want. We'll have the papers with us and kind'a just go from there, OK?"

At the same time Will and his two friends were seated in the Quarterdeck Lounge, Tyrone was pulling up to the gas pump of an all-night convenience store along Victory Drive in Thunderbolt. He was driving Shinika's car, and she was in the passenger's seat, more than a little nauseated from too much Colt 45 Malt Liquor. When he got out to gas up, Tyrone noticed a couple of white boys who had been hanging around the Dumpster on the side of the store. They had come in from Bryan County earlier in the day and had quickly scored in their hunt for some crack but were now semistraight and totally busted. They knew where they could make another quick buy if they had some cash. Tyrone's fancy sneakers and thick, gold chain soon caught their attention.

Earl, the taller of the two, had scraggly brown hair, a Fu Manchu mustache, and a Confederate flag tatooed on his right arm. When Tyrone finished at the pump and started for the store, it was Earl who elected to follow him inside. Dewayne, who was wearing a faded Dale Earnhardt T-shirt with a big number three on it, positioned himself between the store entrance and Shinika's car.

Earl watched as Tyrone pulled out Lane's money and peeled off a twenty for the gas. He was right behind Tyrone when he walked out the door and signaled to Dewayne that Tyrone was well fixed. Tyrone had been drinking, too, and was oblivious to the setup until Dewayne blocked his path.

"Gimme whatcha got, nigga, or your ass is gonna get stomped," snarled Dewayne.

"Fuck you, you cracker motherfucka!" shouted Tyrone, as he started to push Dewayne out of his way. Tyrone hadn't even finished spitting out his epithet before Earl was grabbing him from behind and Dewayne was forcing his hand into Tyrone's pocket. When Earl saw Dewayne running away with Tyrone's money, he reached up, snatched Tyrone's gold chain from his neck, and took off in the same direction.

Tyrone wasn't large, but he was fast, and he caught up with Earl at the corner of the building. He started pounding Earl in the face, telling him what a dirty, low-life white boy he was while he tried to pull his gold chain from Earl's hand. Earl was strung out, desperate, and disinclined to having his teeth knocked out, so he reached for the Charter Arms Thirty-eight Special he'd stolen from a house in Brooklet and jammed it into Tyrone's stomach.

The report from a Thirty-eight Special is usually quite loud, but this time its explosion was largely muffled by Tyrone's midsection. Earl pulled the trigger twice, sending the 110-grain Winchester hollow points into Tyrone's gut.

Tyrone came to rest faceup on the oil-stained concrete surrounded by a graveyard of cigarette butts and beer bottle caps. Before he turned to run, Earl stuffed the gold chain Tyrone had given his life for into his pocket then spit on him.

"Fuck you, you stupid jive-ass nigga," hissed Earl, before he faded into the night.

While Tyrone struggled for his last breath, less than ten minutes away Will was finishing his second draft with Bubba and John-Morgan. At the same time, out on Jesus Island, Lane was seated with Sister Mystery in her cabin waiting for Dr. Divine.

"We always have some tea 'n' benne cakes to welcome the spirits into the house," said Sister Mystery as she put out a plate of small brown cookies and four cups of her herbal tea.

Lane had the camera mounted on his shoulder and kept the old woman in his viewfinder as she shuffled around the kitchen.

"There's just three of us tonight, right?" asked Lane.

"Yes, suh," replied Sister Mystery, as she placed a kerosene lantern on the table and pulled back her chair.

"Well," said Lane, "how come you've got four cups of tea set out?"

"That other one there," said Sister Mystery, "it's for the spirits that comes. Gotta have somethin' for them if we gonna go ask 'em to join us."

Just as he was about to ask when Dr. Divine was going to arrive, a tall, dark figure appeared at the back door.

Dr. Divine didn't say a word as he took his place at the table. He was still wearing his dark glasses, and Lane could see the lantern reflected in the lenses. Without acknowledging Lane, Dr. Divine began to chant in what Lane guessed was an African tongue. Soon Sister Mystery took up the chant and began swaying from side to side in rhythm with Dr. Divine's incantations.

After a couple of minutes, Dr. Divine stopped chanting and raised his hands upward, saying, "I commands you spirits who inhabits this here island to come forth and sit at dis table. Your nourishment is waitin'."

Dr. Divine sat back in his chair and placed both hands on the table, adding, "We can't drink 'til da spirits have partaken."

"How will we know?" whispered Lane.

"Jus watch dey teacup," said Dr. Divine. "You'll know when dey sips dey tea."

There was silence around the table while Lane kept his eyes on the cups. After a few seconds, Lane saw a tiny ripple appear on the surface of one of them. He was also sure he'd felt somebody hit the table with his leg, causing it to shake slightly.

"Now we can drink our tea an' eat our cakes," announced Dr. Divine.

"Got to eat thirteen of these little things," said Sister Mystery, as she reached out and counted off the same number onto her plate.

"Sista right," said Dr. Divine, as he put thirteen on his plate. "Thirteen special in the spirit world. Dey responds to that number."

Benne wafers are about the size of a quarter. They come from an old recipe said to have been brought from Africa to Savannah by the slaves. The main ingredients are molasses, flour, butter, and sesame seeds. Sister Mystery's recipe had all that and more.

Dr. Divine and his ancestors on Jesus Island had been well acquainted with the properties of marijuana and from slave days had maintained a small number of very potent plants deep within the confines of the island. They regarded use of the plant as sacramental and had long employed it in their various concoctions for the herb's mind-altering powers.

Lane had never tried the drug, considering it to be the domain of hippies and ghetto blacks. Since he had no prior experience with marijuana, the effect it would have on him might be profound.

"You gotta partake of this here offering to the spirits," said Sister Mystery, as she ate the benne cakes on her plate, "if you is wantin' to have them visit."

Dr. Divine stuffed several of the wafers into his mouth, took a sip of his tea, and said, "Sista right. Spirits is finicky and easy to be offended."

After watching Dr. Divine and Sister Mystery consume all of their benne cakes and tea, Lane decided they wouldn't administer dangerous substances to themselves and quickly ate his thirteen wafers and drank the tea. Dr. Divine knew it took about twenty to thirty minutes for the marijuana to be absorbed from the intestinal tract, and this period was occupied by another round of chanting, praying, and invoking the spirits of the dead.

Lane's eyes fell on the flame inside the lantern; and as he watched its flickering movements, he became absorbed by its simple beauty. He didn't know it, but he was beginning to feel the effects of Sister Mystery's benne cakes.

Dr. Divine kept an eye on Lane, watching for the signs of marijuana intoxication; and when Lane continued to stare at the lantern, he knew the spirit-calling potion had taken effect. He stood and said, "It's time to go to Salvation Lake. That's where I summons up da spirits."

When they arrived at the dock on Salvation Lake, Dr. Divine walked to the end, put the lantern down, and stood facing the lake. Lane set up his camera equipment, focused on Dr. Divine, adjusted for a wide-angle shot, then pressed the record button.

The night air on Salvation Lake seemed heavy and thick to Lane as he watched Dr. Divine thump the dock with a heavy stick then start into a particularly animated chant full of deep, guttural sounds punctuated by high-pitched wailing and swaying. This continued for several minutes until he stopped abruptly and turned to face Lane.

"Da spirits is ready to rise outta Salvation Lake," said Dr. Divine. "Come an' stand by me, 'cause I can feel 'em a-stirrin' and callin' your name."

Dr. Divine pointed to the end of the dock then the lake and said, "You is standin' right on the edge of the spirit world." Then he moved forward until the front of his shoes were hanging over the end of the dock and said, "Ya gotta get close to da edge, almost fallin' in, for da spirits ta know you is wantin' 'em to come out da water."

Lane obliged Dr. Divine's directive and moved to the very edge of the dock and let the front of his shoes hang over the side. Dr. Divine removed his sunglasses and picked up the lantern with one hand, while producing a small, dark bag from inside his coat with the other. Then he elevated both over his head.

"Come forth, Lucifer!" shouted Dr. Divine. "I commands you in the name 'a him what governs da spirits in dis here lake!"

As soon as he'd heard the thumping of Dr. Divine's stick, the Devil Himself had swum to the end of the dock. It was the signal that a meal was forthcoming.

The old alligator had grown to fifteen feet in length, was three feet wide, and weighed almost a ton. His jaws were nearly two feet long and almost the same distance across, with a crushing power that could rival an industrial press, and he hadn't had a full meal in two days.

When Dr. Divine raised the lantern and that familiar black bag, the Devil Himself was partially submerged about fifteen feet from the end of the dock, with only his nostrils and eyes showing above the water. Dr. Divine had seen him, but in the darkness, Lane had no idea what was lurking just yards away.

Lane instinctively turned to look at Dr. Divine. He'd never seen him without his sunglasses, and the old root doctor was capable of putting a frightening look on his face, something that he always saved for the climax of his spectacular spiritual solicitations.

Dr. Divine looked deeply into Lane's eyes and said, "You is stained by evil, an evil dat only the waters of Salvation Lake can cleanse from your soul."

Just as Dr. Divine said, "cleanse from your soul," the Devil Himself opened his enormous jaws and lunged toward the dock. Lane jerked his head to the sound of splashing water to behold an open abyss surrounded by rows of jagged teeth. Lane's knees buckled in fright, causing him to lose his balance and fall into the saving waters of Salvation Lake.

In an instant the Devil Himself clamped down on Lane's right thigh. One set of teeth crushed his femur only inches from the hip joint, while the other crunched through the bone just above Lane's knee. When he knew he had a good hold on his victim, the master of Salvation Lake violently shook his head from side to side, causing his teeth to cut completely through Lane's thigh, tearing it off at the hip. Then he threw his head back; and while Dr. Divine watched from the dock and Lane thrashed around in a froth of his own blood, the Devil Himself gulped down Lane's entire right leg.

The last flicker of awareness was fading from Lane when the Devil Himself closed his jaws across Lane's buttocks and pulled him into the deepest part of his kingdom, where he hid Lane's corpse under a submerged log, saving it for a royal feast later the next day.

Tony Torillo's ring name had been Tiger Torillo; and back when he was still in the wrestling game, he'd done everything he could to live up to his moniker, from growling during TV interviews to the tiger-striped leather mask he wore.

Eugene T. Snipes, also known as "T-Bone" or "Honkey T," had been a member of the Hell's Angels since his eighteenth birthday. He'd made a living working as a Harley mechanic up in Fayetteville and did part-time work at a locksmith shop that also ran a home security business. It was there Eugene had learned to pick locks and defeat burglar alarms.

T-Bone and Tony had been working for Vinnie Magesto since 1991 and made a pretty good team. Both were large men who knew how to fight and enjoyed it.

It was ten o'clock when they eased their car into the dark end of the condo parking lot and trained their binoculars on Francis's windows. When they saw all the lights go out, they waited for another half hour before making their move.

T-Bone didn't have any trouble with the lock on Francis's door. Once inside, the two stood silently for several moments and listened to the rhythm of Francis's snoring.

"Fucker's out cold," whispered Tiger, who then motioned for T-Bone to follow him. They moved out of the front hallway and into the living room, where T-Bone picked up a large throw pillow from the sofa and fell in behind Tiger as he moved toward Francis's room.

Francis wasn't in the habit of drinking and taking his Halcion at the same time and knew it wasn't safe, but the anxiety he'd felt over the scenes with Monsignor Mulvaney and Will had driven him to seek the solace of a rapid and deep sleep. He was lying on his back when T-Bone and Tiger entered his room and stoood quietly by his bed.

With a nod from Tiger, T-Bone put the pillow over Francis's face and covered it with the weight of his entire body. At the same time, Tiger hopped on top of Francis, straddling his legs while he lay across his midsection. A combined weight of 513 pounds road atop Francis, pinning him to the bed. It would be just what Vinnie Magesto had ordered, a whack job that looked like death from natural causes.

Francis had been dreaming about Margaret Mary and the first time he'd seen her at the Brass Rail when he felt the pillow over his face. He knew immediately what was happening and why; but no matter how hard he tried, he could neither breathe nor break the hold his killers had on him. Soon there was a profound burning in his chest as the carbon dioxide levels in his blood increased and the oxygen content decreased.

From his earliest days, Francis had been schooled in Roman

Catholic theology. For many years he had accepted and practiced his religion. At the beginning it had been the love of his life, the core of his being. However, the allure of the world and all the easy pleasures it offered had blinded Francis and changed him. But those early beliefs had been imprinted on his mind and were indelibly there, always just below the surface.

At about ninety seconds into death by hypoxia, a darkness begins to descend on the victim. In the moment before he lost consciousness, the words Monsignor Mulvaney had spoken only an hour earlier came bursting into his head. *You went wrong when you quit believing you'd be held accountable for the evil you've done in your life.*

An instant before the world went black, when he knew he was at his end, Francis remembered the lessons from his childhood and struggled to say, "God, forgive me."

It was one in the morning, and the big red-and-white RC cola thermometer nailed to the side of Sister Mystery's house still read eighty-five degrees. She watched silently as Dr. Divine knelt in front of the parlor fireplace and touched a big kitchen match to the fat lighter. Somewhere far away out in the deep woods and thick night that surrounded their cabin, Lucifer and Jezebel were howling at a treed coon.

"Did da spirits rise out da lake for dat man?" asked Sister Mystery.

"Yes, sista'," responded Dr. Divine, as he tossed the cassette he'd removed from Lane's camera into the fire. "Dey come right up, jus' like I knowed dey would."

When he was satisfied the visual record of Lane's encounter with the Devil Himself was completely destroyed, Dr. Divine loaded the camera equipment into the Jeep and drove to the dock. Uncle Moses was waiting, and neither said a word as they carried the camera to Lane's boat.

Moses started the boat and eased out into the center of Doomsday Creek, with Dr. Divine following in his old wooden bateau. Just before reaching Wassaw Sound, Moses nudged Lane's boat against the side of the creek and got marsh grass wrapped around the propeller, stalling the engine. Then he walked to the stern, opened the door on the transom, and stepped into Dr. Divine's bateau.

There was a spring tide that night, almost eleven feet high, and it was rushing out of Doomsday Creek into Wassaw Sound. Moses and Dr. Divine watched as Lane's boat got caught up in the current and carried into the sound. The two old men drifted along with the tide until they'd seen Lane's boat float past the southern tip of Jesus Island and out into the Atlantic.

"If you was to find that boat," asked Moses, "what would you think done happened to the fella what's supposed to be drivin' it?"

Dr. Divine gave a little more gas to the old Evinrude twenty-five hanging on the back of his boat. After it coughed and sprang to life, he replied, "I'd be inclined to believe that the operator of that fine-lookin' craft went an' got his propeller tangled up in some marsh grass; and when he was workin' at freein' it up, why da poor fella', he slip and fall overboard. Most likely drown and washed out to sea with da tide, just like his boat. What'cha think, Moses?"

Moses looked up above the dunes, noticed a light come on in Will's room in the big house, then said, "I think our lamb gonna be safe now."

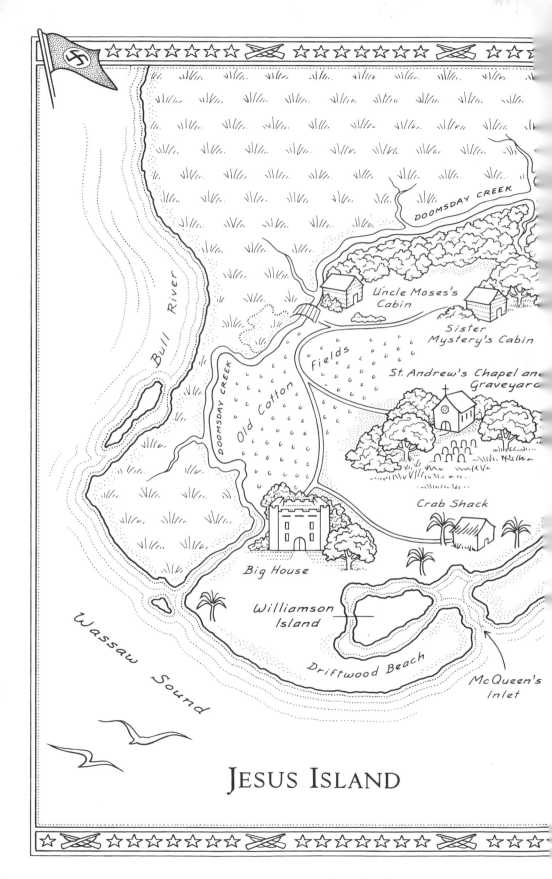

JESUS ISLAND